The Diamond
Bracelet Club

ISBN: 0615848540
ISBN 13: 9780615848549
Library of Congress Control Number: 2013945920
The Diamond Bracelet Club, DeLand, FL

www.thediamondbraceletclub.com

Kay, here's to us. Cheers!
Ginny

Thanks to all those wonderful friends and family members who endured the development of this story. Most of all to Ginny, aka "Girl."
Kay Whitehouse

www.thediamondbraceletclub.com

The Diamond Bracelet Club

Ginny Knight-Simon and Kay Whitehouse

Prologue

"Look out! She's gonna blow!"

"Andy! Get back! All teams clear the area!" Red Sanderson was screaming into the bull horn as he leaped to the top of his black Bronco with the agility of a mountain lion. Red's tall, slim figure was drenched in perspiration and dirt, making him look like a wild man as he waved his dust-covered Stetson from atop his perch. Red tried desperately to catch the attention of the crews, even before the emergency sirens began to blow their danger warnings.

"Run like hell! Run like hell!" he shrieked into the horn. The earth beneath his truck erupted from the magnitude of the explosion, jarring the vehicle so hard that it knocked Red to the hard, dusty ground. Fortunately unhurt from the fall, he used the front bumper of his Bronco to pull himself up. As he ran toward the destruction, he began to shout orders like a military sergeant in combat.

"Get on the radios. Get help anywhere you can. Get me an airlift! Get firefighters! Get ambulances! All hell's broke loose out here!"

The smoke was dense, and fires were springing up everywhere. "Where the hell is Andy?" Red shouted as the hot, dry air burned his eyes. Help began to arrive almost immediately. News of a disaster in the oil fields travels faster than lightning.

"Red...Red, here. Over here."

The smell of burning flesh penetrated the smoke. Red, looking over the carnage, began to realize the amount of waste. Men, covered in oil and blood, moaned in agony. Some on fire, running, out of their minds, like live torches. The roar of the flames and the shrill of the emergency sirens that shredded the air were playing havoc with Red's mind.

"Red...Red...here. Help me, Red."

Red followed the weak voice to what was left of a blown-out shed. Looking down into the rubble, he saw Andy Lewis, president of Lewis Oil Company.

"Andy! My God, it's good to see you! Thought I'd lost you. Give me your hand and let me pull you outta this mess!" The weight of Andy's body as Red pulled him free from the debris sent both men staggering to the ground. It was then Red felt the warm blood of his best friend trickle down his arm. Terror shot through him as his eyes caught sight of a two-inch steel rod protruding from Andy's back.

"Pull, Red...pull it out," pleaded Andy trying to stay conscious as the hot pain punished his weak body.

Red didn't hesitate. Knowing it had to be done, he worked quickly, running high on adrenaline. He laid Andy face down, straddling the small of his back to get at the enemy gleaming between his shoulders. Sure that the pain would be incomprehensible, Red quickly placed a knotted handkerchief in his patient's mouth.

With fires still blazing around them, Red manipulated the hand pliers he had found in the wreckage to pull the blood-covered rod from its sucking hole. With the end of the rod finally in sight, his chest still heaving from the exertion, Red let the pliers and its prize fall to the ground and motioned down a helicopter.

Andy was in and out of consciousness en route to the hospital. The pain clawed through every vein in his body, and the roaring in his brain sounded like a tidal wave. The hot, heavy pain. The weight of it kept pulling him down, under.

"Red, where are you?" rasped the now unfamiliar voice.

"Here, man, don't talk. We're on the way to the hospital in a chopper. Things are gonna be just fine. Trust me." Red was choking on his emotions.

The blood oozed from under the dying man, and he seemed to be afloat in his own warm, sticky liquid. His face, normally exceptionally handsome, was contorted almost beyond recognition, reflecting his agony.

The raspy voice repeated, "Red, where are you?" Andy's weak hand clutched Red's wrist. "In my safe…a brown envelope…a tape…get it to them."

Red knew without question who he meant.

The heavy pain was gaining on him, pulling him down deeper. "Red, you know it's all yours now." The air felt hot and stubborn as Andy sucked harder to fill his lungs.

"Hey you ol' sombitch, pull yourself together. We've got an oil field to rebuild!"

"Red…I love you…like the son I never…"

"Hey, man."

Glazed eyes fixed on Red as the weight of that hot and heavy pain pulled Andy Lewis away.

chapter

ONE

"Oh, Tom!" Lily gasped. She realized the meaning of what Tom was saying when she saw him slip on his overalls. A shower of excitement hit, and the urgency settled in around her. She thought of the medical tray Tom had stocked earlier that morning with all the necessary equipment and carefully placed on a table in the storeroom. The sound of Arizona's quickened breathing made Lily half-dizzy with anticipation. The flared nostrils, the pacing, Tom's excitement.

"Oh no, Tom! She's too early. She's in trouble!" Lily couldn't hide it—the crack in her voice gave her away. She was scared, and Tom knew it. Did she sense his anxiety? Oh, dear God, was Tom scared, too? Tom knew how much the beautiful mare meant to Lily, and he wanted everything to go smoothly when she was ready to give birth. Her mother, Golden Run, had died a few hours after giving Arizona life, and Lily had raised the filly like a baby, feeding her with a bottle every few hours, sleeping with her in the barn, and giving her constant attention until the little gal was out of danger. The filly grew up strong, magnificent, and solid black. When Arizona was bred months earlier with Jet Stream, a jet black thoroughbred racer with excellent bloodlines, Lily hoped to produce a colt that would out run its father. If Lily's plans turned out, the Kentucky Derby winner three years away would belong to Gray Meadow Farms.

"How much longer do you think she'll go, Tom? Tom, you know nothing can go wrong with this baby." She didn't give him time for an answer. "I can't wait till it gets here! And Alexander is simply out of control. He even brought his sleeping bag out to the barn and slept here last night. I ended up out here, too." She laughed nervously. "I couldn't let a five-year-old boy sleep in the barn by himself, now, could I?"

"Aye, girl, I don't know who the child is in this situation." Tom laughed as he felt the mare's stomach and rib area. "Lily, why don't ya go on up to the house and fix us somethin' cool to drink. You could rest a little and then—"

"Tom McNally! I can't believe my ears. If you think I'm leaving this barn for one split second, you are one mistaken Irishman! Tom, I thought you knew me better than that."

"OK, OK, Lily Girl, we'll both stay right here." He knew he should have saved his breath. "It won't be long now. She's a little early, but by my calculations, it's only by a little more than a week."

"What about the vet?" Lily's black eyes, enlarged with excitement, stung as Tom looked into them.

"Not to worry. A week isn't really early. I'll not have a thing go wrong with your pride and joy. We've got plenty of time. Tom began to organize and, knowing he had to get Lily busy, sent her for the medical tray while he reexamined the mare. He couldn't help but notice when she brought the tray how the humidity made her perspiration-soaked blouse cling to her full breasts. The red cotton top fit like a second skin, with trickles of sweat disappearing just where his imagination began.

Lily Gray and Tom McNally had spent all day in Barn F, the two-stall foaling barn at the southwest border of the farm. They watched as the big, black thoroughbred paced off the hours before her time to foal like the slow ticking of a clock.

As they watched Arizona, the dark clouds tempted the sky to let go of the much needed rain. Summer in Kentucky could be rough, and this one ranked right at the top. There had been no rain to amount to much for several weeks, only enough to keep the humidity up to around 90 percent.

The breeze was no longer gentle as it whipped over Gray Meadow Farms this exciting afternoon. The 570 acres of emerald green pasture had turned brown and brittle, and the heat was taking its toll on the livestock and hired help as well. The air felt thick and close as breath. The sky darkened and the wind picked up, but the chance of rain today still wasn't likely.

"Tom," Lily said tightly, trying not to scream, knowing it could upset Arizona. The mare's breathing suddenly quickened to a rapid panting. The pacing slowed as Arizona began to paw the straw, making her place. Suddenly, the huge mare collapsed her heavy bulk on the bed of fresh straw Lily had fluffed for her. Lily felt almost as if the beautiful horse was her daughter. They had been through a lot together since the day she was born. Now, Lily felt so helpless. "Dear God, please help us," she prayed aloud.

The water bag broke, soaking the fresh bed of straw with its warm fluid. Tom slipped on the rubber gloves and dropped to his knees beside his patient. "It's gonna be OK, Arizona, baby," he whispered.

Tears streamed down Lily's cheeks as she swabbed Arizona's face with a cool, wet cloth, consoling her all the while. Arizona's enormous, black eyes expressed the love she had for Lily. Most horses might have preferred to be alone, but Arizona and Lily were a unique pair. "You'll be just fine, pretty girl," Lily cooed, drawing calmness from Tom's gentle nature. "Tom is here. He'll take good care of you."

Tom, with his broad smile and Irish brogue, had been a godsend when he showed up in answer to her newspaper ad three years ago. He became her confidant and friend, as well as her foreman. He'd been through rough times with Lily, and there had been many since she bought Gray Meadows. He had never complained. Lily loved Tom and trusted him totally. He knew everything about a horse farm, from animal medicine to the mechanics of the machinery.

Lily was extremely grateful for the lifetime of knowledge he had taught her. He was very well paid, and he was liked and respected by the other employees. Tom's active workday kept his six-two frame lean and muscular. At fifty-three, Tom was still a double take with his sandy hair and ice blue eyes that could melt stone.

Arizona whinnied. She panted. She pushed. "Any minute now and you'll be a gramma, Lily," Tom whispered.

"Alexander is going to be mighty disappointed he missed this," Lily whispered back.

A normal birth presented front feet first, with the head tucked between the legs. Tom, although usually very independent and not one to ask for divine help, prayed silently that this would be normal. He knew his prayers were answered with the first appearance of the little hooves and, moments later, the shoulders. He spoke gently to Arizona, guiding the little ebony bundle out into the world.

Her colt was perfect. A white blaze flamed up the bridge of the small nose. Black fuzz crowned the top of his head, the beginning of a thick, beautiful mane. Big brown eyes strained to see the strange new world around him, while four white-knee-socked feet each went their separate ways.

Lily was crying joyfully as she hugged the tired mare. "You did a great job, Mom!" she cooed. "We are going to make you queen of Gray Meadow Farms!"

Tom's job was coming to an end as he cauterized the umbilical cord with iodine. Finishing up, Tom gave the foal his shots of streptomycin and penicillin to "help him off to a good start."

"Tom, I just can't wait any longer, let me at him!" Lily gushed. "Ooh, you are the most gorgeous little creature alive," she said with pride as she began to rub the foal down with a big, fluffy towel to dry him off and get his blood circulation pumping. The frisky newcolt took to the attention immediately, rubbing his head against her. It seemed to Lily that Arizona was smiling at the whole scene going on before her.

After a checkup from Tom, Arizona was on her feet already tending to her motherly instincts. She began to inspect her squirming bundle of legs, which had begun to lick, snort, paw, and whinny. They were so funny together, almost as if they were playing a game. She would lick, and he would snort. Then, he would paw at the straw, and she would snort. Tom and Lily laughed until their sides were sore. Then the new arrival decided to check out his long appendages to see if they really worked. First, up came the round, little rump, then the left front leg and finally, the right front leg. Lily scooted back in the stall to give him room.

"He's up! He's down!" Lily and Tom chanted in unison. The legs sprawled in four different directions as he landed in the straw once again. Relentless in his effort, the colt struggled to his feet, and this time he wobbled his first steps.

"Tom, the time?" Lily called out, not letting her eyes leave the colt for a minute. He went straight for his mother.

"Exactly fourteen minutes, two seconds from the time he was taken from his mother. Lily Girl, we're lookin' at a winner for sure." Tom said, waving his stopwatch at her.

Having done everything they could, Tom and Lily left the two to get to know each other. Lily gave Arizona one last hug, whispering in her ear what a great mom she was. The young mare with her nursing foal made for a truly magical scene in the barn that afternoon. With one last survey of the stall, Tom and Lily, worn out, walked arm in arm toward the house.

"Boy, I'm hot and tired. I can't wait to get a shower." Lily sighed. "Why don't you come back to the house after you get cleaned up? I'll fix sandwiches and lemonade."

"You got yourself a deal, Lily Girl," Tom called over his shoulder as he headed for the small four-room house that was his residence.

Lily's horse farm was not as large as most farms in Fayette County, but it ranked at the top for quality and beauty. Gray Meadow Farms was more than a livelihood for Lily; it was life. A life she had worked hard for and given up much for. This life, so dearly loved that the feeling spread to everyone involved.

The farm could pass military inspection at any given time. The barns were cleaned daily, and the exteriors were always snow white. There were patches of flowers everywhere, and the hired hands often teased Lily that she was running a nursery instead of a horse farm. Lily knew every employee personally, their wives, husbands, children, boyfriends, and girlfriends. She knew because it was good business, but most of all, because she cared. She never forgot them at Christmas and other special occasions and set aside a whole acre for a pool and community house for their use. Her employees admired and respected her. She made them feel like family. She was their Lily. She had come up the hard way, and they knew it.

Lily still worked as hard as anyone she employed. She knew it kept her in touch with the land she loved, and she loved being with the horses. From the quarter-mile, treelined lane that curved gently up to the white, two-story house down to the very last acre, Lily knew every inch of the earth and every velvet nose that stuck over a fence. And today, Arizona had come through for her, just as Lily had known she would.

The huge screened-in back porch was an oasis in the heat. The big white ceiling fans circulated the air made cool by the many plants hanging in pots from the rafters and the tall trees that shaded the house. Showered and tired to the bone, Lily and Tom collapsed on two white wicker lounge chairs lined with green cushions.

"Thank you, Tom. You were wonderful with Arizona today." Lily smiled at him. She looked as if she hadn't lifted a finger all day, the way she leaned back with her feet propped up.

"She had an easy time of it, she did. That's all. What are ya goin' to name the little fella?"

"Alexander and I have a few names picked out. I'll let him make the final choice."

Tom looked toward the door and asked, "Hey, where is Alexander today? I thought he'd be down in the stall as my right-hand man." Lily's son loved Arizona, as he did every other creature he ever met. He was a handsome five-year-old and as full of curiosity as they come.

"He went to the Strehls' to see Randy's new golden retriever, Tandy, this afternoon. He should be back anytime now. He's going to be so disappointed!" Lily replied. Alexander had seen many mares foal, but Arizona was special to them all.

"Mom? Mom? I'm home," called Alexander as he rounded the corner of the house, shattering the peace of the moment. "Can I eat out in the work kitchen with the guys tonight?" he asked, bouncing onto the porch. "Hey, Tom!" He flashed him a big grin.

"I guess so," said Lily, "but you might want to take a look at Arizona's little beauty first."

"Wow! What is it?" he squealed anxiously.

"A beautiful, frisky, four white—" Lily teased him, knowing he wanted a male so badly.

"What, Mom? What!"

"—ebony colt!"

"Yahoo! A colt! Oh man, I missed the whole thing. When did it happen? I'm going on out to see them."

"Just a second young man," Lily said, grabbing her son and pulling him down into a bear hug. "I need a kiss."

"Aw, Mom!" Alexander said, trying to act as if he minded.

"You know not to go in the stall yet, right?" Lily reminded her son as he dashed out the screen door, letting it bang loudly behind him, as usual.

"Right, Mom." In the middle of his run he turned, running backward so as not to waste a moment.

"Can I eat after I see the colt—with the guys, that is?"

"Yes, yes, go on. Make sure you feed George, too."

"Don't worry, He'll get plenty, won't ya boy?" Alexander called to George, his 135- pound Saint Bernard loping along with him.

"Be back before dark, Alexander, not after!"

"OK," came the answer, his voice fading as he ran down the path to the barn.

"You know, Tom, I've noticed lately that Alexander always wants to eat out 'with the guys' on Sue's day off, and I am the one cooking. Do you think he's trying to tell me something?"

"Now, what can I say? I'm sure looking forward to that sandwich ya mentioned. Aw, Lily, he just enjoys the food fights and cowpokin' stories. They all love him, and he eats it up."

The thought of Alexander preferring any company other than her own saddened Lily. But she knew it was healthy. He seemed to have grown up a lot since starting kindergarten. Where had the time gone? He had always looked like Lily. Black hair and hazel eyes atop a long frame that had the promise of height. But she had begun to see more of the boy's father in him lately. How long would it be before he started asking questions? She was much too happy to think about all that right now.

"Thank you, God, for this wonderful life I have here," she was thinking when Tom interrupted her.

"A penny for yer thoughts, Lily Girl," Tom said as he touched her gently on the hand.

"I just can't believe it sometimes, Tom. How lucky I am to have my son, this beautiful farm, and a good friend like you."

"Luck wasn't all that got ya here, my darlin' girl. Ya worked damned hard for every bit of it."

"Oh Tom, what would I have done without you these last three years!" She bent and gave Tom a quick kiss on the head. Lily's thoughts made her wonder what Tom would think if he knew how she had almost lost Alexander through her own hard-hearted, selfish ways.

"Now, relax here while I fix us a sandwich and something cool to drink."

As Lily entered the kitchen, she flicked on the small television set on the counter to catch the news and weather while she prepared their sandwiches. She slipped the white chef's apron on over her blue chambray shirt and jeans. Humming an old Beatles favorite, she took the plate of ham from the refrigerator. Suddenly, the kitchen began to echo, and everything shifted into slow motion when she heard the news that surely could not be true.

"Senator Andrew M. Lewis, Democrat from Texas and leader in the oil industry, died this morning in a tragic oil field explosion..." The platter of ham slipped from her hand and crashed to the tile floor. Lily felt her heart shatter at the same instant.

"God, no! Not Andy!" Lily screamed inside her head. Her ears pounded. She couldn't hear the rest of what the blond news commentator was saying. She heard Tom shouting her name somewhere in the distance.

A nauseating, choking feeling overcame her, and she leaned into the sink and became violently ill. She splashed cool water on her face and neck, trying to regain her self-control. How could this have happened to Andy? Lily's mind was racing as tears cascaded down her honey-tan face to the diamond bracelet Andy had given her so many years ago. It was a token of their special friendship. She was never without it.

"I have to get to him," she whispered. "I've got to contact Red..." The shrill scream of the phone jolted Lily out of her craze. She groped wildly for the phone with a silent hope, a prayer, that it would be Andy telling her everything was all right, it had been a mistake. "Hello?"

"Hello, Lily? This is Red. I've been trying to reach you for hours."

"Oh, Red, no!" Tell me it's not true...Tell me, Red! There's been a mistake, hasn't there? Red, please?"

"No, Lily. I wish I could tell you there's no mistake. God, how I wish I could tell you that. I tried to get to you before you saw the news."

"Red, what happened? Was he...did he suffer? Red knew what Lily was trying to ask. "No, Lily, he never knew what hit him," he lied. "He caught a piece of metal in the back and was gone instantly." Red paused, wondering if he'd said too much. "Lily, are you gonna be OK?"

"Oh, Red," she said, sobbing softly. "I'll be there on the first plane out, but that will be tomorrow."

"Lily, are you sure?"

Feeling heavily the loss of someone so dear, Lily replied, "Yes, I'll—Oh, Red! How selfish of me. Are you all right? I know how much Andy meant to you."

Red Sanderson, a tough-looking John Wayne type, had been with Andy more than twenty years. Except for the black hair, he even resembled John Wayne. Red liked the tough-guy image and lived up to it in every way. No one crossed him; they knew better. He picked up the nickname Red when, as a young boy, he fell in love with the little red-haired girl next door, and his brother got everyone to calling him Red. His brother died of pneumonia the following winter, and James Earl never answered to anything but Red after that. Red had respected his brother and Andy Lewis. As far as anyone knew, they were the only two people who had ever gained that status with Red. Now, out of respect, he felt it was his duty to help two of Andy's other closest friends through this difficult period.

"Hey, I'll make it. See you tomorrow," said Red. As Red hung up, he saw the button on his phone light up indicating that the other call he was dreading so much had reached him.

Lily slowly replaced the receiver and turned to the face of her foreman, Tom McNally. Tom loved Lily in every sense of the word, but she could only see the love of friendship. He was mesmerized by her dark eyes and her ways. Ways that were innocent, yet sophisticated and tough.

He overheard the tail end of the news broadcast when he rushed into the kitchen to check on Lily "Once again. In Texas, Andrew M. Lewis, dead at forty-two," the box blared. Tom reached to the television and turned it off. The abrupt silence was like a slap in the face to Lily. She ran to Tom's understanding arms.

"Oh, Tom, he's dead! Andy's dead!"

"And not a minute too soon, either," Tom snarled to himself as he comforted the woman he loved.

chapter

TWO

Lily stood at the closed casket, still in shock, wondering why on earth this had to happen. She was alone in the cool, quiet room of the funeral home. It allowed her time to study the beautifully framed picture of Andy on top of the carved oak vessel. She tried to convince herself that it was truly him lying there under the lid. Because of the blast, the coffin would remain closed, but she would never forget how he looked. She could not picture him cold, hard...dead. Yes, dammit, dead. Dead. Dead!

Her sobs reverberated off the walls and ceiling. When her hysteria began to subside, Lily tried not to notice the huge, pale-blue room with the ten-foot ceilings and the "ever-so-peaceful" murals on the walls. She didn't want to see the endless arrangements of flowers—shaped in every form from oil derricks to the Texas state flag—or smell their sickening fragrance. She stood silently for a long time, then placed a single white lily on the coffin holding the man she loved.

Caught up in thoughts of Andy, she didn't hear the door open in the back of the chapel. She was not aware that she was being observed. Kathryne Langford had quietly entered the room. Taken off guard at the sight of Lily, she quickly settled in a chair to collect her thoughts before she was discovered. Kathryne took in every detail of Lily.

Lily's long, black hair, which Kathryne remembered so well, was elegantly swept up in a French braid woven with tiny seed pearls. The simple, black dress she wore showed a model-like figure, hugging her slender body. Kathryne's throat hurt as she swallowed the emotions brought on by seeing Lily. Sitting in the back of the room, out of Lily's view, she reflected on the past. Her mind reached back to a lifetime ago in Atlanta, when they first met.

Kathryne had been at the Gayle White Advertising Agency for a little over six months and was working on a big account, the Jeff Baker Rolls-Royce dealership, when her assistant quit without notice.

"I can't meet my schedule and deadlines without an assistant!" murmured Kathryne, rushing from her office to keep a noon appointment. She let her long legs carry her swiftly to Pierre's, the plush French café two blocks away. The Peachtree Street streetscape, completed the year before, was beautiful, with small oaks and patches of flowers along the brick sidewalks. Enhanced by the glorious spring sunshine, it was just what she needed. By the time she got to Pierre's, she was starving.

Her appointment was crawling out of his Rolls-Royce just as she stepped under the canopy in front of the restaurant. Jeff Baker was good-looking and tall, with a full head of black, wavy hair and wonderful blue eyes framed in thick, black lashes. His body was straight, lean, and perfect. His movement gave the impression that he had complete command of every muscle. Women really went for Jeff. He was, as he called himself, "a country gentleman." His black, Western-style leisure suit and snakeskin cowboy boots cut a handsome picture as he stood by the Rolls giving his driver instructions.

The black Rolls-Royce, a brand-new 1971 Cloud, had the traditional twenty-eight coats of paint. Each coat was hand rubbed to perfection before the next coat was applied. It was like looking into a black lagoon. Jeff had gone to great lengths to explain this painting process to Kathryne, and when he talked about a Rolls-Royce, it was as if it were his woman. It was "she" this and "she" that. Kathryne loved it. It reminded her of her father; he talked about cars the same way.

Jeff spent a lot of money advertising his Rolls-Royce dealership, and it certainly paid off for him. His clientele included Liberace and Tom Jones. He made sure everyone knew it. It was a great account for Kathryne.

Over lunch, Kathryne reviewed with Jeff some ideas for his campaign. She only wanted to tease him with ideas and name-drop a couple of her new accounts. After he signed the new contract, she would roll out a campaign that would knock the skin right off his boots.

As Kathryne felt Jeff's hand on her leg, she looked up to see that same old shit-eating grin all men get when they make their play.

"Jeff, now behave yourself," Kathryne said in a patronizing tone as she removed his hand. "You know I'm married to a wonderful man," she lied. She was a tall, good-looking woman with shoulder-length, red hair and green eyes. Her sexy figure and gregarious personality were never shielded by her business attitude as completely as she thought. She was accustomed to men's advances.

Kathryne always thought it was a good cover and not like a total rejection to pretend to be in love with her husband. "You've got to be so careful of the precious male ego," she told her friends. Kathryne thought the male ego had been Eve's real punishment. It was certainly more difficult to deal with than monthly cramps and childbirth.

Kathryne, signed contract in hand, went back to the office and tried to finish some of the work she and her assistant had started together. Just after seven o'clock, there was a knock on her door.

"Mrs. Langford?" A voice said.

"Yes?" answered Kathryne.

"I have a delivery for you from Ellen's Height of Beauty Boutique."

"Oh, yes!" Kathryne had forgotten about the lovely linen suit she purchased earlier in the day and almost thought the girl was in the wrong office.

The young woman delivering the suit was strikingly beautiful, about five feet ten, with long, black hair and hazel eyes. Kathryne assumed by her high cheekbones and peach complexion that she must be part Indian. The effect of her coloring was outstanding.

"You must be Lily," Kathryne said. "You are just as lovely as Ellen said you were. I appreciate your bringing this over. I was in such a rush this afternoon, but I didn't want to pass up this suit." She was trying to decide if it would be appropriate to tip Lily for the delivery.

"You have great taste in clothes. I love it." Lily handed the package to Kathryne. "The color will be wonderful with your hair."

"I was standing on the corner waiting for the light to change on my way back to the office from lunch when I saw it in Ellen's window. It looked so good on that blonde mannequin, and it seemed to be calling my name, 'Kathryne, I'm for you...come in and get me.' You know how clothes do that sometimes," Kathryne said. They both laughed at the idea of a talking suit.

"I'm sure you'll get your money's worth out of it," Lily said, looking around Kathryne's office, feeling a little ill at ease for taking too much of Kathryne's time.

Kathryne, on the other hand, had been working nonstop since the middle of the afternoon and felt the need for a nonwork-related chat.

"Ellen's was a real find for me. I like being six feet tall, but tall women's clothes with any kind of style at all are so hard to find." Noticing Lily's height, she added, "Well, I guess I'm not telling you anything you don't already know."

"I know what you mean. I was glad to get the job for the clothing discount alone," Lily confessed.

"Ellen has such good sales, too, and she is so good about giving me a little advance notice. When you are married to an accountant, everything has to be on a budget," said Kathryne, rolling her eyes.

"Ellen told me your assistant quit," Lily said, as if trying to confirm the information.

"Yes," said Kathryne, "and I am going crazy without her!"

"Well, it has been very nice meeting you, Mrs. Langford. I'd better get back to the store." Lily said rather abruptly. Turning to leave, she added, "I've tucked something inside your package. I hope you don't mind. See if you find it interesting. If you do, would you let me know?" She closed the door behind her, and a puzzled Kathryne turned to answer the ringing telephone.

Kathryne finally arrived home in time for a light dinner with Joe and their daughter, Becky. She remembered the suit again and went upstairs to try it on. It was navy-blue linen with red topstitching on the lapel. The jacket had small breast pockets that were also topstitched in red. The side seams of the skirt were topstitched with a double row of red. She knew her red blouse and navy shoes would complete the outfit.

Knowing Becky would love it, she pretended to be a model and pranced around in front of her and Joe in her new purchase. Becky was still clapping over the performance when Kathryne went upstairs to take a shower.

As she was hanging up the suit, an envelope fell to the floor. "Attention: Mrs. Kathryne Langford" was written across the front of the envelope in beautiful script. The handwriting reminded Kathryne of her mother's beautiful penmanship. Inside the envelope was a piece of paper labeled, "Résumé." The opening paragraph said, "Lily E. Gray, age twenty-five, five feet nine, 125 pounds, single, no disabilities."

Too excited to wait until the next day after reading Lily's résumé, Kathryne placed the phone call nine o'clock Friday night to Lily asking if Monday would be too soon for her to start.

"Of course not. Monday at eight will be just fine, Mrs. Langford." Lily's answer had a smile with it ample enough to accommodate a whole slice of watermelon in one bite.

At the end of the conversation, Lily went immediately to her closet. She stood and surveyed the contents, then began to try on every professional-looking piece of clothing she owned. At one o'clock, she finally decided to wear a plain, navy-blue suit with a white blouse and a string of pearls.

Lily was ecstatic to land a position with an advertising firm the size of the Gayle White Agency while she was still in college. She switched all her classes to night sessions, which left her little social life, but she enjoyed her work so much that most of her spare time was spent at the office anyway. She had found in Kathryne Langford a very special type of person. One who was very detailed and patient. She knew Lily was studying advertising in college and had no real hands-on experience in the working world.

Kathryne could see the great potential in Lily and knew the boost of self-confidence she gave her would be a tremendous asset to both their futures. Kathryne was very generous with her time and had a way of helping Lily overcome her inexperience. She made Lily feel like a genius after she learned a new trick of the trade. She was a walking wealth of knowledge. With her driving ambition to be equally good, Lily constantly picked her brain. Kathryne knew after a few short weeks that she had found an undiscovered pro in her new assistant.

Lily put in long hours. By researching the background of some of the major accounts, she realized that since Kathryne had taken over as executive manager, the account retention was up to 95 percent, and new accounts were flooding in.

Kathryne and Lily's close professional relationship quickly developed into a genuine friendship. Many times they would work until late at night and order from Dell's Deli around the corner from the office. They would unwind from a hectic day, talking and laughing for hours. Their need for personal contact was fostered by the amount of time they spent together, and it became very evident that they drew strength from each other.

Lily's family was in Kentucky, and even though she never felt a real part of them—except for her paternal grandmother, who was precious to her—she would sometimes get homesick to see familiar people and places. She always seemed to see things differently from her mother and sister. After the death of her father, she felt like a total outcast. She always wanted more. Not material things necessarily, but more from herself. She was constant in her goal to do better.

Kathryne could relax with Lily and not have to think about the pressure at home with Becky, her beautiful daughter. Becky's medical problems were massive. Lily could sense Kathryne's marriage to Joe was not made in heaven, but Kathryne never talked about it.

Both women had a driving force to be the best in whatever they did. For different reasons, both wanted to make the agency the best in the country. The two women worked in perfect harmony, like a finely-tuned instrument. They worked quickly, handling the pressures of deadlines, last-minute changes, and temperamental clients. And they cussed together when the good-ol-boy system screwed them out of an account. They mixed business with fun, and the entire staff enjoyed working on projects with them.

The ideas between the two of them sparked creativity like bolts of lightning, and they knew they had in themselves a winning team.

chapter

THREE

The agency really grew the following year. Kathryne had been able to lease more space and would redecorate as soon as she could talk Gayle into it. Gayle White had started the agency from absolutely nothing, so she had a tendency, although they were doing very well, to be conservative. Gayle had married her high-school sweetheart, Buddy White, right after graduation. Not realizing what a loser he was until three years later and thousands of dollars of debt, Gayle finally divorced him. Although friends told her to file for bankruptcy on the debts Buddy had run up and start over, her main goal was to pay them all off. It took Gayle a few years of working two jobs to get the finances settled. With a clean slate, she was able to open the Gayle White Advertising Agency.

Accustomed to hard work by then, Gayle put in long hours, which paid off handsomely for her. She became one of the most successful, prestigious agencies in Atlanta. She was recognized four years in a row as Atlanta's "Most Outstanding Businesswoman."

In January, Lily finally completed college, after what seemed like an eternity to her. Without that expense, plus the increase in salary Kathryne had recommended for her, she was able to move out of her crackerbox-size apartment and into a small town house of her own. She loved it.

Kathryne visited the first night Lily moved in. They unpacked boxes to the tunes of Elvis and the Beatles. Lily brought out her own private stock of Boone's Farm Strawberry Hill wine and served it in her finest Dixie cups.

"My gosh, Kathryne, it's eleven thirty!" Lily remarked as she passed the Boone's Farm. "We've been at this since four thirty this afternoon! Don't you have to get home to Becky and Joe?"

"They won't miss me," Kathryne replied as she flipped the Beatles' Abbey Road album to side two. "Besides, your not having the phone hooked up yet is like a sanctuary to me."

Lily stretched out on the Indian rug she found at the discount market downtown. She was thinking how much better the living room would look when she got curtains up and the hardwood floor waxed.

Lily yawned. "Kathryne, do you know what this place means to me?"

"Well, it means a backache to me at this point," Kathryne cracked as she stretched out on the floor.

"No, I'm serious. It means that I finally have something of my own. I am going to make the big time. When I was growing up, I never had any real encouragement that I could ever do anything besides grow up, get old, and die."

Lily poured another cup of Strawberry Hill. Studying the contents as if reading tea leaves, she went on, "Daddy worked hard making a living for my sister, Valerie, and me. But back in Kentucky, you were rich, or you were poor. We were poor, but I really didn't realize it until I went to high school. There, it was either the in-crowd or the out-crowd. I was the "out" and everybody knew it. My sister had gotten by on her brains, so I seemed to be constantly trapped in her shadow. Mother pushed her into all the right social circles. She was in law school. Amen."

"But Lily, there certainly isn't any need for you to live in your sister's shadow," Kathryne interrupted. "You are the sharpest advertising mind I have ever worked with. Already you are getting your own accounts. And you have a fantastic personality to go along with it." Kathryne was very defensive of the best friend she'd ever had. She just could not believe anyone calling themselves family could actually treat Lily that way.

"Well, now when people speak of me, it will be with reverence and awe," Lily said, with mock dignity, letting the word "awe" linger. "I wasn't even expected to go to college, since I wasn't an A+ superbrain. Then, of course, there was Tommy Hawkins. I went steady with him all through high school. We knew we loved each other, but neither of us ever voiced it. Everyone assumed we would get married. When he went to Vietnam, I cried every day for a solid month. Tommy was my first kiss, my first love…everything. I missed him so much…really missed him. Still do."

Kathryne was curled up beside Lily with her head propped on Lily's back. They no longer noticed how hard the floor was or the late hour.

"After my daddy was killed in a car accident," Lily said, "my mother just fell totally dependent on Valerie. Valerie handled all the funeral arrangements, Mother's money, and even where, or if, I would go to college. They acted like I was three years old." Lily let out a long breath. "Naturally, when I announced that I was going into advertising they rolled their eyes and wanted to know where I would get a job in Owensboro, Kentucky, in advertising."

"If you need something"—Lily turned her head and pursed her lips, mocking Valerie—"Honey, you just go and buy it. You don't need someone to tell you where it is or what to buy. Besides, there is only one choice anyway—the best!"

"My life was beginning to fill up with bitterness and hatred. I was unhappy and confused. At the time I was living with my grandmother. If it had not been for her, I probably would never have come to Atlanta."

"That's your Indian grandmother, the one you think so much of, right?" asked Kathryne.

"Yes. She's the only person whom I feel really in tune with. I think it's because I seem to have more of the Indian traits that Mother always seemed to dislike so much."

"Is it your mother who's Indian or your dad?"

"Daddy was Cherokee. Everyone always said Mother had a daughter and Daddy had a daughter, because of the distinct differences in Valerie and me. Mother always detested my allegiance to Daddy's family."

"Why does your mom dislike Indians? She married one, didn't she?" Kathryne sounded aggravated.

"I'm not really sure. At first, I guess Mother thought it was romantic to marry an Indian. He was so strong and independent. Then her family started to run him down so badly that she finally agreed with them…another in-crowd thing. Her mother always called Daddy 'that Indian.'"

"Daddy even shortened his last name to help conceal his heritage, just to shut Mother up."

"You mean Gray isn't your last name?" Kathryne was astonished.

"My name is really Lily Gray Dove. Mother almost shit a brick till Daddy agreed to drop the Dove part. This was done shortly after their marriage, according to Grandmother Gray Dove."

"Well, good grief!"

"Anyway, after a summer sabbatical at Gray Dove's, I never went home to stay again. She is so good and wise. I want you to meet her sometime."

"What is her name?"

"America Gray Dove."

"Oh, Lily, that's beautiful."

"Well, to make a long story short, she gave me the inner strength to stand up for myself. I decided to come here and go to school and get away for a while. So you see," Lily said, looking around the room, "this little town house and my job at the agency mean the world to me. And so do you, Kathryne, for giving me the chance."

"Didn't you have any high-school friends?" prodded Kathryne.

"Yes, I had one close girlfriend. We would skip school and go to the GE parking lot and steal her sister's car while she was working. We would drive to the horse races thirty miles away. The funniest time was the day we took the car, and her sister came to use it only to find it was gone. She called the police and turned in a stolen car report. You know, the whole nine yards. Of course we didn't know we were fugitives and just drove the car right back to the very same parking spot where we got it. It wasn't hard to get through the police dragnet. I think Barney Fife trained them.

Anyway, her sister comes out after work, and there it is, just exactly where she left it, gas and all. It was hilarious! Of course, it was all news to us. As far as I know, she is still goin' on about it to this day. We got pretty good at betting, too. We would always win enough to put the exact amount of gas back in the car and stop for pizza on the way home. With no more than we had to bet, that was pretty good. That's where I learned to love the sport and horses so much."

Lily was still smiling, thinking about the days of car theft and horse races, when Kathryne brought her back to reality with a serious tone of voice.

"I had no idea things were that bad for you at home. Have you gone back recently?"

"No. I want everything to be just right before I go back."

"But you've seen Gray Dove since you've been living in Atlanta, haven't you?"

"Oh, yes. She lives in Cherokee, North Carolina, now. She moved there just after I left Kentucky. I couldn't go without seeing her. She seems more like my mother than my real one."

"Valerie doesn't have much to do with her?"

"God, no. Valerie has Mother's brain. She's only close to the women's clubs, money, and Mother. She even treats Mark, her husband, like a lapdog."

Changing the subject, Kathryne continued to prod Lily. "Have you dated much since you've been here?"

"Oh, I've gone out one or twice—a concert, a movie, nothing special."

Turning to Kathryne with a "now it's your turn" look, Lily asked, "What about you? Do I detect a void in your life that you're not telling me about?"

"Maybe, maybe not," Kathryne replied slyly. "The subject tonight is Lily Gray. Let's see now…a puppy love in high school, nothing special since you've been in Atlanta…so, does this mean you're still a virgin?"

Lily looked at Kathryne as if horrified. "Oh my gosh, I guess it does. Well, I think it's high time I did something about that." They both rolled on the floor laughing uncontrollably.

"You know," Kathryne said, "Joe says there's nothing more disgusting than drunk women!" With that, they laughed even louder.

"Hey, let's order a pizza, I'm starving."

"That would be great if I had a phone."

"Well, shit. And I don't suppose there's anything edible in the house either?"

They prowled the kitchen like starving wolves, only to find a limited choice of popcorn or ketchup sandwiches. The popcorn won.

"Hey, let's build a fire. Do you have any wood?"

"Yes, I do. My Realtor brought some by yesterday as a house-warming gift. Appropriate, huh?"

The fire was roaring. The popcorn was salted. Lily, not wanting to be the only true confession of the night, asked, "How did you meet Joe?"

"Are you trying to ruin a perfect evening, or what?" Kathryne said, avoiding the question.

"No, really. Don't close the door on me. I know you don't like to talk about it, but I just care about you," Lily said.

"All right then, we met in high school and got married in college."

"Love at first sight? Oh, and just when did you lose your virginity?" Lily asked, giggling through the wine.

"No, not love at first sight. Joe was a football player, and I wanted him because all the other girls wanted him. We went steady our senior year and in our second year of college, Miss Virginity, I got pregnant with Becky, and we had to get married."

"I...I didn't mean to pry." Lily wanted to bite off her tongue.

"Oh, don't worry about it. I was happy to get the man I wanted anyway I could. Everything was OK for a few months, but as my stomach grew larger with Becky, Joe seemed to be turned off by it. Then, after she was born, he seemed OK again, for a while. Becky was born in late November, on my birthday. She was a beautiful baby. I was overwhelmed by my responsibilities as a mother, but I was determined to be the best."

"During a routine checkup, I became aware that the doctor was taking an unusually long time with her. He repeatedly examined her eyes with a light and bent and released her little arms and legs. I'll never forget that day. The doctor turned to me and said, 'Mrs. Langford, are you aware of your baby's slow development and lack of eye movement?' I felt my stomach begin to crawl up my throat. As I searched his eyes for some meaning to his words, I knew we were in serious trouble.

"Becky's needs became far too complicated for me. She needed professional care. You know, doctors, nurses, special teachers, and all, but she was really happiest at school, where she was constantly learning new things. Joe thought if I tried harder I could teach Becky, but I couldn't seem to get the hang of it. One day I became so exasperated with one of Becky's violent outbursts that I hit her. Later, after I got her to bed, I sat on the floor in the bathroom and cried until I threw up.

"After years of hospital and costly operations, we had to take a second mortgage on the house. Our insurance only covered a portion of it, and the medical expenses continued to mount. Joe just couldn't handle it and flipped out. By then he was drinking so heavily he lost his job. I knew what I had to do—earn the money needed to cover the exorbitant costs and pay back the second mortgage so we wouldn't lose the house.

"I had become anxious to build a career. I had to have something to fill the deep, growing emptiness. I searched for a job for weeks. No one wanted to hire me, because I had no experience. Finally, Gayle White gave me a chance to prove myself. I went to work scared but determined. That first day I left Becky, I cried all the way to work, on every break, and for my entire lunch hour. Every ad I worked on had tear smudges on it."

The women were still lying on the floor. Tears ran down Lily's cheeks, but Kathryne's vow a few years back—never to cry again—held fast. They gazed into the hypnotic fire.

"Life ain't easy, is it, kiddo?" sniffed Lily.

"Nope," came her brave reply.

Kathryne had just come from a breakfast meeting with her client and good friend, Andy Lewis. She had first met him a few years before in Texas. He had made millions in the oil business and was developing a chain of gas stations. Convenience stores, he called them. She made a presentation to him that was exactly what he was looking for. His idea came across just as he had envisioned it, and the gas stations were a tremendous success throughout the

Southeast. She had told Andy all about Lily, but somehow their schedules had never worked out for them to meet.

"What a trio we would make," she thought. She was still smiling and fighting laughter over Andy's joke about Texas politicians when she swung open the office door and stepped inside. Looking around, her smile faded quickly.

It was only nine thirty, and the office was already full of roses. Usually it was around noon before the "daily dozen," as they were called around the office, arrived. But today, roses were everywhere. Yellow roses, red roses, white roses. The front reception area looked like a flower shop. Sal always went to extremes. If Gayle would pay as much attention to her business as she did Sal, they could redecorate or even move to a nicer building.

Gayle had met Salvatore Martino at a cocktail party for the governor six months before. Dignitaries from all over the country were at the party, and Salvatore Martino was one of them. He looked like a movie star that night, with his long, white-silk scarf, cigarette holder, and gold-and-diamond watch. He was mildly attractive, not too tall, with black hair and a Clark Gable mustache. But he was charming. So very, very charming. He and Gayle hit it off from the beginning. A very good friend of Sal's, Tony Campbell, was a client of Gayle's. He raved to Sal, when he introduced them, about what a remarkable job she had done for his custom yacht company.

Sal and Gayle had been on a whirl ever since. They would have lunch in New York and dinner in Palm Springs. Sal would get lonesome at a business meeting in Canada and send his Learjet for Gayle.

"I guess I can't really blame her," thought Kathryne. "But one day he's going to drop her for some young thing. And then what?"

Gayle was losing accounts every day. She would not let anyone else handle her clients, and consequently, the work wasn't getting done. Major accounts were going elsewhere. There wasn't enough time to service accounts and be with Sal every second. Sal always won.

Now, walking into Gayle's office, one of those rare days when she was in, Kathryne had to acknowledge how truly beautiful Gayle was. She was a young fifty-three, about five feet four, with a flawless complexion and big blue eyes. She always wore just a little too much makeup. Her golden blonde hair was always done perfectly in the latest style.

"Kathryne!" Gayle squealed. "I'm so glad you're here. Look!" Gayle said as she leaned across her huge mahogany desk sticking out her left hand. Kathryne found herself looking at the biggest, most beautiful diamond ring she could have imagined.

"Sal has asked me to marry him!" Pacing back and forth in front of the large windows overlooking Peachtree Park, she spluttered out details of how Sal had proposed, the wedding plans, and the two-month honeymoon he had arranged for them in Europe. It was indeed a Cinderella story. "Gayle, I'm so happy for you," stammered a surprised Kathryne, sinking into the nearest chair.

As Gayle was rambling on about the wedding, Kathryne suddenly realized that she might be looking for a new job. What would she do? There wasn't another agency in Atlanta she liked. She and Lily had always considered them the enemy; plus, she couldn't relocate because of Joe and Becky.

"Well, shit," Kathryne was thinking. "Why does one person's happiness seem to always be someone else's misery?"

Gayle sat down beside her and took her hand. She told Kathryne that she wanted to sell the agency to her. Kathryne had proved that she had what it took to make the agency grow. And Gayle felt comfortable turning her life's work over to Kathryne.

Kathryne was flabbergasted. "Boy, things could sure take off like a bullet and always when you least expected it," she thought as she tried to grasp what was going on in Gayle's mind.

Kathryne moaned. "But, Gayle, Becky's care takes so much money I haven't been able to save—"

Gayle interrupted Kathryne with her plan to sell the agency to her and also finance it. Kathryne could hardly sit still. She couldn't believe her ears. But she was beginning to get the picture. Gayle was going to be married to a multimillionaire and would never have to worry about work, or money, or anything ever again.

"Kathryne, I know you have held this agency together for me these last several months, and I want to show you how grateful I am."

Kathryne tried to protest, but Gayle told her instructions for the deal had already been given to her attorney, and the papers would be signed at her bachelorette party.

"Now, can I show you my ring again?" Gayle asked.

Kathryne smiled at Gayle as she took her hand to gaze once again upon the three-carat, blue sapphire diamond and was amazed at how much prettier it had become.

"Yes, Virginia, there is a Santa Claus!" Kathryne shouted to herself.

chapter

FOUR

Gayle's wedding was a month away. Kathryne and Lily had taken over just about all of her accounts, and the clients were delighted with the attention they were getting. The papers to transfer ownership of the agency over to Kathryne were to be signed in a couple of weeks. Kathryne was about to buzz Lily on the intercom when the door to her office popped open.

"Well, how do you like it?" asked Lily as she twirled around in front of Kathryne's cluttered desk. Lily was modeling a sleeveless, white dress with a narrow skirt, a matching jacket, and a wide-brimmed, white hat complete with a royal-blue sash.

"It's gorgeous," declared Kathryne as she leaned back and looked at Lily. Kathryne had been in Colorado for the past two weeks, working on the Mountain View Ski Resort account. It was good to see Lily, and she was obviously up to something.

"Do you have a hot date, or what?" Kathryne asked.

"No, next Saturday is the first Saturday in May!"

"Yes, and the next day is Sunday, then Monday, and so forth. They go that way, Lil." Kathryne laughed.

"Girl, don't you know anything?" Lily chided her friend. "It's only the most exciting two minutes in sports—the Kentucky Derby! And this kid's going, and this is what I intend to wear." She pranced like a model on the runway. "I'll be dressed to kill when I rub elbows with the racing royalty and movie stars who are always there. Ooh, I just can't wait!" Lily went on. Her whirling sent her into the white leather chair in front of Kathryne's desk, breathless. "I've missed the derby since I've been living here in Atlanta, but I wouldn't miss it for the world this year."

"What's so special about this year?" Kathryne asked, while pouring herself a cup of coffee from the bottomless pot she kept brewing on her credenza.

"Well, for one thing, I've got box seats!" Lily said like a little girl who had the biggest cookie. "And, get this—an invitation to the Derby Ball! Man, I just can't wait. I dreamed of this every year I stood in the infield on top of a beer cooler, trying to at least get a glimpse of the horses."

"Lily, I don't think I've ever seen you so excited. What's the derby like?" Kathryne asked. Excitement was beginning to grow in her own mind.

"It's grand, Kathryne, just grand. It's hard to explain, but the city comes alive the week before the derby. There is a certain feeling in the air throughout Louisville. Excitement, anxiety, a high that continues the whole week, right on up to the draping of the blanket of red roses on the winning horse."

"Go on." Kathryne sipped her black coffee.

"Oh, let's see. There are celebrities everywhere. Jack Klugman, Bob Hope, Lee Majors. I saw John Wayne there once, too. Only at a distance, but still, I almost died! There's the Pegasus Parade down Broadway Street, the Derby Ball, the steamboat races between the Belle of Louisville and the Delta Queen of Cincinnati, and there's the Kentucky Colonel's Bar-B-Que the Sunday after the derby, just to name a few of the highlights. The derby is just steeped with tradition. The one thing that stands out in my mind most is the singing of 'My Old Kentucky Home' during post parade. It never fails to bring tears to my eyes."

"But most of all," Lily went on, unstoppable. "The horses, Kathryne, it's the horses. It's their day, and they know how beautiful they are when they strut by in post parade, each one's coat glowing like fine satin and as soft as velvet. They just kind of look like soft jazz sounds before it really starts cookin'."

"Well, I've never been to a horse race in my life," Kathryne announced to Lily's horror.

"Oh, I'm so sorry for you," Lily said with genuine sympathy. "Then you've never heard the sounds. There is just no sound on earth like the sound of the hooves as the horses come thundering down the track, and the crowd goes into a frenzy, all the people chanting for their horse to win. I think it was Irvin S. Cobb who said, 'Until you go to Kentucky and with your own eyes behold the derby, you ain't never been nowhere, and you ain't never seen nothing,' and I completely agree. You see, Kathryne, it's really more than a horse race. It's also a feeling of great emotion and sense of belonging to a part of history, even if it's just for a split second."

Kathryne leaned over the desk and looked into the seriousness in Lily's eyes. "Lily, are you high or something?"

"Oh, Kathryne, you are disgusting, absolutely! Here I am describing the most wonderful event in the world to you, and you've got your mind on drugs."

"Well, it sounds to me like I ain't never been nowhere and ain't never seen nothin'."

"There is just no way for you to understand until you have been there," Lily said removing her new white pumps.

"Say, then, why am I not going with you?" Kathryne asked, realizing there was a piece missing from the puzzle.

"Because I'm being escorted by a gentleman." Lily threw her head back in a snooty flip.

"Who is he? Do I know him? Where did you meet him?" Kathryne could not get the questions out fast enough.

"Seriously, no. I don't think you would remember the Dressler account. They manufacture horse equipment. You know…saddles, whips, bits, bridles, etc. Anyway, as I was saying before I was so rudely interrupted, Bill Dressler, president of Dressler Manufacturing, and I got to talking about the derby last week, and one thing led to another, and…well, we're going!"

32

"Whoa, horse," Kathryne said, throwing her hands up as if she were going to stop traffic. "It sounds like I've been missing some action between ol' Bill and you. Anything I should know about?"

"Nothing really," stammered Lily. "I do enjoy his company though, and I've been riding with him several times. He keeps several horses at Thoroughbred Stable on the north side so he'll have something to ride when he's in town. You do know how I love horses. He's just someone comfortable to be with, that's all. Not a heartthrob or anything."

Lily popped up from the chair in a jack-in-the-box fashion. "I have some loose ends I'll need to get Laurie to help me with before I leave. We'll be gone Thursday through Sunday."

"Oh yeah? If the derby is on Saturday, why are you going to also be gone Thursday and Friday with someone you only feel 'comfortable' with?" Kathryne smirked good-heartedly.

"The derby itself is Saturday afternoon, but it entails a whole weekend of activities. Thursday night we will attend a party given by some of Bill's friends in Louisville. Friday is the Running of the Oaks, which is the race that is always the Friday before derby. Friday night is the Derby Ball. Saturday, of course, is race day, followed by parties. We will return Sunday. Got it, boss? Who knows, with all the parties to attend, I might just pick up a new client or two." Lily winked at Kathryne and floated out the door singing, "My ole' Kentucky home...here I come." As the strains of the song faded down the hall, Kathryne jotted down a note to get derby tickets for next year.

Bill arrived on Lily's door step promptly at one o'clock Thursday afternoon, giving them plenty of time to make their two thirty flight. Bill was always very prompt. They were seated in first-class. Lily leaned back and tried to relax. She began to think about Bill and the relationship that had developed between them. Her feelings were mixed, but the word "comfortable" kept coming to mind when she thought of him. She wanted to feel more, but somehow the chemistry wasn't there. He would be a good catch, if that was all she wanted, but she was just not sure at this point.

Tommy Hawkins, her high-school love, always seemed to be in the back of her mind.

The sun was warm and shining when Lily and Bill deplaned at Standford Field in Louisville. The airport was already filled with derby goers. Bill had arranged for his friend and branch manager of Louisville Operations, Kevin King, to meet their plane. They were all staying at the Galt House downtown. Kevin, like Bill, was tall, good-looking, and from a very wealthy family.

The traffic slipped along the crowded streets like a slow-moving ooze. Lily, totally removed from the business conversation Bill and Kevin were having, fondly reminisced about times in Louisville. "Could this be how Cinderella felt when the prince found her and brought her back to his kingdom?" she wondered, watching the people and buildings from the window of the plush, white town car. The city of Louisville seemed to be saying to her, "Hello, old friend! Where have you been? I've missed you!"

Like the airport, the lobby of the Galt House was packed with people already in the spirit of derby week. After checking in, Lily entered the lovely sixth-floor suite with Bill. She was relieved to see it had two bedrooms, each with a separate bath. She and Bill had been seeing quite a bit of each other over the last few months, but she wasn't ready to go to bed with him. To her, that would mean a commitment her feelings would not let her make at this time. Lily knew Bill well enough to feel sure that he was too much of a gentleman to expect anything from her before she was ready.

Lily realized suddenly that she was actually pacing the sitting-room floor, jabbering to Bill about all sorts of dumb things. She knew it was her nerves. She was about to take the biggest gamble she had ever taken in her life.

Lily had been very thrifty, saving money every month since she had gotten to Atlanta. Even when she was going to school, she had saved money and managed to buy the little town house she loved so much. Now, every dime she had in the world had been withdrawn from First National Bank of Atlanta before she left.

Lily put her nervous energy to use after Bill went to Kevin's suite to check over some business reports. As Lily unpacked her bags, she checked the wad of money she had secretly tucked away in the lingerie compartment of her overnight bag. She felt like a thief sneaking into her room to secretly count her money. Her entire life savings, and she was going to blow it all at the track. "Oh God, what a thought!" she said aloud.

Lily had never had anyone to depend on but herself, and this money meant a great deal to her. It was her constant assurance that she would not have to go back to Owensboro and hear Valerie and her mother say, "I told you so."

She always had good luck at the track, and this time she had researched the horses she planned to bet, especially Secretariat, the big, red horse that was getting so much news coverage.

Lily pulled back the luxurious, royal-blue drapes and looked out over the Ohio River and down on the city of Louisville. It happened just as she knew it would, the moment she stepped off the plane. "I'm so homesick," she said to herself. "Dorothy was right. There is no place like home. Dear God in heaven, please get my horses to the finish line first so I can come back home a *somebody*," she prayed.

Bill came in and slipped his arms around Lily's slender waist. "We had better get ready. It is getting late, and we don't want to keep everyone waiting," he said as he kissed her neck. She brushed a tear from her cheek before turning to give him a big hug. He would never know how grateful she was to him. Lily hoped the party that evening would end early. Tomorrow was going to be a big day. Lily had plans.

Friday morning started with a big breakfast at the hotel, sponsored by Dressler Manufacturing. The top person in every department was invited. Thanking them for a job well done, Bill handed out tickets for both race-day events. Lily couldn't believe the size of the buffet. There was country ham with redeye gravy, sorghum molasses, silver-dollar pancakes, eggs, cheese grits, biscuits, marinated strawberries, and Bloody Marys. Lily, delighted with a breakfast that wasn't wrapped in cellophane, ate as if it were going to be her last meal. She listened to Bill's brief talk and realized how intelligent and well received he was. She felt proud.

"But why isn't it there? Why can't I love him?" she wondered. "He's tall, he has blond hair and blue eyes, and he's well built— every mother's dream. Maybe I just need to give it more time. At least until after Tommy comes home. That's it. Then I can compare." At any rate, she couldn't think about that now. She was too interested in getting the early copy of the *Daily Racing Form* to check her picks in today's races.

Bill had a little schmoozing to do before the afternoon races, so Lily had time to get away and revisit some old haunts in Louisville. Lily walked downtown, visiting shops she'd frequented years ago. The sky was clear blue with big puffy clouds. The cool morning breeze had a hint of spring. Lily felt like a winner.

She was to meet Bill back at the suite at noon to change and get ready for the afternoon race. Giving herself plenty of time to check the racing form one last time, she got back early. Lily's plan was to bet the daily double in each race, the track favorite, and the three long shots she had researched. If she won Friday, she planned to bet it all on Saturday. Of course, all that could change after she had one look at the horses. If they didn't look right to her, she would change her strategy. She always got a special feeling when she looked at a horse she wanted to bet on. If it wasn't there, she didn't bet on it.

She didn't want Bill to know that she was betting a lot of money, much less her life savings, so she would only let him see her two-dollar ticket. Lily was ready to go when Bill knocked on her door.

"Did you enjoy revisiting the city today?" Bill asked in the elevator.

"Yes, I really did," Lily replied. "So much has changed since I was here last. The city has grown so much."

Kevin had brought his girlfriend, Holly, and they were waiting in front of the hotel with the car when Bill and Lily got to the lobby.

"The company has had box seats at Churchill Downs for forty-three years," Bill explained proudly to Lily as he escorted everyone to their seats. "Mom and Dad will be here for tomorrow's race. They'll be at the ball tonight, too. I'm very anxious for you to meet them."

Being at the derby in a box seat was an intoxicant to Lily. She was seeing everything this year from the other side of the proverbial tracks. In years past, when she had come to the derby with friends, they partied in the infield, where it was a privilege to see the wisp of a tail go by. But this time, she was going to see the whole race.

Holly was from Detroit, and Lily had no compassion for her lack of interest in this historic weekend. She didn't even know who Secretariat was, for God's sake. Lily would rather have been nibbled to death by ducks than sit beside the conceited, spoiled brat.

When the racing started, Lily made sure to place her bet away from where Bill was doing his wagering. Lily plunked down $600 on number four in the first race and number five in the second race. She bet them both to win for the daily double. "This one is a shoe-in…I hope," thought Lily. The odds were four to one. She bet a hundred dollars on the long shot to place and the token two dollars on the track favorite to show for Bill's benefit. "Poor Kevin," thought Lily, as she settled back in her seat. "He'll never get to see a race for getting drinks and trying to explain to the little space cadet that win is the winner, place is the horse that comes in second, and show is the horse that comes in third."

"And they're off!" bellowed the track announcer. Lily had never been so scared to watch a horse race in her life

"The number four horse, Gala Queen, is on the inside moving up."

"Oh, good Lord, get him there first!" prayed Lily. Goose bumps made her feel as if it were the middle of January.

"Comin' down the stretch, it's Dino's Boy and Gala Queen, neck 'n' neck, Gala Queen movin' in, and Gala Queen, tha winna by a neck!" called the track announcer. Lily jumped for joy. Half of her double was home! Her long shot did not materialize until second to last, however. Lily was undaunted and placed $300 on the number three horse at five-to-one odds in the second race.

"It will only take one," she thought. Lily was so nervous that she excused herself to the ladies' room until the second race was over. When she managed to get her stomach under control and reappear, to her jubilation, number five, Sweet Pleasure, had come in first, and the long shot placed. Lily rushed to the window to collect her winnings, quickly stashing the money in her purse and zipping it tightly. She could not believe it. Number three paid $43.20 to place. Lily had similar luck in all the races the rest of the day. By the time the last race was over, Lily was totally exhausted. She worked herself into a screaming fury, and now she could relax… until tomorrow.

The foursome finally arrived back at the Galt House after fighting traffic for well over an hour. Bill and Kevin went to the bar to have a drink with some good ol' boys, and Holly went to have her nails done before the ball. Lily was relieved she didn't have to baby-sit Holly the rest of the afternoon. The Derby Ball was the social event of the spring. Everyone who was anyone would be there, and Lily was looking forward to hobnobbing with the elite of the horse world.

But for now, she couldn't wait to be alone with her loot. She had not had time to count it at the track. She rushed into her bedroom like a child to a Christmas stocking. Bills flew out in wads as Lily leaned over the bed emptying her purse. First, she just gathered it up close to her and lay down across the bed, loving the smell and feel of it all.

"Mmm," she said aloud. "The wonderful smell of money." She rolled over and spoke directly to her green companions. "You are the ticket to my little Kentucky in Atlanta!" Lily had her heart set on twenty-five acres just outside Atlanta. It was just right for raising a few horses, but selling her town house could only raise a portion of the money she needed to buy the land and get a barn up. She didn't care if she had to sleep in a tent, as long as the horses had what they needed. There was enough room to build a house later. And after that, another barn and stable. Lily could see it in her mind's eye, always the same. The curving, treelined lane leading up to the white, two-story house on the right.

Winding back and to the left, the lane curved first to the white barn and then to the training corral. Already she could see a horse or two grazing within the white-fenced boundaries.

These two days of horse racing could mean the fulfillment of that precious dream for Lily. Totaling her winnings, she jumped up and down on the bed as she used to do when she was a little girl. $22,138.60! "Not bad for an afternoon's work, ol girl," she told herself. Before she could wallow in her glory any longer, she heard the key in the door. It was Bill. She ran into her bathroom and turned on the shower so he wouldn't bother her. Then she hid her winnings.

chapter

FIVE

On that same beautiful spring night, as Gayle and Sal started into the curve, she knew they would not make it.

Francoise, one of Sal's closest and craziest friends, had given them an engagement party to be remembered. She was noted for having the best of parties at her elaborate Spanish villa in La Jolla, California. Movie stars as well as popular business tycoons looked forward to them. From the limousine-studded driveway to the band playing loudly near the pool, where party lights decorated the shrubs and palms, the party was swinging. Gayle had coaxed Sal into leaving their friends around one o'clock so she could have him to herself.

Francoise's parties could also get out of hand. Booze, food, a little cocaine, and some crazy games could sure make you wild. When they left the party and started up Highway 1 through the mountains, she and Sal were laughing and carrying on like a couple of kids on a joy ride.

The top was down on the bright-red Mercedes Sal had bought Gayle as an engagement present, and the sky was beautiful with stars sprinkled across it like diamonds.

As the car left the road and spun wildly down the mountainside, Gayle felt herself become airborne. Sal's last kiss would linger upon her lips forever. Why had she so drunkenly continued to play with Sal as they drove along that dangerous road in the dark?

When Gayle's body was shattered against a tall majestic pine, the last words she heard herself mutter were "Sal, my love!" An explosion in the distance splattered sparks high into the night, and then the woods were quiet, as if the end of time had dropped its finishing touch.

Unbelievable pain awakened Gayle, as she lay against the tree in the damp woods. She heard sirens and then men yelling information to each other. "Over here!" she screamed in her mind. "Oh my God, the pain!" Gayle felt tears streaming from her eyes. She wanted to call for help, to crawl toward the sounds, but no movement would come. She had not even the strength to open her eyes. She heard men talking as they scrambled past her.

"God in heaven, they can't find me!" Was she watching a movie, dreaming maybe? No, the pain reminded her that these feelings were hers and very, very real. Just then, she heard someone say, "What's that shining over there?" Gayle's beautiful three-carat, blue sapphire diamond engagement ring had caught the flashlight, giving off a reflection that hit the eye of an alert, young paramedic.

She could hear the snap of branches as help worked its way toward her. "Johnny! Get that stretcher down here fast. This gal is trying to make it. She's got to be in some serious pain, too. Bring the medic bag with you." Johnny scurried down the side of the ravine, dodging tree branches and rocks on his way to Gayle.

The soft hands, the smell of Old Spice, and a kind, wooing voice. "Come on, sweetie, it's OK now. I'm going to give you a shot for that pain. Help me now, baby. We're gonna get ya outta here." His affectionate words reminded her of Sal and the way he continually babied her. "You're pretty busted up, but you'll be OK." Gayle felt the needle slide into her arm. Tears poured from her eyes.

"Sal?" she asked as she began to feel the effects of the shots. "Sal?" she said again as she drifted to a semiconscious plane, where she felt like she was watching everything on television.

The gentle man was still speaking to her, but she could no longer make out what he was saying. She felt them pull something out of her side. They placed her on the stretcher on her back, strapping her on tightly. A rope was attached to the stretcher, and a member of the rescue team began to pull her up toward the road, where red lights flashed and radio-dispatched messages echoed through the night. The easy-talking man seemed to hover right along with her like an angel, but Gayle knew she was hurting too badly to be dead.

It seemed to take hours for them to get her up the side of the mountain. Finally, they were in an ambulance screaming down Highway 1 where, somewhere in time, she and Sal had driven along, laughing and planning their honeymoon. Paramedics gave her oxygen, more shots, lots of blankets…everything but what she wanted the most.

"Sal? Sal?" she asked them. Nothing. They could not hear her over the sounds of all the monitors they had hooked all over her.

chapter

SIX

Lily felt like Cinderella again as they entered the huge ball-room. Never had she seen so much glitz and glamour crammed into one place in her life. There was enough jewelry on display to take care of the national debt. As Bill guided her through the medley, Lily could see that the political community, as well as the racing world, was well represented. As Lily and Bill made their way to the table, all the male heads turned to stare. The women openly glared with jealously. They made a handsome couple, Bill in a black tuxedo with his red bowtie and carnation, and Lily in a black-taffeta, tea-length party dress designed with a fashionable "V" back, accented by a red sash at the waist.

"Look at them, slobbering like dogs!" Bill crowed. "I told you I would be the envy of all the men here tonight Lily, and I am!"

"Oh Bill, you exaggerate so! But, don't leave me alone for long. I'm afraid I won't have much in common with these people. I'm not from the same social background, and I'm no good at small talk."

"Just be your sweet self, Lily, and give them that million-dollar smile. You'll be wonderful. Don't worry, you'll see," he said reassuringly.

"I'm glad you're so sure!" Lily said with a big smile to cover her insecurity.

"Besides, when you meet Mom and Dad, you won't have time to make small talk They'll do it all for you."

"Thanks...I think," whimpered Lily."

"Here they are now," Bill announced as they approached his parents' table.

"Lily Gray, these are my parents, Jacob and Doris Dressler."

"I am so pleased to meet you," said Lily, extending her slender hand.

"The pleasure is ours, my dear," said Doris. "We have heard so much about you. Haven't we, Jacob?"

"Yes, Doris, we certainly have. And Bill, my boy, you were right. She's a beauty, a real beauty. Pleased to meet you, Lily." Jacob's smooth voice gave Lily a warm, comfortable feeling. Jacob Dressler was the epitome of a true gentleman, of whom, in Lily's opinion, there were few and far between.

"Well," gushed Bill's mother, "let's all sit down and get acquainted!"

Kevin and Holly finally made their way through the crowd to join Bill and Lily at their table. Holly was very impressed with the wealth that filled the room and was quick to suggest that she and Kevin get champagne and mingle in the crowd. Lily wasn't sure yet if she liked Kevin or not, but she was sure about Holly. She did *not*. To Lily, she was a pretentious social climber.

"She's not just a Yankee, she's a damn Yankee!" thought Lily. Lily never cared for anyone who didn't like animals—especially horses.

"You can't trust them either," she said under her breath watching Holly flirt with Phil Dressler, Bill's younger brother.

Bill's parents were very active in the Democratic Party in Texas, where they had lived for forty years on a twenty-three-hundred-acre ranch called the Circle D. Jacob had more or less retired. He and Doris were deeply involved in Texas politics, and they enjoyed traveling. When they were away, they left the cattle ranch in the capable hands of Phil.

The evening was pleasant, and Lily met politicians and horse people from all over the county. After meeting some of the politicians, it reminded her of the quip that nowhere did the champagne and the bullshit flow equally freely as at this particular event. Now Lily understood the saying. Also there was a lot of back stabbing to go along with the backslapping. Bill and his parents were busy mingling, so Lily made her way to the ladies' room to check her hair and makeup, but mostly to get a breather from all the conversation.

"Even the ladies' room is ritzy," she thought, sitting back on the plush, crimson-colored sofa to relax awhile. Listening to the other women in the ladies' room, Lily discovered that, like everywhere else, the talk was all about the big red horse named Secretariat.

As Lily strolled back to the table, mint julep in hand, she could see Bill in an intense conversation with several men. Knowing she would be alone for quite some time, she made her way back to the Dressler table to enjoy one of her favorite pastimes, people watching.

"Do you mind if I join you while Bill is otherwise engaged?" asked a smooth, deep voice.

Startled, Lily turned to look over her shoulder at the intruder. "I'm sorry if I have frightened you," the extraordinarily handsome stranger said as he pulled out a chair and sat down next to her, uninvited.

"I'm Andy Lewis. Aren't you Bill's date?"

"Well, ah, yes," stammered Lily, trying to think where she had heard that name before. She couldn't help but stare. She thought maybe her jaw dropped, but she couldn't be sure. She knew one thing, though. This man was beautiful. And exotic. Yes, exotic... there was just no other way to say it.

"This is my first derby, and I had no idea it was really all it is cracked up to be." Andy spoke as if they had known each other all their lives. "Are you a novice or a pro at this?"

"Well, I guess I'm a little of both."

"What do you mean, Miss...?"

"Gray, Lily Gray."

"Miss Gray?"

"I'm a pro at the derby because I have been here almost every year since I can remember. But I'm a novice at the ball and all the fancy festivities."

They sat silently for a moment, looking over the crowd.

"Mr. Lewis, do you know Bill?"

"It's Andy, please. And yes, you could say that," Andy said with a hint of a smile that sent goose bumps up Lily's spine. "I'm from Fort Worth, not far from the Circle D. Where are you from, Miss Lily Gray?"

"I'm from Kentucky, a little town west of here called Owensboro. That's why I claim to be a pro at attending the derby. It was always a great time to load up a bunch and come to the derby." Andy roared with laughter and, encouraged, Lily continued to talk about the derby and Kentucky until Andy interrupted.

"Lily, you are a very beautiful young woman." The way he said it was unintentionally exciting. He was just being honest.

"Thank you, I…" Lily stammered, searching in a mind that had left her helpless for a reply. He completely intoxicated her.

"I'm sorry if I've embarrassed you. You're blushing," he said jokingly. "I didn't know women still did that. OK, let's talk about horses and get the color out of those cheeks. Let's see. How about Secretariat? Is he any good, or is it all hype?"

"No, I don't think it's all hype. As a matter of fact, I think he'll win tomorrow," Lily said, relieved to get the conversation back to the derby. Maybe now she could begin to feel normal again.

"Why? What makes him so good?"

Lily hoped she was impressing him with her confident knowledge of the sport. She told her mesmerized listener that Ron Turcotte, one of the best jockeys around, would be aboard Secretariat for the big race. And Secretariat's bloodlines came from a previous derby winner, Bold Ruler, and Something Royal.

"Kentucky must be proud of Secretariat, especially if he turns out to be the winner tomorrow."

"Oh, Secretariat isn't from Kentucky. He's out of Bay Meadow Stables in Virginia."

"Well, I know when I'm outta my league." Andy laughed. "I think I will have another one of these julep things. Care for another?" he asked, holding up his empty glass.

"Don't mind if I do." Lily said, feeling at ease and forgetting all about Bill.

"I'll just be a moment," Andy said, stepping away from the table toward the bar. Lily watched him as he made his way through the crowd. He put her in mind of a panther, sleek and aggressive. A more attractive man she had never seen. His dark coloring made her wonder about his nationality.

"Man, he sure is something to look at." She sighed as she saw him turn to walk toward her.

"Here we go, Kentucky Beauty," Andy said, handing her a fresh drink. "By the way, what is the proper name for these concoctions?"

"Mint julep. I'm not finished yet," she went on, holding up her hand to keep from being interrupted. "A genuine Kentucky mint julep should be served in a frosted silver julep cup, and all the ingredients must be native of Kentucky. Ice from limestone-spring water, Kentucky bourbon at least eight years old, and mint picked after the most recent dawn while the dew is still on the leaves," Lily explained authoritatively, laughing all the while.

"You certainly know your mint juleps, Lily, and your horses too, I might add," Andy said, smiling. The sparkle in the smile seemed to leave Lily somewhat tongue-tied. "I'll bet you would have input on just about any subject."

"Well, Mr. Lewis, maybe I'll see you at the races." Damn, she thought. My face is beginning to flush again. I can't think of one sensible thing to say.

"Please. My friends call me Andy, and I'm sure we will become friends."

"Yes…" Lily's brain was burning. She would be miserable until she remembered where she had heard of him. Suddenly, out of nowhere, Bill swept down on her like a vulture.

"Lily, get your purse. We are leaving. Now!" Grabbing Lily by the arm, he pulled her out of the chair.

"Bill, what on earth? You're hurting my arm!" Angrily, she wrenched her arm free.

Utterly calm and unalarmed, Andy stood up. "Hello, Bill. You should know better than to leave a jewel like Lily unattended for so long. You'd better watch out, or you will end up losing her, too."

"I'm not planning to lose anything," snarled Bill.

"Lily, it was indeed a pleasure to meet you," Andy said, bowing slightly from the waist. "Good luck tomorrow."

"Thank you," Lily replied over her shoulder as Bill pulled her toward the door.

"Bill, what in Sam Hill is wrong with you, dragging me out of that room, causing a scene? You are embarrassing me! Have you lost your mind?"

"That is Andrew Lewis. He is director of the Texas Railroad Commission and a strong contender for the Democratic congressional seat nomination." By then Bill was hollering. "He is the lowest scum in Texas!"

"If he is so low, how did he get elected to the Texas Railroad Commission? Somebody must think he is OK," Lily shot back, sounding more defensive of Andy than she had wanted.

"He bought his way in and is buying his votes. I am trying to get elected by the people," said Bill. "He's not a politician, he's an oilman. He also has several other ventures of questionable repute. I've got him under investigation right now."

Lily knew that the Texas Railroad Commission was a very powerful group in Texas. Created to regulate the oil industry and rising freight costs, it had grown into a strong state governmental force. Three elected commissioners controlled the oil business in Texas. She was also aware of the bitter resentment between the old-money cattle ranchers and the new-money oil companies.

Bill always chose to ignore the fact that his grandfather got the money to buy their cattle ranch by betting on an oil well in the early nineteen hundreds. The Texas Railroad Commission would make an excellent springboard for Andy Lewis's political goals.

"Bill, I'm sorry," Lily said. "I had no idea he was running against you for the nomination. He seemed so nice and polite, I—"

"Dammit. Just forget it Lily," bellowed Bill. "His very presence infuriates me." Bill was still raging when they arrived at the hotel. It was only eleven o'clock, and Lily regretted having to leave the ball so early.

As soon as they got inside the suite, the interrogation began. "Just what was he saying to you, anyway?" Bill became more demanding as he poured a double shot of bourbon, straight up.

"Bill, I really can understand your intense dislike for him, but you are being absolutely ridiculous. And," Lily continued, "you are drinking too much."

"I've only begun to drink, my dear." Bill growled as he held up his second round of bourbon, as if daring her to stop him.

"Bill, I have never seen you this way, and I don't like what I'm seeing." With that, Lily stormed into her bedroom, slamming and locking the door behind her. After a long shower she put on the Kentucky Derby T-shirt Bill bought for her that afternoon.

Sitting cross-legged in the middle of the king-size bed, she recounted the fortune she had won that day. She went over the figures again in her head. She was beginning to get nervous. This was her future. And she was planning it all by herself. Valerie would not be able to chime in with her unwanted advice.

She lay on the bed for a long time, planning her future and replaying the look Kathryne would have on her face when she told her about the luck she had had at the Kentucky Derby. Her thoughts turned to the next day's race.

"Yipes!" Lily said aloud. "I don't know if I can handle all this pressure." She quietly got out of bed and listened at the door that adjoined the sitting room, trying to hear if Bill was still there. The room was silent. Easing open the door, she quickly stole across the floor to the bar and poured herself a small glass of good old Kentucky bourbon. "This should help me sleep," she thought. She downed it and slipped back into her room.

Lily slept without movement until she heard her alarm at 5:30 a.m. Getting up quickly, she donned slacks and a jacket and eased silently out of the room. She was on her way to the corner newsstand to pick up the early edition of the *Daily Racing Form*. Stepping onto the sidewalk in the blue-gray before dawn, Lily could feel the city yawning and stretching awake as newspapers were thrown to the curb for delivery, buses spewed their black fumes, and yellow taxis began an ant-like train bringing early arrivals for this special day. Lily stood taking in all the sights and sounds of the chilly early morning as a mother watches her baby wake.

She chatted patiently with the young man while he unbundled the stack of *Daily Racing Forms*. "Keep the change," she called over her shoulder as she hurried to the coffee shop next door. Lily slid into a booth to read her future. She ordered black coffee and a Danish from the sleepy-eyed waitress. She noticed she wasn't alone in future planning. The coffee shop was full of people reading the racing sheet. There was a silent electricity running throughout the place. The excitement felt almost touchable.

There was no doubt among this group that Secretariat would be the winner of today's ninety-ninth Kentucky Derby. Lily glanced at the big Coca-Cola clock over the counter. It was seven thirty. "Bill will be up, and I had sure better be there," she thought.

Folding her paper and tucking it under her arm, she stepped out of the booth. Feeling like one of the guys, she took a deep breath and strode confidently back to the hotel.

When Lily walked in, Bill was sitting on the small sofa with his head resting in his hands. Lily shut the door noiselessly.

"Are you OK?" she asked, sitting down on the arm of the brightly colored, plaid sofa.

"No. I'm sick over the fool I made of myself with you last night," he said sheepishly. "I apologize, Lily. Please accept. Please."

"Bill, you know I do. I guess I just didn't realize the way you felt about Andrew Lewis. Let me call room service for a pot of coffee and some toast. In the meantime, I'll fix you a seltzer. You look awful." Lily felt sorry for Bill, even though he had really upset her the night before.

"Lily, you are so good to me. You know I have fallen totally in love with you," he told her, pulling her down onto his lap. He tried to kiss her, cradling her in his arms like a baby. "Lily, do you love me?"

"Bill, I really don't know." She tried to explain, struggling to her feet. "I do know there is no one else, and I am very fond of you. Can we give it more time?" She kissed Bill's aching head and fixed the seltzer for him.

By noon, they had arrived once again at Churchill Downs, along with the other hundred thousand people who turned out for this annual event. It was a beautiful day, and the air was crisp. The downs was dressed in its Sunday best with thousands of recently planted flowers bursting in colorful blossoms.

Kevin and Holly were already seated with Bill's parents when they arrived. Lily was so excited she could hardly contain herself. The crowd was a kaleidoscope of spring colors. Women wore huge hats of flowers, and men, bright jackets. It was rumored that Liz Taylor and Richard Burton were there. Lily had not seen them, but it wasn't for the lack of looking.

"Good afternoon, Miz Lily. You look fresher than the morning dew on a mint leaf," said the silky smooth voice.

"Oh no! Not him again," thought Lily, slowly taking the binoculars from her eyes to see Andy Lewis's broad smile. Her face reddened, because she just couldn't keep from smiling back.

"Bill, what's that black son of a bitch doing here, and why is he speaking to Lily?" blurted Jacob.

"Jacob, please," said Doris, holding her husband's arm in restraint. "You'll make a scene."

"It's a public function, Dad, anyone can attend," Bill snapped.

"Lily," he said turning to her, "do you have to speak to him? Can't you understand that he is bad news?"

"Did your dad say black?" asked Lily, dumbfounded.

"Yes, he did." Bill sounded like a growling tiger.

"I thought he was…well, I guess I didn't—I mean, I couldn't really tell."

"Yeah, I know." Bill sneered. "His mother was colored and his father white of some kind. I don't want him hanging around you. Is that clear?"

"He just spoke to me on the way to his seat. Just a casual thing, that's all," said Lily, trying to calm the close-to-explosive situation.

"What was all that 'Miz Lily and dew on a mint leaf' shit?" Bill was starting to get ugly again. "And where had you been this morning when you came in at seven thirty?"

"Bill Dressler, I resent being given the third degree, especially right here in front of everyone. I'll take this up with you later. Right now, I'm going to the ladies' room."

Lily was embarrassed to be treated so crudely in front of four people whom she hardly knew. She went in the ladies' room to regain her composure. She was fighting her temper. She could let nothing upset her now. She had her future to think of, and the first race was soon to start.

She went to the window to place her bets. She put $2,000 on Jeff's Treasure, the long shot to place, and another $2,000 on the track favorite, Luxury Ride, to win. Lily bought a watered-down mint julep and walked around in a daze, too scared to listen to the race. She had started back to her seat when a horrifying chill swept over her as she heard the track announcer call Full Speed to win and Boss to place. Lily was sick.

"This is a bad sign," she said to herself. "My luck isn't holding today. Oh God, don't let it fail me now, not today." Lily wondered if God would hold it against her for praying about a horse race.

Shaken but determined, Lily went to the window to make her wager on the next race. This time it was $3,000 on the long shot and $3,000 on the favorite. On the way back to join Bill, she ran into Andy.

"Lily, I've been looking for you. Can you help me pick a winner?" he said flirtatiously.

"Andy, I had better not be seen with you. I had no idea last night that you and Bill were enemies."

"Have I done something to offend you, Lily?" he asked solemnly. "If so, I apologize most humbly."

"No, not really," Lily admitted nervously, "but as Bill's guest, I feel I must respect his feelings. Can you understand that?"

"And can you understand that this has nothing to do with Bill?" asked Andy. "I have made your acquaintance, and I like you. Besides, you've only heard one side of Bill's story. I'd like a chance to tell you mine."

Lily sighed. "I'm going back to my seat. Please don't speak to me there again. Bill acted like a raving maniac last night, and he has already started again today. Please. It will only make it miserable for me." Lily turned and gracefully ascended the stairs to the box-seat level, knowing as she went that she would see Andy Lewis again.

Her luck was gone. The second race proved no better than the first. Two races, and she had lost $10,000. She quietly seethed, reading the form as her blood raged through the veins in her head. Lily realized she had missed the third race when the buzzer sounded.

"Hell, what to do now?" she asked herself. "I've got one last chance, and if it doesn't work, I'm going to quit. My luck is gone."

"Bill," she said, "I am so restless. I want to walk around a little. I need to stretch my legs."

"Honey, I'm sorry about what happened a little while ago with Dad and what I said," Bill said pathetically. "Is that why you are so restless?"

"Not really," Lily lied. "I just want to walk around a little. Maybe I'll see Liz and Richard." She faked a big smile.

She went quickly to the window to place her bets using the same strategy, bought another drink, and walked around to see whom she could see, trying not to think of her massive losses. She walked toward the paddock area, as close as she could get, to see the horses. "You are so beautiful. Why can't you win this one for me?" she was thinking.

"Trying to use ESP on them?"

"What?" Lily said turning quickly to see Andy's big smile.

"Lily, do you need to sit down? You look pale." Andy took her hand and tried to coax her to sit down on a bench close by.

"No really, I'm OK. Just a little queasy." Lily smiled. "Maybe too many juleps."

Andy looked down to see Lily's knuckles were white she was clutching her tickets so tightly.

"I think I know an antidote for you," Andy said, smiling.

"What's that?"

"Maybe a smile from Lady Luck. How much have you lost, Lily?"

"Ten thousand! I don't know what I am going to do, but I have to regain my losses. I just have to." Tears began to well up in her eyes.

"Now, now, Lily." Andy consoled her, patting her trembling shoulder. "Tell me how you have been betting."

Lily told him about her run of good luck the day before and how she had wagered. And now, today, her luck was gone.

"If you are so hell-bent on betting to regain losses, I'll tell you my plan. I just pray to the Great Horse God in the sky. It works." Andy told her to wait until the race, the actual Kentucky Derby race, and bet everything she had left. The order in which to bet was Secretariat to win, Sham to place, and Our Native to show. Betting in that order would give her some leeway in case they did not come in just right.

"Everything? What makes you so sure about this?" Lily asked, almost whispering.

"Just say I have a feeling. Just do it," he insisted. "If it doesn't come out as I said, I'll insure your bet."

"You'll what?"

"I'll make good my advice. You can't ask for more than that, can you?"

"But," stammered Lily, "you don't know what I have left."

"It doesn't matter, Lily. A deal is a deal. Are you in?"

"Well, I guess."

"Since I'm insuring you, how about telling me what all the money is for, anyway? Plan on retiring this year?" he said in a kidding manner.

"No, I have a dream to fulfill. This money is for something I want more than anything else in this world." Lily said it in a way that let Andy see into her soul and know how important this was to her.

"Is this something a bank could help you with?" he inquired.

"No, that didn't work. It's too much money, and there are other circumstances," Lily said, starting to clam up. She did not want to go into the details with this man of how a banker feels about making a loan to a single, inexperienced woman with very little money who wants to buy a piece of property and start a horse farm.

"This thing you want so badly," Andy inquired further. "Is it here in Kentucky?"

"No, I live in Atlanta now. I guess I didn't have a chance to tell you that. I am in advertising. I've been with the Gayle White Advertising Agency for three years now, and I feel like I have roots. Kathryne and I—oh, that's the woman I work with and my very best friend. Anyway, Kathryne and I have established some very good accounts, and I am enjoying my work tremendously."

"You're kidding," Andy mumbled.

Maybe she had bored him with her humdrum story. Well, he did ask, she thought. "I feel like I lost you to the clouds," Lily said with a smile.

"No, no," he stammered. "It's almost time for the big race. Bill will come looking for you. We don't want that, do we?"

"No, we don't," she readily agreed. Turning to leave, she paused and touched his arm. "I thought you were a novice at horses. You are either a fast learner or a great liar." Lily gave a mischievous smile, curling her lips.

"Well, I had to seize the moment the best way I knew how." His eyes held hers as he spoke. "One more thing before you go. I want to tell you that meeting you has been a very pleasurable experience. If the race doesn't turn out as I said, I'll be right here to take care of that insurance claim."

"Andy, I don't know about that insurance business, OK? But thanks for restoring my betting confidence. It sure has been interesting meeting you, to say the least." She gave him a special smile she just could not hold back.

"Lily, don't tell anyone, especially ol Bill, about the insurance I offered you. I am sure the investigation committee would have a field day with the information. Can I get a promise?"

"Yes, sure, I promise," she said, and as much as she hated to, said good-bye to Andy Lewis. Watching him walk through the crowd, her heart sank. He was the most handsome man she had ever seen, even if he was colored, which she still found difficult to believe. The way he carried himself, the way he dressed, his hair, his eyes, his butt. Butt? Get a grip on yourself, girl. He is a married, colored man. As if someone had just slapped her in the face, she said, "Get to those betting windows. Now!"

Feeling calm and reassured, she placed her last bets at the window just as Andy had instructed. She bet all of it. Her entire future.

She joined Bill in time for the singing of "My Old Kentucky Home." The song never failed to bring tears to her eyes, and today was no different. Lily knew her life would never be the same after the finish of the ninety-ninth race of the Kentucky Derby. As the horses walked by in post parade, Lily was on her third Hail Mary. The horses were out of the gate at 5:37 p.m.

"And they're off!" bellowed the track announcer sending goose bumps all over her.

Lily stood, binoculars affixed to her eyes, never missing a second. "There are too many to watch all at once," she groaned to herself. Secretariat dropped back leaving the gate as the field broke in order. The race was so fast, Lily couldn't keep her eyes on all three horses. When the field turned on the back stretch, Sham was nowhere to be seen.

"Oh God, please let them come in one, two, three, as they are supposed to. Please!" prayed Lily aloud.

"Secretariat, leading the field at a good distance, coming on, with Sham dominating the remainder of the field!" the PA system blared.

Lily's heart was pounding so hard, she could hardly hear the announcer call the race. She couldn't look. With tightly shut eyes and held breath she heard the thunderous hooves and the wild screaming from the crowd. But she couldn't hear the last call. She opened her eyes. There it was—her future coming across the tote board.

Lily read the results on the board, knowing how the Olympic teams must feel when they are reading all tens from the judges. First place, Secretariat, winner paying $5.00; second, Sham, paying $3.20; Our Native was third, paying $4.20.

"Oh my God. I've done it!" yelped Lily. Tears poured down her face. She could hardly believe her eyes. She felt dizzy and week in the knees. She was going to have enough money to buy that property just outside of Atlanta. And even some left to get the farm started. The dream she had had all her life was finally coming true. She would have a horse farm of her own. It would be small, but it would be all hers. All these thoughts were running a race of their own through Lily's mind when Bill's embrace brought the excitement to a screeching halt.

"How did you do?" he asked excitedly.

"Fine. Just fine. I bet Secretariat." Lily tried to answer with some manner of coherence, since she did not want to reveal her windfall.

Turning, she saw Andy several boxes away holding up his mint julep in congratulations. Lily raised her hand, thumbs up, and mouthed, "Thank you." She gave him a look she didn't even know she could give and couldn't help wishing she could celebrate with him.

Her attention was drawn to the winner's circle, where her magnificent, red horse was being draped in a blanket of red roses. The cold chills up and down her spine gave way only to the hot tears streaming her face.

Kentucky Governor Wendell Ford was presenting the trophy to a jubilant jockey still astride the beautiful winner of the 1973 Kentucky Derby. As she looked upon this glorious sight, Lily Gray knew she could not die without first raising a horse that ran in the Kentucky Derby.

chapter

SEVEN

Kathryne looked forward to the Spring Art Festival near Waleska, Georgia, where her mother lived. The professional artists were there, of course, but what intrigued her most were the local amateurs. Their artwork was so simple and uncomplicated, and to Kathryne, so much more valuable.

Her mother, Jessie, lived in a small rural town about twenty miles north of Atlanta. Her dad bought half an acre six years ago when he retired and built them a three-bedroom, country-style home. He did all the work himself. He liked to stay busy; said it kept him young.

The property had lots of trees, and he helped Jessie put in her flower beds and bird feeders. She would putter around the house and fuss with her flowers, naming the birds things like Gobble Guts and Gabby. Kathryne loved to go see her. To sit at her mother's kitchen table drinking coffee with her, smelling the flowers, their aroma drifting in with the breeze, was more relaxing than anything she knew.

Two months after her daughter, Becky, was born, Kathryne drove with her up to visit her parents for the day. As Kathryne's dad helped them out of the car on that beautiful sunny day in January, he looked down at Becky, sleeping in her car seat, and said, "This is the most beautiful baby I have ever seen."

Kathryne would never forget him saying that and the look in his big brown eyes as he said it. He was a man of very few words. Oh, he would ramble on about the garden or a house he once built, but he was never openly affectionate. That day Kathryne knew how very much he loved her. He died in his sleep four months later, and the world lost a talented craftsman in Hardy Wright. He never knew about any of Becky's health problems.

Now, driving back to Atlanta, Kathryne smiled as she thought about her mom and the special weekend they had shared. Jessie Wright was the most giving person she had ever known. Always on Kathryne's side, always understanding, somehow, about business and how it all worked. Kathryne treasured the time she could spend with her.

Did she really have to go home? Back to that damn charade with Joe? They had such a fight before she left. But what made it so bad was that it was such a bland fight. When lovers fight, there is passion involved—a "Hey, I love you enough to care whether you pay too much attention to the guy at the party" kind of fight. Not with Joe. With Joe it was, "Is your work your whole life now?" which is just what Joe had mumbled at breakfast Friday morning.

"Oh, Joe," Kathryne had said, "do we have to go over this again?"

"I guess not," Joe spluttered. "I don't know what to do about it anyway." Kathryne felt like screaming to him at the top of her lungs, "A little romance would work wonders!" But that would be like telling a blind person to see. How could anyone be so loveless? Kathryne had cried herself to sleep in the early years of their marriage, craving the love that all the books were written about, that all the murders were committed over, and that all the babies were conceived in.

As Kathryne pulled into the driveway of her comfortable, ranch-style house, she could hear Becky's squeals coming from the pool. She had chosen not to take Becky with her because she had been running a slight fever. Now Joe had her in the pool. Dammit, could he refuse her nothing? They had been able to capitalize on a tax-deductible heater for the pool for Becky, but if she wound up in the hospital again on a respirator, Kathryne would personally beat him to a pulp. "Oh hell, he is a pulp already," Kathryne said as she turned off the motor.

Joe loved Becky so much, it was becoming sickening. He had actually taken cooking classes at the community college so he could make her special dishes. Becky's appetite was so poor; they were always trying to find a way to get food into her system. Joe had become such a good cook that Kathryne had just turned the whole kitchen over to him. Coming through the family room from the garage, Kathryne yelled a hello to Joe and Becky from the patio door and said she would put on her suit and join them. She decided to rake Joe over the coals later.

"I think I'll give Lil a quick call and see if she is back from the Kentucky Derby," Kathryne said aloud, as if talking to an invisible person, while she pulled on her azure bathing suit. She left a message with Lily's answering service for her to call as soon as she got back.

Kathryne joined a happy Becky and a sullen Joe in the pool. After they swam and played water games, Joe fixed Becky's favorite dessert, strawberry shortcake, for them all. Becky was exhausted by then and ready for bed. After tucking her in, Joe came into their bedroom as Kathryne was pulling a lightweight blue sweater over her head.

"To the office?" he asked.

"Yes, Joe, I have to check over a campaign before the meeting tomorrow, and I don't want to hear anything about it, OK?"

"Dead-end street, anyway," he muttered. He headed for the shower and Kathryne for the door. She knew he would drink himself to sleep as usual, with or without her company.

Lily was popping at the seams to tell Kathryne her news. It made landing at the airport in Atlanta and getting to the phone feel like slow motion. She was the one person in the whole world who would be as happy as Lily. The dream would not be complete until she had shared it with her best friend.

Trying to keep her cool, Lily dialed Kathryne's number at home. "Joe? This is Lily, is Kathryne in? At the office? OK, thanks, Joe, I'll call her there." Whew, was he a drag. Even on the phone, he was a drag, she thought as she hurriedly dialed the private number used after hours.

As Kathryne reached for the phone, it rang, and she almost screamed. "I am as nervous as a cat tonight," she thought. She had done the same thing a moment ago when Lily called saying she was back from the derby and on her way to the office with details of a great weekend. She smiled as she reached for the phone, recalling how excited Lily sounded.

"May I speak with Kathryne Langford, please?" the caller asked.

"This is Kathryne Langford. Who is this?"

"Kathryne, your husband was kind enough to give me this number. You may not remember me. I am Vincent Martino, Salvatore Martino's brother," the voice continued with a heavy Italian accent. "I met you a couple of weeks ago at a party for Gayle and Sal's engagement."

"Yes, Vincent. How are you?" Kathryne asked, puzzled as to why Vincent Martino would be calling her on a Sunday evening at the office. And why in the hell had Joe given him her private number?

"I am afraid I am not too well." Vincent hesitated, clearing his throat. "Kathryne, I've some very bad news for you."

"What's wrong, Vincent?" Kathryne rose slowly from her chair, very anxious from the tone of Vincent's husky voice. "What do you mean, bad news?"

"Sal and Gayle were at a party last night in California. It was late, and they were drinking. On their way back to the hotel, they had a terrible car crash."

"Oh no! How are they? Are they hurt badly? Are they OK?" She kept firing questions at him, but he was overcome with emotion, mumbling something in Italian.

"My brother is dead." Vincent's voice cracked. "Gayle is in very critical condition. She is in the hospital undergoing some type of emergency surgery. I thought you should know, Mrs. Langford." His voice was almost a whisper by now.

Groping for the chair, Kathryne sat back down and tried to think of what to say to Vincent, who had started to cry again.

"Vincent, where are you? What hospital is Gayle in? Vincent, please pull yourself together. I have to know where you are!" Finally, she was able to get him to speak English. She copied down the information she needed.

"I am really sorry about your brother, Vincent, and I know this is terrible for you. Could I ask you to do something for me?" Kathryne asked.

"Yes, of course." His accent was even heavier now.

"Don't tell Gayle about Sal until I get there. She has no family. No one else. I want to be there for her." Kathryne was choking up now as the realization hit her that Gayle might not even make it until she got there.

"Yes, of course," he repeated. He seemed to draw strength from knowing she would be there soon.

Kathryne still had the receiver in her hand and was staring mindlessly at a huge painting of the ocean breaking against a rocky cliff when Lily entered her office with her mouth running like a 45 rpm record on 78 speed.

"Yoo-hoo, Kathryne, I've got a story you're not gonna believe, and in these brown bags are a feast fit—Kathryne, what is it? What's wrong?" Lily dropped her bundles on the small conference table just inside the door.

As she gently shook Kathryne's shoulders, she asked, "Is something wrong at home? With Becky. Who is on the phone?"

"It's Gayle. A terrible car accident after a party in California. Sal is dead. Gayle is critical, Lil."

"No, oh no!" Lily gasped as she took the phone receiver back to the base. "Kathryne, where is she? You'll have to go to her. I will take care of everything here." Lily took over in a crisis in a very authoritative manner. It was almost callous, in a way. It was just her way of handling a difficult situation. She chose to deal with sorrow or pain in private. She would do just that, too, later that evening, alone in the seclusion of her town house. She felt she got her inner strength from her proud Indian ancestors. Or perhaps it was due to the favoritism shown to her older sister when they were growing up. Sometimes that inner strength was all she had to help her hold onto her dreams.

"Let's get you some flight arrangements for tomorrow morning," Lily said, picking up the phone with one hand and patting

Kathryne on the shoulder with the other. Lily looked over the information Kathryne had hastily written on the note pad beside her phone as she told the airline, "I need the earliest possible flight."

Kathryne had gone into the bathroom to try to pull herself together. The cold water helped her realize that she needed to be as strong as possible in order to help Gayle, the woman who had pulled her through more than one rough ordeal over the past several years. Now it was her turn to help, and she wanted to give it all she had.

"Are you OK?" Lily inquired, gently tapping on the bathroom door.

"Yeah, come on in. I'm trying to pull my thoughts together."

"Kathryne, what do you know about Gayle's condition? Is she stable, conscious, what?"

"I know very little. Only what Vincent told me, and he was so broken up he could hardly talk. What kind of flight did you get for me?"

"An 8:15 a.m. TWA tomorrow. Can you handle that?"

"Sure, sure."

"Do you want me to take you to the airport? I don't mind."

"Oh no, Joe can—on second thought, yes, you'd better."

"Come on. I'll take you home. You are in no condition to drive. Get your purse. I'll get the lights and lock up."

Walking down the hall toward the elevator, both women had the same thing on their minds. Deciding to share her thoughts, Lily spoke. "Kathryne, I don't know how to say this without sounding selfish, but what will this do to our purchase plans for the agency? I mean, if Gayle doesn't pull through. I mean—"

"I know." Kathryne broke in. "I've thought about the same thing," she said glumly as she pushed the elevator button for the parking garage.

Lily had the top down, and the cool night air seemed to help the women think. Neither had much to say, each lost in thoughts unknown to the other. "By the way, what about that weekend of yours?" Kathryne asked absentmindedly.

"Oh, it was fine. Just great," Lily replied. They were just pulling into Kathryne's driveway. "I'll tell you all about it when you get back."

"Well, I'll see you in the morning," Kathryne said, giving Lily an assuring slap on the leg. "You OK?"

"Oh, sure. Try to get some sleep, kid. You're going to need it."

When Lily left her friend, she headed for the country and an open road. The events of the evening had Lily wound tight as a clock. Driving seemed to help her relax and put her troubles out of her mind. She loved to drive. Her dad had taught her. When she was too young to reach the pedals, he would sit her in his lap behind the wheel and let her steer. She could drive anything with wheels by the time she was twelve.

"The salesman was right," Lily thought as she cruised down the highway. "I never want another car after driving a Corvette." The low body of the car hugged every curve. She could feel the power of the engine surging through her body, releasing the tension and stress of the day. Lily loved driving fast and the feeling of being in total control.

"Man, I wish Daddy could be here now. He would sure make you do your stuff," she told the car, feeling as if it would fully agree. Her dad had always wanted a Corvette but could never afford one. And since a sports car would not have been practical, her mother would not have stood for it anyway.

As Lily slipped through the crisp night air, the smell of honeysuckle along the road kept her thoughts on her dad. Honeysuckle was his favorite flower. Her mother always argued that they were just weeds harboring snakes and mosquitoes.

"That woman could nag Jesus Christ right off the cross," she told the night.

As Lily looked back, she wondered just where along the way her mother had gotten the upper hand. Except for the times Lily and her dad spent alone, his spirit just seemed to vanish. Lily missed him tremendously tonight and looked at the stars, wondering which one was his. Her Indian grandmother, Gray Dove, had told her that each star belonged to a spirit and was used to see into the night and watch over loved ones still on earth. Lily took comfort in that thought tonight, as she always did when things were troubling her.

Gayle's accident took Lily back to the night Sonny Gray Dove was killed in a tragic car crash. She relived the phone call in the dead of night, knowing what had happened even before her mother said a word. She still felt the loneliness as it enveloped her that night when her mother said, in a cold, matter-of-fact way, "Well, Lily, your father has gone out and gotten him killed."

He had hit a bridge abutment on a dark country road and was apparently knocked unconscious. He lost control of the car and veered into a culvert. The car burst into flames, and he was burned beyond recognition. Lily could not believe she would never get to see him again. She lay awake the rest of the night hugging her pillow tightly and tried to remember everything he had ever said to her and everything they had ever done together.

Lily stayed with her grandmother for a few weeks after her father's death. One sunny afternoon, they were walking hand in hand in the field of wildflowers behind Gray Dove's house, enjoying the soft wind that had picked up. Suddenly, her grandmother stopped and said, "His spirit is with us now." Lily felt it sweep over her. A feeling, strong with love and warmth, seemed to blanket her, and she only had to close her eyes to see her father's smile and twinkling eyes. At that moment the lonely void that dwelled within her core vanished.

"His spirit is settled. He is at peace," Gray Dove whispered.

After that day, Lily never again felt she was without him. She missed his physical being, but she knew his spirit was with her.

Lily suddenly realized she had been driving for quite a while and headed for home. After a hot bath, she tried to relax in her recliner with the newspaper, but could not keep her mind on it. Finally, she began to cry. She let it all out. Exhausted, she went upstairs to bed. She was still unable to relax enough to sleep. After some tossing and turning, she realized that one face kept popping into her mind—Andy Lewis. How mysterious, exciting, handsome! Lily felt somewhat aglow with thoughts of him. She was agitated when the phone disturbed her.

"Lily, I tried to call you earlier. Where were you?"

"I went to the office. Bill—"

"On a Sunday night? Weren't you tired after our trip?"

"Yes, I was tired, but I wanted to stop and see Kathryne." The call was more like an interrogation than a conversation. Even after she told Bill about Gayle and Sal, he still seemed only interested in Lily's whereabouts between the time she left him and when he got her on the phone. The call did not suit Lily at all. She punched her pillow an extra time or two and settled back to her dreams. "Now, where was I?"

The drive to the airport the next morning was full of last-minute instructions. "Call me as soon as you can, Kathryne, and don't worry about a thing here," Lily assured her as she waved good-bye.

"If only I could be so sure myself," Lily thought. She turned toward the office into the early-morning traffic, fighting the feeling that she was headed into an arena with a ten-headed monster.

The next two weeks flew by. Lily was so busy, it felt like she spent every waking hour at the agency. She called her Realtor to tell her she would have to wait on the property outside of town that she wanted so badly. She was in daily phone contact with Kathryne in California, getting reports on Gayle's condition, and giving updates on the office. Gayle was slowly pulling out of critical condition, but remained in devastating pain.

Bill's calls were also daily. Lily could not put her finger on the feeling she had for him. He was different, but in a way she was not comfortable with. He could be so wonderful, yet other times he was moody and hard to talk to. She told herself it was just because she was so tired and had so much on her mind.

On one of her busiest days, Joe called and left a message that a package meant for the office had been delivered to the house by mistake. He said Lily could pick it up anytime.

"What idiots!" fumed Lily as she drove to Kathryne's house. "Those people in New York can never get anything right! Like I have time to do this."

Lily mumbled aloud about why Joe wouldn't bring it by the office, Rose, the housekeeper, let her in the front door. Lily was shocked and quite disturbed at what she saw next. Becky, now ten years old, dressed in Kathryne's green strapless minidress, painted up with makeup like a two-dollar whore, came stumbling into the room. She looked hideous. But the worst was yet to come. Joe, looking for Becky, appeared similarly clad in another one of Kathryne's dresses.

"Aunt Lily, we're all dressed up!" yelped Becky.

"Yes, honey, I see you are. You look lovely, too," Lily lied, trying to hide her disbelief.

"Rose, bring the damn package!" Joe yelled, visibly uncomfortable to be found in this situation.

Seeing the look on Lily's face, Joe tried to explain. "Well, Lily, ah…I…Becky likes for me to play dress-up with her. You know her mother is never here to do it."

Becky had always been pretty. She had Kathryne's long curls in a pale-copper tone that was the envy of every woman who saw her. At first glance, Becky's retardation and crippling bone structure was unnoticed. A second look, however, revealed the problems of the child who could, otherwise, be on her way to the rewarding life of a beautiful woman. It was glaringly obvious to Lily that Becky was, in spite of it all, developing into a young woman.

Just then, Rose came back with the long-awaited package. "Thank you, Rose," Lily said genuinely, thrilled to see the package and her way out of the awkward situation.

"Thanks, Joe, for calling me," she mumbled as she hurried out the door. As the door closed behind her, Lily could hear Joe bellowing at Rose. "How many times have I told you not to let people in this house without telling me first?"

That scene stuck in Lily's mind for days. She wondered if she should mention it to Kathryne. But little girls *do* like to play dress-up, she told herself. But with their dad, on a workday afternoon? She argued with her little voice. What about Joe? Were the dads supposed to dress up, too? Like another mommy? Finally, thanks to all the work that had to be done, she was able to push the incident out of her mind.

After five and a half weeks, Lily got the call from Kathryne she had been wanting. "I think I will be able to come home this Friday. Gayle is stable and has private duty nurses to stay with her. She needs to stay for some therapy and some minor repair work before coming home."

"Oh, man! I've never heard such good news," Lily yelled out as she spun around in her leather chair, tossing her pen in the air. "Let me know when. I'll pick you up. Give Gayle my love."

"Hey, gang! The cavalry is coming Friday!" Lily shouted, walking into the front office.

Working with kids and animals was always a pipeline to sheer torment. Given a choice, though, Lily would pick the animals over the kids every time. But the kids themselves still weren't as bad as the mothers who thought their little darlings were destined to be the next Shirley Temple.

As the work at the office became more and more demanding, Lily valued her time as if it were a precious gem. Finally, after finding out Kathryne would be back at the end of the week, she gave herself an early night off. It was rare lately to get home before midnight, so she planned an evening of pure self-indulgence. Wrapping herself in a long, white terry robe after enjoying a relaxing hot bath, Lily's mind was on the pan of brownies she'd left cooling on the kitchen counter.

"Ahh, perfect timing," she thought as she switched on her new color TV set and the tune to *Happy Days* hit her ears. "What could be better? A new TV, warm brownies, and the Fonz," she said aloud, curling up on the couch. The phone interrupted the first brownie en route to her welcoming mouth.

"Damn thing," she said, grabbing the receiver. "Yes?" she answered abruptly.

"Is this Miss Lily Gray?"

"Yes, it is. Who is this?"

"This is your insurance agent, specializing in Kentucky Derby winners," answered the smooth, deep voice.

Lily had the phone halfway to its cradle when she heard the words Kentucky Derby.

"Who…is this? Andy? Is this Andy Lewis?"

"Yes, Lily, how are you?" said the playful caller, chuckling.

"Oh, fine," she stammered, embarrassed by her prior rudeness.

"Am I calling at a bad time?"

"No, no, not at all," she replied, her mouth watering for the brownie promised seconds earlier.

"I'm going to be in Atlanta tomorrow evening, and I was hoping I might have the honor of your company at dinner."

"I'd be delighted! It's been so long since I've had a conversation with someone who's not trying to 'up' a deadline, sing a new ad jingle, or rearrange a layout. I may not be able to handle the pressure of casual chitchat."

A hearty laugh from her caller assured Lily that she, as hoped, had been successfully witty.

"I'll bet you can handle it," he retorted. "How does eight sound?"

"That's fine. It will give me a good excuse to leave the office early." She asked if they could make it casual dress, and he agreed.

"See you at eight."

Lily hung up the receiver, smiling. She sat for a few moments, thinking of how good it would be to sit and talk to Andy without looking over her shoulder every moment for Bill. Satisfied with the mental picture, her attention turned once again to the pan of patiently waiting brownies. She put her hands together like a diver and spoke to the delicious goodies. "Here I come, ready or not." She groaned with pleasure as she bit into a warm morsel.

The next day was as chaotic as all the ones since Kathryne left. The fill-in receptionist called in sick. Bridgemont Game Company, a new client, showed up a day early to go over the rough promo brochure, and the cameraman shot an entire dog-food segment with no film in his camera.

"No film in the camera. Where the hell do we find these people?" Lily asked herself as she nervously tapped her pink nails on the steering wheel, waiting impatiently for the traffic light to change. "Seven fifteen. Just enough time to shower and change," she thought, running up the stairs to her bedroom. The phone rang just as Lily was stepping out of the shower. It was Bill.

"Hi Lily, home early tonight, huh?"

"Yes, everything went bananas at the office, so I decided to knock off early," she replied.

"Hon, I can't talk but a minute—quick break in a meeting—wanted to say hi and make sure you remember the party Saturday night."

"Sure, I'll be looking forward to seeing you, Bill."

"OK, sweetie, see you then."

If only Bill could always be so nice and casual, she thought, brushing her hair. He was like Dr. Jekyll and Mr. Hyde. One thing was for sure, he would shit a brick if he knew whom she was having dinner with tonight. Lily giggled. The deception made her feel foxy. Dressed in bell-bottomed blue jeans and a tunic top, Lily grabbed her purse and was going downstairs when the doorbell rang. Giving herself one last look in the full-length mirror, she opened the door with a wide sweeping motion.

"Boy, you're right on time"—she stopped mid-sentence—"Oh! You are not who I expected to see!" She was shocked to find a muscle-bound man, dressed as a chauffeur, standing in her doorway.

"Are you Miss Lily Gray?"

"Yes. Who are you?"

"I'm Derrick. I've been sent by Mr. Lewis to deliver you to the Plaza Hotel. He sends his deepest regrets and apologies for not being able to come for you himself." He recited the message as if it were an announcement he had been rehearsing. He smiled from ear to ear and handed her a beautiful white rose with a blue envelope attached. "Lily" was written across the front in flamboyant penmanship.

Lily,
Please forgive me for being unable to be there myself. Derrick is the second-best man for the job. See you soon.
A

After presenting every credential he could find to prove himself, Lily finally consented to get into the white limousine and go with Derrick. When Lily slid into the back compartment of the huge car, she found another blue note attached to a bottle of champagne.

Maybe this will help you handle the pressure of the upcoming chitchat.
A.

Next to the champagne, a huge arrangement of white roses filled the limo with heavenly perfume. Lily took in the entire scene with a deep breath, which also served to convince her that she was still alive.

Derrick wound the long vehicle through the city traffic with ease, arriving at the Plaza Hotel, the most elegant hotel in Atlanta. As he pulled up to the front door, Lily wanted to soak into the soft velvet seat. The entrance to the hotel was done in black marble and brass with sixteen-foot double glass doors, also embellished with brass. Over the doors hung a crimson awning, extended to the street by three shiny brass poles on each side of the matching red carpet that led to the doors. When Lily saw the words "Plaza Hotel" in bold script on the awning, her eyes lowered to her requested casual outfit.

"Mother of Mercy!" she whispered, rolling her eyes and leaning her head back. "Are you sure this is the place?" she asked Derrick hopelessly.

His proud smile confirmed it. He nodded and said, "Penthouse suite, miss." He circled the car and opened the door for her as if she were royalty.

Everyone stared as she made her grand entrance in jeans and flats. She walked to the elevators as fast as she could without actually taking off in a dead run. Just as she reached for the button marked penthouse suite, the door opened, revealing her host. He was dressed in tan slacks, a red polo shirt, brown loafers, and his ever-present, melting smile.

"Good evening, Lily! I'm sorry…I wanted to be waiting out front for you when you arrived." Andy led her by the hand into the elevator. He was even more handsome than she remembered. "I hope you don't mind having dinner in my suite. The hotel is too full of foreign dignitaries and their guests for the British ambassador this evening."

"No, no this will be fine. Especially since I'm *so* dressed up." Lily shot Andy a look to kill. She was going to let it go at that until he howled with laughter.

"Andy Lewis, I can't believe you sent that car for me and knowingly let me parade through a wall of furs and tuxedos. Why, those people were staring at me like I should be using the back delivery door." Lily's face reddened as she realized Andy might not appreciate the reference to the back door.

"Don't be so rough on yourself, Lily. You look sensational." Andy was still laughing as they reached his suite. "Come in and sit down. I see my little ice breaker worked!"

Andy had left the double doors of the suite wide open for them. Entering the room reminded Lily that she was still a country girl. She had never seen anything to match the refined elegance of her surroundings.

The suite was beautifully decorated in white and pale blue, contemporary art, mirrors, and countless bouquets of fresh flowers. The rooms, which were really areas instead of rooms, were separated by different levels, giving the suite a spacious atmosphere. Beginning with the sitting area, two small steps led to the dining area, and billowing alabaster curtains defined the opening onto the balcony.

A leisurely dinner, with courses from turtle soup to fresh lobster, was served by the waiter. After a final dish of strawberries drenched in molten chocolate liqueur, it was all taken away. The couple was drawn to the balcony by the magnificent view of the city lights. The mood was totally relaxed, and each felt they'd known one another for years. The warmth spreading through Lily was disturbing. It took very little alcohol for her to feel the effects. She was infatuated with Andy, even though he was not only married, but colored as well. On top of that, he didn't look colored at all, and she kept forgetting.

"The view is breathtaking," mused Lily.

"Almost as breathtaking as your beauty." He was refilling their wine glasses as if nothing he said was unusual. "Kathryne told me you were very attractive…"

"Kathryne…that's it!" Lily said, finally remembering. "I have heard Kathryne mention your name. You don't know how I've been racking my brain to figure out who you are. I haven't had a chance to tell her I met you at the derby. Everything has been so crazy since I got back. You heard about Gayle's accident?" Barely allowing him time for a nod, she continued with excitement. "She will be home Friday. I can't wait to tell her. How long have you two been friends?" He was more exciting than ever now. If he was a friend of Kathryne's, he must be OK.

"I'd say about five years," Andy answered. "I remember the first time I met her. She was as nervous as a pregnant nun. Oh, but she was doing one helluva job covering it up."

"Kathryne nervous? I can't imagine."

"She really wanted my account," Andy said, "but, she was so cool, so professional. I admired her for it. Hell, there wasn't an agency in the country that had a chance after I talked to Kathryne. I knew we would work well together, and we have, too. I seem to have a sixth sense about me. I can read people. See inside them, what they want, what they need. Not just what they say. I could tell there was a lot riding on her getting my account."

Lily smiled into Andy's big brown eyes as she counted the hours until Kathryne came home and she could get the lowdown on the story he had just given her. Kathryne had told her of an account she landed about five years ago that had kept her from losing her house. Soon after she borrowed heavily against it to pay Becky's operation, Joe went on a two-week drinking binge and lost his job. Was it Andy's account that saved her? Andy excused himself to take a phone call in the living room.

Lily took a deep breath and whispered to the night sky, "Kathryne, get your butt on back to Atlanta!"

Lily stood leaning against the rail of the balcony as she watched him talk quietly into the light-blue phone. A soft, warm breeze tossed her hair. Were Kathryne and Andy lovers? Would Kathryne be mad if she knew they were having dinner alone in his hotel suite? What would it be like to touch him? What kind of past had he had? What was the deal with his wife? Her imagination was running wild as her eyes watched his every move.

He emitted an urgency. One that pulled you toward him. There was a streetwise worldliness about him that let it be known he had been around. Yet a genuine goodness came through as well. Not wanting him to catch her eye, she had turned to view the city when he returned to the balcony.

"I'm sorry for the interruption, Lily."

"Oh, it's OK, I was enjoying the night air." She felt the chemistry between them and wondered if Andy's sixth sense was penetrating her thoughts. She felt herself blush.

They lingered on the balcony, talking for hours. The twinkling stars reflected against the ebony sky. He was so easy to talk to. Lily found herself telling him stories of her childhood she had never told anyone. How kids made fun of her in school because of her Indian blood. "I guess I'm not telling you anything you don't know about being treated differently."

"No," he answered quickly. He told her how much he enjoyed hearing her story.

She continued by telling him of the wonderful times spent with America Gray Dove and could not hold in her emotion as she gave her grandmother's account of the Trail of Tears and the indignities suffered by a whole nation of people. The injustices man bestowed on man.

"My grandmother gave me a journal her great-grandmother kept during the removal. That's what it was called. It was the real story, left untold in American history books, portrayed by pictures and in the Indian language."

"The Indian Removal was enacted by President Jackson in the early eighteen hundreds, right?" Andy asked.

"Yes. You know your history, don't you?" Lily answered, a little surprised.

"My wife, Pearl, is very active in the civil rights movement, and it has made us aware that black people aren't the only ones to have ever been treated unjustly. I'm kind of a history buff, too. How long did it take to move them? I'd like to hear more about the journal."

"Are you sure? I can really get wound up on this subject."

"I want to hear what really happened," Andy said, unable to take his eyes off Lily. She was so beautiful. Full of energy and excitement.

"It was a horrible trip. It took the government ten years to move the tribes from the east all the way west of the Mississippi River to the territory of Oklahoma. A population of over a hundred thousand people were uprooted from their homes and moved in a herd. Like a huge cattle drive. They walked the entire two thousand miles. Through cold, rain, sickness, birth, and death. Their provisions were very limited. The soldiers kept the best for themselves and sold what was left to the Indians.

"Sold it to them?" Andy interrupted, looking into Lily's eyes as if what she was saying was the most important thing on earth.

"Yes. They had to pay their own way. The ones who had more bought for the ones who had nothing."

"Where did they get the money?"

"They sold all they couldn't carry before they left. Over the course of the trip, they began to trade their last belongings for blankets and necessities."

"My God." Andy breathed out slowly.

"Thousands died en route. The old and sick were left behind to wait for medical wagons. The wagons were a day behind, stopping to pick up the sick and bring them the rest of the way. They died waiting for that day. The Indians were told that lie to make it easier for them to leave their loved ones. Those who questioned the soldiers were beaten with rawhide whips. Made from hides bought from the Indians, I might add."

She told Andy how the beautiful young Indian women painted their faces in mud and rubbed their bodies with animal feces from the trail to make themselves repulsive to the soldiers. "But," she continued, "they were still pulled from their groups and raped repeatedly. The children were toyed with like trained animals only to be rewarded with old, tainted meat. The journal spoke of the many deaths from broken hearts at the realization of what was happening to this country's original people. A nation was dying. Slowly, helplessly, and very, very painfully."

"Lily, this sounds like the Jews going to their death during Hitler's reign of terror."

"I know. It's unbelievable. And no one cared, and they still don't."

"Who were the tribes that were removed?"

"The Cherokee..."

"Aren't they your ancestors?"

"Yes, they are. Anyway, the Cherokee, Chickasaw, Choctaw, Creek and Seminole. The government called them the five civilized tribes, because they built villages and stayed in one place. They raised their food and had a community with leaders, similar to small towns. They were forced to give up their land and all they had worked for to move west, leaving it for the white settlers."

"Were they offered anything to do it? I mean, did the government make a deal or a treaty or something to get them to go?"

"Oh yes. They were promised the rights to all the area known as Oklahoma for 'as long as the grass shall grow and rivers run.' But that was a farce. Soon after the Civil War, Oklahoma was considered Twin Territories. Indian Territory and Oklahoma Territory. By the turn of the century, white settlers had infiltrated the Indian Territory five to one. Oil was discovered, and the government acted quickly to negotiate for the Indian Territory. In the meantime, the Five Tribes had adopted a constitution to propose their territory as the state of Sequoyah. Congress would not accept them. They knew the Indian nations would have to be recognized and treated equally. Oklahoma became a state and quickly became productive in oil. The Dawes Act had been passed, enabling Congress to purchase land from the Indians. Having nothing and no way to make money, the Indians sold their land and their rights that would last... *as long as the rivers ran.* They were forced to live on reservations in poverty-level conditions. By that time, the population had dwindled to less than half of the original one hundred thousand."

"Your great-grandmother, I take it, was quite educated for her time. She had the foresight to keep a journal for future generations."

"Yes, I think she was. My grandmother's family was well educated. They had their own teachers in the villages. The art of 'tale telling' was their education, each story having a moral. They were also all taught to read and write their own language. It took people a long time to forget the stigma attached to Indians. I would like to see one good Western in which the Indians win and are not depicted as savage, blood-lusting renegades."

"Maybe in time, we will." Andy took her hand in his, but offered nothing of his past.

As the stars began to fade from the sky, and the dawn slowly crept in, Lily was aghast to realize the time. On the way home, relaxed in the back of the limo, she rested her head against Andy's shoulder and he kissed her lightly on the forehead. She felt so close to him. She sensed a special friendship...security. But was that all?

"Lily, I wish I didn't have to say this, but our friendship will have to be a secret one. Can you understand..." Before he could finish, Lily assured Andy, just as Kathryne had, that she understood. They would keep it among the three of them.

He attempted to explain how the press would sensationalize an innocent friendship during a campaign. Anything could be misconstrued by the opponent.

They both realized that Lily's date at the derby, Bill Dressler, was that opponent.

As Lily closed and locked the front door behind her, she paused for a moment in the dim glow of the night light she always left on and reflected on the evening she had just spent. She knew her whole life had changed somehow.

Pulling her red-flannel sleep shirt over her head, she went into the kitchen for a snack. Too nervous to eat much at dinner, she had become suddenly famished. Pouring herself a Diet Rite cola, she sat down with a bag of potato chips to read the weekly letter she exchanged with Gray Dove. As Lily read the letter, she could almost hear her words and the sweet rhythmic flow in which her grandmother spoke. Lily's heart ached to feel the old arms around her once again and to share the love and wisdom America Gray Dove exuded. What would she think of her friends, Kathryne and Andy? Would she approve of her new lifestyle? Lily missed the old woman greatly. She felt her life beginning to move ahead, and she missed the simple pleasures she'd loved so much and was taught to enjoy by Gray Dove.

"I've got to go home, just for a while. I have to see her," Lily whispered as tears stung her tired eyes.

chapter

EIGHT

The weeks Kathryne had been away seemed longer than the actual time that had passed. It had been a trying, demanding time. She missed Becky and her work, and she knew how badly she was needed at the office. She missed her routine, her clothes, Andy, and Lily, and she missed her own bed. She was just plain tired and needed to go home.

As she pulled open the curtains and the warm sunlight filled Gayle's mint-green, flower-filled room, she knew just how badly she had been needed here. It was amazing now to see how peaceful Gayle looked as she slept. Gayle's recovery had come such a long way in the time since the accident, thanks to Southern California Memorial. One wing specialized in multiple-injury patients who were left paralyzed.

The first sight of Gayle so near death, with tubes penetrating what looked like every part of her body, hit Kathryne hard. Gayle had been left partially paralyzed, and the doctors were unable to determine if physical therapy would help her walk again. Kathryne had stayed at her side faithfully.

Gayle awoke when Ginger came in to change her IV. "Good morning, sleepyhead," the young nurse said cheerfully as she retaped her patient's arm. All the staff loved Gayle and went out of their way to make her as comfortable as possible.

"Do you want anything?" Kathryne asked, fluffing Gayle's pillows. Scooting up in the bed, Gayle smiled as much as possible. Her jaw had been broken and was still wired together, but she moved her head slightly to indicate no.

"Interested in a manicure this morning? I can't leave this afternoon knowing you have naked nails!" Gayle's tired eyes smiled somewhat as Kathryne pulled the chair over to the bedside.

Gayle's aching heart showed in her eyes as she painfully tried to ask. "Sal...dead?"

Kathryne knew the day would come when she would have to tell Gayle that Sal had died in the accident. The doctors had kept it from her, fearing she would not survive. Tears came to Gayle's eyes as she squeezed Kathryne's hand.

"Yes, honey, he is. I'm so sorry, so very sorry." Gayle's eyes closed as the tears streamed down her face. Kathryne held her hand until she fell into a deep sleep brought about by the pain medication Ginger put in the IV. Kathryne put off leaving her dear friend as long as she could. The flight was early the next morning, and she would not be able to get back for a couple of weeks. She knew the office needed attention. Physical therapy would start soon, and Gayle would need her company intact when she recovered.

The next morning, Kathryne stretched out in the roomy first-class seat of the Boeing 707, and started to relax. She was confident Gayle would be OK and was strong enough now, with the doctor's help, to accept Sal's death. For the first time in six weeks, she felt at ease. Daydreaming out the window at the fresh morning sky, she thought how good it would feel to have Becky's little arms around her neck. But almost immediately the happy thought was darkened by the image of Joe's sneering face. She wished now she had asked Rose to fix the spare bedroom for her. The thought of sharing a bed with Joe was more than she could handle. She decided she would just sleep with Becky for a couple of nights.

After spending a long weekend at home, Kathryne returned to the office to find everything in great shape. Lily had done a terrific job keeping the work flowing. New accounts continued to pour in and Kathryne, acting as the president in Gayle's absence, found it necessary to hire two new employees.

"God almighty, I'm dead to the bone," Lily moaned as she collapsed on the sofa in Kathryne's office. "I mean, my mind is too full, you know?"

"Yes, I believe the term is brain dead." Kathryne laughed, propping her feet up on the desk. "Hey, let's go to the movies. We haven't been out for a long time. Joe and Becky have gone to father's night at the clinic."

"Yeah, and then we'll get pizza! We've got so much to catch up on." Lily checked out the movie selections in the newspaper. "What do you want to see, *Paper Moon* or *The Exorcist?*"

"*Exorcist.*"

"Oh no, Kathryne. I live alone. I'd be up for weeks drinking holy water!"

"OK, cry baby! *Paper Moon* it is." Kathryne laughed. "Anyway, Ryan O'Neal is cuter than a kid throwing up pea soup!"

After the movie they struck out for Papa Guido's and their favorite round-the-world pizza, baked twice, with everything on it. Papa's wood floor, red-and-white-checked tablecloths, and centerpiece candles could make you forget you were not in Italy.

"Well, I guess you are seeing quite a bit of Bill now, right?"

"No. To tell you the truth, we have both been so busy lately that between my long hours at the office and his campaign, we really have to work at getting together."

"So, does he turn you on? Have you finally fallen for him?" Kathryne was ready for some girl talk, far remote from ads, payroll, and hospitals.

"Oh, Kathryne, not really." Lily knew this was coming but felt as if she was on a hot seat. She wanted Bill to turn her on, but it just wasn't there. Maybe thoughts of Tommy Hawkins were in the back of her mind. Anyway, it made her nervous even to talk about it. "He is so jealous and wild tempered. I don't feel comfortable around him sometimes. He's so…so…"

"Possessive?"

"Yes, I guess that's it. He wants me to be his ideal instead of myself. Obviously, they are not the same."

"Bad news," said Kathryne. "Get rid of him."

"I don't want to talk about Bill, anyway," Lily said with disgust. "Oh, let me tell you! You won't believe who I met at the Kentucky Derby. We've been so busy I haven't had a chance to tell you about it." Lily was dousing her pizza with juice from the hot peppers.

"Ooh, you met someone! Tell me everything!" Kathryne teased, winding the thick strings of cheese around her fork.

"Andy Lewis!"

"Andy? You did?" Kathryne was surprised, her fork of cheese suddenly forgotten. Gayle's accident and recovery had pushed Kathryne's talk with Andy before the Kentucky Derby far back in her mind. She had not thought another thing about it until this moment. What is she leading up to, Kathryne wondered? And, what did this have to do with how she felt about Bill? She was almost afraid to ask, "What do you think of him?"

Lily told Kathryne how they met at the derby, the terrible things that happened with Bill and his dad, and the shock at finding out that Andy was colored. She left out the story of her winnings and quickly skimmed over their dinner in his hotel suite, not quite ready to talk about that either. Anxious for details from Kathryne, she asked, "Did you know he was colored when you first met him?

"Nope." Kathryne was trying to absorb Lily's story.

"So weren't you a little shocked to find out?"

"I'll say!"

"Tell me how you two met. Andy thinks you're the greatest thing since sliced bread. Is it a secret? Are you lovers? Tell me, tell me!" Lily begged, refilling their beer mugs from the pitcher.

Kathryne's thoughts took her back five years when she saw a young man standing on the dock of an oil well, drenched in black film. She began telling Lily her story. They had just hit oil, and everyone on the dock was cheering and slapping each other on the back.

"The oil made his clothes cling to him like a second skin and the outline of his physique literally took my breath. Honest to God, Lily, he was the most sensuous man I had ever laid my eyes on." Kathryne told Lily she had gone to Texas to set up some oil field shots for an account she had just signed up. Andrew Lewis, president of Lewis Oil 3 Company, wanted an elaborate advertising campaign for a chain of cut-rate, self-service gas stations he was building all over Texas. Kathryne's idea for the campaign was a "straight from the oilfields to you—no middle man to pay" approach to convince the customer he was getting a real bargain.

"So, Lily, here I am, standing in the middle of an oil field trying to control my racing hormones and screaming corpuscles so I won't make a complete fool of myself."

Lily felt flushed. She was on that oil field with Kathryne, picturing how Andy must have looked. She laughed with Kathryne, but hormones of her own had begun to race. Lily knew Kathryne wasn't easily distracted by a man. She seemed to always have her mind on business. Lily wondered if alcoholics like her husband, Joe, could even have sex. All Joe cared about was being with Becky and getting drunk. In that order.

Kathryne took a sip of beer and smiled. Looking over Lily's shoulder as if in a trance, she continued. "Since the contract had been negotiated over the phone and executed by mail, I wanted to impress the owner by going right out to meet him and start the campaign. Lily, this was my first real break. I had to pull it off. Not to mention that the bank was getting ready to foreclose on my house. I arrived at his office early that morning and was informed that Mr. Lewis had been called out of the office on an emergency and would meet with me in the afternoon. The foreman, a real cowboy type named Red Sanderson, had been elected to show me the oil fields and some of the wells. Red is what you would call a good ol' boy. You know what I mean?" Pausing and looking into Lily's eyes, she waited for an answer.

"Yes." Lily chuckled.

"He is a rugged, big guy with wavy, black hair. I never have figured out why they call him Red. So anyway, here I stood, staring at that handsome, oily hunk of a man laughing with the guys over the oil strike. I know I was blushing when Red finally quit cheering with them and directed me back to the Land Rover. I was hoping he couldn't read my mind. I stumbled and glanced back every few steps, managing at last to crawl up into the Rover and finish the tour with Red."

By now, they were the only ones left in the restaurant, and Papa was closing up around them. "When Red and I got back to the office, Mr. Lewis had called to say he should be there in about thirty minutes. I was still shaken by this 'oil god,' so I freshened up in the ladies' room and then had a cup of coffee with Red. I was my tough, business-minded self when the secretary announced that Mr. Lewis was ready to see me.

"You should have seen me strut down that hall to Mr. Lewis's office." She sat up straight in the chair, swinging her shoulders back and forth as she illustrated. Her height of six feet gave her an edge on staying slim and also on strutting. "I felt like I had the bull by the horns, until I stepped into that office. Lily...my smile froze. There, walking to meet me with an outstretched hand and warm smile, was that same man I had seen earlier standing on the dock drenched in oil!"

Their eyes just locked together, Kathryne remembering and Lily imagining what it had been like.

Kathryne did not share with her best friend the weeks she had spent wrestling with the attraction she felt for Andy. "Get it off your mind, Kathryne," she would tell herself. The afternoon she saw Andy at Well 212, she had no idea he was colored. Later that day when she realized he was not only colored, but also the Mr. Lewis with whom she had contracted to do an advertising campaign, she was astounded. His skin was beautiful. It was very light and creamy colored. Kathryne couldn't sleep for dreaming about how badly she wanted to touch him, to discover if his skin was as soft as it looked...as soft as his voice, as inviting as his eyes.

Kathryne was strongly opposed to crossing the racial barrier in a romantic relationship, and as she got to know Andy better, the attraction she felt became friendship.

Leaving Papa's brought the girls back to reality, and Lily asked, "Have you had a chance to find out what Gayle's plans are?"

"No, I really haven't. She was always so busy telling me about her progress, I was afraid to mention anything that's going on here. It might show down her recovery."

"I guess she probably plans on coming back to the agency. I mean what else does she have now, right?" Lily asked, unable to hide her disappointment. She had hoped Kathryne would still take over the agency.

Kathryne agreed.

As the weeks turned into months, Gayle's progress continued. Kathryne and Lily watched her come slowly through rehabilitation, learning to walk again, and basically learning to live again. Gayle was a survivor. In six months she was back in the office. She knew she had to pick up her life again as it was pre-Sal. She was welcomed back to the office on her first day with a party and a gift from the staff of a special desk chair that, with the push of a button, helped her up discreetly.

Gayle settled into a routine. She seemed fine, at first.

"How's the campaign going?" Lily asked Bill on one of his daily phone calls.

"Well, I'm givin' your buddy a pretty good run for his money."

"My buddy?" Lily asked, playing dumb. She knew exactly who Bill meant.

"Yeah, ol' Andy Lewis. I've got an investigating committee diggin' pretty deep into his shit. You know, a lot of people don't know he's a nigger, since he doesn't have that dark skin."

That kind of talk made Lily's skin crawl. She hated Bill when he was this way.

"Where were you Tuesday night? I tried to call you all night." Bill was grilling her again.

"Oh, that must have been the night I stayed at Kathryne's. Joe was away overnight."

"I gotta go, sweetie. I love you, and I'll see you next week."

"Take care," Lily said sweetly, hanging up the receiver.

"Knock, knock. It's me," called Kathryne, opening the door to Lily's office. "Busy?"

"No, I was just talking to Bill."

"How's his campaign going?"

"Oh, I think there's quite a bit of mudslinging going on, from what I can get from Bill."

"Really? What do you mean?" Kathryne checked her hose for a run.

"Well, I don't know that much about politics, but Bill has an investigation committee checking out Andy."

"What's there to check?" Kathryne asked, as she abruptly turned to face Lily.

"Bill says he's a notorious womanizer. Do you believe it? Also, his wife was a great follower of Martin Luther King, Jr., so Bill says Andy would just carry on as Dr. King's puppet through his wife." Lily mocked Bill's Texas accent. "Also there is supposed to be something crossways with how Andy became such an oil tycoon. Have you heard a word I've said, Kathryne?"

Kathryne was lost in memories all flashing together at once. Small bits and pieces of things she'd heard and fragments of articles she'd read about the credibility of Andy Lewis, rich oil tycoon and hopeful political leader. Something about an oil lease and a poker game...a suicide.

"Yes, I've heard everything you've said."

"Well, do you think it could be true?"

"I suppose it could be," Kathryne said thoughtfully. She changed the subject. "The reason I came in—get this. Gayle wants to chuck the entire Majestic Cruise Lines account!"

Lily was planning to get Kathryne back to the subject of Andy until she realized what she had said. "Kathryne, you've got to be kidding."

"No. No, I'm not."

"My God, why? We all worked our asses off on this one!"

"I know. I know. Jim and Eddie are simply livid over this. They've worked on that jingle and mixed the sound a thousand times. They were here the last three Sundays, not to mention the nights till midnight and one."

"Why would she do that?" Lily raged. "We've got to get her straightened out, or we will miss the deadline!" Lily was headed for the door and Gayle's office.

"Wait! She doesn't want to do it, she has. It's chucked...out... gone."

"Kathryne, we'll lose thousands of dollars. Can they sue?"

"You better believe they can, and they will. She isn't even going to give the deposit back."

"Well, you've got to give it to them. They'll murder us!"

"I can't. She took me off the signature card at the bank. I found out this morning. My checks started coming back, and I called the bank to find out why. She didn't even tell me."

"Damn! What is she doing? What is wrong with her?" Lily began stomping around the room waving her arms as she recapped the hard work everyone had put in on the Majestic account.

"I don't know. But, if this keeps up, the Gayle White Agency will be down the tubes quick!"

In a few short days it dawned on Kathryne what was going on. "Lil, have you noticed how Gayle comes to work every day and just sits, staring out the window in a dazed stupor? Or, she's wild like a raving maniac?" They were having lunch at Pierre's so they could talk freely outside the office.

"Yes, and have you seen that creepy, glassy-eyed look she gets sometimes?"

"I know exactly what you're saying Lily, and now I know what's happening. She's hooked on drugs—pain killers, morphine, and God only knows what else."

"Oh, Kathryne. How do you know?"

"I was on my way to her office yesterday to confront her about some of this shit. The door was open a little, and I overheard her on the phone to her doctor. From what I could gather, Gayle has been hooked ever since the accident. Apparently, the doctor won't buy her unbearable-pain story anymore and refused to renew her prescription last week. He wants her to go to the hospital's drug dependence therapist. From the way Gayle was carrying on, she has no intention of going."

"Well, what's next? Are we just supposed to sit idly by and let her lose her shirt and ours right along with it?" asked Lily, watching the dessert cart go by with lust in her eyes.

"No, we've got to get her to talk about selling the agency again. But, how I don't know. Lord, look at the time. I've got a client due in my office right now." Kathryne grabbed her purse.

Lily spent the rest of the week snooping and soul searching and decided it was time to talk to Kathryne about a solution to their problems.

"Hey, come home with me tonight. We can fix something to eat." She was in her office talking on the phone to Kathryne. "I've got some carpet samples for my bedroom, and I need a second opinion. Besides, you need a break. I couldn't help but overhear you on the phone with Joe this morning. Whew, that was some argument!"

"Don't I know it," Kathryne replied. "I'll pick up something at Dell's though. I know what the inside of your refrigerator looks like."

"See ya later, then." Lily said replacing the receiver. Carpet samples were the last thing on her mind, but she didn't want to say too much at the office for fear of being overheard by someone who shouldn't know the problems at hand.

Arriving at Lily's, Kathryne came in the front door and went straight for the kitchen. "Hey Lil, where are you? I've got lots of food, and I'm starving."

"I'm in the kitchen," Lily called. Barely waiting for Kathryne's nose to get through the door, Lily started. "Kathryne, I've been doing some sleuth work at the office for the past few days, and I found out why Gayle took your name off the signature card at the bank. She's been taking money out of the account on a daily basis. I know she's using it to buy drugs from Vinnie, the creep we saw her with at lunch that day. Also, we aren't going to be able to meet payroll by the first of the month. And the bank is ready to repossess her car."

"Holy shit!" Kathryne gasped. "I'd say you do very good sleuth work." Lily's kitchen looked like a page out of a country cookbook. It seemed unnatural to have a business conversation amid the gingham and copper decorations. "Well," she said with a deep sigh, "I have thought this over a thousand times. I don't have the money to buy her out without the terms she offered me before Sal died. This could be the end, Lily." Kathryne had to look away. She felt her throat tightening. She stared at the floor as if for a solution, her face displaying her feelings of disgust and desperation. Kathryne was slumped in the chair at the kitchen table. Lily began to circle the table, too excited to sit down. "I have a plan," she announced. "How much do you think it would take to buy the agency? I figure," she continued, not waiting for an answer, "that on the basis of the net profits of the accounts under contract at the present, taking into consideration the value of the name, the furniture, equipment, lease, and trained staff, the value should be right at $750,000. Wait a minute now," Lily said, as Kathryne started to protest.

Kathryne couldn't help noticing how pretty Lily looked. She was still dressed from work in a cobalt-blue pantsuit. The pants were slightly belled and the blouseless jacket was made like a long tunic, flared just below the hips. The cut of the jacket made Lily's already slim waist look even smaller. Her beautiful, black hair was pulled back from her face in a low ponytail, but strands of loose curls framed her face like ribbons on a lovely package. She continued her presentation to Kathryne.

"If we deduct from this amount the accounts you have brought in and all the ones I have landed myself, which we could take with us if we started our own agency, I might add, I would say Gayle would be damn lucky to get $350,000 to $375,000."

"Good Lord, Miss Agnes!" exclaimed Kathryne using one of her mother's favorite expressions. She was shocked at Lily's accuracy about the value.

"I'm not finished," Lily said with that look she always gave her client when she was ready for the signature on the contract. "I met this morning with Nick Bryant at Atlanta National."

"What!?" Kathryne's mouth gaped in astonishment. Expressions of surprise and excitement played leapfrog on Kathryne's face as Lily showed her a copy of the spreadsheet for the business plan she had presented to the president of the bank that very morning.

"Nick said," Lily continued, "that he would approve a loan of $250,000 with two points, which he would add to the principal. The interest would be 13 percent on a fifteen-year payback period, with monthly payment to be arranged."

"Lily Gray!" screamed Kathryne. "You're kidding! No, you're not kidding! Oh, Lil!" They jumped up and down and ran around the room like two teenage wallflowers who had just been invited to the prom.

Suddenly Kathryne stopped in the middle of the floor. "Oh, shit!" She looked like she had been shot in the stomach. "Lily, I don't have enough money to make up the down payment. I agree, and I am impressed all to hell with your calculations, but even if I sold my lot at Lake Sydney and scraped up every dime I could find, the most I could hope for is $50,000! That's only half of what we need. Lil," Kathryne said sadly, "you have done an outstanding job of evaluating this whole situation. I am so grateful, but I feel my hands are tied. Nick is a real peach, too, and I know he shot you the best deal he could..." Kathryne continued to ramble. As she paced the room, she could feel the tears gaining on her. Her motto, "Professionals don't cry," kept rolling around in her head like the clapper of a giant bell.

"Kathryne, Kathryne, wait." Lily took her by the arm. "Come here and sit down. I want to tell you a story about the Kentucky Derby and a magnificent horse named Secretariat."

chapter

NINE

Dressed in their most impressive suits and feeling more confident than they had ever felt in their lives, the anxious pair presented their plan to Gayle and her attorney. Gayle hungrily snapped up the proposal, afraid they might change their minds. During the meeting, Lily noticed the absence of Gayle's beautiful engagement ring and was sickened by the thought of what might have happened to it. The meeting went smoothly, the final papers to be signed within the next two weeks. Closing the door behind them as they left the attorney's office, their professional sophistication went out the window. Trying to be soundless, they silently jumped up and down mouthing their words like mimes practicing a skit.

"Let's get out of here!" Kathryne exclaimed, trying to whisper. "Are we doing the right thing?" she asked on their way down in the elevator. There is something about finally reaching a life-long goal that gives you the shakes. Kathryne was wondering if she had acted prematurely. Had she paid enough dues to justify such a leap?

"Damn betcha!" Lily grinned. "I never felt better in my life!"

Her confidence regained, Kathryne chuckled. "With a partner like you, success is a given!"

They strode down Peachtree Street arm in arm, both excitedly talking at the same time about the changes they wanted to make in the office, how proud Andy would be, and whether or not they could save the Majestic Cruise account. They decided to change the agency name due to Gayle's recent damage to its name.

After they signed the final papers on the agency, the new owners of the Langford Gray Advertising Agency took Gayle White to lunch. Lunch was a high for all three, each one starting life anew. Gayle looked beautiful. The plastic surgery done on her face made the scars untraceable. Gayle had been faithful to her physical therapy program and was walking now with only a slight limp. The drug and alcohol dependence department of Atlanta Memorial had been a godsend three months ago; Dr. Snow had insisted she start counseling or he would have her committed. Gayle's happiness assured her two friends that she was finally getting her life back together. The women sat and talked for hours, Kathryne and Gayle reminiscing about the days before Lily joined them. Kathryne's emotions were evident when she thanked her mentor for the guidance, the training, and the encouragement she had so desperately craved. She credited Gayle as the person who had done more for her than anyone in her whole life.

Each of them had her own story to tell. Most of them, although not humorous at the time, were funny now. Lily laughed until her sides were hurting. She even chimed in with her own story about trying on everything she owned the night Kathryne called to tell her she had the job. It was a wonderful afternoon.

The luncheon turned out to be a good-bye party for Gayle. On the way back to the office, she told Kathryne and Lily that she had booked herself on a cruise to the Bahamas the next day. Then she was moving to Phoenix where a new concept called cluster homes was very popular. With some of the money from the sale of the agency, Gayle planned to buy stock in the real estate company developing the cluster home project.

As a surprise, Joe and Bill planned a celebration for the new partners that night. Joe was sober but remained touchy about his work and resented even a friendly inquiry. Bill was becoming more obsessed with his love for Lily. But, much to everyone's amazement, the four had a wonderful time. They toasted Lily Gray, Kathryne Tabor Langford, and the Langford Gray Advertising Agency over dinner at Oscar's, Atlanta's newest dinner club. The group dined and danced to Herb Albert and the Tijuana Brass. Then, after closing the Jazz Lounge on Thirty-Third Street, they declared the celebration a success. Joe and Bill had been complete gentlemen all night, and there was no argument from them when the women wanted to stop by the office for a drink to properly christen the partnership.

With Joe and Bill busy finding glasses in the break room, the new owners walked through the office with a kind of reverence.

"I can't believe it, Kathryne Tabor. We did it." Lily laughed defiantly under the influence of the champagne. "Hey, I like that Kathryne Tabor name. Hmmm, I think I like KT even better!"

"You shit." Kathryne giggled. "You are just plain drunk."

"Oh no I'm not! I'm just feelin' festive. Aren't you?"

"Flying high would be the better term," Kathryne said. "You Indians never could hold your firewater."

With grandiose plans for redecoration, they all decided to call it a night. Out of habit, Kathryne checked the message box on the way out and found a note in Gayle's slot. Knowing the message probably would pertain to an account that Kathryne would now be handling, she took the note and stuck it in her purse.

Feeling giddy and interested only in getting home and into bed, she threw her head back and said to Joe, "Oh, Rhett, I'll think about that tomorrow!" She flipped off the lights and closed the door behind them.

Kathryne slept very late, feeling slow and lazy and good. She was enjoying a second cup of coffee on the patio when the pink note in her purse came to mind. Grabbing a cinnamon roll and the note, she read Gayle's message en route back to the patio, her weekend haven.

"Vinnie called. OK for 6."

"Now where have I heard that name?" She squinted at the paper trying to remember. She picked up the newspaper, but the name Vinnie kept returning to her mind, making it impossible to concentrate. Knowing Lily would probably have one helluva hangover, she was reluctant to call her, but she just couldn't shake a bad feeling. Lily answered the phone amazingly alert.

"Hey, are ya up and movin' yet?" Kathryne inquired mischievously.

"Oh, I'm slowly coming to life. How much champagne did you feed me last night, anyway?"

"I lost count after we left Oscar's. Listen, does the name Vinnie mean anything to you in connection with Gayle?"

"Yes, it does seem familiar. Let me think a second. I've only had one cup of coffee."

"Well, I've got a strange feeling..."

"Wait. I remember now," Lily blurted out. "He's that awful guy we saw with Gayle at lunch a couple of months ago. Don't you remember? We saw his picture in the paper after that. He was picked up for dealing drugs and got off on a technicality."

"That's it!"

"Why? What about him?"

"Lily! Oh shit, Lily! The note I picked up for Gayle last night. It was from him confirming an appointment with her—for yesterday."

"Kathryne,"—Lily's voice was shaky—"are you thinking what I'm thinking?"

"Oh my God, Lily! I'll meet you at Gayle's."

Kathryne pulled into Gayle's driveway right behind Lily's bright-red convertible. As they got out of their cars, the two women's eyes locked. They each felt the dread they shared. They realized that the appointment with Vinnie was to buy drugs, and Gayle once again had money to buy them. Lots of them.

Lily banged anxiously on the front door of Gayle's two-story, colonial-style house.

"Come on, come on! Open the damn door!" Kathryne screamed impatiently. Her tousled red hair seemed to flame with excitement, revealing how she felt inside.

Gayle's housekeeper, Mr. Ling, finally opened the door. Unaware of any trouble and happy to see them as always, Mr. Ling bowed as he waved them into the house.

"Ah, good day, ladies, please come in. May I fix you some tea?" Mr. Ling was a small Asian man, about fifty-five, with black eyes and hair. He had been Gayle's housekeeper for a little over nine years.

"Is Gayle home?" Lily asked, trying to keep her voice from quivering.

"Oh, she still sleeping. She go to bed early last evening. Say no disturb. Need beauty sleep for long journey." When Mr. Ling smiled his eyes seemed to disappear. He was unaware of any crisis.

"Ling, call an ambulance!" Kathryne screamed at him as her long legs took the stairs two at a time. Lily was right behind her. Kathryne stopped abruptly at the bedroom door. Her heart was pounding so hard, it felt as if it would come out of her ears. She was trying to get her breath and gain some composure before entering the room. Lily was beside her as she slowly twisted the doorknob. They stared into each other's fear-filled eyes. Kathryne slowly stepped in, afraid to see what might be waiting.

Entering the dark room, a strong, bitter smell hit them, almost taking their breath. The heat was stifling. Gayle did not have air conditioning. She believed the theory that it caused premature wrinkling. She even used a humidifier in her bedroom to keep the air moist, thereby keeping her skin from drying out. The humidity hung in the room and in the fiber of the ever-present pink-and-white ruffled curtains. Lily fought with the ruffles to get the window open, letting in some air and light. As the sunlight suddenly filled the room, Kathryne saw Gayle lying on her side amid more pink-and-white ruffles. Her back was to her.

"Gayle. Gayle..." Kathryne's firm voice broke the thick, hot silence. Lily noiselessly crept to Kathryne's side by the bed.

"Is she...?"

Kathryne could not answer. She stood frozen at the sight of the woman who had given her a chance when no one else would, who had taught her how to live again, who had stayed at the hospital with her through Becky's last three operations.

She was dressed in the ice-blue pants and matching silk blouse Sal had bought her for their honeymoon. She had worn it yesterday for the closing.

Kathryne knew she was dead before she touched her. She gently pulled Gayle's shoulder, causing her to roll onto her back, face up. She was rigid, swollen.

"My God, Gayle, why?" whispered Kathryne. She searched for an answer in the ashen face of her mentor. Gayle's bulging blue eyes seemed to fix on a picture of her and Sal taken at a dance several months ago. The dark stains of her body's final excretion were evident on the once immaculate pink-and-white comforter. The heat from the humidifier seemed to suddenly enhance the odor. Deterioration was apparently accelerated. Leaning slightly over the bed, Kathryne saw the needle still in Gayle's arm, just beneath the silk scarf she had used to pop up the vein.

Kathryne was so stricken by the hideous sight that all she could do was stand there and stare. The ambulance attendant clanging the stretcher up the stairs startled her. Turning toward the door, she saw Mr. Ling standing just inside the room, tears dropping from his small black eyes. Lily, now somewhat revived, stood with Kathryne. The Medical Examiner pronounced Gayle dead of an overdose of heroin. She was zipped into a bright-yellow body bag and carried off like a sack of garbage.

Kathryne and Lily would never forget the sight. Nor would the feeling they shared at that moment. It was a feeling that would bond them forever.

❧

The next day the Atlanta *Sentinel* read, "Gayle White of Gayle White Advertising Agency, named four times as Atlanta's Businesswoman of the Year, was found in her home dead from an apparent drug overdose." The same paper simultaneously ran the half-page announcement, "Gayle White, ready for early retirement and a carefree life, announces the sale of her advertising agency to Kathryne Langford and Lily Gray. The agency name will be changed to Langford Gray Advertising Agency and plans to continue the same great service…"

❧

A long, black limousine crept slowly up the winding sandy lane behind the hearse. The afternoon sky was dark and gloomy, as it should have been for such a sad occasion. Headlights stretched through the old cemetery like a long, twinkling snake.

Kathryne and Lily, Gayle's closest friends, rode in the family car that customarily followed the hearse. They shared the blue-velvet-tufted coach with Gayle's only living relative, an aunt on her mother's side. Aunt Iris, a homely chemistry teacher from Valdosta, was as delighted to be there as a buzzard at a road kill. She was sure she had inherited a large sum of money.

Bill was in Texas busy with his almighty cattle, and Joe, using Gayle's death as a good excuse, was drunk. What sorry support they had been for Lily and Kathryne. The days following Gayle's death had been horrid. The suicide overdose had been big in the news.

Andy was there, of course. He played it low key, but Kathryne and Lily knew he was there as much for them as to pay respects to Gayle. His driver, Derrick, stood leaning against a black limo, his eyes never leaving Andy.

Gayle's family, lying next to the gaping hole over which the coffin had been suspended, waited for her to join them. Her beloved, Salvatore Martino, had been buried in Italy right after the accident.

The preacher had his final say, and a robust woman who resembled Kate Smith sang a chilling rendition of "Amazing Grace." The wind from an approaching storm rustled the stately oaks surrounding the gathering as if to announce the end.

People began returning to their cars. Andy walked over to the solemn pair lingering at the graveside. He knew they were asking themselves if they should have paid more attention...if they could have somehow prevented what happened.

"I asked Gayle's aunt if I could take you home," he said softly. He stepped between them, linking his arms in theirs. "Let it go. There is nothing you could have done."

"I'll always wonder," Kathryne replied sorrowfully. Her voice broke. "She had grown to depend on me so much."

They turned and walked hesitantly to Andy's limo. It seemed so cold to leave her. So final.

"Derrick, let's drive over to the park," said Andy. Kathryne and Lily numbly rode along in silence, gazing out the window.

"You girls are sure going to disappoint Gayle if you keep this up," he said as they pulled into the park. Peachtree Park consisted of twelve beautifully landscaped acres. The dogwoods were blooming, and buttercups were popping up in plant beds throughout the park. The centerpiece fountain was a Civil War memorial to the fallen South.

The wind had settled down now, and they walked together to the fountain. Andy talked to them about Gayle. Her accomplishments, her attitude, her charm. He talked about how Gayle had always looked forward, not back, and that she had a right to die without being someone's guilt trip.

"Let her go," he told them again. "You have to take what she has given you of herself and carry it through. Gayle saw something special in you two. Now, you must be the women she saw in you. She told me once that the two of you were every agency's dream team. There was magic between you. She was very proud of you both."

Kathryne and Lily knew what he said was true. They did have magic between them. They had felt it too many times to ever deny it. As Andy spoke, they began to feel new energy surge through them. Accounts came to mind that needed work and employees who needed attention.

"Well," said Lily, nudging Kathryne and grinning, "she ain't seen nothin' yet, has she?"

They were all smiling as they walked through the park back to the car. Kathryne and Lily would never forget the day they found Gayle dead, but they were ready to begin putting it behind them. Seated in the back of the limo facing Andy, Kathryne smiled at him. "Thank you." Her eyes, puffy and dark, showed how deeply she meant it.

"Well, there is another matter," he said, reaching into his jacket. "I wanted to give you both something as the symbol of a new beginning. I am very proud of you. The way you figured it all out, put it together, and bought the agency. Heck, you didn't even ask my advice. Not once. You could have crushed my ego, you know." He was holding two small red-velvet boxes.

"Andy Lewis!" they exclaimed in unison. The sight of the red-velvet boxes took their minds off Gayle and made them feel better immediately. "What is it?"

"Wait just a minute."

"Oh sure," Lily said huffily. "He whips out two little velvet boxes and then says wait. How sadistic!"

"I designed these myself," he continued, ignoring her, "and had them hand made by an old man in the French Quarter of New

Orleans. He is about seventy-five now and truly the last of the real craftsmen. He was bursting with pride when he showed them to me." Andy gave a box to each woman and, holding their hands in his, said, "No matter what ever happens, Lily Gray and Kathryne Langford, remember always that this ol' boy from Texas loves you both." Those warm, wonderful brown eyes showed his sincerity.

They opened the red-velvet boxes to discover matching diamond bracelets. Quarter-carat diamonds were set in continuous, closely-fitted, white-gold Tiffany settings around the entire bracelet. Among the diamonds, right in the middle of the bracelet, was a slightly larger ruby. The ruby made a statement. It said "Never forget me!"

Andy fastened the bracelets on Kathryne and Lily, and they showered him with hugs and kisses.

"I can't believe you!"

"You shouldn't have!"

"It's beautiful!"

"Only you would have thought of something like this!"

"There is something else," he said. "With Gayle gone and the agency in your hands"—he looked from Kathryne to Lily—"things may get tough occasionally…you can probably count on it. I am dubbing a team." He lifted the sleeve of his jacket to reveal a similar bracelet, a little heavier, more masculine. "I had one made for myself. We are now the Diamond Bracelet Club. We can draw strength—"

"Oh my gosh," Kathryne spluttered. "Just like in the movies!"

Well, she had done it again. Kathryne's remark broke the serious shadow that had crept upon them. They rode home laughing and, with their imaginative nature, Lily and Kathryne made up scenarios in which they would tap their bracelets or press one of the diamonds to signal one of the others for help.

It had been a full day and Lily was exhausted, but the need to claim the long-awaited, "I am so proud of you!" from her mother was too strong to put off until morning. Knowing her mother would still be awake watching television, she dialed her number in Kentucky. So many things had happened since the closing on the agency that Lily hadn't had a chance to tell anyone back home about it. Lily had wanted to make sure it went through before she called them.

"Did I wake you?" Lily asked the voice on the other end.

"Heavens, no. I am baking bread for the St. Stephen's Spring Festival," her mother replied energetically. "Is anything wrong?"

"No, quite the opposite. I wanted to tell you that Kathryne and I have bought the advertising agency we have been working for. It is so exciting, Mother!"

"Let me check my bread."

Lily waited patiently for her mother to return and continued, "We are planning to double the operation within two years, add a lyric department, and well, we just have all kinds of plans."

"Oh how nice, dear," came the monotone, limp reply. The only interest her mother showed in the whole conversation came as she talked about Valerie and her husband, the grandchildren, and how wonderfully Valerie's law practice was doing. "She even had to hire an extra part-timer!"

"Well, I thought for sure you had called to tell me you were engaged and had given up your little job. Aren't you even dating anyone, dear?"

"Oh, listen, Mother, someone is at the door…I'll call you right back." Lily couldn't stand it another second. "God, I hate it when she calls me 'dear,'" she thought. It was so condescending. Tears ran down her face. What was it about her that her mother did not like? Why was it like this? Unable to handle the thought that her mother did not love her, or loved Valerie more, she decided her mother simply did not understand the important step Lily had just taken.

Living in Owensboro, Kentucky, her mother could not understand why a single woman could possibly want anything but a husband. A woman's husband and family should be first. Then, if she wanted to work, and it was all right with her husband…Maybe she was right. Maybe Lily *was* missing the most important ingredients. Feeling broken spirited and confused, she called Bill.

"Yello," slurred Bill, obviously awakened from a sound sleep.

"Hello, honey," she said in her sweetest voice.

"Lily? Wha…is something wrong?"

"No, I just wanted to talk to you." As she continued, she told Bill that buying the agency from Gayle had put her where she wanted to be in her career, and she was now ready to make a personal commitment.

"Does this mean...Lily, are you saying you will marry me?" Bill was fully awake now, and he was elated.

"Yes. Yes, Bill, I will marry you."

By the time Bill hung up the phone, he had an erection that felt like a Louisville Slugger.

Lily had flown to the Circle D Ranch to attend the annual Dressler Bar-B-Que. It was always a great party of rich, affluent horse people and politicians, and it was, according to Bill, the perfect time to announce their engagement. She pulled on her red-lizard cowboy boots and gave herself a long look in the full-length mirror.

"You are one lucky woman, Lily Gray." She was looking forward to the party. She also had a business hook to set. J. J. Long of Long Haul, Inc. didn't have a chance.

"You ready, baby?" Bill called through the door of the magnificent guest house. Bill made sure Lily stayed in Cottage Three. She had teased him on the phone about how much fun they could have, now that they were engaged. He knew she would not turn him down tonight. The proximity of Cottage Three to the house would give them plenty of privacy. Bill's parents were staunch in their morals and believed the whole world should be virgins on their wedding night. Bill, of course, had other plans. He would slip into Lily's cottage tonight after the barbeque.

William Tyler "Pappy" Dressler, Bill's great-grandfather, began the family's oil empire as a twenty-year-old driller on a roughneck crew in East Texas, near Beaumont. They worked day and night through rattlesnake infestation, heat, cold, and the skeptical jeers of pessimism from the townsfolk. On a tip from an old Indian, the rickety derricks and makeshift sheds were erected. Drillers from coal-mining crews were brought in to penetrate the hard, dry Texas land. Pappy Dressler, Ty back then, could smell the oil from the first day of drilling. He offered his labor and exceptional skill on the drill for a 5 percent piece of the hit. In order to keep their expenditures as low as possible, the wildcatter from Australia jumped at his offer.

The vibration from the first oil strike in Texas was so great that men fell to the ground as they ran to clear the area. Ty knew it was payday when he felt the ground soften slightly under his drill. He had to shut down the drill, eliminating the danger of a spark that could ignite the oil, and then he had to get the hell out of the way. And he had to do it fast! To the day he died, sixty-four years later, just after his eighty-fourth birthday, Ty never thought about that moment without getting a chill. He had turned to his foreman with the gravity of death itself and said, "If you want to live, get the hell outta here!"

The gusher on Spindletop Hill shot up two hundred feet with tremendous pressure. It was January 10, 1901. The strike gushed for nine days and was the beginning of six decades of prosperity for Texas oilmen. With his 5 percent of Spindletop, Pappy Dressler bought fifty thousand acres twenty miles west of Ft. Worth and one thousand head of cattle. The oil business had never really interested him, and as a little boy he had dreamed of a cattle ranch. He named it the Circle D.

In 1940, Pappy built a Texas mansion. He wanted a home where his guests could spend the night or the weekend, and where his four children could live comfortably with him. So he built the estate with five wings, one for himself and his wife, and one for each of his children, Jacob, Jonathan, David, and Rachel. Then, he built three large guest cottages. The cottages were located behind the pool and tennis courts, giving privacy to those who stayed.

She was the life of the party. Bill announced their engagement immediately, so he was busy all evening being exalted by his buddies, as well as all of the old cronies. Lily enjoyed the food, the people, and dancing with Bill's friends and family. Her future father-in-law was the first to get her on the dance floor. He was a marvelous dancer. Then, Bill's brother, Phil, took over with the

Texas two-step. Three hours later, Lily opened the door to her guest suite and for even more fun.

She wanted everything to be just right. She was nervous; there was no doubt about it. Her soft, blue teddy lay on the little satin stool in her bathroom. The water was running for a warm bath. A bath that would relax her, as would the red wine she sipped. She stepped into the large marble tub.

Ah. The water was perfect. It felt wonderful. She began the program. "Yes, Lily, you do love Bill. He is handsome, successful, charming, and he loves you very much. And, of course, he is very rich." She chose to ignore the volatile side of her fiancé and her mother's influence in her decision, confident she could change him.

She closed her eyes and relaxed. Stretching her naked body in the big tub, her thoughts turned to sex. It would be good to have sex in her life again. It had been so long. Actually, her sex life had always been a little askew. She and Tommy had wanted to wait until marriage to have sex, but their teenage bodies would burn with passion when they were together. They did just about everything but go all the way.

Every Wednesday night, his parents played canasta at Roberta and Ted's house. Tommy was crazy about Ray Charles. He would ceremoniously put the *I Can't Stop Loving You* album on the record player. As the music enveloped them, the den would become their own special place. They would dance for a while and then settle into making out until Lily decided it was time to stop. The words to those old songs still aroused her.

How had they been able to hold back? And how had she gone so long without it? She had tried to bury her desires with work and striving for her now-obtained career. Tonight her thoughts had brought it all back. Using the bath, the wine, and the reflections of those days with her high-school sweetheart to set herself up, she thought she was ready for Bill. She pulled on her teddy, and the creamy lace snuggled her full breasts.

Five minutes later, she lay in the bed next to a collapsed Bill with her teddy still intact. When she came out of the bathroom, he had been lying on the bed, uncovered and visibly very aroused. He had switched off the small lamp as well as the soft music she had carefully planned for ambiance.

"Jeez, you're beautiful," he had said pulling her onto the bed. He immediately was on top of her, fumbling and breathing heavily. She had never had intercourse, and Bill was having trouble. His breath came faster and faster. He fumbled with her clothing. It was hurting. Suddenly, Bill groaned. Lily thought he had, at last, realized he was going too fast, that she was still a virgin. But, when she felt the warm wetness on her leg, and he slumped beside her, she knew it was over.

She lay there, shocked. Bill had not even kissed her. So much for romance, she thought. She began to rationalize. "Look Lily, give Bill a break. He has been on edge for this for two years. Men are like that. They get too strung out sometimes. He will settle down, and it will work out."

The two-carat diamond ring he had given her at dinner was looking up at her. "It'll work out," she told herself.

Bill awoke again during the night, only to repeat himself. By morning Lily was on the verge of screaming. Just before dawn, she slipped out of bed. She had to get out of there, especially before he woke up again. She dressed quietly and went to the stables. The stable hand was already working with the horses. He saddled a beautiful, white stallion named Lookin' Good for her. She cried as she rode—tears of frustration, disappointment, and fear.

"What have I done?" she asked Lookin' Good as she rode. The sun was beginning to peek through the morning darkness, casting a gray hue around them. They opened it up, and Lookin' Good ran as if he knew how Lily felt. As if he was trying to run off the terror growing inside her. He was a magnificent horse.

chapter

TEN

It was weeks before Bill calmed down enough to listen to what Lily was trying to tell him. Although he seemed to pay attention as Lily coached him in caressing her and holding back so she could be involved also, there was still a lot of room for improvement. As she inched along in the morning rush-hour traffic on her way to the office, she admitted to herself that sex had to be better than this. If not, no one would ever want to do it. Last night's mental replay repulsed her. Maybe a talk with KT would help.

Kathryne and Lily had succeeded in pulling the agency back together. With the company now properly staffed, they were stronger and more creative than they had ever been. Many of the people who had worked with Gayle since the beginning took her death very hard. The new owners spent a lot of time with them and helped them get through it. Guilt plagued them all. Could they have done something or prevented it somehow? That question would remain forever.

"Good morning," Lily said, more like a proclamation than a greeting as she burst into Kathryne's office. "I'm on my way to the break room for a cup of coffee and a 'still warm' cinnamon roll. Interested? KT, did you hear me?"

"Oh, ah…yes, of course, still warm. I want two."

"Two it is." Lily mimicked a waitress taking an order and turned quickly on her heel. "I'll be back in a flash, honey," she said with a heavy country accent. Kathryne was still staring out her office window in deep thought when Lily returned with the good-ies. Lily went to the window and looked out at the beautiful, cloud-less sky as if searching for something.

"So, what's up? I don't see Clint Eastwood out there." Seeing the look on Kathryne's face, she added. "Didn't you have a good afternoon off yesterday?"

"Yes, I did. Well, no, I didn't."

"Joe?"

"Yes and no. Maybe it's—"

"Well, what happened? What, what?" Lily prodded her impa-tiently. She had completely forgotten about discussing Bill's prow-ess—or lack thereof.

"I wanted to spend the afternoon alone with Becky," Kathryne began. "It's been quite a while since we did anything together, just the two of us. I wanted to take her to Benji's, her favorite restau-rant, and to the beauty shop for a trim. Then maybe a matinee." She was still standing at the window as if she was reading a script from a cloud. "Well, when I get home, Rose tells me Joe took off with Becky. Shopping. He said he was taking her shopping. The man hates to shop!" With that she turned to face Lily. "What the hell does he know about shopping with a ten-year-old girl?"

Lily tried to reason, tried to make her feel a little better. "Maybe he just felt like buying her something."

"A bra?"

"A bra?"

"She doesn't need a bra. Much less a padded one. She's still too young, for God's sake! And she certainly doesn't have peer pressure like that at *her* school. Oh, it was awful, the fight Joe and I had when they got home."

Kathryne's voice began to pale compared to Lily's own thoughts. Thoughts of a daddy and a little girl playing dress-up.

A sickening feeling began to envelop Lily like an invisible vapor. Should she tell Kathryne about it, or was it just nothing?

"Lily, are you listening?" Kathryne was saying softly. "I know you must get tired of hearing all the—"

"Yes, of course I'm listening. I was just wondering why a father would take time out of a workday to take his daughter to buy her first bra and not let her mother do it. What did he say when you jumped him about it?"

"You mean when World War Three started? He just gave me the same old song and dance about me never being home to see how Becky is growing up. As far as the padded bra goes, the salesgirl must have given him the wrong package. He said he didn't pick out a padded one."

There were a few minutes of silence. Lily did not know what to say, and Kathryne turned to stare out the window again.

"Listen, KT," Lily said affectionately. "Do you want to cancel tonight with Andy? We can just make it the two of us, and we can talk all night." Andy was in town on business, and they had planned to have dinner with him at Lily's.

"Oh God, no! I need to put this out of my mind, and an evening with you guys is the perfect way to do it. Thanks, though," she said, looking straight into Lily's eyes. A look that said more than thanks. They knew if Kathryne ever figured out what to do with her personal life, it would only be with Lily's help.

Laurie interrupted to announce that Lily's first appointment was waiting in her office.

"Whoops. Tell him I will be right there." Lily said as she quickly cleaned up her cinnamon roll and coffee feast. "You OK?" she asked Kathryne.

Kathryne nodded and gave her some get-out-of-here hand jive. She was picking up her phone as Lily left. Their conversation was never really finished, and it stayed with Lily all day. Maybe her imagination was running wild just because she disliked Joe so much. Or was it?

The incident left Kathryne with a feeling of unrest. Something wasn't right, but she couldn't put her finger on it. Rose had also told her that it was not unusual for Joe to come home during the day for a couple of hours. He would usually send her on errands during that time, since he could be there with Becky while she was gone. She was so astonished that she forgot to ask her what kind of errands. She found herself phoning home more often during the day and keeping closer tabs on Becky on the days she went to the clinic.

Lily fixed her famous country-fried steak for her two best friends. The trimmings included mashed potatoes, lima beans, gravy, and biscuits. Lily loved to cook for Andy, because he always ate so much, sighing with every bite.

"This is so good!" he would say. "How do you fix this, Lily?" Kathryne would accuse him of trying to find out the secret of an old family recipe.

When they had finished dinner, Kathryne brewed a pot of deliciously strong coffee. They drifted out to the pool and the warm night air, and the music from *South Pacific*, Kathryne's prized album, gave them the feeling of being on a tropical island. Lily's love for plants and flowers was tastefully displayed on the colorful patio area that surrounded the small, intimate pool. The red, blue, purple, and gold of the different varieties garnished Lily's haven. They bloomed in every nook and cranny available. The smell of jasmine filled the air. They drew their chairs in a semicircle. Kathryne, as usual, sat in her favorite spot on the side of the pool with her feet in the water.

"Ah." They all exhaled as if on cue. Talk of the beautiful night and delicious dinner was dwindling. The lingering fragrance in the soft night air, coupled with the moment and their full bellies, created a kind of reminiscent mood.

"Andy, were you born in Texas?" Lily asked, suddenly surprised that she didn't know.

"No, Mississippi. A little town on the gulf called Pascagoula."

"What was it like for you then? People are still so prejudiced, it must have been horrible when you were a kid."

Kathryne quickly looked to see his reaction. As long as she had known Andy, they had never discussed his childhood. She had not known how to bring it up. But, leave it to good ol' blunt Lily. She could ask a June bug about his June. She moved closer.

The wine at dinner had really relaxed him, and he felt like talking. He had put it all so far back in his mind that he had almost managed to forget it. As he leaned back in the chaise lounge and took a deep breath of sweet jasmine, it came rushing back to him as if it were yesterday.

As a child, Andy had felt like an ugly duck. He wanted to be darker-skinned like his family, especially like his mother. He thought there was something wrong with him, because he was so light. Maybe he had something called iron-poor blood. He heard his grandmother say that you could get it if you didn't eat a lot of vegetables. He ate every vegetable he could in hopes that his skin would turn dark.

He began to notice how he was treated differently from his family. The whites would call him son, but they called his brother, Todd, boy. One afternoon when Todd, his mother, and Andy were returning from town on the bus, the driver told Andy he could sit on the front seat right behind him on the way home.

"Great!" Andy was delighted. "Come on, Todd. This is gonna be fun!"

"No, son," the driver said, "the little colored boy will have to sit in the back."

Andy was stunned. Not really understanding what was going on, he took the seat up front and rode there all the way home. But, instead of enjoying the ride, his tear-filled eyes roamed constantly to the back of the bus where his dear mother and little brother sat with lowered eyes and solemn faces.

Andy had nightmares for weeks. Why, he asked his mother again and again. Finally, as the summer days dwindled and preparations for his first day at school began, Andy's mother took him in her lap as she rocked the last of the day into twilight and answered all his questions. Mommy explained to Andy that his real father was a white man she used to work for.

"In those days, shugah," she explained to him, "if a white man wanted you, you had to oblige him." After the Civil War, labor remained cheap and plentiful in the South. Mississippi led the nation, second only to Texas, in cotton production. Sadie's family worked cotton and she, at age thirteen, was one of the best pickers.

She did not share with her inquisitive son the memories of those late afternoons deep in the cotton field. When cotton is ready to be picked, the ripened cotton balls pop open, exploding the plants into a field of snowy white. It was there, during cotton season in the heart of an unpicked field, that Andy's father, the owner's son, had taken away her innocence. He took her to the fields every day for several weeks, an experience that was not at all unpleasant for Sadie. He was very gentle with her and she was in love with him. He would arrange the snowy white cotton into a bed for them. He always told her she was beautiful and whispered such wonderful things to her. She wanted to believe he meant them. She never spoke to him, or about him. She knew when she didn't come down that month that her baby would be a real looker. She also knew that her lover's blond hair and fair complexion would produce a light skin—a ticket out for her child.

She had been Willie's girl for about a year. He was a hardworking neighborhood boy who treated her real nice. When he got a job in Pascagoula and asked her to marry him, she did. They moved to Pascagoula the next day. Willie was very proud to have a son so quickly and never suspected a thing.

Andy loved to sit on the porch cuddled in Mommy's lap in the old creaky caned rocker. She sat there every evening after the dishes were washed and left on the drain board to dry. She called it her special time. The crickets and frogs kept time with the rocker, and when Mommy began humming her songs, it must have been a signal for the stars that it was time to appear, twinkling and darting through the sky. That evening, Mommy held him long into the night. She hummed and rocked, soothing away his little sobs. As he drifted off to sleep that night, Andy's tears were replaced with an assurance that it would all be OK...he would make it so. If he couldn't be mommy's color, he would fix it so it didn't matter. Somehow he would fix it.

In school it was hard to make friends with the Negro kids because they resented his light skin. He stayed pretty much to himself until the third grade, when Todd entered school. Todd was outgoing and made friends easily. Even though he, too, was somewhat sensitive about Andy's light skin, Todd would include Andy in games at recess to help him get to know the other kids. By the end of elementary school, Andy was accepted as one of the gang. But then came junior high and integration. What hell that was for Andy.

Choosing his words carefully, Andy told his beautiful friends about his high-school days. How he worked in the oil refineries in Pascagoula, made good grades, and went to Biloxi to join the army as soon as he graduated. What he didn't tell them was how he learned to fight dirty in high school. In the army, he learned to use his lighter skin to his advantage. He did not tell them of the countless number of white girls he took to bed or the college courses and promotions available to him when he no longer denied that he was white. He returned from the army a changed man. A white man.

By then, Willie had died, and Sadie moved to Austin to be close to her brother, Josiah. As a teenager, Andy had spent a couple of summers in Austin with his uncle working in the oil field. He was glad to join his mother there when he returned from the army. Andy went back to work in the oil fields and, determined to make something of himself, enrolled in night classes at a white college. Good grades would be useful. But not as useful, as it turned out, as a colored girl named Pearl Banes.

The daughter of a Baptist preacher, Pearl had grown up fast when her daddy was accused of preaching to his congregation about equal rights for colored citizens. The white segregationists wanted to put a stop to it once and for all. Reverend Elijah Banes was beaten to death in the Negro cemetery next to his church in Dallas when Pearl was eleven. Mrs. Banes took Pearl and her brothers, Nathaniel and Sam, and fled to Austin, leaving behind everything they owned.

Pearl and her brothers had to drop out of school and worked odd jobs to help their mother. Eventually, Pearl's mother got a full-time job as housekeeper for Dr. William Drake, the dean at the University of Texas. With Dean Drake's help, Pearl was able to graduate from college with a bachelor of arts degree in prelaw.

Dean Drake was one of the few whites who would help a Negro student at that time. But, he saw in Pearl a mind so sharp, he equated her to an uncut diamond just waiting to be honed into perfection. He liked Pearl's family and enjoyed their company. The university provided him with a huge two-story house. He let Pearl and her family have the upper floor. He had not used it in the five years since his wife had passed away.

Many nights the dean would come home late and find Lettie, Pearl's mother, in the kitchen, working over the ironing board. She called it "doin' up" his shirts. They were done to perfection. Pearl would be sitting at the table studying. She would get so excited about her lesson that she would read half aloud and half to herself. Both were unaware of the late hour.

"Evenin', Dean Drake," Lettie would say. "I have your supper still warm. Made you a cherry pie today, too. I declare though," she would say, laughing and shaking her head, "I'm liable to get me an education just standing here ironin' and listenin' to that girl!" He would always ask Pearl about her studies and help her no matter how late the hour or how tired he was.

It was at her college graduation party that Pearl met Andy Lewis. She was twenty-six. He was twenty-one. Andy had been invited to the party by a girl he had met in a local jazz club in the colored section of town. There were still some things Andy couldn't deny, and the blues was one of them. Andy was drawn to Pearl immediately. She was different from the other Negro girls. He was really impressed by her education. They started dating, and Pearl helped Andy with his business classes.

Dean Drake was on guard the moment Pearl brought Andy home. He was too smooth for Pearl...too handsome. Pearl wasn't noted for her beauty. She wasn't ugly, just plain. But her genuine honesty and ability to talk and make people listen and agree with her made up a hundred times over for what she lacked in looks. She would be a successful lawyer if—because of her color—she ever got the chance.

He knew Dean Drake had no respect for him, but Andy went to every lecture of the dean's he could. Dean Drake was brilliant when it came to public speaking. Andy copied his style. It was a style of presentation, content, and call for action. Every politician's game for getting votes.

Lettie was taken by Andy's charm, too. He would waltz into the hot kitchen on a summer afternoon with a bouquet of daisies, ill-gotten from a neighboring garden, hidden behind his back. "My, my, Lettie Banes, you sure do make a heavenly aroma throughout this ol' house with them pies of yours," he would say, producing the flowers from behind his back.

Lettie's face would light up. "Andy Lewis, you're a rascal, and I know it!" She would put her prize in the big, green vase on the windowsill over the sink. Then Lettie would sit him down at the big, white table with a piece of warm pie while he waited for Pearl. Andy had a knack for working his way into people's lives and then just taking over.

When Andy made love to Pearl in the back of his pickup, he could not believe it was her first time. Pearl had been determined to wait until she was married so she would not fall into the trap some of her friends had, but she was so in love with Andy. Just the thought of him made her hot. She adored him.

Andy had returned to the oil fields, intending to stay just long enough to save some money and relocate to an area where racial prejudices were at a minimum. He had gotten too used to being white to go back to the race game. He had games of his own he wanted to play. He identified with white people more than he did with the people who were his family. As long as Mommy was there, he would always be a part. After that, he would be gone forever from the colored side of town.

One night after they'd made love, Andy and Pearl lay on a sleeping bag in the back of his truck. He told her about a contract a guy he knew had on a piece of property. He wanted Pearl to look at the contract for him to see if there was anything wrong with it.

"This guy has four pumps working on the property," he explained to her, "but he hasn't found any oil. He is out of money and has to sell his contract on the property to recoup some of what he has lost." He didn't tell Pearl he had gotten the guy drunk and won it from him in a poker game. Andy knew the property and made sure he had a winning hand that night. He needed to make sure the contract was good and also scrape up the payment that was coming due.

"Baby, I know there's oil on that land," Andy had told her excitedly. "If I can raise the five hundred dollars, I want to buy him out. Would you just look over the contract and make sure I'm OK to give him the money?"

The contract turned out to be an option on two thousand acres forty miles south of Fort Worth. Pearl checked it over and loaned Andy $500 she had been saving for law school, with one stipulation. She wanted her name on the option contract right along with Andy's.

Forty-eight hours after he transferred the option to their names and made the payment, Andy Lewis and his partner Pearl Banes hit one of the largest oil strikes since Spindletop. He was a twenty-one-year-old black millionaire. The first thing he did was ask Pearl to marry him.

Kathryne and Lily went inside to fix dessert, and Andy walked over to the pool. Retrieving an overzealous grasshopper from the pool, Andy caught sight of himself in the water's mirror. Lingering there, he studied the face of the man looking back at him. The years were still replaying in his mind's eye. They began to roll together like a kaleidoscope. Thoughts he did not want tumbled over and over, but he had pushed them away for too long. He seemed naked and alone, with no protection from his memories.

He wondered what was taking them so long in the kitchen as the picture of the dead poker player hit his mind. Then sweet Mary Ann Montgomery showed up to haunt him. He could see her long, blonde hair and blue eyes. She stood beside her brand new '57 Chevy, which he drove more often than she, taking out other girls. Her breakdown when he told her he was a Negro had infuriated him. What did she think he was, a leper?

Then, Beth Walters. Red hair, big boobs, big bank account. He needed no collateral for loans at her father's local savings and loan. The secretaries, models, daughters of business associates— all of them white.

Andy wondered if he had been as ruthless as it now seemed. When along the way had he started to love Pearl, and how on earth could she still love him? Who was this man in his reflection?

The sound of clinking dishes made him realize, thankfully, that he was daydreaming. "What do you call a nightmare in the daytime? A daymare?" he was asking himself as he literally ran from the patio.

"Mm, Lily, this cherry cobbler is luscious!" Kathryne rolled her eyes as her taste buds reacted to a sampling of the warm dessert.

"KT, I need to go home." Lily said abruptly as she dished up the cobbler. She sounded as if she were arguing with herself. "It is time now. I can be proud. I've succeeded. I want you to come with me." She was spitting out the words so fast, Kathryne couldn't get a word in. The faster Lily talked, the more ice cream she heaped on each bowl of cobbler.

"Well, do you want to go tonight?" Kathryne teased her, just as Andy popped in the kitchen door as if something was after him. Lily laughed and asked him if he was afraid they were about to eat all the dessert. They finished the evening with generous helpings of warm, crusty cherry cobbler and French vanilla ice cream.

chapter

ELEVEN

Kathryne had never seen Lily so strung out. They were on their way to New York to make a presentation to a new Japanese company. Andy had set it up for them, and Lily wanted to make absolutely sure everything went perfectly. The account would be a dream come true for them. They would be able to set up a branch office in New York.

Lily looked gorgeous. Her silky hair hung loosely around the shoulders like black trim on her red dress. She was arranging her luggage with the skycap, but it looked more like she was trying to do his work for him. She was like that when she was nervous, and she was certainly nervous today.

Leaving the poor guy ready to quit his job, they hurriedly set out for the gate, almost missing their flight. Once on board, Lily asked the stewardess for some red wine, which seemed to calm her a bit.

"KT," she said, "I hope you don't think I'm rude, but I knew I would be extremely anxious during this flight, so I brought work to do. You know, some reports and all. Do you mind?"

Kathryne laughed softly. "No, darlin'. Do whatever you have to do. To tell you the truth, so much has happened these last couple of weeks, I would just like to close my eyes, relax, and try to mentally file everything away."

As the plane became airborne, Lily reached for her brief-case. Kathryne closed her eyes with a deep sigh and began to think about the fast track they were on these days. The trip made her recall her plane trips to see Andy when she did the cut-rate gas stations for him.

After weeks of planning, telephone conferences, and taping, Andy and Kathryne had met in New York to review the first of the tapes for his campaign. After spending a long day reviewing and editing, Kathryne went back to her hotel to dress for dinner. She had intended to dress down, try to keep it business, but could not resist the emerald-green crepe she had brought with her. Her long, red hair and svelte figure even drew attention from little old ladies when she wore it.

The candle on the table seemed to flicker to the beat of Kathryne's heart as she and Andy toasted the campaign and the new phase of their friendship. Their next toast was for what Andy called "a new life."

Kathryne and Andy were having dinner at Luigi's in New York. The green dress she wore wrapped in the front. Two deli-cate rhinestone buttons secured the bodice tightly under her breasts. Her curls fell freely to her shoulders, almost obscuring the emerald-studded necklace and earrings. When the light from the candle caught her earrings, sparks shot across her face and bare chest. She felt good. Damn good. She had waited for this moment for a long, long time. Andy smiled across the table at her and said, "Let's go dancing. I want to hold you in my arms."

The electricity between them could have lit New York City for a year. The way he held her on the dance floor made her breath-less, and when their eyes met, Kathryne felt drunk. They danced until two o'clock. Then, as if drawn by a silent force, they walked hand in hand to the limousine. They rode to Andy's apartment in silence, searching deep into each other's eyes. Andy unlocked the door, and they stepped into his elaborate twenty-fifth-story pent-house apartment.

"Kathryne." He took her hand and stepped close to her. She could feel his breath on her face. "Kathryne?" Andy's voice was husky as his eyes searched hers for his answer.

"Yes." She breathed into his parted lips. "Yes." The lips she had dreamed of, longed for, were finally hers. Lust raced through her as their bodies locked passionately.

Things fell, clothes melted away, and they became adrift on a bed-like cloud. Kathryne heard herself scream, she heard Andy groan, and her whole world turned into the Fourth of July as he reached deep within her, again and again.

"Kathryne! Wake up!"

She awoke with a jerk, looking into the concerned faces of Lily and the first class flight attendant. Other passengers were trying to see what was causing the commotion.

"KT! My God, you were dreaming! You scared the pee wadden out of me, screaming like that. Are you OK?"

Kathryne looked sadly at the two of them. It was a dream. But it was so real. Where had it come from? What kind of a trick was her subconscious playing on her? "I….uh, sorry. I guess so. Whew, there was this bear…" she stammered. She was throbbing all over. She had to get up.

"You would not believe how often this happens," the flight attendant said. "Can I bring you something?"

"Vodka, please. Straight."

"KT, are you OK?" Lily repeated. "You are so flushed."

"I think I will go to the ladies' room," Kathryne replied as she scrambled out of her seat.

Locked into the small compartment, Kathryne had difficulty pulling herself together and shuddered as her body finished what the dream had started.

She splashed cool water on her face and refreshed her makeup. Andy was her friend, nothing else…wasn't he? she asked herself. She studied herself in the small mirror and snapped her compact closed. She took a long, deep breath. Damn! It had been so real...so wonderful. She knew it was a cheap trick of her subconscious. Did she need a man's attention that badly?

Andy was waiting at LaGuardia and whisked them off for lunch at the Russian Tea Room. Kathryne had great difficulty looking him in the eye. She was afraid something would show. Would it ever be the same?

The presentation with the president of Yamamoto, Inc. went very well and he said he would have his attorney review their contract for acceptance. Mr. Yamamoto told them, as a change from the custom in his country, he was looking forward to doing business with two lovely women.

Lily asked Kathryne on the way home if she was mad at Andy about something. Kathryne denied anything was wrong, and they discussed Andy, his gubernatorial campaign, and Pearl.

Kathryne promised herself she would do something about her sexless life. After all, that was the only reason she had that dream, right?

She arrived at Jeff Baker's plush office punctually. "Hi, Jennifer."

"Mrs. Langford. How nice to see you again. Mr. Baker is expecting you. Go right on in."

"Thanks, Jennifer. Oh, by the way, my presentation is very intense. Would you hold his calls until we are through?"

"You betcha." Jennifer winked.

"Jeff?" she called softly, opening the door.

His mouth gaped when he saw her. Kathryne stood just inside his office next to the closed door she'd locked as she entered. She wore a calf-length, black cashmere coat with five-inch black heels. Her long, red hair fell loosely across her face. The cashmere was held together by one of her black-gloved hands.

"Damn, Kathryne! Whatever it is you are selling...show me where to sign." He walked toward her. "Let me take your coat," he said with outstretched arms.

"Thank you," she said, dropping her hands and letting the coat fall open. He froze, savoring the moment. She wore nothing but the coat. Their eyes met. He started a slow grin, his eyes excited and dancing. "Well Kathryne, are you—" he began.

"Am I going to have to draw you a—"

"Let's go," he said suddenly. She clutched her coat as he took her arm. "See you tomorrow, Jen," he mumbled as he rushed her from his office. In the elevator, he kissed her softly and held her gently against him. He tucked her into a silver Rolls-Royce and drove a few blocks north to an apartment he kept for out-of-town clients. It was a beautiful apartment, designed for a good time, with a whirlpool bathtub, mirrors, and a well-stocked liquor cabinet.

As soon as the door closed behind them, Jeff slowly slid the coat from her shoulders. She was nervous, trying to relax, and realized she was holding her breath.

"Baby, I've wanted this for so long." He breathed passionately. She closed her eyes as they eased onto the bed. The feel of a man's body pressed against her was like therapy. She relaxed and let dormant feelings spring to life.

Two months ago, when she'd experienced the dream about Andy, Kathryne decided she was spending too much time at the office. Even though she loved her work, she longed for someone to hold her, to make love to her. She could not run the risk of vulnerability. It might show in conversation or jeopardize a business relationship. Most important, she finally admitted to herself that she had to fight her attraction for Andy.

Jeff Baker's Rolls-Royce dealership had been an account of hers for years. He was a nice guy, and he had always been attracted to her. There was a warmth about Jeff that always made her think he would be a good lover. Of course, he was pretty good at crowing about himself, too.

She had suppressed her desires for so long, but letting go was surprisingly easy. Jeff slowly removed her hose and garter and wore the garter on his arm the rest of the afternoon. She fought thoughts of her dream about Andy and eventually, as she had hoped, desire took over. Jeff made good on all of his promises to her over the last couple of years. He promised to satisfy, and satisfy he did. He had been crazy for Kathryne since the first day he saw those long legs stride into his office.

As they relaxed in the whirlpool bath, Jeff played with the curls that hung in her face. "Can you get away for a weekend?" he asked.

"Mm," she said dreamily. "Not this weekend."

"Let's go to the mountains. Leave Thursday afternoon, come back Sunday. Baby, you've only whet my appetite."

"I'll see what I can do." She sighed, leaning back against him. She ran her finger through the hair on his chest and giggled at his physical reaction to her attention. She felt better. She was glad she had made this decision.

∾ψ∾

It was late afternoon when she returned to the office. Kathryne wanted to see what she had missed during her afternoon of much needed R and R. She chuckled under her breath. A note taped on her phone from Lily read, "KT, take this thing and give me a ring." Kathryne smiled. Lily was working on a new jingle, so everything she said or thought had to rhyme. There was a knock and the door opened.

"Yo, partner of mine. Oh, you look so fine!" Lily sang happily.

"Oh, brother." Kathryne laughed.

"I thought I heard you come in. What are you doing? Gonna stay? Got time to talk?" Lily asked, cutting through the small talk, straight to the point, as she was so prone to do.

"I just wanted to see what happened this afternoon and get home before Becky goes to bed. What's up?"

"Oh, I just wanted to see if you would drive up to Kentucky with me for a couple of days."

Kathryne looked at Lily thoughtfully. She had known this was coming. Lily had been talking about going home a lot lately, and they both knew she could not do it alone. After all, this was the family who belittled, scorned, and ridiculed her every goal and achievement. She would have to take one of her two best friends with her, and it sure as hell couldn't be Andy Lewis. Or, for that matter, Bill Dressler.

"It's a great idea," she replied. "I tell you what. Come on out to the house and have dinner. We can talk about it."

"But, Joe might not—"

"Oh, don't worry about him. He goes to bed about nine, when Becky does, and besides, Rose made cheesecake today." She knew how much Lily loved Rose's cooking, especially her cheesecake.

"Below the belt, KT." Lily smirked. "Below the belt. Let me know when you're ready, and I'll follow you out."

After dinner Becky wanted Lily to see her room, which had just been redecorated like *Sesame Street*. They tucked her in and then sat by the pool and made plans to drive to Kentucky in three weeks. It would be the first of October, a beautiful time of the year to make the trip.

They left Atlanta just as the sun peeped over I-75. The eight-hour drive zipped by as they caught up on girl talk and sang a jingle Lily was working on for Delta Airlines. No songfest was complete without the jingle Lily had written for Andy's convenience stores, sung like a chant:

"Gas 'er up, wipe 'er down,
Get the best price in town,
Stop at....ANDOCO!"

The closer they drew to Owensboro, the faster Lily drove, and the more Kathryne complained of leg cramps from having them folded into the little sports car.

"Lily, if you don't slow this thing down, we are going to be hearing a radio report about a red comet hurtling up the interstate. Just think, they can call it Lily's comet instead of Haley's."

Finally getting to Owensboro, they went straight to the Executive Inn, a new seven-story hotel on the Ohio River. Kathryne was very impressed to find such a modern complex in the small town. She was ready to poke around in some of the little shops that encircled the lobby and have a relaxing drink in the bar before meeting the family.

"Oh, KT, let's do that later. I'm really anxious to see them," Lily pleaded.

She was surprised to see Lily that excited. "Let's get there." She laughed, taking Lily's arm.

They pulled into the circular driveway of Valerie's house in late afternoon. It was a gigantic, colonial-style house with white columns and a porch edged with golden mums.

"Holy shit!" Kathryne whistled as she stepped out of the car. "You didn't tell me they lived at Tara!"

"I know. It's huge. Valerie would never have been satisfied if she had been unable to live on Griffith Avenue. It's the super snooty section of town. I've never been here before, but Mother actually sent me fifty-two pictures of the house, inside and out, when they all moved in. I feel like I know it intimately," she said with a roll of her eyes.

They stood in front of the front doors, Lily smoothing her blouse nervously, forgetting that they should knock or something.

"Will they sense we are here, or do we have to ring the bell?"

"Oh…right. Right," Lily stammered as she pushed the doorbell. Almost immediately, the door was thrown open with a grand gesture, which was abruptly halted when Lily and her mother's eyes met for the first time in nine years.

"Lily? What on earth…are you all right?" her mother said. After a few awkward moments, her mother seemed to recover from the shock of Lily's surprise visit.

"Come in, come." Her mother coaxed them in, shutting the door behind them. "Valerie isn't here right now. She is still at her office. I know she will just be thrilled when she finds out you have come back."

"Back?" Kathryne mouthed to Lily behind her mother.

"Oh, let me take you in to see Valerie's children." On the way to the TV room, proper introductions of Kathryne and Lily's mother were made. Lily noticed that her mother had put on some weight. Her hair was still blonde, Clairol blonde, and she was wearing those funny little half glasses that she absentmindedly alternated between hanging from her neck on a chain and putting on the very end of her nose. Maggie Lou pushed them right in the door to the den where Valerie's two children, Peggy, ten, and Travis, eight, were watching *The Brady Bunch*. The room was as big as one whole floor of Lily's town house and was completely without warmth or character. It was Valerie.

Peggy paid no attention to the threesome, but Travis was immediately interested in his aunt Lily. It was instant adoration.

He bounced off the couch and walked to her. He wanted to hug her but instead stuck out his hand. He stood and stared after her when they left the room.

Maggie Lou led them into the large, white, sterile-feeling kitchen, where she busied herself making coffee in an elaborate automatic machine.

Speaking for the first time to Kathryne, she said, "Would you like sugar in your coffee, dear?" Scooting the sugar bowl to Kathryne, she excused herself and went to the phone in the study to call her older daughter. Valerie, somewhat less than jubilant to hear the news, told her mother she would be late but to hold dinner for her. Maggie Lou returned to the kitchen and began fussing over dinner in a never-ceasing chatter.

Kathryne marveled. No hug, no "tell me all about what you've been up to…to what do we owe this wonderful visit." Nothing.

"It's a Corvette, isn't it?" Lily was surprised to see Travis standing right beside her.

"Yes," she replied softly, "it is." Somehow this little boy was tugging at her heart.

"Oh no, Travis, you go on back in and watch TV. Aunt Lily doesn't feel like talking to you right now." Maggie Lou said scooting him out through the white swinging doors.

"But, Mother, I would like to talk to Travis."

"Don't be silly. What on earth would you have to talk to him about? You have no children, nothing in common with him. Kathryne"—she turned her attention to Kathryne—"Has Lily told you how proud we are of her sister, Valerie?"

"No, no…" It was all she could manage while choking coffee out all over the pristine white counter top in answer to her question.

Lily was cleaning up the coffee, telling Kathryne under her breath to behave herself.

Maggie Lou rattled on. "Yes, we sure are. She is chairing the women's club this year, she's a past president of the Junior League, and she was just installed as the first and *only* woman officer of the local attorneys' association." She actually held up her fingers imitating quotation marks when she said *only*.

Behind Maggie Lou's back, Kathryne pretended to throw up while Maggie Lou continued to brag about the fine crystal and linens that filled the cabinets and drawers throughout the house.

Kathryne and Lily were glad when Valerie's husband, Mark, came in the back door, giving them much needed relief from Maggie Lou's ongoing tribute to Valerie.

"Hey, Trav, that your 'Vet out front?" Mark teased to Travis who ran to greet his father. Lily had always felt that Mark and Valerie were mismatched. Also apparent was the closeness he shared with his son.

"Dad," Travis said softly. "It's Aunt Lily's. That's her, isn't she beautiful?"

Kathryne and Lily enjoyed their talk with Mark while Maggie Lou labored over dinner. Travis stood next to his dad and never took his eyes off Lily. The arrival of Valerie put an immediate damper on the pleasant atmosphere. She barely acknowledged the fact that her sister, whom she had not seen for several years, was there. Her main interest was in what they were having for dinner and if Maggie Lou was preparing it to suit her. Valerie, like Maggie Lou, had put on several pounds. Somehow, she seemed shorter, but her blue eyes and enhanced-blonde hair were still pretty.

Maggie Lou sat them down in the formal dining room to a dinner of fried pork chops, green beans, mashed potatoes, gravy, rolls, and pecan pie. Mark's whole demeanor had changed since his wife, the major wage earner, arrived on the scene, but apparently trying to lighten the mood, he made the mistake of asking why Valerie had kept her beautiful, younger sister such a secret. Valerie shot him a look-to-kill, and he shriveled. Lily could not help losing respect for Mark. After all, there is such a thing as divorce.

"Mommy, I thought your sister's name was Pocahontas," Peggy blurted out and, glancing under the dinner table, added, "and I thought you said she wore moccasins."

Peggy's comments seemed to set the stage. Valerie and her mother had a good laugh. It became dig Lily night. Valerie, Maggie Lou, and Peggy made one "injun" pun after another. Mark kept his eyes fixed on his green beans, as if they would form a line and march right off the plate if they were not carefully watched. He did not want to risk being reprimanded again in front of company.

"Well, what kind of little ads do you sell, Lily?" Valerie chuckled as she asked.

Kathryne could hold it in no longer. She threw her fork onto her plate, hoping to break the damn thing. Lily began to tremble. She knew nothing short of a lightning strike would stop Kathryne.

"Hey, folks. You seem to be on the wrong track here." She looked directly at Valerie with the fiery eyes of a she-devil. "Lily doesn't sell 'little ads.' She *owns* the largest advertising agency in Atlanta. She creates ads, she writes songs for advertising campaigns. Her clients are worth millions of dollars!" She was beginning to hiss. "Have you heard this year's Ford Motors jingle? You know, the one that is being played on every radio and television station in the country?" She sang it as if she were an opera star on stage, holding the last note eight counts, while her eyes dared anyone to move. They sat like statues, eyes glued to Kathryne.

"Lily wrote it. Ford Motor Company is her client. She worked out the advertising strategy and wrote the slogan in an hour—in one hour!" Kathryne couldn't keep her voice from rising. "She made more money on that one 'little ad' than you made in the last five years, Lady Lawyer with mashed potatoes on your chin!"

Valerie was mortified, and Mark smiled slyly behind his "fine" linen napkin.

"KT, don't!"

"Lily, I can't help it!"

"Well, I never!" Lily's mother spluttered indignantly.

"Dad, why don't Mom and Aunt Lily look alike? Her hair is so black and Mom's is…" Travis whispered innocently.

Silence hit the room like a too-tight turtleneck sweater—hot and choking. Unfortunately for Peggy, it was she who interrupted the mute gathering by awkwardly reaching for her milk as she stared first at her mother, then at her newly acquainted aunt. Her hand knocked over the glass, spilling its contents right into the middle of the linen-clad table. Valerie, at the brink of ignition, struck Peggy across the face with the back of her hand. Maggie Lou and Mark voiced loud protests. Peggy, seeing an opportunity to vent her own frustrations, screamed and cried like a catamount.

"Oh, Lily," Maggie Lou implored. "What do you want here, anyway?"

"I am still your child, too. I just wanted to see you, I guess." In tears, Lily ran for the bathroom.

"Holy Christ!" Kathryne exploded. Standing to leave the room, she hurled one last morsel to the still seated coterie. "Watch the news, guys. Lily will be married to Congressman Dressler in the fall."

"Sure, sure." Valerie smirked, wiping Peggy's face hard enough to strip the skin.

"If you had not been so busy making fun of her, maybe you would have noticed the two-carat diamond on her finger. I guess you thought it came out of a Cracker Jack box. That's about your level of taste."

"I noticed the ring."

"Mark!" Valerie barked. He obeyed by looking back at his beans.

Kathryne met up with Lily coming out of the bathroom. "Let's get the hell out of here before they form a lynch party," Kathryne whispered hoarsely on the way out the front door. The crowd had followed.

Lily stood on the front-porch steps outside the huge double doors to her sister's house, inside the invisible shell she could pull out when needed for total control. Her cold, black eyes imprisoned each of them like steel beams. The beams seemed to crush Valerie as Lily's disgust raked over her.

"Keep climbing that social ladder of yours, Valerie. That's right where you belong."

"Mother, Maggie Lou"—the steel from the beams had penetrated her voice giving it a flat, hard tone—"I'm not sure about all of this, but I'm going to someone who will give me the truth. I'll never come here again. There is no reason to ever see you again or know anything about you. To me, you will no longer exist."

"Mark."

"Lily I...," he stammered, avoiding Valerie's eyes, trying to bring some kind of feeling to the grisly scene on the porch.

"Mark," she said, "you poor thing. You have my sympathy." She turned, gracefully descended the porch stairs to where Kathryne waited, joined hands with her, and walked calmly to the car.

She came around to the driver's side of her car and was surprised to see a solemn Travis standing by the door. He was a good-looking boy about five feet tall. The blue-plaid shirt he wore brought out the blue in his eyes. His sandy-brown hair had started to curl around his temples in the damp night air. Without a word, he turned and opened the car door for her. She squeezed his arm and smiled down at him, hoping to convey her affection. She prayed he knew none of this mess involved him.

When she was seated, he leaned in and kissed her on the cheek. For some reason, this little boy loved the woman he had met today for the first time. Tears glistened in his eyes as he watched her drive away. He promised himself he would find her again as soon as he could.

Kathryne was astounded. No one had said a word to Lily when she walked off that porch. They didn't call her back to apologize, ask if she was OK, try to explain. Nothing.

Lily gripped the steering wheel so tightly, the knuckles on her hands turned white. She bit her lip and fixed a dead stare into the street, her eyes burning with the tears she was determined not to shed. She was trying to see the road, but she could only see replays of the scene at the house and ask herself the burning question, "Why am I treated so differently?" She did not realize she was swerving all over the road until she heard a horn blasting in her ear.

"Pull over, Lily. Right over here by the curb."

Kathryne wrestled Lily into the passenger's seat and took off down Frederica Street. They drove in silence to the Executive Inn. Lily was still quite upset, and Kathryne hoped she would feel better if she could get her to eat. Thinking back, it had been morning since either had eaten. They ordered a club sandwich in the Patio Room of the luxurious hotel lobby.

The big, open dining area had cathedral ceilings, skylights, and potted palms. The palms had small twinkle lights strung through them, which made them look festive. Lily was trying to act as if nothing had happened, and Kathryne went along with it.

Lily wanted Kathryne to meet her long-time friend, Ginny Knight. They had gotten their first jobs together at an insurance agency. They had stayed in touch through the years. Ginny was able to meet them after dinner. Kathryne liked her immediately. Lily and Ginny filled Kathryne in on things that happened while they worked together.

"Ginny, remember when we reorganized the office and moved all the tax records and company accounts to the back room and told Mr. Peacock someone had stolen them?

"How could I forget?" Ginny snorted with laughter. "We almost got fired over it!"

"Oh, girl, it was hilarious. Before we could get control of the situation, he had the building superintendent—whom we called Clark Kent—and his helper lined up out in the hall, interrogating them Gestapo style. He was marching up and down the hall like Hitler!"

"Before we knew it, the city detectives were there."

"You're kidding!" Kathryne's ribs were splitting.

"We never did know when Mr. Peacock called them. Anyway"—Ginny snickered, finishing the story—"when we told him we were just kidding and that we had rearranged them to a different area, he stood perfectly still for a couple of minutes and then went in his office and slammed the door. He didn't speak to us for two days. Not one word! On the third day, he told us never to pull a stunt like that again. We didn't, not like that, but plenty of other stuff he never knew about."

"Wonder why he never fired us, Ginny."

"Who would run the office?" They were bordering on hysteria.

Strains of music from the lounge drifted through the dining room, and Ginny suggested that an Absolut on the rocks would be delicious. Kathryne agreed, wanting to continue keeping Lily's mind off her nightmare of a family. Dancing would help, too. For some reason, Lily could always dance. No matter what was bothering her, how tired she was or how sick, dancing would always make her feel better. It made Kathryne wonder if it had something to do with her Indian blood. They entered the dark, smoke-filled room and found a small table toward the back. A friendly waitress in a blouse so tight her buttons threatened manslaughter took their drink orders.

"An Absolut on the rocks, bourbon and Coke, and a screwdriver. Back in a jiffy," she assured them and bounced off. An off-key country band was playing an almost unrecognizable version of "Night Fever." They discussed what the Bee Gees might say if they heard it.

The lounge was full of young, energetic men ready to jump the attractive trio. While Lily danced, Ginny filled Kathryne in on some stories about Maggie Lou's treatment of her when she was younger. Ginny assured Kathryne that Lily had a lot of friends. Everyone knew she wasn't like Maggie Lou and Valerie—bullies who tried to use everyone to their own advantage.

The girls closed the bar. Lily and Ginny parted with hugs and promises to get together again soon. The next day, Lily drove Kathryne around town. The early fall air was crisp and refreshing. They rode around with the top down, letting the wind blow through their hair as if to erase thoughts of the previous evening. Lily spoke not one word about the fiasco. She showed Kathryne the high school where she and Tommy graduated and the building that housed the insurance agency where she and Ginny tormented poor old Mr. Peacock. She drove past the houses on Monarch Avenue where she and Tommy had grown up. Then they took flowers to her daddy's grave.

Later, Lily drove out of town toward the rural community of West Louisville, where Sonny had lived with Gray Dove before his marriage to Maggie Lou. And where Lily had spent so much time as a child and teenager. As Lily turned her car onto Crooked Creek Road, Kathryne, barely able to hear her friend sniffing, could see tears welling in her eyes. Lily's heart was breaking, but she continued to fight it.

The little house was dark. Weeds had overtaken the old gravel driveway. Lily slowly got out of the car and walked up the small incline to the house. She stood for a moment and just stared at the weather-beaten small wooden structure. She could still see her daddy and Gray Dove sitting on that porch, he in the wooden rocker and her on the swing, laughing and talking. Absentmindedly, she plucked a goldenrod and started up the four wood steps to the porch. The second step broke when she put her weight on it. The swing too, she felt sure, was unable to bear weight. She tried the door, and it opened reluctantly. There, in the middle of Gray Dove's front room, Lily stood, alone. She felt hollow. Her heart felt like one of the hollow gourds her grandmother used to decorate the front porch.

She sat on the hearth in front of the stone fireplace, resting her head on her knees, and began to cry. A more mournful cry Kathryne had never heard. It drifted out into the late-afternoon air sounding like a hurt animal, fragile from its wound. When something really got to Lily, she would go off by herself to deal with it. It was an Indian custom to seek out the spirits and let them help you with your grief.

Kathryne stayed outside, sitting on a big rock next to the driveway. The sun had started to set, and the colors were magnificent. Big, billowy clouds had begun to move in, casting a blue-black shadow across the sky as the rays of orange and yellow light shone through. The wind rustled some golden-yellow and brown leaves from the treetops and sent them floating to the ground in splendid gusts. Kathryne sat on the rock, surrounded by the leaves, as long as she could. Just before dusk, she knew it was time to go to her best friend. She quietly entered the house and walked slowly to the hearth. She sat down beside Lily and put her arms around her. Sitting there beside her like that, Kathryne could feel the comfort of the spirits surrounding them. She thought of the tales Lily had told her about Gray Dove and this house and could see why Lily had loved it here so much. Even now, the empty house was still alive with love's spirit.

"Let's stop and see Gray Dove on the way home, huh?" Kathryne knew Lily needed more answers.

Realizing suddenly that darkness as well as hunger had settled on them, they drove back to town. Lily stopped at Moonlite Bar-B-Que on the way, and Kathryne had her first taste of mutton and burgoo, a barbecue-type soup. To her surprise, she liked it. They ate until they were stuffed. Feeling guilty about their calorie intake, they decided to swim a few laps in the Olympic-size indoor pool at the hotel.

It was eleven that evening when they returned to their room. Lily was exhausted. All her tension had been worked out, and she was relaxed and ready to get a good night's sleep. Kathryne, on the other hand, was restless and could not sleep. She tried to watch TV in the sitting room of the small suite, but the *Tonight Show* and Johnny's "Carnac" routine could not hold her attention. She stepped out on the balcony for a breath of cool air. The night sky was beautiful. The stars were on full wattage. She watched a lonely barge push its load up the Ohio, the rustling ripple of the waves barely audible. She became acutely aware of how lonely and homesick Lily must have felt over the years, and how she felt tonight.

Kathryne found herself overcome with loneliness as she stood there in her white gown, gazing out over the river. She would be glad when morning came so she could call her mother. Her mother's love had always given her such strength. How horrible it must feel when your mother's love did not include you. She could not understand it.

The house America Gray Dove occupied in Cherokee, North Carolina, was quite similar to the little house in Kentucky. It was a small, four-room, white, clapboard house built on a slight hill. From the driveway a brick walk curved up to the porch, which ran the entire length of the front of the house. It was a natural weathered-wood color and, of course, it had a swing. The yard was well kept, with herbs in a garden beside the house and a weeping willow tree on the bank of a little creek in the back. The entire scene suggested a Norman Rockwell painting, which became complete at the appearance of two frisky, brown pups from under the willow tree.

Lily was so excited she hardly had the motor turned off before she was out of the car and up the walk. "Come on, KT!" she called in a schoolgirl manner as she ran up the two wooden front steps.

The sun made the late-morning air warm. The front door of the house was open. Kathryne could see a figure moving toward the screen door, and a feeling of excitement mounted. What would she look like? Would she have feathers sticking out of her hair? Would she smoke a pipe and have animal pelts for clothing? Her imagination was running wild. Gray Dove would never allow herself to be photographed, so Kathryne only had a mental picture of her appearance.

Then, there she was, holding the screen door open. No feathers, pipes, or pelts. She was beautiful. The old woman still had perfect posture. She stood straight and tall. Her gray hair was pulled back into a tight braid that hung well below her waist. She wore an ankle-length, brown, tunic-like dress, sashed in the middle by a white apron. She wore long, silver earrings, many strands of colorful beads, and a copper bracelet. On her feet were brown moccasins. Her dark complexion was still quite good and had fewer wrinkles than Kathryne expected.

"Oh, Momma," Lily cried as she ran to her grandmother. Lily called Gray Dove Momma when she addressed her. She had always called Maggie Lou, Mother. She said it sounded more rigid and seemed to fit better.

"My precious Lily. Come to my arms." Gray Dove spread her arms as if opening her heart.

Kathryne stopped at the bottom of the steps, not wanting to intrude. She watched the playful puppies, trying to avoid tears.

"There is something troubling you, my child," Gray Dove observed, lifting Lily's chin in her brown, weathered hand.

"Yes, Momma, there is. We have just come from Valerie's." Kathryne caught the sad, wistful look in Gray Dove's eyes, as if something she had dreaded was now upon her.

"First, we must invite your lovely friend into our home. You must be Kathryne. Or KT, I guess it is, huh?" she said, taking Lily's hand in hers and moving toward Kathryne. "Please. Won't you come in?" Kathryne could immediately see the special quality in Gray Dove that Lily had been talking about all this time. She was wonderful.

The house was a giant curio cabinet. Never before had Kathryne seen so many things. Wooden carvings, pictures of Lily throughout her life, figurines, carved-driftwood pieces, and colorful afghans. There was a table set up in the corner where Gray Dove still made jewelry. She sold it to the gift shops in Gatlinburg. The pieces she made were unique, and they sold quickly. On the table by the front window was the phone. Alienated from everything else, the phone sat alone, as if to say, "I don't fit in, but I am being tolerated because Lily insists." Kathryne chuckled to herself, remembering the ordeal Lily had getting her grandmother to accept it in her house.

Gray Dove babied and pampered both women as if they were small girls, and both became comfortable with it very quickly. She served them herb tea and roast beef sandwiches accompanied by homemade pickles and ketchup. Her dessert specialty was lemon sugar cookies.

She sat on the swing stringing beads as she mesmerized the women with the story of Maggie Lou and Sonny. Lily sat beside her with her legs folded under, picking out beads for her grandmother from an old wooden box. Kathryne's lap had become the afternoon napping spot for one of the pups as she rocked gently in a big wooden rocker.

Picking her words carefully, Gray Dove began the journey back in time to remember the first day she saw Lily's mother. Kathryne was keenly aware of how close Lily was to Gray Dove. Although she never asked her the question that was burning on her heart, somehow the old woman knew that Lily needed to find out why she was so different from her mother and sister. Maybe it was because she knew Lily had just come from Valerie's house. Nevertheless, the closeness was profound, and now Gray Dove was telling her the answer to a question she had not even asked.

"Sonny was so young and handsome then, standing straight and tall. He was very lean and muscular, too. His hair was black as jet, and his dark, sparkling eyes danced with life. He was painfully shy. He worked at Short Brothers' Chevrolet Garage on Main Street in town. He had been working there for two years when he met Maggie Lou." Her voice flowed with feeling, bringing the story to life as it unfolded.

"It had always been Sonny's way to take his lunch to work every day. I'd prepare it for him and put it in a brown paper sack. He would come to the kitchen, give me a peck on the cheek, take the sack, and as he went out the back door, he'd say, 'What's it gonna be today?' Knowing he never waited for an answer, I would always just say, 'Wait and see.' It was kind of a ritual we would go through every morning." She smiled, remembering her son alive and affectionate.

"One particular morning, he went out the back door without picking up his sack and said nothing about it. This went on a little over a week. Finally, I said, 'Sonny, who's the girl?' He wanted to know what I meant, and I just told him a mother knows her son. He spoke of this beautiful creature who worked at the lunch counter at Kresge's Five-and-Dime, which was just up the street from Short Brothers'. He had met her when he and one of the fellas he worked with walked up there on break one afternoon. She had the blonde hair of an angel and blue eyes that would shame the clearest of skies. And, of course, a quite pleasing figure. He was completely taken in by her looks, but at this point, I don't think he had ever said anything to her except, 'I'll have a hamburger, fries, and a Coke.' Needless to say, the lunch sack days were over."

They all laughed at the remark.

"This had been going on for some time when I was in town one hot afternoon and decided I'd stop at the lunch counter for a vanilla cone and see Sonny's new girlfriend. Sonny's description was accurate, all right. She was lovely."

What Gray Dove couldn't tell her audience was what a siren Maggie Lou was. She was beautiful and knew it. That she was using a God-given gift as a weapon to get what she wanted from any man. The men crowded her lunch counter every day. Gray Dove knew she had to tell Lily the truth, but she saw no need to make the story worse. It was not her way to gossip or cause needless grief. Besides, Lily was bright enough to read between the lines. She wanted to tell Lily all the funny, happy things about her son and Maggie Lou. She used them to make the story worth telling.

"By that time, Sonny had worked up enough courage to ask her out," Gray Dove continued, "but she declined his invitation. He was crushed. He was strong willed though, and he persisted for a long time. He had saved up enough money by then for a car and bought himself a brand-new, shiny-red Chevrolet..."

"What year, Momma?" Lily asked as she wistfully glanced at her own red car.

"Oh my, too many years have come and gone to still be able to remember that." She laughed, swatting Lily's leg. "Anyway, one Friday afternoon Sonny came through the back door like a shot. She had asked him to the church picnic that Saturday. He was steppin' high! I remember he shined that car of his until I know he wore a coat of paint off it. He had a new suit, and when he was ready to leave, he was the most handsome man I'd ever seen. I could see so much of his father in him that day. John Henry was a snappy dresser and every bit as handsome. From then on it was Sonny and Maggie Lou."

Suddenly, the brown pup in Kathryne's lap yelped. The second pup had decided he had been in the lap of luxury long enough. It was his turn. He had bitten down on the tip of his brother's tail. They laughed as the frisky puppies ran around on the porch and out into the front yard.

"Momma, before you finish the story, I want to get us some tea."

Gray Dove did not hear what her granddaughter said to her. She was back when Sonny courted Maggie Lou. It was when Gray

Dove made a lot of jewelry for the people in town and got to know them and their friends. Margaret Louise Roberts's family lived up on the east end of town. They weren't well-to-do, but gave airs of being so. They weren't poor either, but Emma, Maggie Lou's mother, was just never satisfied with the financial status her husband, Lester, had achieved by that time in his life. Emma was always trying to push her daughter into society, but she just wasn't society material. After that picnic, Maggie Lou had a hold on Sonny as tight as a field mouse caught in a hawk's claw. He was wild about her.

A short time later, Sonny's boss sent him to St. Louis for a week of school. Gray Dove remembered Sonny thinking he would not be able to live through the separation from his beloved that long. But he did, and so did Maggie Lou. Gray Dove had ridden into town with Mrs. Snyder to deliver some jewelry while her friend did some shopping. On the way home, Mrs. Snyder stopped at the little store on the highway just at the edge of town. Once when Gray Dove and Sonny were in the store, they heard whispers about "stupid, dirty, superstitious worshipers of voodoo injuns." Gray Dove preferred to wait in the car for her friend. While she was waiting, she saw Maggie Lou and an older man in a black sedan cruise out the highway and turn left just past the store onto a secluded gravel road. The sorrow Gray Dove felt for Sonny was sickening. She felt cold through and through. The girl was no good.

When Sonny returned home from the school, she casually asked what Maggie Lou had done to keep herself occupied while he was gone. He said she had been visiting a sick aunt in Evansville, Indiana.

"She is such a giving person," he said. Gray Dove knew that to be true. About two months later, Sonny bolted in one evening and announced that he and Maggie Lou were to be married as soon as possible. They were very much in love and couldn't wait any longer. Gray Dove knew it would do no good to try to talk him out of it. He was strong willed like his father, who had passed away only three years prior.

John Henry's spirit had always remained close to Gray Dove in times of need. His spirit had been with her constantly since her first visit to Kresge's Five and Dime. America Gray Dove missed her strong, handsome brave greatly. Even in his older age she still referred to him that way.

The wedding took place at the St. Stephen's Cathedral downtown. It was small. Emma Roberts was very unhappy with her daughter's choice in a husband and did not want to spend one penny more than necessary on what she considered a lost cause. Her thoughts had turned to her next eldest daughter.

Sonny and his new bride moved to a tiny three-room house in town close to Sonny's work. She was discontented from the beginning. She quit her job at the lunch counter and quickly adapted to the status of lady of leisure. The new red car became hers, and Sonny bought an old brown pickup to drive.

One Sunday Gray Dove fixed dinner for her son and his wife. Maggie Lou had never been in her mother-in-law's house before and wasn't looking forward to it. When she came in the back door that day, Gray Dove knew that the older man in the black sedan had been Hobart Davis, vice president of Owensboro Commercial Bank. The day before, she had seen Maggie Lou going out the highway, Gray Dove had delivered a wide silver necklace with special handwork on it to Mr. Davis in his office. Maggie Lou wore that very necklace to Sunday dinner. She had no idea that Gray Dove was the old Indian who crafted jewelry. After that Sunday, the necklace was never seen again.

In the following weeks, Maggie Lou's waist began to expand, and Sonny understood her haste in wanting to get married. He knew the child wasn't his, but it made no difference to him. He was still crazy about her. He never let on if he knew who the father was.

"Ready for tea, Momma, KT? It's ready," Lily called from the kitchen.

Gray Dove was lost in her thoughts. "Tea?" Kathryne asked, gently touching her arm. Kathryne felt sorry for the old woman. How painful it must be for her to talk about her dead husband and son. Also, she realized that Gray Dove was trying to pick and choose her words in order to spare Lily's feelings. She could tell it was not Gray Dove's way to ridicule and run other people down, even if she despised them as much as she most certainly did Maggie Lou.

"Momma...Valerie mentioned that she had no Indian blood in her. How can that be? Is it true?"

Gray Dove put her arms around Lily and held her tightly. Putting it simply and as plain as possible, she told Lily that Maggie Lou had an unfortunate experience with an older, married man before she met Sonny. He was older and took advantage of her youth and gullibility. Sonny loved her so much, he married her when he found out she was pregnant. Valerie had a different father.

"So you see, she is different from you. She doesn't have the gift of Indian blood in her veins," she whispered softly to Lily.

Kathryne saw a slight smile touch Lily's eyes.

"She doesn't, Momma? You mean Daddy is all mine?"

"I guess you could say so, yes."

"Why did Daddy change his name?" Lily asked, trying to grasp the depth of what Gray Dove was telling her.

Gray Dove remembered it as if it had happened yesterday. Maggie Lou threw a crying fit, saying she did not want her children to endure the same kind of prejudice Sonny had. And besides, why should she have to put up with snide remarks? It would just be better all around if the name was shortened to Gray. Sonny was totally blinded by his love for her. His fear of losing her prompted him to legally change his last name. Gray Dove did not find out about the change until much later, when she saw Lily's birth certificate. She felt John Henry's heart break.

The battle won, Mrs. Gray was happy for a while. Then, right after Valerie was born, an article in the business section of the local paper announced the requested transfer of Hobart Davis to the new facility in Covington, Kentucky, as president. Maggie Lou became unbearable. But Sonny seemed happy with Valerie in spite of it all. He loved her like his own and took pride in showing her off. Maggie, on the other hand, took to the comforts of alcohol. Sonny asked Gray Dove to come and help with the baby and the housework until Maggie Lou got back on her feet. She stayed several months, until her tongue got the best of her.

There were things going on that should not have been. Too many secret phone calls. Too many long lunches with friends. Friends, Gray Dove knew, were in short supply. Other days were spent sleeping after drinking all night. She was slipping out to meet the banker when he was in town for meetings, which was frequently. Hobart actually came to Sonny's home one afternoon while he was working. Gray Dove told him who she was and that she knew all about him. He learned rather quickly that America Gray Dove was no stupid renegade when he was threatened with a paternity suit as well as alienation of affection. His decision was evident when he left and was never heard from again. Maggie overheard the conversation and flew into a rage. She went at Gray Dove with both fists and ordered the "meddling old Indian" out of the house. To spare her son more grief, Gray Dove left before he got home from work.

The drinking got worse. Maggie Lou took no pride in herself, the house, or Valerie, and she all but totally ignored her husband. Sonny would take Valerie to Gray Dove's on the weekends and stay sometimes until time for work Monday morning. He was hurting so badly. They would talk long into the night, and he would seem to find enough strength to make it another week. Finally, after a long, hard battle, Emma Roberts got Maggie Lou off the alcohol. Maggie Lou began to fix herself up, and the blonde angel's brown roots became blonde again.

She and Sonny seemed happy for a while. She joined several women's groups and helped at church functions. She even became civil to the "meddling old Indian." Sometime during that brief, happy time, Lily was conceived. That was a miracle in itself since Maggie Lou had vowed there would be no more children. Her figure was too hard to regain. She hated the thought of being fat and unattractive, unable to wear the latest fashions. Her confinement with Lily was torturous to all involved. She stayed in bed and demanded to be waited on. This time, Emma stayed with her until her delivery date.

When Lily was born, Sonny brought Gray Dove to the hospital. The moment she saw Lily, she knew she was his blood.

"From the first moment I held you in my arms, I knew you were special," she told her granddaughter. "Your father would bring you to me in the summer and let you stay until school started. You would cry to stay when it was time to go home. Those summers were the most joyous times I have ever spent. Sonny would always come down for the weekend to join us. Sometimes, he would even come out during the week and spend the night."

The difference Maggie Lou made between the children was heartbreaking, and Gray Dove tried to make it up to Lily. Valerie was taught to be aggressive and vain. She was spoiled and pampered. Lily was taught her father's ways, the Cherokee ways. Gray Dove never liked Valerie as a child, and the passing of the years did nothing to change her feelings.

"Momma, why was I never told?"

"I never told you these things, Lily, because I knew it would hurt so deeply. Also, it was Sonny's duty. He was going to tell you when you started high school, but his time was cut short. He told me a few weeks before his death that he planned to leave Maggie Lou. He was going to bring you, of course, and we were going to move down here. She had broken his spirit, and the only happiness he knew was watching you grow, Lily. He loved you so much. But as you know, the Almighty had other plans for him. And, in my old age, I took the easy road. Not wanting to hurt you, I kept my mouth shut."

"This explains a lot of things that I used to just put out of my mind when I was at home." Lily seemed lightened, almost happy over the news that Valerie was only her half sister. "Valerie would always get the pretty dresses and all the attention and praise. I never told Daddy that I noticed, because I didn't want him to think I was a baby. I guess, too, I thought I would get those things when I got a little older. I remember he worked late most nights for the extra money to pay for all of Valerie's necessities."

"Are you all right, my child?"

"Yes, Momma. I'm fine," Lily said, kissing the tanned cheek. "Somehow I feel so much better to know for sure that I am different from Maggie Lou and Valerie. I have always been afraid that I would wake up one morning and be like them. Now I know I won't. Thank you for telling me. I know it wasn't easy for you. I love you so much."

"Could I hear about this man of yours now? When do I get to meet him?" Gray Dove was anxious to change the subject to a happier theme.

"Oh my gosh! I haven't even shown you my ring!" Lily squealed, sticking out her left hand. "Isn't it a beauty? We haven't set a definite date yet. I'll get him up here as soon as I can. And I won't get married unless you promise to be there."

Kathryne and Lily stayed two more days with Gray Dove. They visited the shops in Gatlinburg, drank herbal tea, and took long walks with the puppies in the woods next to Gray Dove's house. Not once did Kathryne feel like an outsider. She became a part of the spiritual peace that surrounded Gray Dove. She could not get over the change in Lily since they'd arrived at Gray Dove's. Instead of being upset over the sordid story, she was happy and relieved. She never liked Valerie and always felt guilty about it. The depth she had as a person, and as a woman, helped her understand Maggie Lou. She understood the profound difference when one of your children was conceived in love and the other was not.

They all cried when they hugged good-bye. Lily was ready to face the world. Kathryne could have spent a month with America Gray Dove. She was so warm and loving.

chapter

TWELVE

The Kentucky trip had been almost a month before, but Lily still could not shake her depression. Friday had come as a lifeboat to a sinking ship. She was tired and irritable. The afternoon had turned unusually warm for this time of year, and the wool of her gray skirt suddenly became a thousand tiny, prickly needles attacking her legs.

Now, fumbling for her keys at the front door, Lily could not wait to get inside and lock out the world. Shifting the grocery bags to one arm, she retrieved the mail from her mailbox beside the door. Finally, she was inside.

Immediately slipping out of the itchy skirt and silk blouse, she kicked off her too-tight gray pumps and put away the contents of the brown bags. Pouring herself a glass of red wine and getting comfortable in her La-Z-Boy, she sorted through the mail.

"Mmm, just what I need," she said aloud, dropping the rest of the mail to the floor beside her. It was a small package from Gray Dove. Her grandmother still preferred writing to using "that thing," the telephone. As it turned out, Gray Dove's package was not at all what she needed.

The letter brought her news of the suicide of Tommy Hawkins. As Lily read, tears dropped to the page, causing the ink to blur the words. Closing her eyes, she could see two young children at play, riding stick ponies, playing tag, and sharing each other's excitement on Christmas morning when Santa left them each a red-and-white Western Flyer.

"Oh, God, why did you let this happen?" she cried out accusingly. Holding the crumpled letter to her heart, she remembered how in the fifth grade they had pledged their love forever. And it was only yesterday, wasn't it, when he took her for a ride in the black '57 Chevy he had saved for so long to buy. Time had passed too quickly. High-school graduation, Vietnam, and now suddenly he was gone, gone forever.

In 1965, when President Johnson ordered troops sent to South Vietnam to fight communist North Vietnam, the Vietcong, antiwar protests broke out on college campuses throughout the United States. News of peace rallies and marches took precedence over every other public event, from the largest cities to the smallest towns. The country as a whole was not behind this war, and the troops, thousands of miles away in a different world, could feel it.

Most Americans felt the country was involved in the war only for political status and recognition as a "world policeman." By 1969, 543,000 American troops were in Vietnam.

The Vietcong used guerilla warfare, practicing barbaric tactics in their dense jungles that were unfamiliar to the US troops. The inability of the troops to recognize their enemy presented another serious problem with which to cope.

President Nixon began troop withdrawal in the early seventies, and a cease-fire agreement was signed in January 1973 between the United States and Vietnam. The fighting continued between North and South Vietnam until the South surrendered in 1975. This seemed to confirm to a large percentage of Americans that the conflict in Vietnam was a civil war, and the United States should have stayed out of it from the start.

Over two hundred thousand US troops were listed as dead, wounded, or missing in action. But what about the Tommys of the war? The ones who couldn't cope and ended their own lives? Or the ones who left mind and spirit behind in another life, with only a body to return with?

"Damn the politicians!" Lily screamed defiantly, as if to be heard in Washington. "Why do they have to use people to feed the almighty economic fires?" She had saved the few letters Tommy had sent. They always made her feel like someone in hell was reaching out to her for help. Each letter was full of horrors and fears. Fears, Lily sensed, that were as constant as the air they breathed and as visible as the lives being lost every day the war continued. She cried when she read every letter and regretted never telling Tommy just how much she really loved him.

When the letters quit coming, Lily learned Tommy had been wounded and was in the VA hospital in Louisville. She called him immediately, but the Tommy she talked to wasn't the one she had known. He was old and angry. She wanted to visit him, but he had said no, not ever. Confused and hurt, she had gone to his parents for answers. Tommy had lost both of his legs in a minefield. One leg could have been saved, had he gotten medical attention in time, but his platoon was under such heavy fire that the wounded had to wait a long time before being picked up.

Tommy had told his parents about the horrible moments that changed his whole life. His platoon had been instructed to play dead and try to hold on to their weapon if they were badly wounded. The chance of survival would be better that way. Frequently, however, the enemy would make a random check and stick bayonets in the bodies on the field to make sure they were dead. Tommy had done as his sergeant instructed that day. His weapon was positioned just under his right arm, ready, waiting. He lay motionless on the ground, numb from the waist down. With steely eyes he watched the approach of two from the enemy bayonet squad. They laughed as they stopped for a smoke. Making random stabs, they laughed and made fun of the dead, searching them for cigarettes and money. They were close now, one behind the other. He could take them. He could blow the smiles right off their slimy gook faces.

"Assholes!" They turned toward the sound—an American GI. They knew what hit them. Their faces were blown into a million bloody pieces. With sweat dripping from his face, Tommy smiled as he rested his head on one arm to wait for the rescue chopper.

He had learned to kill, and he enjoyed it. He received a Purple Heart for his bravery.

Tommy's mother cried as she told Lily the story. He was waiting to be fitted for a new type of artificial leg, but so far he'd had no luck. The mobile unit was deluged with torn bodies by the time he got there, and in the frantic conditions under which they worked, the doctors had hurriedly and recklessly removed too much of his lower limbs. There was not enough left to attach a prosthesis.

Her lifelong sweetheart was bitter and full of hate. His physical condition improved, but mentally he deteriorated fast. He allowed no visitors, and Lily received no answer to her regular letters. Wiping her eyes on the now soggy Kleenex, Lily refilled her wineglass and began to read the remainder of Gray Dove's letter. Tommy's mother told Gray Dove, who was her dearest friend, the actual account of his death and the thoughts he left on a note pad beside his bed.

He was scheduled to be released from the hospital the day after he was found dead. He was a star athlete in high school and now felt only half-alive. The immobility of his body had spread to his mind, and suicide became his only answer. Feeling he would be unable to cope with the outside world, Tommy had electrocuted himself in a makeshift electric chair designed around his own wheelchair. The hospital orderly who found his stiff, ashen body the next morning surmised that Tommy had used the elevator to get to the basement generator room, where electrical supplies were kept. After cutting the end from a heavy-duty extension cord and scraping off the insulation, he wrapped the exposed wire once around his waist and then twisted them to the chair arm.

Thinking of everything, not wanting his plan to fail, Tommy removed the pad from his chair and used his own urine as an electrical conductor. When he plugged the end into a 220-volt outlet, death came quickly. Tommy's last wish was a private funeral with a closed casket—family only. His wish was carried out.

In her distress, Lily had not noticed the small envelope that fell out when she opened the package. Reaching for another tissue, she saw Tommy's familiar script written on the envelope lying on the floor:

For Lily's eyes only.

My sweet Lily,
I've loved you from the moment I first threw mud on your baby doll. I
wanted to marry you when I got home, but the gooks screwed me up.
I couldn't bear for you to see me this way. Remember me always as the
first guy to steal a kiss from you. I'll always love you. Lily, the mental pain
is unbearable. I know of no other way. Please forgive me.
I love you,
Tommy

"My sweet Tommy, I love you, too." Lily was near hysteria as she cried and rocked back and forth, holding the letter. Not knowing how long she had cried, she finally got a grip on her emotions and sat up. She began to press out the crumpled letter with her hand, and her engagement ring caught her eye. Lily held her hand in front of her eyes as if she were an infant discovering it for the first time. She stared at the huge diamond and realized she absolutely was not in love with Bill Dressler. She couldn't jump into a marriage just to try to win her mother's approval.

"Who the hell is Maggie Lou Gray anyway? Just a slut. An old whore," she said, pouring herself a water goblet of wine. She slipped the ring off her finger and put it on the mantel over the fireplace. Tears filled her eyes again as they met Tommy's, watching her from a small golden frame. He looked so handsome in his uniform with his deep blue eyes and what was left of his dark brown hair. Her mind began to play what-if. What if Tommy had come home uninjured? What if they had married?" Had the phone been ringing? Yes.

Andy knew Lily wasn't herself after the brief phone conversation they had twenty minutes earlier. Something was not right. He walked briskly up the front steps to her town house. After several knocks, she finally opened the front door.

He had never seen such a sight. Mascara and makeup was smeared all over her face. She had red, puffy eyes, and her hair was stringy. All this mess was standing there in a wine-stained, pink silk slip.

"Lily, what in God's name has happened to you?" Taking the glass from her hand, he led her to the couch. "Sit here and tell me what's going on. Did Bill…?"

Without saying a word, Lily handed him both letters. After reading them, Andy gently folded each one and put them on the coffee table. Lily sat staring at the picture of Tommy across the room on the mantel. Putting his arms around her, Andy pulled Lily to him. "I'm sorry. So sorry."

Kathryne had told Andy about the trip to Kentucky and what an effect it had had on Lily. Now, this. He felt totally helpless, not knowing what to do or say. Why had Kathryne picked this weekend to go to her mother's?

"Have you had anything to eat?" Andy asked, trying not to count the empty wine bottles. He wondered why Lily wasn't passed out.

"Yes, I had a Twinkie at noon."

"No, I mean tonight, dinner. It's ten thirty. Listen, you go in the bathroom, wash your face, brush your hair, and put on something warm, while I fix you something to eat. Go on now, you'll feel better. Besides, you will be sick as hell in the morning if you don't eat." Andy slipped off his Armani jacket, loosened his tie, and began looking through the fridge. He found eggs and made an omelet, while strong coffee brewed. Lily was still in a daze on the couch. He coaxed her to eat a bit, and she began to sober some. Lily's emotions were running wild. She felt lonely and sad. All the good things in her childhood were gone now, except for Gray Dove. Her father, the true family she thought she had, and now, her lifelong sweetheart. Lily wanted to scream, to laugh, to cry, and to run away. Mostly she wanted to go back in time. As she stared into the black coffee thinking of Tommy, the memories overwhelmed her as the melody from the stereo rushed to her with nostalgia euphoria.

"Dance with me."

Without question, Andy obliged.

"I need you to hold me. Hold me close," she whispered. They danced in the soft glow of the fire lit room to all their favorite old songs. They danced as Tommy and Lily had done so many times before. Lily closed her eyes as her lips met Tommy's, and the closeness of their bodies became one in the shadows on the wall.

Andy held Lily in his arms and looked down into her face. He had never known a more beautiful woman. Her skin was so flawless and smooth. He held her close, feeling every curve of her subtle body as it met his. His hands were drawn to the long, black silk draping her soft, bare shoulders. He wondered just how far he would let Tommy go. His lips moved down her neck as gently as a floating feather. He wanted to be Tommy, if only for one night.

As they kissed, she was overwhelmed with the passion of their high-school days. Tommy's hands stroked her body like a harpist who knew every string by heart. Her body ached for fulfillment. Ray Charles was singing.

"I can't stop loving you,
I've made up my mind…
To live my life in dreams
of…
yesterday…

"I can't stop loving you," she whispered passionately. Her mouth was starved for his kiss.

"I can't stop." She breathed into his open lips.

For the first time in his life, Andy had to measure up to another man. He had to be as much of a man as Tommy had been; had to know when to stop.

When the sunlight crept through the lilac curtains in Lily's bedroom the next morning she became acutely aware of her aching head.

"Oh, my head," she grumbled, slowly rolling on to her side. Leaning toward the clock on the night stand, her hand on her head as if to keep it in place, she was startled to see Andy sitting on the white chair beside her bed.

"Oh, Andy! I—"

"Here, drink this. It's great for hangovers. It is an old oil field recipe. Cold tomato juice, lemon juice, and a dash of Tabasco sauce."

"No! Oh no, I just couldn't..." He gave her little choice, so she gulped down the concoction quickly to get it over with.

"Now you just lie back in bed, and I'll get a cool washcloth for your head."

"But I'll be late for work." Lily protested.

"Quit worrying, it's Saturday," Andy reminded her, scurrying from the bathroom with the cool compress. She pulled the floral sheets up around her, embarrassed at having Andy see her like this.

"Are you going to be OK?"

"Yes, I'll be fine. I will probably stay in bed a long, long time. Andy, about last night. I..."

Leaning over the bed, Andy put his finger across her lips. He smoothed the hair from her forehead ever so gently, knowing her head must feel like a giant bruise. His big brown eyes smiled warmly at her.

"I'm going to get out of here. Call me later if you want to talk."

He eased himself out her front door. Lily stared after him until she realized she was holding her breath. Letting out a long exhale, she reluctantly tried to reconstruct the previous evening.

chapter

THIRTEEN

In the following weeks, Kathryne did all she could to keep her best friend's mind off Tommy's death. She pressed her intercom button and spoke into the speaker. "Miss Gray, could I see you a moment? In my office?"

"Yes, ma'am, Mrs. Langford!" Lily, replying like an errand boy being summoned by the president of the company, dropped what she was doing and took off running out of her office.

Langford Gray Advertising Agency now occupied the whole tenth floor of the Atlanta National Bank Building. Kathryne and Lily's offices were in the back overlooking the courtyard, separated by the executive assistant and personal secretary they shared.

Lily threw open her office door and ran as fast as she could in her bronze suede suit and matching pumps. Reaching Kathryne's door, she opened it immediately and ran in, leaving their office staff wondering what in the world they were up to now.

"Yes, boss!" Lily said, pretending excitedly to be out of breath.

"Miss Gray. There is a huge sale at Macy's today, and we are not there!" Kathryne stated in her most formal boardroom manner.

"No! It cannot be!" shrieked Lily. They looked at each other and screamed. Then exploded with laughter.

"We will be out the rest of the afternoon, Theda," said Lily. She and Kathryne prissed out the door. "We have to do a site inspection for a new account."

Laughing like bank robbers getting away with the loot, Lily drove like a bat out of hell. They shopped for hours and then went to Brandywine, a small restaurant specializing in gourmet salads. The cozy atmosphere was enhanced by the hanging philodendron and soft lighting.

"KT, I'm in serious trouble!" Lily said. "I have spent way too much money!"

"I know what you mean. It will take months to get out of debt. Oh, but the treasures we found!"

"Do we have any money for lunch?" Lily inquired.

"I'm not sure." Kathryne laughed. "And if we have to do dishes, it will mess up my manicure!" They were giddy, thoroughly enjoying the afternoon. They knew it was their hard work that enabled them to engage in such carefree antics.

As they left the restaurant, a flyer in one of the store windows caught Lily's eye. She glanced at the blue sheet of paper and quickly jerked Kathryne back.

"KT, get a load of this." Lily was still holding Kathryne by the arm. "Mrs. Pearl Lewis, wife of oil magnate, Andrew Lewis, and director of public relations for Southern Christian Leadership Conference, SCLC, formed by Dr. Martin Luther King, Jr., will be the guest speaker, five o'clock, Thursday, June fourth, at the post-graduation celebration for Spellman College. Mrs. Lewis will be speaking about the advancement of black women..."

Lily stopped reading and looked at Kathryne. They looked at their watches simultaneously. It was four thirty. Tearing down the street in a dead run, they crammed their packages in the car, jumped in, and sped off to get a bead on the woman who had intrigued them for so many years.

Arriving behind most of the crowd, they had to park quite a distance from the auditorium. Their feet, already sore from shopping, took more abuse as their high heels hit the asphalt. Once inside, they had to stand in the back of the packed auditorium.

Pearl was seated to the right of the podium, waiting to speak to the young women. Her thoughts returned to her childhood. She remembered greasing her stout legs with Vaseline as she looked at herself in the mirror hung over her dresser.

"You're just at a gawky age," her mother had told her the month before, on her eighth birthday. She hated the kinky, black hair that Mommy made her grow long to cover her huge ears. Pearl would have kept it cut close to her head so it would not hurt so much when brushed and braided. Her lips were big, her nose was big, and her feet were so big she couldn't even fit into her mommy's pumps to play dress-up anymore.

It was 1948 in Dallas, Texas, at the height of the summer. Pearl was dressing for Sunday school. She heard her brothers, Nathaniel and Samuel, reciting the daily Bible verses they were required to memorize for their daddy. Unlike Pearl, who always knew her verses frontward and backward, they stumbled and stammered, finally finishing barely on the edge of approval.

It was only while alone in the bedroom she shared with her brothers that Pearl scrutinized herself so closely. She dreaded her unattractiveness—no, ugliness—and was working on a plan whereby she could overcome it. Although only ten years old, Pearl was very bright. She was already planning her life, how to change it, and who she wanted to be. One thing was for sure, she did not want to be a preacher's wife. She wanted to be somebody special. She had to be. She just had to be. She felt a driving force deep within her all-black soul that would not relent or let her alone.

When she recited her verses for the morning, including the verses for the next two weeks, her daddy was so astonished and proud he asked her, as she had hoped he would, to recite them for the congregation in the church services.

Pearl's father, Elijah Banes, had been the pastor for the All Soul's Methodist Church in Dallas for ten years. He had quite a following. Pearl had overheard some murmuring that white folks thought he was building a rebellion. The membership had reached five hundred in a church that only seated two hundred. Brothers and sisters stood at the open windows and the front and back doors to hear Reverend Banes. He was a gifted teacher of the Word.

When Pearl was in front of the congregation, which she tried to be as often as possible, it made her feel wonderful. She had the people in her power. Her careful placement of tone variation, pauses, and diction became a magnet for their attention. She would no longer be aware or accept herself as an ugly black girl. Instead, she was certain to be that mental picture of herself: a beautiful, powerful woman. Somebody special.

As she grew up, always excelling, always in control, other people began to tell her she was special. When her daddy was mercilessly killed by white vigilantes one night as he walked home from his beloved church, her mommy, brothers, and she moved to Austin, and the opportunity for which Pearl was born fell into her lap.

They moved in with her uncle, sharing one room of a small clapboard house in the heart of Austin's colored town. Pearl had to help her mommy clean and do laundry for people, so she could not attend school. She thought at first that her life was over. But that voice within her would not give up. She saved old newspapers from the beautiful homes she and her mommy cleaned and memorized every word in them. Even the want ads. She would make her brothers sit and listen as she recited. She had to have an audience to survive, and she grieved for the large congregation in Dallas.

One night at bedtime, Pearl's mother told her children that they would be moving the next day. She had been working for the last month as the housekeeper of a widowed college professor. His huge home included an upstairs apartment. It had not been used in years, and he felt Lettie could take better care of things if she and her family lived there.

Pearl's life began the day Dean Drake asked her why she wasn't in school.

"Mommy needs my help, sir," she replied, using perfect diction.

"Have you ever attended school, Pearl?" Dean Drake was well aware that many Negro children were deprived of schooling.

"Oh, yes, sir. I love school. Would you like to hear my favorite address?" Without waiting for him to answer, because something inside told her he would, she recited for Dean Drake the Gettysburg Address, followed by the entire United States Constitution. She was ecstatic. She was a queen. She was beautiful! Her big ears were gone, her kinky hair gone. Then, she noticed tears in his eyes.

"Oh, I am sorry. I am so sorry that I—" She ran from the room, mortified for having bored such a kind man to tears. She sat in her closet and cried until she fell asleep. She learned later, almost to her disbelief, that she had touched Dean Drake so deeply with her love for school and scholastic achievements that he made arrangements for her to attend a school for academically gifted students. Pearl was thirteen years old.

She was in heaven. Memorizing the newspapers had honed her mind like a razor. She excelled in her work and, oddly enough, the white students accepted her as an academic equal. They never invited her to their parties or into their clubs, but they were cordial and friendly. Pearl was the only colored student in the school.

She kept busy with homework, housework, and church work. Dean Drake would spend hours with her, working on a project or discussing a topic. She would play with her cousins when Mommy took them to visit Uncle Josiah in the colored section of town, but she always knew she was not just another little colored girl.

In high school, Pearl began work with the local Southern Christian Leadership Conference set up by Dr. Martin Luther King, Jr. Unlike the NAACP, which concentrated on legal action and court battles, the SCLC operated through southern Negro churches to coordinate local civil rights activities. The SCLC stood, as King did, for nonviolence. Pearl's effort with the group was in getting Negroes to register to vote, a dangerous activity in the late 1950's. They set up voting clinics, transportation to register, and campaigned for white supporters.

Pearl graduated from Dillard High School at the top of her class. She was asked to read scripture at baccalaureate and won a five-hundred-dollar scholarship for college tuition. Dean Drake had slipped Lettie a little extra in her pay envelope to buy Pearl a new dress for graduation. A large Negro turnout at the graduation services of the all-but-Pearl white school caused a temporary state of confusion as to where they should sit. Once the faculty realized they were all sitting together on one side of the auditorium, everyone relaxed. Although Pearl was well liked and respected in the school, it was 1958, this was the South, and integration was new, very new.

Pearl entered the University of Texas as a prelaw student and again made the honor roll. She was on the debate team and the Students in Government Club, and she stayed very active with the SCLC. She was infatuated with Martin Luther King, Jr. and followed his every move through the newspaper. She read everything written about him and longed for the day she would get to meet him in person. That day came when she was chosen as the Texas delegate for SCLC.

It was a month before graduation. The SCLC Annual Conference was in Atlanta, Georgia. Lettie had been sewing for weeks as the four-day trip approached. Pearl traveled by train and was met by Jimmy Johnson, one of Dr. King's directors. On the way to the hotel, he asked Pearl if she would say a few words at the conference about being a black, 4.0 prelaw student in the South.

"Yes, sir, I will be happy to." This was the calm reply from the woman who knew, at last, she was somebody special.

"Great. I will tell Dr. King. Can you meet with him and the other speakers in the morning after breakfast?" Pearl was trying to keep from floating out of the car. "Oh," Jimmy added, "he will want a summary of your speech. Can you have it by then?"

"Oh, sure." Pearl pinched herself on the arm. Well, it must hurt even when you are dreaming, she thought, because surely I am asleep.

Checked in and alone in her room, she stood in the middle of the beautiful suite going over in her mind again and again what Mr. Johnson had said.

"I should call him. He has me confused with someone else," she told the room. "Is this happening? Pardon me, ma'am"—she mimicked Mr. Johnson—"would you be available to meet the famous, wonderful, sainted Dr. Martin Luther King, Jr. after you have had your breakfast tomorrow morning?"

She switched places with an imaginary person to assume the opposite role. "Why certainly, Mr. Johnson. Please tell Dr. King I will be delighted to meet with him."

She ran around the room, turning on the television, the radio, the shower, and the faucet in the sink. She tried to drown out the sound as she jumped on the bed on all fours with her butt high in the air, buried her face in the pillow, and screamed loud and long.

Her meeting with Dr. King was brief but profound. He wore an impressive gray pinstripe suit and had such a kindness about him that Pearl felt at ease immediately. He shook her hand and congratulated her on the accomplishments she had made scholastically and with the SCLC. She briefed him orally on what she planned to say, and he told her something that she remembered and repeated to herself for the rest of her life: "Pearl, that is perfect."

Her short speech only fueled her fire. She had to have more. She talked to Jimmy Johnson about her love for SCLC and her eagerness to do more. Pearl Banes left Atlanta as the national spokesperson of the SCLC.

Pearl Lewis was introduced and took the podium as the all-black, all-female student body roared with applause and a standing ovation. She was beautifully dressed in a white suit, navy-and-white spectator pumps, and a white bellboy hat. She was short-waisted, but her five-foot-six-inch frame stood tall and strong. The navy face net of her hat provoked respect. Kathryne and Lily were spellbound.

She began her speech with a quote from Jesse Jackson, president of the People United to Serve Humanity, PUSH, and PUSH Excel, founded to promote the advancement of education for minorities.

"I am somebody. I may be black, but I am somebody. I may be poor, but I am somebody. I can learn. I am somebody. Down with dope, up with hope. I am somebody."

The students whistled, clapped, and chanted, "Yes, Jesse! Yes, Pearl!" The emotion in the auditorium could have raised goose bumps on chrome. Kathryne and Lily, as if on cue, reached to rub their arms in a shivering gesture.

Pearl said, "We must end the questions of the quality of the Negro race and rise above the lingering stigma of a lesser status. The lazy, loafing, uneducated Negro of the past must be replaced through goals, education, and the commitment to be the best we can be. Rise above the haunts of yesterday, divorce yourselves from those who would drag you back. Feel like a Stradivarius in a jug band? Today, my friends, that can change. You don't have to stay in the jug band anymore!"

The crowd went mad. Chants rocked the auditorium. They cried as they sang, "I have a dream, Lord, I have a dream!"

When they were finally quiet, she remained strong. "Dr. Martin Luther King, Jr. said, 'Now is the time to rise from the dark and desolate valley of segregation to the sunlit path of racial justice.' The very evidence of your attendance here today tells me you are on your way to reaching that goal!" The students cheered again. Pearl continued by explaining the SCLC and PUSH Excel organizations, the progress made in racial equality, and the strides being taken. Her thanks went to Dr. King and his movement. She explained how the students there today could play a part individually as well as collectively.

Excitement surged through Washington Hall as hundreds of young Negro women were encourage to strive for their dreams, directed to reach for their birthright, for equality. Kathryne and Lily found themselves somewhat disappointed that they would not be a part of this grand victory.

By the end of Pearl's speech, the auditorium rocked with chants. "Yes, Pearl! Tell us, Pearl! We're gonna do it now, Pearl!"

She concluded, as she always did, by thanking the sainted, late Dr. Arthur Drake for believing in her, thereby enabling her to believe in herself.

Awestruck, Kathryne and Lily lingered in the lobby watching and listening to the students as they left. They talked briefly with a young colored girl who worked in their art department. Then Pearl came parading through the lobby flanked by professors and staff members of the college. Kathryne and Lily could hear their conversation regarding scholarships and programs available for their students through the SCLC and PUSH Excel.

They longed to talk to her, to the woman who had just made such a rousing call for action. And to the woman whose life was so intricately entwined with Andy's.

Slowly descending the stairs from Washington Hall, Kathryne murmured, "I wouldn't take a million dollars for that experience."

"No way." Lily replied.

chapter

FOURTEEN

The doctor's office smell and the anxiety that she felt were almost more than Lily could handle as she sat flipping nervously through a well-worn copy of *Ladies' Home Journal.* The horribly depressing view of all the big-bellied women waddling in and out of the squeaking door did not help either.

"Oh Lord, let me out of here." Lily was praying under her breath when the nurse interrupted her plea.

"The doctor will see you now, Miss Gray," she said so sweetly, almost as if she were talking to a baby. "Please follow me."

As Lily followed Nurse Sweetness down the hall, she could not help but wonder how in the world any woman could dress so plainly and be so homely. From her drab, brown hair to her white, boxy shoes, she was homely. Lily decided that was why she was so sweet. She was concentrating on her inner beauty. Lily wanted to stay in the hall and talk to Nurse Sweetness some more, but she knew she couldn't put it off any longer and followed the hand that waved her into the doctor's private office.

"Hi, Lily, please have a seat," said Dr. Thomas. He motioned Lily to a high-backed, green leather chair. The whole office was done in the same puke-green color. Since Lily felt a little queasy anyway, she was afraid the color was going to act as power of suggestion to her lunch. She silently prayed that it would stay in her stomach.

"Well," she said, "let's get right to it. Am I pregnant or not?" Lily demanded the information as if she had caught the doctor doing something wrong and wanted him to own up to it.

"Yes, you are, Lily," Dr. Thomas said with a big smile. "About eight weeks."

"Oh, for God's sake," Lily screeched. "How can this be? What are those stupid little white pills I have been taking? Vitamins?" She was pacing the office, waving her arms like an Indian doing a rain dance. She was mad at someone. Or was it something? "This is so unfair!" She glared at Dr. Thomas as if it was all his doing. "I don't want to be pregnant. That's why I take precautions. Damn! Damn, damn, damn."

"Lily, calm down." Dr. Thomas pressed the intercom button on his phone and spoke into it. "Jean, would you bring in a glass of water for Miss Gray, please?"

"Oh God, Nurse Sweetness again," Lily said through her clenched teeth.

"I know it seems bad now—"

"Bad, hell!" It was like throwing gas on a fire. Lily had started to sit back down in the puke-green chair when Dr. Thomas began to assure her. Now she was pacing the floor again with a new rain dance. "It's horrible! I don't want children." Lily spoke if she were a five-year-old talking about the spinach on her plate. "I don't even like them. This is going to ruin everything!" All of a sudden it was as if she ran out of steam. Sliding into the chair, she turned to Dr. Thomas for a solution, knowing before she asked there wasn't one. "Dr. Thomas, what am I going to do?"

Just then Nurse Sweetness arrived with the same smile and a glass of water. Lily wondered as she took the water from her if it would be too sweet to drink.

"Lily," Dr. Thomas said, "I am surprised at your reaction. I guess I thought you would be happy. But since you're not, we can approach the matter differently." As Dr. Thomas talked, his

Adam's apple bobbed up and down, making his stethoscope do the same. Lily tried to force herself not to watch it. It made her feel insecure about this man who seemed to hold her future in his hands.

"The fetus," he said, "is within the legal time frame to abort, and as healthy as you are—"

"Wait just a minute here!" Lily interrupted. "OK, OK. I can see I have overreacted, but"— Lily suddenly felt delicate—"there is no way I can kill a baby."

"Oh, it isn't recognized as a baby until—"

"Dr. Thomas"—Lily pointed to her midsection—"this is a baby. This is a life." She got up slowly from the chair, her rage subsiding. She felt drained and exhausted. "I'm sorry, Dr. Thomas, I am just…confused."

"I understand, Lily." Dr. Thomas was trying to go easy to prevent another outburst. "I suggest you go home, get a good night's sleep, and think things through. Let me see you here next Thursday. We can go over the results of the tests we did and discuss this further."

Lily stepped outside the door of the doctor's private office and leaned against the wall to regain her composure. The tears running down her cheeks felt like boiling water. "Get it together," she told herself. "Get it together, kid." Lily just wanted to make next week's appointment, calmly walk out the door, go somewhere, and cry her guts out.

"Please make a late afternoon appointment for me next Thursday," Lily instructed the receptionist. "Thank God it isn't Nurse Sweetness," she thought as the receptionist looked at her appointment book.

"Yes, Miss Gray, how about four thirty?"

"Fine," Lily mumbled.

"Oh, congratulations! I know you must be *so* excited!" squealed the young girl.

Lily picked up her appointment card and looked at it. She leaned over the desk and smirked into the anxious face of the young receptionist. "Excited isn't the word."

As Lily stepped from the elevator on parking level four, her legs were so weak she barely made it to the car. Glad to be seated at last, she threw her blue suit jacket in the passenger side, slipped her American Graffiti tape into the recorder, put down the top, and took off down Thirty-Third Avenue.

She drove aimlessly for hours, agonizing over her predicament. About midnight she realized tearfully that she was somewhere on the west side of town and pulled into the graveled parking lot of a seedy little bar.

"The Brass Rail," read Lily from the rainbow-colored neon sign flashing the name across the front of the small building. "This looks like a good place to get blitzed," she said. She observed a couple of pickup trucks with rifle racks on the back and redneck license plates on the front. Still talking out loud, she said, "I wonder where the dog is that goes on your toolbox." She sauntered past the trucks and opened the rickety screen door to the bar.

Crossing the threshold, Lily was greeted by Hank Williams singing about a cheatin' heart from an old Rockola jukebox in the dimly lit corner. A play for a blood game of pool next to it never missed a beat. Her body seemed to make a path through the smoke-filled room as she headed toward the bar. She felt like a lamb looking for invisible passage through a pack of wolves. The watchful eyes of the "good ol' boys" glowed at her from the dark corners.

"A double bourbon and Coke, please," Lily told the bartender when she reached her destination at last.

"Sure, lady." The one-room shack had wood floors, a long bar across the back, and a television set to the left on a high shelf. The windows were so caked with sludge, you couldn't tell if it was night or day outside them.

Lily paid for her drink and found an out-of-the-way booth on the far side of the room. The booth sat beneath a partially lit Budweiser sign that twinkled the threat of burning out altogether. The cheap bourbon blazed a trail all the way down as Lily took the first big swallow.

"Whew! This really is firewater!" thought Lily, gasping for the breath she had lost. "Oh, well, I want to get drunk anyway, so here goes. Bottoms up, ol' girl." Downing the remainder of the bourbon, Lily hoisted her glass in the air, signaling the bartender for another one as she gasped again for breath.

"Look, lady, this ain't the Ritz. We ain't got no waitresses here. Ya wanna nuther drink, you'll hafta come an git it," squawked the squatty, stubble-faced bartender.

"Hell's bells," snarled Lily under her breath. "Might as well sit at the bar." She took a stool at the end of the bar next to a rack of glasses. This seat gave a view of the entire room.

"Could a person get killed in here?"

"Wouldn't have ta try hard," said the bartender. "Matter o' fact, last fall some ol' guy kept a settin' on Luke's truck out ter in tha parkin' lot and jus wouldn't get offen it. Luke had to shoot him to get him off. They never did find the body, so they couldn't convict ol' Luke. 'Nuther bourbon?" The bartender's broad smile made it evident that dental care was not one of his priorities. He was about fifty, short, and bald.

"Yes, please," Lily told him as she glanced slowly around the room, wondering which pair of glowing eyes belonged to "ol' Luke."

"Say, what's a good-lookin' broad like you doin' slummin' around in here anyway?" he asked Lily, setting down another glass of cheap bourbon and charging her for the expensive brand.

"Just wanted to step out of my world for a while, I guess," she mumbled.

"What's your name?"

"Lily. What's yours?"

"Jack," he replied with his never-seen-a-toothbrush grin.

"Well Jack, glad to meet cha'. Now how 'bout I buy you a drink?" slurred Lily. "And... gimme another while you're at it."

Lily and Jack talked off and on between customers about the weather and the new bypass around Atlanta. Lily wanted to ask a question or two about the shooting last fall, but she never could work up to it. Then a real heavyset woman about thirty came in and wanted one of the pool players to leave with her. Jack said the pool player was afraid of her, because she was part Indian. Lily was dying to talk to her. It was then she found out that the floor in that bar wasn't stable. It seemed to be built like a roller coaster. Wonder why she hadn't noticed that when she came in? She quickly sat back down but decided not to mention the floor to Jack. It might hurt his feelings.

Lily began to drink, holding the glass with both hands. As soon as her glass was empty, she would buy a fill-'er-up. She kept saying to Jack, "Fill 'er up, Shack!" As Lily drained the glass one more time, she felt herself losing her balance and could not stop herself from falling. She slipped rather gracefully off the barstool and fell almost in slow motion. She was out cold before she hit the old wooden floor, sending the barstool she had been sitting on flying across the room.

Jack heard the thud of Lily's head as the barstool skidded to a stop at the jukebox. "Lady! Lily, are you OK?" cried Jack, as his short legs carried him around to her side of the bar as fast as they could.

Between Jack hollering and the barstool making such a racket, all attention in the room was drawn to the classy lady, passed out cold, sprawled on the floor in front of the bar. Jack was trying to figure what in hell he was going to do with her, when a few of the good ol' boys decided to be not quite so good. One was going through Lily's purse while the other one was trying to get her skirt up. "Hey, Spike!" Jack yelled to his clean-up man. "Come over here and give me a hand." He turned, snatched Lily's purse from one jerk, and backhanded the one crouching over Lily like a buzzard still working on her skirt. Jack was not a big man, but he was strong. He could out-wrestle anyone in the place, and they knew it.

"Dumb sombitches!" he spat at them as they strolled slowly back to the pool table.

Jack and Spike carried Lily as gently as they knew how into the storeroom and laid her on a cot Jack kept there for the nights he was too tired to drive home. He covered her with clean bar towels so she would not get chilled and then sat down with her purse, praying there would be some sort of identification in it. Jack was looking for someone to call to get him off the hook. He certainly did not want to be held responsible for this one. There in the front section with her credit cards was what he was looking for. Kathryne Langford, a number and the magic phrase: Please call in case of an emergency. Jack made sure Lily was OK and then rushed to the phone.

Kathryne was stepping out of Becky's room after kissing her goodnight when she heard the phone ringing from her bedroom. "Can't you even answer the phone?" she sniped at Joe as she came into the room and reached for the phone. He was tucked into his side of their king-size bed, watching a movie. In order to carry his laziness one step further, he had put a television set in their bedroom. Kathryne wondered how much more she could take.

"Why should I waste my time? It's always for you anyway." He yawned in his usual blasé manner.

"Hello?" Kathryne said into the receiver flashing him a drop-dead look.

"Do you know a Lily Gray?" a gruff, unfamiliar voice asked.

"Yes. Yes, I do. Who wants to know?" Kathryne felt panic mounting as flashbacks from the call she received about Gayle and Sal's horrible accident began flooding her mind.

"This is Jack at the Brass Rail bar, ma'am. I found your phone number in Miz Lily Gray's purse that in case of an emergency, you ought to be called. Well, I guess I thought—"

"Dammit, man, what's happened? Where is Lily? Is she all right?"

"Uh, well," stammered Jack. "She's here, ma'am. In pretty bad shape, though."

Kathryne's whole body was trembling. "What do you mean, 'bad shape'—has she been in an accident?"

"Well, ya might say that, ma'am." Jack chuckled. "She's, well, she's just plain shit-faced drunk, ma'am. Scuse me. Anyways, she's gone and fell offen tha bar-stool. She's here in the back room, out like a light. Thought ya might wanna come on outten here an pick 'er up."

"Oh God." Kathryne gasped in relief. Without stopping to wonder why in God's name Lily was in some bar called the Brass Rail, she wrote down all the directions Jack gave her and told him she would be right there.

Joe had become mildly interested in the conversation. He sat up in the bed. "I guess you will be gone all night," he said accusingly. He was jealous of Lily and would more than likely need a drink to get through the night. Then he could blame Kathryne for upsetting him.

"Why don't you find a rock to crawl under, Joe," Kathryne said vehemently as she stepped into her tennis shoes and tried to tie them. She was shaking like a leaf. How dare he, she thought. Lily was in trouble, and if it took all night, then it would just have to take all night.

"Shit-faced drunk?" Kathryne repeated aloud as she jumped in her car. She drove for what seemed like an eternity trying to follow the direction the voice named Jack had given her.

"What in the world could make Lily come out here?" Kathryne was mumbling, staring wide-eyed at the Brass Rail as she pulled into the parking lot. "This sure doesn't look like a prospective client."

Stepping over beer cans strewn everywhere, she approached a short, squatty man who had been sweeping in front of the doorway when she pulled in.

"'Lo, ma'am. Are you Kathryne Langford?" Jack said, leaning the broom against the wall.

"I'm Kathryne Langford. Where's Lily?"

"Pleased to meet you, ma'am. I'm Jack. I'm the one what called."

"Yeah, yeah, yeah. Where's Lily?" It had occurred to Kathryne that this could be a trick. She couldn't wait to get Lily and get out of this place.

"Just follow me, ma'am," Jack said, motioning her through the dimly lit tavern. Jack had no idea that a small pearl-handled Walther PPK 380 tucked inside Kathryne's purse was pointed straight at him as they walked to the back room. Her father had given it to her as a twenty-first birthday present, along with weekly Saturday morning trips to the firing range until he was completely satisfied with Kathryne's marksmanship. The automatic pistol contained a magazine of six cartridges. If Jack so much as burped, she would shoot him for sure. She followed Jack cautiously to the back room, where Lily was stretched out like a dead woman on an old army cot between stacked cases of liquor. Kathryne held her breath and prayed for a pulse as she reached for the pretty little neck of her best friend. And there it was, beating like an athlete.

"What happened?" she asked when she found her voice.

"Well, now, ma'am. She come in here early on. A real looker she is. Caused quite a ruckus. Looked all down in the mouth about somethin'. Just sat there at the bar drinkin' double bourbons till she just fell clean off the stool. Me and Spike, we packed her back in here to get her away from them night crawlers out front."

It seemed pretty evident that Jack had tried to take care of Lily. "Thank you, Jack. It was very kind of you to look after her." Kathryne was gathering Lily up, trying to get out of the horrible smelling hellhole as quickly as possible.

"She seemed so depressed, ma'am. Do you know what's plaguin' her mind?" asked Jack worriedly.

"It's a puzzle to me, Jack," said Kathryne, struggling to get Lily up, hoping to reach the door in one piece. She had just asked Jack to hold the door for her when Lily woke up.

"KT, I'm so glad you dropped in. Didja meet my friend, Shack?" She was just awake enough to try to carry on a conversation. "Let's buy Shack a drink, KT," she said, trying to lean Kathryne toward the bar.

"The bar is closed, Lily," Kathryne explained. With Jack on one side and Kathryne on the other, they managed to get Lily into her car.

"Someone will pick up my car in the morning." Kathryne said, deciding that her tan Thunderbird might have a better chance of making it through the night than Lily's red Corvette convertible.

Jack smiled. "It'll be fine here tonight. I'm gonna bed down in the back, so it'll be safe enough."

"Thank you, Jack," she said, trying to maneuver Lily's car out of the parking lot.

"Weren't no trouble, ma'am. Kinda fun, tell ya the truth."

Lily passed out again as soon as she hit the car seat. Kathryne got lost twice on the way, but finally managed to get Lily home and awake enough to get her up the stairs to her bedroom.

"What in the name of God is wrong, Lily?" Kathryne asked as Lily began to sober and wake up. "You nearly scared the shit out of me!"

Kathryne was trying to help Lily get her clothes off. "Oh, my head. I'm gonna be sick," cried Lily, heading for the bathroom. Kathryne held a cold washcloth to Lily's head, just as her mother had done for her when she was a little girl. Lily vomited and cried, cried and vomited. The bathroom smelled like sour mash, and Kathryne was beginning to feel like vomiting herself.

Finally getting her stomach to stop heaving, Lily rinsed her face with cold water. "OK, kid, hit the shower," said Kathryne with authority. "While you're in there, I'm going downstairs and make a big pot of coffee. I want to hear what brought all this on."

"Oh my God, how could things get so screwed up?" thought Kathryne. She was in that same living room of Lily's where they had worked out the plan to buy the Gayle White Advertising Agency. Now Lily sat there in her white terry-cloth robe crying hysterically.

"Are you sure?"

"Yes, how many times do I have to say it? I am pregnant. I am sure. I am pregnant!" cried Lily.

"Does Bill know?"

"No!" Lily cried even louder. "He will never know, either, and I have no intentions of marrying him or any noble thing like that!" With that Lily, laid her head on her arm and cried harder. "I don't want this baby," she spluttered through the sleeve of her robe. "I never want children. I don't like them!"

Lily's face was swollen from crying. Her hair was stringy. A more helpless, pathetic face there never was than the one Kathryne looked into as Lily said, "KT, please help me. All I want to do is go away, have the baby, and give it up for adoption. Then I can come back to work and forget this whole damn nightmare ever happened."

Three days later Lily and Kathryne arrived at the Daytona Beach airport in Florida. Poor Lily had thrown up four times during the flight and still looked pale.

The cute flight attendant was so nice to Lily. She and Kathryne cleaned up after Lily every time she was sick, and the older flight attendant kept bringing cold cloths with instructions to put them on Lily's throat to make her feel better. The other passengers in first class commented that they had never seen anyone so airsick.

Lily was so embarrassed that all she could do between bouts of throwing up was sob. Although it was a normal one-hour flight from Atlanta to Daytona, Kathryne felt that the trip should go in the *Guinness Book of World Records* as the longest flight ever made.

Their plans were to look at the beach house Kathryne had told Lily about. After picking up their rental car, they headed down A1A. "How far down here is this place?" Lily groaned as she stretched out, making a recliner of the seat.

"New Smyrna Beach stays relatively undeveloped because of the restrictive zoning," said Kathryne trying to get Lily's mind on something else besides the reason they were there. She continued the explanation to her pale, impatient passenger. "Apparently the city fathers wanted to make sure it did not turn into another Daytona Beach. Also, the city has never approved another bridge to the mainland, making it more difficult to reach. That, my dear, is why it takes so long to get there."

"Well, thank you Mrs. Know-It-All, Smyrna Beach!" Lily snorted.

The sharp remark caught Kathryne by surprise, and she turned suddenly toward Lily. Lily glared back for a moment. Then the love between them broke through, and they started laughing. "I guess I was on one of my toots, huh?" Kathryne said through the laughter.

"And I was being a bitch!" exclaimed Lily, tossing her hair back as if to throw off her bad mood.

They rode along, smelling the sea air and listening to the waves hit the beach. The narrow winding road with its thirty-mile-an-hour speed limit and beautiful palm trees forced the two women to relax and go with the flow. "KT," Lily began after a long silence, "Herb Grossman, the attorney I use in Atlanta, is arranging everything for the adoption."

"Lil," Kathryne interrupted, "are you sure?"

"Listen, Kathryne!" Lily flared up. "So help me God, if you ask me that again, I am going to—"

"OK, OK, I'm sorry. No more, I promise. You are a grown woman and know what you want to do."

"As I was saying before I was so rudely interrupted," Lily continued with a raised eyebrow look to Kathryne. "Herb is handling everything for me. He says he has a, to quote Herb, 'wonderful couple' who are dying for a baby."

"Will you get to meet them and interview them or anything?" Kathryne inquired, knowing that her next question would be, "Can I come?"

"Oh no, that isn't the way it is done," Lily said. "Don't you know anything about adoptions? Herb has checked them out completely and will handle everything. He will notify them when the baby is born and where to pick it up." Turning to Kathryne with a look of "I dare you to approach me on this again," she said, "and that will be that!"

Just as Kathryne stared to make another comment on the situation, Lily said, "Look, KT, there's an oasis." She was pointing to a little ice cream stand just ahead on the right. "Let's get an ice cream cone." So they stopped at the ice cream stand, and the subject was closed.

◦◣◦

"It's perfect," Lily said in a flat tone of voice.

"Listen Lil," Kathryne said, "I'll be down here every chance I get. It won't be so bad really."

"Easy for you to say."

When Kathryne and Lily had pulled into 75 Sailfish Drive about an hour earlier, an unexpected longing for Andy overwhelmed them both. Lily did not want to tell Andy about the pregnancy. She said it would upset him, because he loved children so much. Andy's wife, Pearl, had had three miscarriages, and he knew they would never have children. When Andy told them of his agony each time Pearl lost a baby, tears welled in his eyes. She did not want to break open any old wounds, and she sure did not want to hear another lecture about her decision. The three of them had become unbelievably close. The problems each of them had endured—Lily's horrid experience with her mother and sister, mixed with the confusion she felt about her Indian father and the loss of Tommy; Kathryne's disgusting marriage and heartbreaking experiences with Becky; and Andy's background of racial prejudices, torn between the white race he looked like and the black family he loved so dearly—gave them a closeness incomprehensible to anyone else.

"KT, where are you?" Lily yelled impatiently. Lily found her friend on the deck, looking at the ocean. Lily began throwing her arms around in the Indian-war-dance way she had of expressing herself. "It's perfect. It will work. Now, let's get outta here."

"And perfect it is," thought Kathryne as she closed the doors that opened onto the deck. "A one-bedroom hideaway on the Atlantic Ocean," the ad had read. The little house sat back off the road behind a clump of palmettos. The main room was like a big family room with cathedral ceilings, wood floors, a fireplace, and French doors covering the entire front facing the ocean. The bedroom was large and roomy. Beach pictures covered the wall. Pine decking ran across the front of the house, and steps led down through the sea oats to the beach.

Kathryne would have loved to stay a couple of days, but Lily was already in the car. She was sitting out there like a reluctant Indian chief being led off to the reservation.

"God help us all," said Kathryne aloud as she started for the car and a long trip home.

chapter

FIFTEEN

Two subjects, Lily's condition and Bill Dressler, were forbidden. Lily hated the situation she was in and found it difficult to hold her tears and her temper. She was embarrassed each time she had to excuse herself in the middle of a morning meeting to go to the ladies' room and throw up. Kathryne continually tried to cheer her up.

"I can't wait to tell Lil about this," thought Kathryne excitedly as she stared proudly at the signature of the president of Coca-Cola. They worked night and day for two months on this one. The ideas between the two of them flowed strong and endless, like a river current. They knew their client would love it. The advertising game was a hard, continually changing business. They were always aware of being women in a man's world. Keeping a jump on the competition meant never letting it leave your mind. Never relaxing a minute, and never, never taking anything for granted. That is what made Kathryne and Lily so good. They went to movies and conventions, and they often took Becky to the coast, but they always worked business into fun or fun into business, whichever way it was.

When Kathryne got back, she burst into Lily's office, waving the signed contract, singing, "We're in the money!"

"Whoopee!" shouted Lily. They uncorked bottles of champagne and served everyone in the office. The whole art department was ready to collapse from exhaustion from putting the proposal together for this account. Lily gave them the rest of the day off.

"Do you think Dan knows yet?" asked Pete, one of the most talented artists Kathryne had ever worked with. He was talking about Dan Spencer, his former employer.

Dan owned and operated Progressive Advertising Agency, Lily and Kathryne's biggest competitor in Atlanta. Dan was good at what he did, but he was a real son of a bitch. He was the type of businessperson who gave meaning to the phrase "dog-eat-dog." Kathryne had not really run into him but had heard the horror stories of those who had. She and Lily had been able to keep about a half a step ahead of Dan so far, but their goal was to widen that step to a mile. The local Coca-Cola account would get them closer to that goal. Dan's agency and an agency from New York had also vied for the account. The president of Coca-Cola had told Kathryne he liked her ideas because they were fresh and new. Dan Spencer would just have to get used to losing accounts to the Langford Gray Advertising Agency.

Early the next morning, Kathryne was sitting at her desk going over the final copy of a perfume layout when the door burst open. Without a doubt it was Lily. She was the only one who ever did that.

"KT, it's me." announced Lily. "It's time to go."

"I didn't have anything written down," replied a puzzled Kathryne, checking her appointment book.

Lily closed the door tightly behind her and rushed to Kathryne's desk. "I can't zip my black leather pants!"

Their eyes met and then Kathryne realized what Lily was telling her. "Already?" Where had the time gone? How could three months slip by so quickly?

"I plan to go this Saturday. That will give me three days to get things cleared up here. Of course, I'll be able to do some work from the beach house. Lord knows I will need something to do."

"You want to drive down, right?" asked Kathryne rising from her oversize chair.

"Yes, I'll want my car there." For some reason all of a sudden, she felt a little strange about asking Kathryne to help her. She had been such a bitch. Maybe her best friend was sick of the whole thing.

"KT, would you mind—that is, if you're not busy this weekend—driving down with me?"

"Lily, I've planned on it. You didn't have to ask."

"Oh, KT." Lily began to cry. "What would I do without you? You're always here for me. You always understand. My family never—"

"Oh, cut it out!" Kathryne put her arm around Lily, and they sat down on the white leather couch. Lily cried harder, letting out the anguish she held in over the last few months.

"KT, I am so scared. I don't want to go through this. I'll be so lonely," Lily spluttered between sobs.

"I will be there so much you will never get a chance to be lonely," Kathryne whispered, trying to console Lily. She brushed Lily's black mane from around her wet eyes and cradled and soothed her like a mother. Lily felt the strength coming from Kathryne and accepted the handful of Kleenex in front of her. She knew, as they had so many things in the past, they would get through this together.

The phone on Kathryne's desk rang, and they both jumped. "Kathryne Langford."

"Hey, kid, it's Andy. Can anyone there have dinner with me Saturday night?"

"Andy! Hey, yourself." Kathryne searched her mind for a reply. "You will never guess what just happened!"

Lily pulled herself together as she listed to the imagination that made Kathryne a leader in her field. She was explaining to Andy how the European account they worked on for over a year finally came through and how excited they were. Lily could hear Andy's voice coming through the receiver, full of questions and excitement.

"Yes, yes!" Kathryne was saying. "Lily is leaving right away. They want her there by Monday, so she is flying out Saturday."

By now, Lily was signaling Kathryne not to tell Andy she was there. Andy wanted to know more, and Kathryne promised to tell him all about it. He was disappointed to hear she had other plans Saturday night. She assured him Lily was planning to call him before she left.

"What am I going to do in Atlanta Saturday night all by myself?" Andy kidded her.

"Change your appointment to next week," Kathryne retorted.

"By golly, that's just what I'll do! See you Saturday week." He laughed and hung up on an astonished Kathryne.

Lily sniffed. "Whew."

"The nut," said Kathryne.

What a gorgeous day for a journey to Incarceration City," thought Lily as she double-checked the lock on her front door. She strapped a single dark-blue suitcase onto the back luggage rack and took a long look around. Apparently satisfied with the memory she found necessary to store within her mind, she crawled into her sports car to start the longest ordeal of her life.

Joe and Becky were coming out the front door when Lily pulled into the treelined, circular driveway. She waved at Becky. "How's my girl?" She gave her a big hug on the way in the house.

"Hi, Joe. KT ready?"

"If you are referring to Kathryne, she is upstairs," he snarled.

"Thanks, I'll just go on up," Lily muttered with contempt. She patted Becky on the back, gave her a big grin, and went into the house.

"Hey, are you up here?" she called, ascending the stairs.

"Yeah! Come on up. I'll just be one more minute." Kathryne's voice rang from her bathroom.

Lily watched from the upstairs window as Joe and Becky loaded the station wagon. Poor Kathryne, she thought. She realized the only thing that came to mind when she looked at Joe was a slimy slug. Although he was really a good father to Becky, she wondered why Kathryne stayed with him.

"Where are Joe and Becky off to?"

"Joe is taking her on a weekend camping trip sponsored by the therapy clinic. The children really love these trips. There are games and other activities for all the children, according to their level of comprehension and dexterity. Next month, it is the mothers' turn to go," she huffed, finally getting her suitcase closed.

Lily was dressed for a long trip in casual, wide-legged slacks, a matching, rust-colored top, and low-heeled shoes. "Is Joe mad because you are going with me?" She was trying to help Kathryne down the stairs with her luggage, but Kathryne insisted she shouldn't be lifting anything in her condition.

"Who knows—or cares, for that matter—about Joe? He has such a negative attitude, anyway. What difference does it make?"

After Kathryne hugged and kissed Becky good-bye, Joe pulled the station wagon out of the driveway, turning north for Camp Setting Sun. Kathryne loaded her suitcase on the back of the Corvette with Lily's.

The drive to Florida was fun. Both gals talked nonstop about the agency, layouts, and the new script writer. They stopped to eat and sang along with the radio, but never mentioned the reason for the trip.

The stretch of highway from Daytona to New Smyrna Beach seemed to unfold endlessly before the headlights of Lily's little red car. The constant roar of the ocean combined with the shadows cast by the full moon began to give Lily a feeling of hollow longing. She already felt homesick; now desperation was setting in fast. If only she could awaken from this horrible nightmare, she thought. About that time, the beach house came into view.

They wrestled their luggage from the car. "I can't believe you only brought one bag, Lily."

"I only need a few things to get by. I will buy more clothes as the need arises, if you know what I mean." She might as well have said, "Oh, hell, KT, I won't need much here in solitary confinement."

The house had a musty smell that dissipated once the doors were opened and the ocean air filtered in. The women were exhausted, and after hot showers they collapsed on the double bed in the only bedroom. They slept side by side like sisters, neither one moving until just before dawn.

"Let's go watch the sun come up," whispered Kathryne when Lily stirred. She had been awake for about thirty minutes watching Lily sleep, wishing she were the one pregnant.

They wrapped blankets around their shoulders, went outside and sat on the deck in the dark like two lizards waiting for the first fly. The waves pounded the shore as if to say, "It's coming! It's coming!" A mist hovering at the horizon turned deep pink... then, slowly and beautifully came peeping over the water. Streaks of color hit the sky like outstretched arms.

Whoever said that God is dead would have changed their mind had they been on the deck that morning. As the sun continued to rise, it created a golden pathway on the water to somewhere in the future. Kathryne and Lily were filled with promise as they left the deck in full light for the kitchen and a cup of coffee.

"What time does your plane leave tomorrow, KT?" asked Lily. She stood in front of the dresser mirror brushing her long tresses.

"Noon. That will give me time to help you go to the grocery and get settled."

"KT, I am not an invalid. I will manage," snapped Lily. Kathryne made no comment and went back to the kitchen to make a grocery list.

"KT, I'm sorry." Lily slid into the kitchen. She leaned against the refrigerator. "I am acting like such a bitch. I'll do better, I swear. I am just so damn mad, and I don't have anyone to be mad at but myself. And, of course, the drug company that makes those stupid pills. Oh well, let's go get something to eat. I am as hungry as a wolf, as Gray Dove would say."

They drove down Highway A1A to the little town of New Smyrna Beach and stopped at the Red Rooster for breakfast. It was a small cafe in a remodeled house with red-gingham curtains and terrazzo floors.

"Mornin', ladies." The statuesque waitress greeted them. Setting down the coffee cups on the plastic red-and-white-checked tablecloth, she said, "Here's your menus. Ah'll be back to get y'all's orders in just a sec." They could hear her chewing gum popping as she hurried away.

"Mmm, everything sounds so good." Lily was almost drooling. Kathryne giggled behind her menu, remembering that only a few weeks ago, Lily wouldn't have touched breakfast.

The tall, cheerful brunette returned about the time Lily finished reading everything on the menu aloud to Kathryne. She had never seen Lily so excited about food.

"Y'all ready?" Pop! Snap! went her chewing gum. Kathryne wondered how she could talk, chew, and smile at the same time.

"Yes, I will have the 'He-man Breakfast', a side order of bacon, and extra hash browns. Oh, and extra biscuits, too, please," Lily replied cheerfully.

"I will have orange juice and an English muffin," said Kathryne under a look from Lily.

After watching Lily eat enough for a tribe of warriors, Kathryne wanted to browse through the small shops nearby and enjoy the view of the sand dunes. They found a grocery store and got everything Lily would need for a while. After the awful mess she ate at the Red Rooster, Kathryne was relieved to see that her purchases included an array of nutritious items except for the pork rinds she insisted on eating before they left the store. They did a little sightseeing on the way back to the house, and the rest of the day was spent basking in the sun.

En route to the Daytona Airport the next day, Lily said she told Bill he should find someone else. She was going to Europe for a year to fulfill a lifelong dream.

"How did he take it?" Kathryne wanted to know.

"He was pretty upset. But you know Bill. He accused me of having someone else."

"Lily, are you sure you shouldn't tell him?" asked Kathryne, knowing she was treading thin ice.

"No, I have thought it over to the ends of the earth and back, and it has just got to be this way. By the way, not that they care where I am or what I am doing, but just in case someone from Owensboro should call, tell them the same thing." Kathryne knew she meant her mother. "KT, promise me...this is our secret. No one but us will ever know. OK?"

"If that is the way you want it, you have my word."

That afternoon Lily's finger traced her diamond bracelet as she watched, through tear-filled eyes, her best friend's plane take off. Before going back to the beach house, she found the Halifax General Hospital where she would have her baby. Dr. Thomas had been helpful, finding her a good doctor in New Smryna and sending him her records.

She drove through the parking lot, checking the emergency entrance used by women in labor. The hospital was small, fairly new, but quaint. Compared to the huge hospitals in Atlanta, it reminded Lily of a hospital in an old movie where the leading lady would go to recover or die from some dreaded disease.

The first night alone at the beach house was the most devastatingly lonely time she ever spent in her entire life. The night following her father's death brought with it a deep abiding emptiness, but the aching aloneness she felt throughout the night in this strange, faraway place was worse.

The unfamiliar sounds in and outside the house, the peculiar smells surrounding her, and the unknowns of the future kept Lily up most of the night. Who was the poet who talked about sweet relief? He must have known what it would feel like to see daylight after such a night.

The days and nights began to flow together and meld into one. Lily was so homesick she was literally ill. The only contact she had with the outside world for two weeks was a daily phone call from Kathryne. Standing in front of her dresser, Lily stared with disgust at her growing figure in the mirror.

"There is nothing I can do to stop this," she said aloud. "I cannot quit living, and I won't be a hermit!"

She flung back the drapes to a beautiful morning. The sun was a luminous medallion hanging in front of a crystal-blue backdrop. "You are too wonderful to ignore!" she told the day.

Back at her dresser mirror, Lily put on her makeup for the first time since she got there two weeks ago. She pulled her thick, black hair up into a ponytail and tied it with a white ribbon. Dressed in a pair of loose-fitting pink pants and matching, oversized top, she felt ready to meet the world again.

Lily spent the day poking around town. She picked up a few trinkets in the shell shop and stocked herself with magazines. Her mental attitude had come full circle. She felt healed and somehow no longer so confused. She would take good care of herself and enjoy this beautiful place! Gray Dove's advice from many years past rang in her ears, "Make the most of what you have."

She began to get up early every morning and walk along the beach for a few miles. She wanted to keep as much of her figure as possible. Dr. Nash told her that walking was the best thing she could do to help retain her shape, and she wanted to be able to return to work as soon after the baby was born as possible.

It was the middle of October. The strong sun of the summer was gone now, setting an ideal stage for late afternoon walks. Actually, it was a perfect time for a stay at the beach. Usually her end of the beach was deserted when she walked, but today she saw someone in the distance bent over something in the sand. Lily hurried her pace to see what was going on. As she approached, she saw a very handsome man trying to revive a small black kitten, of all things. The kitten was very skinny and Lily thought that it was probably dead.

"Hi. Can I help?" Lily asked. The poor creature lay prostrate in the sand.

"I don't know if anyone can," he answered. "Poor fella looks like he just dropped here from hunger. He needs something to eat pretty bad. Do you live around here?" he asked bluntly.

"Yes, about a half a mile back up the beach. We can take him there if you like. I have some milk and maybe even a can of tuna fish."

"Great," he replied anxiously. They started up the beach, he carrying the sick kitten, and Lily wondering if he couldn't walk a little faster.

"By the way, my name is Lily. What's yours?"

"Mike Carrozza. Nice to meet you."

"Here we are," said Lily, motioning to her entrance from the beach. "I'll run ahead to get the door open. Then we can fix something for the kitty."

Mike and Lily worked with the kitten for over an hour, force feeding him slowly until life finally began to seep back into his tiny body. He was beautifully marked. He had slick black fur and white feet that made it look like he was wearing socks. He had a white mark on his forehead resembling a star, reminding Lily of something you would see on a racehorse.

"You seem to know a lot about the care of animals," Lily said to Mike as she fixed them each a glass of freshly squeezed orange juice.

"I studied veterinary medicine in college," Mike was standing at the sliding door, looking out at the ocean. "The setting here is something else. Lily, are you here on vacation?"

"Yes," Lily exhaled. She walked toward him, still holding her glass of juice. "Let's go out and sit on the deck for a while."

Then she asked, "What about you, Mike? Are you here on vacation?"

"Yes," he replied in the same flat tone. They each chose a chair, and Mike sighed as he relaxed.

"Do you think he will live? The kitten, I mean," she asked.

"It's too soon to tell, but we have done all we can for him. Cute little guy, huh?"

There was an uncomfortable silence that Lily finally broke. "It's getting about dinner time. Why don't I put a couple of steaks on the grill? I mean, if you don't have to go. I just hate to eat alone."

"Oh, I really shouldn't," Mike said.

Lily interrupted. "I feel so foolish. Of course, you must have plans...your wife is expecting—"

"No, no wife. Actually, I would love to stay." Mike said with finality. He was not much taller than Lily. A stocky build made him appear somewhat shorter, and his warm, handsome face made him immediately likable. He looked right at home on the beach with his sandy-blond hair and sharp blue eyes. His easy manner and interesting accent were so comfortable they made her forget Mike was a complete stranger.

Mike made himself at home, helping Lily fix the salad. She couldn't believe how natural it seemed to be with him. She spread a white cotton tablecloth over the small, round table by the window overlooking the ocean and lit two vanilla-scented candles. He had been assigned steak duty and was bringing them from the grill just as she finished setting the table.

"Hey, you are going to a lot of trouble here, aren't you? This looks great."

"No trouble. I am just delighted to have a dinner companion." Lily smiled, looking through her favorite eight tracks she brought from home.

"Mike, do you like the Beatles?" she called.

"My faves."

"Good, you are gonna hear 'em," Lily called as she popped Let It Be into the player.

The evening went by all too fast for Lily. She was starved for conversation, and Mike was able to talk about so many different subjects. He seemed so wise for his years. She guessed him to be about thirty-five.

"The steak was delicious, Mike."

"Thank you, madam," he said, making a swooping bow from the waist. "Would madam care for anything else?"

Lily found herself really laughing again, and it felt good. They sang with the tapes and even did a few dance steps as they cleaned the kitchen together. The loose-fitting top she wore made her look more heavyset than pregnant. If Mike noticed her condition, he did not let on.

"Lily, it's getting late. I had better get going. If you'd like, I will stop by tomorrow to check on our little friend." He was squatted over the box where they had made the kitten a bed. Socks, as they had named him, was sleeping soundly and even purred a little when Mike scratched his head.

"Please do. Do you think he will be OK?" She asked walking him to the door.

"He should be OK in a couple of days as he regains his strength. Thanks so much for a wonderful evening, Lily. I really enjoyed myself."

"So did I," admitted Lily. They said good night, and she watched Mike walk up the beach in the dark. During dinner he had drawn her a little map of where he lived in proximity to her house. It was two blocks from the beach about a half a mile up.

Lily picked up the box that held the recovering Socks and took it in the bedroom with her for the night. She set her alarm clock to get up in three hours to feed him, like a little baby. She couldn't wait to tell Kathryne about her two new friends.

Bill Dressler was not going to buy the story Lily gave him about the European ad campaign and extended trip. His constant calls to the office and to Kathryne's private phone line at home were beginning to be more than she could handle. Each call became more demanding and now, almost threatening. Kathryne knew this problem would not be dismissed easily. She had kept the calls from Lily, not wanting to upset her in any way.

Bill had been devastated when Lily returned his two-carat ring and told him she would not marry him. She told Kathryne that suggesting to go to the Premier House, a very affluent restaurant where Bill was well acquainted with the owner, seemed like an excellent way to avoid a bad scene. She had been wrong.

Lily told him, as gently as possible, that she was going to Paris for a lengthy ad campaign for a new client and then planned to travel through Europe, alone. She told him she was very sorry, but she realized she just was not in love with him. A marriage would be unfair to them both.

He just could not understand it. He had everything to offer her. Money, prestige, security. There had to be something else... someone else. He would make it his life's goal to find out who it was and destroy him. No other man was going to have Lily.

Lily told Kathryne how loud and crude Bill had gotten at the Premier House that night. His temper had mounted to a pivotal point. He pushed his chair back and jumped up. Circling the candlelit, linen-draped table holding the ring up for everyone in the restaurant to see, he called her a slut at the top of his lungs. He acted insane. None too soon, Bill's friend, the owner of the restaurant, subdued him and talked him into going to the back office with him. As they walked out of the dining room, Bill was mumbling, "...ungrateful little bitch, anyway."

During all the commotion, a mortified Lily managed to slip out unnoticed and hail a cab. Afraid Bill might show up at her house later, she stayed the night at the Hilton.

Lily assured Bill there was no one else. But there was. It was herself. After the scene at Valerie's house, the death of Tommy, and now this accidental pregnancy, she realized it was time to take charge of her life. Yes, she could marry Bill, keep the baby, and live just as Maggie Lou and Kathryne had done. A loveless, restraining marriage was not her cup of tea. The young, lost life of Tommy brought home the vulnerability of one's own existence. Lily still wanted it all. But, first she had to get this baby out of the way.

Kathryne and Andy were in the projection room, previewing the new campaign for his convenience stores, when the door suddenly crashed open. Bill charged in like a maniac. His hair hung on his sweaty face, and he was breathing so heavily spittle splattered onto his chin.

Theda, hot on his heels, was yelling, "Sir, you can't go in there! Sir! Sir! Shall I call security?" she asked Kathryne frantically. Kathryne gave her a nod.

Bill demanded a way to contact Lily. A phone number, an address. He was shaking his fist in her face when Andy stepped from behind the projector.

"Lily doesn't want to see you."

"The nigger and the white whore! So you are both in on this. I bet you talked her into giving my ring back, too!" He was out of control. Bill inched toward Andy, flexing his fists.

"Will you stop bothering Kathryne if we give you Lily's address?"

"Andy, no!" Kathryne begged.

Andy took a note pad and scribbled down an address in Paris. Shoving it in Bill's hand, he took his arm, spun him around, and shoved him toward the door. Bill calmed down immediately. It was as if someone had thrown a switch and cut off the juice. He was leaving just at the security guards arrived. Kathryne asked them to make sure he got in his car and left.

"What address did you give him?" Kathryne gasped.

"Oh, let's just say he is in for one helluva surprise when the door opens." His eyes were lit with boyish mischief.

The surprise Bill got at Lorraine's bordello was a doozy. He picked out a girl who resembled Lily, but he treated her so violently that he was removed from the premises.

chapter

SIXTEEN

Mike stopped by the next day to check on the sick feline just as he had promised. Socks was eating solid food and walking around a little bit. Mike assured Lily that he would be frisky within a couple of days.

Lily and Mike walked along the beach and made small talk about nothing. She thought he seemed evasive and wondered if he thought the same about her. During their nightly phone call, Lily told Kathryne about him. "The only thing I know for sure is that he is from Boston. I guessed that from his accent. Wonder what he is hiding, down here alone and all. I mean, what if he's a hatchet murderer, and he's here laying low?"

Kathryne interrupted before the mystery got out of hand. "Have you been reading those detective magazines again? Has he asked you any questions?"

"Not even one."

"Has he said anything about himself?"

"No, nothing."

"Hmm…Wonder what he is up to," Kathryne mused.

"Ha! Now listen to you!" Lily laughed.

"Well, I'll get a chance to meet him this weekend and see for myself. Give Socks a scratch behind the ear for me. Take care of yourself."

Lily was looking forward to this weekend. She wanted Kathryne to meet Mike. She knew if anybody could get Mike's story out of him, it would be Kathryne. Lily and Socks watched the eleven o'clock news and sipped their nightly milk. The news report was depressing, still full of news about Vietnam. She wondered if Vietnam would just drag on forever. She missed Tommy and was deeply saddened for the POWs, MIAs, and their families. She wondered who the winners would be, if any. Half an hour into the late movie, Lily was bored and decided to call it a night. Socks agreed with the decision and settled immediately into his bed. He was somewhat stronger, but Lily still pampered and spoiled him.

She felt restless and uncomfortable. Thoughts of Mike, the baby, home, and Gray Dove tumbled together in her mind. She thought of Christmas and spending it alone in a strange place, and wondered how could she ever explain to Gray Dove that she couldn't spend the holidays with her. She also wished Mike would still be there. But how could he? No one stayed on vacation that long. Tears stung her eyes. She was feeling sorry for herself. Angry for letting it get the best of her, she got out of bed and walked onto the deck. The ocean was beautiful. The full moon cast a spotlight on the waves. A movement on the beach startled her. A lone figure was moving along the water's edge. She reached just inside the door for the binoculars she had bought to watch the birds and the big ships out on the ocean. She held them to her eyes hoping the moonlight would be adequate. The crisp night wind blowing her hair and the sound of the waves breaking made her feel adventurous. She could see now. It was Mike on the beach.

Why would he come to her house so late? She had never been afraid at the beach house, and in spite of her conversation with Kathryne about the hatchet murderer, she was not afraid of Mike either. But, Mike wasn't coming toward her. He walked slowly, almost aimlessly. The moonlight was so bright Lily could see the painful expression on his face.

She slowly removed the glasses from her eyes and watched as the figure faded from her sight. Staring down the empty beach after him, Lily wondered if Mike really did have something to hide.

The weekend came early with Kathryne's arrival Friday afternoon. Ever thoughtful of Lily's condition, Kathryne did everything she could to make the situation easier for her best friend. She even rented a car at the airport to save Lily the inconvenience. Lily was overjoyed to see that Kathryne had come stocked with office work and bags of her beloved pork rinds, which could only be found at Freddy's in Atlanta.

While Kathryne changed from her business attire into white shorts and a coral top, Lily signed contracts and looked over layouts. They finally settled on the deck with a snack of cheese, fruit, and fresh lemonade.

"Lily, you look wonderful," Kathryne remarked while Lily sliced the apples. "Maybe you should keep a little weight after the baby comes."

"KT, now you are being just plain ridiculous." She dropped a piece of apple in her lemonade. She was the only real friend Lily had in the world. Otherwise, she might have smacked her. "How are you doing at the office?"

"Pretty hectic, but I will get by. We all miss you."

"I am glad you didn't say, 'Just fine, thanks.'" Lily laughed.

Kathryne was very upbeat and talked about Becky and the beautiful weather. She omitted telling her that Joe had lost another job and was home in a drunken stupor most of the time. Nor did she mention the phone calls from Bill, who threatened, then begged, and finally demanded to know Lily's whereabouts.

"Have you bought any new clothes?" Lily asked jealously.

"Not a stitch. I'm waiting for our big shopping spree when you come home."

"Ooooh, I just can't wait to buy something sluttishly tight!" Lily dramatized the effect by showing off her protruding profile. Their howls of laughter woke Socks from his afternoon nap in the sun. He stretched slowly and sauntered toward Kathryne, who scooped him up for some serious stroking. He was purring like a diesel engine when Kathryne asked, "So, what about Mike?"

"It seems to be a closed door. We have seen each other almost every day since we met, and I only know what I told you on the phone the other night. I think he is in some kind of trouble."

"Why?"

"I've seen him on the beach at one and two in the morning, just walking." Lily struggled out of her lounge chair. "Let's do some walking ourselves."

"That makes him in trouble?"

Socks decided to have his lunch, as Kathryne joined Lily and his personal petting session came to an end.

"It makes him mysterious, don't you think? I mean, he walks the beach twice a day with me, so it isn't that he needs the exercise. Wait till you meet him tonight. I'm anxious to get your opinion. Maybe he's in the new witness protection program for the FBI for something."

"One thing for sure, Lily, you have one healthy imagination."

They walked up the beach talking about everything and everybody they knew. Lily wanted the latest on Becky and the office. Kathryne, in competition with the roar of the breaking waves on a windy day, was almost hoarse by the time they reached the cottage.

Mike brought fresh shrimp, which Lily made into kabobs for the grill. Mike did most of the cooking and entertained them with funny little stories. It was wonderful for Kathryne to be able to talk and laugh about everyday things like finding a kitten on the beach. She felt guilty for secretly wishing Lily had longer to go before the baby came. She would miss these desperately needed weekends of total freedom.

Kathryne and Mike hit it off immediately. She liked the way he took care of everything. He was so comfortable there, and he and Lily looked so good together. They seemed like a married couple, and Lily actually seemed happy.

Feeling at ease with Mike, she shot questions at him as if he were a guest on *60 Minutes* in an effort to shake loose some details. He, in his cunningly brilliant ability to banter, gave Kathryne no more of a clue than he had Lily. About midnight, after an evening of fun, kabobs, and Beatles, Mike left the two laughing at a cornball joke he had pantomimed for them.

The next morning, the three drove up to Daytona and spent the day sightseeing and browsing the boardwalk. Feeling exhausted after a full day, Lily stretched out in the back seat and slept all the way home. Kathryne studied Mike. Was Lily safe with him? After all, the beach was pretty deserted this time of the year, and no one would be around for help if she needed it—if he did turn out to be a hatchet murderer. He was hiding something, but Kathryne decided it was nothing as spectacular as Lily surmised. A last-minute change of heart before the wedding, maybe, or even a divorce. Kathryne was sure it was something along those lines as she drove along, unaware that Mike was studying her as well.

A picnic Sunday came and went and with it came the time to go home for Kathryne. The women always choked up when they parted, and today was no different. Kathryne felt more at ease with Mike and, concluding that he was a good, caring person, felt better about knowing he was there if Lily needed help.

As Kathryne stepped off the plane in Atlanta, a sinking feeling came over her at the thought of what was waiting at home. She envied Lily.

Mike and Lily became constant companions. They were both going through a disturbing period in their lives. She would still see him walking alone many nights after he left her. Recently, his mind seemed to be elsewhere when they talked. He seemed so troubled. Finally, her genuine concern led her to start asking the first questions.

They had just spent a full day in St. Augustine. Lily had wanted to see the oldest city in the United States. They stopped in all the little shops, squeezed along the narrow brick streets and laughed their way through Ripley's Believe It or Not! Museum. Lily especially liked the Fountain of Youth and the Indian burial ground at the twenty-one-acre park that claimed to be the landing site of Ponce de Leon in 1513. They went through the oldest framed schoolhouse in the United States and toured the ancient fort. They spent their day down to the last minute.

Lily was exhausted as she lowered herself into the passenger seat of her car. Mike loved driving her Corvette, and tonight she could not have been happier to give him the wheel. They turned south onto US Route 1. The top was down, making Lily feel that she could touch the stars. Several miles into the trip home, Lily felt rested and wanted to talk.

"What's bothering you, Mike?"

"Nothing. Just a little tired, I guess."

"I don't mean right now. I mean what's the deal?"

"I don't know what you mean."

"Come on, Mike. I mean, who are you? What are you doing here?"

"I don't know—"

"Don't give me 'I don'ts.' We have been together every day for, well, I forget how long. I know your name is Mike Carrozza, you are from Boston, which I guessed by the way, and that you were going to be a vet. Period. End of story." They drove a few miles in silence. The ocean's roar and the night air, antidotes for Lily's tension, made her determined to get it out of him. "Mike, talk to me. I have seen you walking the beach at ungodly hours. Lately you're not here when I talk to you. We spend almost every waking hour together, but we don't know anything about each other."

"I know you're pregnant," He said, trying to get Lily to let up.

"That's quite obvious, since my stomach sticks out almost to the dashboard of this car. However, do you realize that is the first time you have ever mentioned it? Could it be that you are afraid to ask me questions, because you know mine will follow?"

Mike took a long, deep breath. Lily thought that he was finally going to talk to her, but he said. "Let's stop here for dinner. I hear their seafood is great." He was pulling into the crowded parking lot of a little restaurant. The light of the neon sign fluttered like a temptress's eyelashes. He totally ignored her questions.

"It will be about fifteen minutes," said the hostess. The crowd at the Seafood Shack had Lily's full attention. People were stuffed into every corner, and the waiting area was full.

"Your name, sir?"

"Carrozza."

"Thank you, Mr.Carrozza, I'll be right back with a chair for Mrs. Carrozza.

Lily started to correct the perky young girl then blushed as she realized what a warm feeling being called Mrs. Carrozza induced. Mike called Lily honey and, when the waitress asked when she was due, proudly announced it was their fifth baby. Lily could not keep from laughing although she wanted to get some answers tonight.

"Damn you, Mike Carrozza," she said over dinner.

"For what?"

"For changing the subject, stopping here, and making me laugh."

"Oh, don't you like the flounder? Mine is good. And isn't the atmosphere just enchanting? Yes, we do need to talk." He took another bite of fish and a drink of wine, wiped his mouth, and began.

"My name is Michael Anthony Carrozza. From Boston, thirty years old, the youngest of four brothers, and I'm a priest."

"A priest!" Her hand dropped. Coleslaw flew in the air. Hush puppies hit the floor and rolled like shooter-struck marbles. The waitress trotted up just as Mike decided to have a good time.

"Honey, is it time? Do you need to stretch out?" he asked a bewildered Lily. "We may have to clear out a section here quickly," he explained to the waitress who was frozen to the spot, having a horrifying thought of being asked to assist in the delivery of a baby on the dining room floor. "Honey, I was hoping this baby could be born in a hospital. She has them so quickly. Our other four were, let's see, one was at the museum…" The waitress thawed and made a dead run for the manager.

"Mike, you are a maniac! That poor girl." Lily was trying to get the table back in order so they could get out without further attention. The manager appeared by their table as if beamed in by Scotty. He appeared to be holding his heart, his stomach, and his breath.

"I guess I'm a little jumpy," Mike explained after Lily had assured the lipless, very pale man that she was clumsy, but fine.

"Mike, or should I call you Father Mike? A priest! Wait, are you kidding? What are you doing here? Like this? No black suit, no white collar. Are you on sabbatical? What?"

"I left the church. Let's get out of here."

Barely back in the car, Lily, not wanting to lose the moment of truth, began, "You left? Walked out? You just threw your robe off and just walked out? Can you do that?" She was trembling. The excitement of Mike finally opening up to her and the meaning of his words made her babble.

Nodding, he asked, "So what do you think of me now?"

Unable to connect her thoughts and feelings, she groped for an answer. "Why did you leave? I know it couldn't have been due to lack of job security. Do I have to call you Father?" It was exactly what was going through her mind.

"No, never. Aren't we the clever one now." He chuckled. After a long sigh he continued. "Maybe the question is why I went in. I wonder now if my thoughts of the Church and priesthood were just an escape that would be an answer to all my problems."

"How long were you a priest?"

"Five years."

"Are you out completely? There's no going back?"

"I can go back."

"Will you?"

"I don't know."

He needed to talk, but his training as a counselor made it difficult for him to talk about himself. Sensing his reluctance, Lily gently prodded and pulled until he told her he had left the Church months before he met her.

He was born in Boston to Frank and Angela Carrozza, a Mafia family. Mike was the youngest son of seven children and the only one not in the family business. Angela, determined to save one of her children, tried to shield her baby from his father's business, but Mike was no fool.

"I remember how I felt when my suspicions that my father was a gangster were confirmed. I was listening at the door of my father's den when he gave my brothers the order. 'I know he can't get insurance on that ol' dump, so let's put him out of business for good. Torch it!' he snarled. I had never heard my father talk like that. Even his voice seemed to change as he spoke. He was totally different. The business he burned was a small grocery owned and operated by an old man and his wife. He wouldn't or couldn't pay his percentage to the family for their protection, so just like that, my own father gave the order to burn it down.

"I couldn't believe what was happening, so I followed them. I saw my brothers break in and put gasoline on everything. Flames danced from one aisle to the other as my brothers drove away. It was their job. All in a day's work. I can still hear the crackling of the old wooden store, the breaking glass, the shouts of the people." Mike could also still smell the garbage from the cans he hid behind. But as he remembered the horrible spectacle, most of all, he remembered the look on the old grocer's face. He never listened at his father's door again.

"A couple of years later, the family moved to Chicago. My mother sent me to live with her sister in Boston. 'Mike is different. He will never come to you. He is pure and good. Keep him out of it,' my mother told my father. It was the only time I ever heard her talk up to him."

"I stayed in Boston, finished high school, and went to college, planning to be a veterinarian. I kept up with the business through relatives and newspaper articles. They were making tons of money. Most of it came from drugs. My oldest brother was caught and sentenced to ten years in prison, but got out six months later on some type of technicality."

He sighed again as deeply as before and stared at the road ahead for quite some time before he continued. Lily was afraid he would not go on if she made a sound. The only move she dared was a careful glance that checked out every inch of her companion. She longed to know what was going on inside of him.

Finally he went on. "Mother spent a great deal of her time in Boston with us. She never mentioned what was going on with my father and brothers, but I could see it was killing her. She aged dramatically between visits. She and Aunt Louisa were very religious and I, too, found great peace in going to Mass. I had been an altar boy when I was younger back in New York and loved the ritual of it all. When I decided to go into the seminary, Mother and Aunt Louisa were thrilled. My father was violently against it at first, but finally gave his blessing and eventually came back into the Church. Mother was so proud of me. She had always wanted a priest in the family. I guess she knew if anyone needed a priest it was our family.

"Boy, I remember the party they gave me the night before I left. I think people are still talking about it. There was a band, more booze than a distillery, and lots of food. Everyone I had ever known, including all of my family, was there."

"Lots of brokenhearted girls, too, I bet," Lily added with a sly look that was returned by Mike. "Mike, this sounds like a movie."

"Should I stop? Are you sick of this yet?"

"No. By all means, please continue."

"I was finally ordained in Boston on June 15, 1970. I loved it. I had found my place. A place where I could escape the corruption that surrounded our family. I was on my own, and the Carrozza name couldn't buy jack. I knew that any other profession I went into, the Carrozza name would take me straight to the top, from fear if nothing else."

"It was a plain, simple, wonderful life. I was assigned to the cathedral in Boston. I was just getting my feet wet, getting to know the parishioners, the staff, just getting the feel. Then suddenly, after five months, I was made pastor. I was furnished a beautiful home and a new car. The bishop took me under his wing, and we became very close friends. Things were happening so fast. Too fast."

Mike recalled feeling cheated. Where had his chance to be a real priest gone? He wanted to set up bingo games, talk to grade-school children, and take the Eucharist to the sick and elderly. He wanted to give. Wanted to serve. So far it seemed to him that he had only been receiving. Mike tried talking to the bishop, but he always left his office as chairman of another committee.

Mike began to notice the grand style in which Bishop Simon lived in comparison to the other bishops. He had a new car, but he also had a limo and a driver at his disposal. He had memberships to country clubs, his own golf cart, a fully staffed, elaborate home, and he had just purchased some property on the ocean.

"I guess things were just looking too good." Picking up where he had left off with Lily, Mike continued his saga. "When I was informed I was to be appointed vicar general the wheels in my head started to roll."

"Mike, I don't understand. What?"

"Hang with me, I'll get there. Although I knew I was a sharp fella, you don't move up that fast. Everyone knew I had planned to spend some time in New York with friends and would not be at the church for a week. Last minute changes delayed my trip for two days. What was going on fell in my lap accidentally the following week. Father Kelly had the flu, and I had to take his confessional. I had only heard confessions a few times and was anxious to do something priestly for a change. You see, Bishop Simon thought his committee work was more fitting for me than the mundane work of the priesthood. Mundane…that's what he called it.

"St. Timothy's was a mammoth old cathedral with three sets of confessionals on each side toward the altar. I was a little early so I went in the first booth and just sat for some quiet time before my first customer. But as soon as I got there, someone was already waiting. The partition slide back and the moment I heard the first word, I knew who it was.

'I'm sorry to be late, but there was a pileup on the bridge. Are you there, Your Excellency?' I realized that I was supposed to be the bishop. I froze. If I spoke he would recognize my voice. I coughed out an answer. I knew something was up, because the bishop does not hear confession. It must have been a prearranged meeting of some sort.

"'I just got over the flu myself,' my father said. 'The package is in the same place. I won't keep you. Take care of yourself.'"

Lily gasped.

"I made sure he was gone before I slipped in the small cubicle he had just left. It smelled like my father, a cigar. I searched and found a manila envelope under the kneeler. Hurriedly I opened it. The contents was fifty thousand dollars in cash, the bill of sale for a new Lincoln Town Car, and a note that read:

'Send Mikey to Rome. He needs to look around if Mrs. Carrozza's son is to be a cardinal. The outcome will be good for all of us.'

"I hid the envelope exactly where I had found it and waited in the balcony. I didn't have long to wait. Bishop Simon quickly stole in and out of the confessional. At dinner that night, I found out Bishop Simon, in his new Lincoln Town Car, was also tied up in traffic on the bridge that afternoon."

Mike told Lily that although his father was buying him the position of cardinal for his mother, there was more to it than that.

He accepted the position of vicar general to access the bookkeeping system and kept close tabs on everything that went on, secretly of course, since he wasn't supposed to know anything. He found out that the Most Reverend Bishop Simon and his greatest benefactor, Frank Carrozza, had set up a charity account through the church called Food for Children. The money came in through bogus fundraisers. Letters asking for money were sent directly to those faithful donors who the bishop knew would write checks and never question him. It turned out the bishop and Mr. Carrozza were bookies. They had been friends for many years, and this was a piece of the action that Mike's father kept to himself. It was a hobby. They used the Food for Children money to back their bets. Evidentially, they had bought several racehorses with money from the church and were making thousands of dollars every week at the track.

"Wow, what did you do?" a wide-eyed Lily asked.

"Well, it almost looked funny. You know. Two old guys betting the ponies with ill-gotten gains. But it went even deeper. The bishop and my father were incredibly greedy. The charity's funds were drained completely, and after careful investigation, I realized the two had been skimming off the Sunday offerings from the entire diocese. Money from the faithful who were not so well-off. Money being taken from real hungry children, schools, the whole gambit."

Mike had to do something. He found out that the bishop had set up a three o'clock meeting with Frank at the confessional. Mike eased the clock on the bishop's desk back thirty minutes. The bishop never wore a watch and depended completely on that clock for his daily schedule. Mike was in the last confessional on the right when his father entered.

"Are you there?" his father inquired.

He slid back the partition as an answer. He had practiced the bishop's voice but did not want to take any more chances than necessary.

"I have the package." His father's voice came again.

"Fine."

"The jockey didn't make it," Frank whispered.

Now it included murder, Mike thought. "No?" Mike stammered almost forgetting his disguise.

"What's wrong with you, Eddie? Don't act so damned innocent."

"I must hurry," Mike replied.

"Wait, one more thing. Bless me, Father, for I have sinned—"

The son of a bitch wanted forgiveness for having some poor jockey beaten lifeless for who knows what.

"No!" Mike shouted.

"Eddie, I must have absolution!" his father begged.

"No, Pop. Not this time!"

"Mikey? Is that you? Mikey? Oh, Jesus, no!"

Mike heard the rustle of him leaving. He wanted to confront him. Mike's rush from the cubicle brought him eyeball to eyeball with the ashen face of the Most Reverend Bishop Edward Simon, who had just heard enough to know it had hit the fan.

"Mikey, I can explain—" his father began.

"No you can't!"

Bishop Simon, holding his chest, slumped into the nearby pew as Frank tried again.

"Mikey, we can fix it. You can come in with us. No one will ever have to know."

"No, Pop. I hid behind garbage once and watched your dirty work. I won't hide behind garbage again.

"That's the day I left, Lily."

"Whew, Mike, that's quite a story," Lily said, trying to absorb it all. "What happened to the jockey?"

"He lived, but he will never be able to walk or talk again. I think he had thrown a race and cost them a lot of money.

"Do they know where you are?" Lily asked, suddenly concerned for their safety. She couldn't suppress a mental picture of being gunned down by a couple of goons in black pinstripe suits.

"Sure."

She had to swallow hard before she could ask, "Are you afraid?"

"No. They won't do anything to me."

"What's next?" She wasn't sure she wanted the answer.

"I have a full report with documented copies of everything. I'm trying to bring myself to send them to Rome. I wrestle with it constantly."

They were turning into the beach house. "Are you too tired for a dessert and maybe some coffee?" he asked.

"Are you kidding? After a story like that, I doubt I'll sleep for a week!"

"On one condition, Lily Gray."

Lily rolled her eyes playing put out. "Now what?"

Mike laid his palm against the top of her protruding abdomen. "Can we talk about you?"

They found some cookies for their sweet tooth. Lily opted for milk instead of the coffee she wanted. She thought Katherine would be proud of her. Mike had a cold Budweiser. They sat on the sofa, her swollen feet in his lap. She asked what his plans were.

"I'm not sure, Lily, but I do know one thing. I'll be here with you until you go back to Atlanta."

"Oh, Mike," she sighed softly. She had found her guardian angel.

chapter

SEVENTEEN

"Hey, honey," Kathryne said affectionately.

"Girl!" her friend replied. Lily began talking so fast, Kathryne could hardly keep up. Mike had finally spilled his guts. And he was plenty gutsy, that was apparent. The long story of Mike's priesthood unfolded in seconds due to Lily's excitement. Kathryne was relieved to know he wasn't an axe murderer, but she felt she was hearing a rerun of an old gangster movie. Did those things really happen?

"Are they after him?" were the first words out of Kathryne's mouth. This question, however, was followed by plenty more until she got it through her head that Lily was completely safe. It became clear that Mike was also safe from that part of his life, but Lily was Kathryne's first concern. They threw the story back and forth until they were both worn out with it. If there was any more to the story, Lily vowed to find out when she could.

"Has our phone bill these last few months affected our profit-and-loss statement?" She chuckled.

Kathryne and Lily talked to each other every day, at least once. They missed each other terribly, personally as well as professionally. They'd worked together so long, throwing ideas back and forth as they created ads, that even now, although 421 miles apart, they were able to continue their collaboration.

Lily was kept up-to-date on every account, and she helped with some of the campaigns. The beach house was great for concentration, but some days Lily's peace and quiet was enough to drive her crazy. Those were the days Mike would come to her rescue with either a new topic to explore or an exciting area of Florida to investigate. Socks, now fully recovered and full of energy, kept her laughing with his constant playfulness.

Kathryne continued in her affectionate tone. "I'm dying to see you, kid. I'm coming down tomorrow."

"But you were just here last week," Lily argued. "And the big day is a little over two weeks from now. Who knows how much longer after that it could be?"

"I know, I know," Kathryne said firmly. "Believe it or not, I can still afford to come back again in two weeks. Besides, this is business. I am flying to Orlando to talk to Brian Little, director of marketing at SeaWorld. He wants to hear our ideas for some marketing in Georgia. So, what do you say, boss, can I come?"

Lily laughed. "Well, I am really busy, but I will try to rearrange my schedule."

"Are you OK? You are really putting up a good front, but I know you too well, my dear." Kathryne could hardly sleep most nights for worrying about Lily, so alone and far away. Thank God she had met such a nice guy. Father Mike was just what the doctor ordered. Lily really liked him. Even though they were helping each other through a tough time, by all appearances, they were enjoying life.

They had been to Disney World, SeaWorld, Cypress Gardens, Bok Tower, Silver Springs, Marineland, St. Augustine, Cape Kennedy, a water show north of Tampa called Weeki-Wachi Springs, and they had even found a Seminole Indian reservation down around Lake Okeechobee. Lily was like a kid, bubbling with stories of their adventures, while Kathryne tried to tell her she was doing too much. "I won't lie to you, KT," Lily admitted this morning. "I don't feel so good today. But what do you expect? I am fat, swollen, and ugly."

"It will pass, I promise," consoled Kathryne. She knew better than to try to tell Lily how beautiful she was pregnant. It was like teasing a viper. "I'll get to Orlando about ten o'clock and meet with Brian. I should see you around three. Can I bring you anything?" Kathryne asked.

"Oh, KT, yes! Please bring me some pork rinds from Freddy's Grill. The hot ones in the red wrapper. Make sure they're the hot ones!"

"You sound like a dope addict," Kathryne exclaimed.

"I feel like one. Make sure they're the hot ones—about six bags."

"Are you supposed to be eating that garbage? I am sure there should be a surgeon general's warning on those things."

"Kathryne Langford, just make sure you get the hot ones!" Lily shouted. "See you tomorrow."

"Lily, you do look very swollen," Kathryne said with concern. "What does Dr. Nash say?"

"Oh, I think the only word in his vocabulary is normal." Lily was fussy. "He says I am normal this and normal that."

They were sitting on the deck of the beach house enjoying the early evening. It was a beautiful afternoon in late January. The tide was in, and although there was still plenty of light, the full moon had appeared. The sea gulls filed across the sky in military formation on their way to Gull Island for their nightly roost.

"Anyone home?" Mike yelled as he came around the side of the house.

"Out here," the two women sang in unison.

Mike came up the steps to the deck dressed, as usual, in Bermuda shorts, a knit shirt, and flip-flops. He looked like an ad for a beachcomber magazine.

"Well, what a lovely sight," he said. Kathryne was watching Mike as he pulled up a chair and sat down. What a doll! She wondered what would become of his priesthood, and if his friendship with Lily would influence his decision. Suddenly, she saw his friendly expression turn to fright. Following his eyes to Lily, Kathryne sprang out of her seat.

"What is it?" she asked Lily.

"Oh, KT, this doesn't feel good," Lily whispered as she grimaced in pain.

"What doesn't feel good? Does something hurt?" Kathryne prodded.

"No, I just all of a sudden feel like a truck hit me.

"Has this happened before?" Kathryne continued to try to figure out what was going on. She didn't have to wonder for long. A scream from Lily electrified Kathryne. Her senses could not comprehend fast enough what had happened. She could only stand there and wait for her brain to register everything and tell her what to do.

"I don't know what happened!" Lily looked scared. Her red slacks were soaked and so was the deck.

"Oh my God, Lily," shouted Kathryne. "Your water broke!"

"But it's not time!" Lily cried, taking hold of Kathryne's arm. "I'm not ready. It's not time!"

"Honey, you are going to have to get ready!" Kathryne said soothingly. Lily was much too upset. She had to calm her down and get her to the hospital immediately.

"Mike?" Kathryne tried not to scream.

"Just tell me what to do, Kathryne! Just tell me what the hell to do!" He was dancing from one foot to the other, wringing his hands.

"What kind of car do you have?"

"A 1974 red Oldsmobile, four-door, automatic transmission, AM/FM radio—"

"All right, all right. Good." Oh, brother, she thought, trying to pretend everything was OK. "Why don't you drive? We'll go on up to Daytona to the hospital and have Dr. Nash check Lily over." She spoke as calmly as possible. "Oh God, please help us. I'm scared!" she silently prayed.

"Absolutely not, KT," protested Lily. Kathryne was trying to convince her to go on to the hospital now and worry about her wet slacks later. "I am not going anywhere like this!"

"Lily, I really think we should—"

A pain hit Lily so hard she had to grab Kathryne's arm to keep steady. Her knees felt like jelly. Lily looked at Kathryne and fear sprang to her eyes. With serene determination, she said, "KT, get me somewhere quick…I am going to have the baby!"

"No shit!" Kathryne exclaimed as Mike ran for the car. They were right behind him. Kathryne helped Lily into the back seat.

"Do you want to lie down?" asked Kathryne. Lily had taken control. She was the one who knew exactly what was happening.

"Yes," she whispered.

As Mike eased the car onto A1A another contraction hit Lily. "KT! Oh, KT!" Lily screamed.

"Head for Halifax General, fast!" Kathryne told Mike. Lily screamed again. Kathryne began to rub Lily's stomach. It seemed so hard. Then she realized it had tightened for delivery. "Mike, let's forget Halifax. Does New Smyrna have a hospital?"

"Oh, Kathryne, I don't know! What are we going to do?"

"Head on up A1A. Stop at the fire station right there where A1A and Flagler meet." He was driving like he had a load of fresh eggs in the back.

"Hit it, man!" she slapped him on the shoulder.

Lily's contractions were a minute apart and extremely severe. Kathryne was smoothing back her hair and giving her false assurance as Mike, on his five-hundred-forty-fifth Hail Mary, pulled into the fire station and jumped out. Seconds later, the paramedic and two fire fighters were carrying Lily to their ambulance. A trembling Kathryne crawled into the ambulance with Lily and the paramedic. They sped out of the fire station with full siren and all lights flashing. Mike was right on their bumper.

The paramedic, about five foot eleven, with brown eyes and hair and a bright-red mustache, was really cute. Lily took a look at him and, winking at Kathryne, said, "Good job, KT."

"Where are we going?" Kathryne asked.

"We are headed for Halifax General, but we're not going to make it." He was pulling Lily's slacks off, talking to Kathryne over his shoulder.

"Wh…what do you mean?" Kathryne was so scared she could hardly speak.

As the paramedic talked, he readied Lily for delivery and instructed Kathryne how to help. Lily stretched out and relaxed.

The paramedic's obvious expertise gave her confidence and the pain seemed to subside slightly.

"Oh, KT, I am so glad you're here. Isn't this a helluva note?" Lily moaned. Then she seemed to get busy. She worked with the paramedic and did everything he said. She breathed, she groaned, and she grimaced, and all the while, Kathryne assured her they would be at the hospital soon.

The arrival of a bloody, screaming baby surprised Kathryne. She really thought they would get to the hospital and have a normal delivery.

"Hold him for me," the paramedic commanded, "while I suck the mucous from his throat."

"Him?" She held out her arms. The paramedic placed Lily's son in Kathryne's outstretched arms. Looking down into his eyes, she was overwhelmed by the love that filled her heart. The paramedic slipped small tubes in his little nose and down his throat, suctioning as he probed. The baby gagged and then slowly opened his big, black eyes. He looked deep into her eyes as if he knew her. He did! He knew her.

Kathryne held the baby boy, wrapped snugly in a soft white blanket, the rest of the way to Halifax General, while the paramedic tended to Lily. He was so kind and good to her, explaining everything that was going on in her body. Lily's sleepy face was one of relief now. The ambulance pulled up to the emergency room entrance to Halifax General Hospital and Kathryne looked down at the baby she nestled close to her heart. His little face smiled up at her. She reluctantly surrendered her precious bundle to the nurse, who insisted he must be checked over immediately.

The next day when Mike and Kathryne, still looking a bit ruffled, came to see Lily, she laughed and said, "You two look terrible!" Lily still looked drowsy and tired, but she was radiant. Her soft, pink bed jacket accented her tan.

"You scared the hell out of me!" exclaimed Kathryne. "Oh, excuse me, Mike," she apologized.

"Well, she scared me, too!" He chuckled to Kathryne as an acceptance of her apology.

Mike and Kathryne went into a frenzied enactment of dashing to the car carrying an eggshell between them. Mike mocked

Kathryne. "Hit it, man! Let's get to the hospital!" And Kathryne imitated him. "Hail Mary, full of grace…"

Lily, trying not to laugh, carefully said, "You crazy idiots, stop it! This laughing is about to kill me!"

Mike smiled and kissed Lily on the forehead. "Thank God you are OK," he said. "Thank God everyone is OK." Kathryne knew Mike was talking about the baby but was afraid it would upset everyone if he mentioned him. "I will see you this evening," he told Lily and winked at Kathryne on his way out.

"So, Miss Scare-Everybody-to-Death, how are you feeling?" asked Kathryne, pulling up a chair. Kathryne wore a green pantsuit and new low-heeled pumps to match.

"Oh, I feel great, KT, just great. It was such an easy birth. I guess that makes a difference."

"What? Easy! Lily Gray, you are the only woman in the world who could have a baby two weeks early, delivered by a paramedic in an ambulance on the way to the hospital, and call it easy!"

"Oh God, KT, you have lost your mind!" Lily looked absolutely breathtaking. She was wearing the white Pierre Cardin nightgown Kathryne had brought her. Her long hair, brushed to a glow, fell across her shoulders, and the afternoon sun brought out the light bronze of her Cherokee skin. Her face, though, was screwed into an expression of disbelief.

"Lily," Kathryne said, "I know the plan was to give him up for adoption, and I know there is a couple waiting for him right now at your attorney's office. I know it sounds preposterous. But, Lil"—Kathryne was pleading now—"I have wanted a baby boy for so long. And when I looked into his little face in that ambulance, we knew each other!"

Lily was trying not to be patronizing. "KT, I realize how dramatic the birth turned out to be, and I am sorry. Don't you think that is what this is really all about?" As Kathryne started to object, Lily put up a stop signal with her hand. "KT, you are my best friend. I love you dearly and would do anything for you. But I don't think this is a good idea. You can have a baby of your own, for God's sake, KT."

"Just listen to me a minute, Lil," Kathryne pleaded. "When I got pregnant with Becky, I prayed for a boy. When I had a little girl, I was thrilled. Of course I knew my next child would be a boy."

"And you can still—"

"Just hear me out, OK?" Kathryne asked.

"OK." Lily sighed, throwing up her hands as she leaned back on the pillows.

"When Becky was three months old, and we found out about all her physical and mental problems, I thought I would die from grief. Lily, the grief came not only for Becky but for the unborn children I knew I could never have."

Lily knew how hard it was for Kathryne to talk about Becky's condition. She never talked about it much. The rare times when she opened up were difficult, because it broke Lily's heart to hear the agony she had been through, operation after operation, hope after hope. When she'd met Kathryne six years ago, there were no more operations. Everything possible had been done to and for Becky.

Kathryne sat on the chair beside the bed, facing Lily. Her height gave them eye-to-eye contact. Looking tired and upset, Kathryne continued her appeal.

"We had no idea what had caused Becky's problems and could not ignore the fact that heredity could have been a factor. So, I checked into Atlanta Presbyterian Hospital the following week and had my tubes tied. I couldn't take a chance on letting it happen again."

"Oh, KT, I had no idea." Tears came to Lily's eyes as she learned why Kathryne had never had more children.

"I have never told anyone. Not even Joe. I forged his signature on the consent papers, checked in at six in the morning, and drove myself home about six that evening. Lily, please let me have him. You know I will take good care of him. He'll never know, I swear! You can be Aunt Lily. Please don't give him away to strangers, Lily." Kathryne's face was twisted into an expression of desperation, and she had lost all dignity. "I've been in the nursery with him the last two days. I've held him, fed him, changed his poopy diapers. He threw up on me, Lily!" With a crack in her voice, she begged, "Please, Lily. I have fallen in love with him."

"KT, how would you explain it to Joe, or my attorney, or the other couple?"

"I can handle Joe, he loves children as much as I do. You said yourself what a good daddy he is. I will pay off your attorney. Besides, the final papers haven't been signed yet anyway. And the other couple are strangers."

"Dear God in Heaven!" Lily exclaimed. She fell against the pillows again, searching the ceiling for an answer.

As Kathryne came through the door at the airport, a sober, clean-cut Joe was waiting for her. The thing about Joe she could always rely on was his compassion for children. He was not even aware that Lily was still out of the office. Kathryne told him that Lily had gone to Europe on a special assignment, but he paid little attention. The office staff even thought she was in town over the weekend from time to time.

When Kathryne called Joe and told him about the baby whose parents, friends of her attorney, had drowned in a boating accident, he was an easy sell. As close friends of the dead couple and executor of their estate, the attorney had been named guardian of the baby, but he could not keep him because of his failing health, and so on.

Joe was full of questions about the baby. How old was he? How long was he? He seemed long, like he was going to be tall. Did she have a line on his parents' backgrounds?

On the way to the baggage carousel, he said, "Kathryne, let's just sit down here a minute. I want to look at him."

Kathryne had urged Lily to suggest a name, but she wouldn't have any part in it. But, when Kathryne mentioned Alexander, she saw a slight smile flicker on Lily's face.

Joe was more excited than she had seen him in years. Kathryne felt close to him again as they sat in the middle of the Atlanta airport and marveled at this new life. Joe smiled at Kathryne and said, "He is really a handsome little guy, isn't he?" This was the Joe she once knew. Had Becky really changed them that much?

As she and Joe sat at the airport cooing at Alexander Langford, life seemed to take on a new meaning.

But as wonderful as things seemed, why did Kathryne have such a strong feeling of impending doom?

chapter

EIGHTEEN

It was thundering, and the lifeguards on the beach were whistling their lungs out trying to get people to come out of the water. A yellow municipal jeep equipped with a loudspeaker system was telling everyone to clear the beach.

Non-Floridians did not realize that after drowning, lightning ranks as the second-highest cause of death in the state. The beach was a magnet for lightning. Lily stood at the Causeway Café window, watching the scrambling beachgoers heading for home. It was time for her to head home as well, home to Atlanta.

The beach was empty now, except for a small sailboat drifting along just outside the break of the waves. It had been five weeks since the pell-mell arrival of seven pounds of trouble. Her coerced decision to let Kathryne take him still haunted her. She dreamed about it every night in some fashion or another. Her doctor said it was postpartum blues.

"Will this ever be over?" she was asking herself just as Mike popped in the door, right on time for what was to be their good-bye lunch.

"Hi. Looks like you just beat the rain," she said as light sprinkles hit the windows.

"Good thing, too," he said. "Sugar melts, you know."

Lily smiled, watching him set his small suitcase down beside the table.

"You've decided to go back?" She had offered him a ride as far as Atlanta if he was ready to return to the love of his life, the Catholic Church.

"Yes, I have. As much as I thought I wanted to, and as hard as I tried to quit, I just can't see my life any other way. I know now that I truly want to live my life to serve the Lord. I think I have learned how to do that. The road will be rough at times, but I can handle it now. I had a long phone conversation with the new bishop last night. I decided I would ride back to Atlanta with you and get a flight to Boston."

"Where will you go? Not back to the same parish." They had placed their order and were doctoring their iced tea.

"No, I made that very clear to the bishop. I have to go where I can serve the people. I'm going to one of the inner-city parishes in New York where the Carrozza name will mean nothing. I'm taking the one in the Bronx. The only desire I have is to pastor a parish and help the kids make something of their lives. Help them move up and out of the ghetto."

"I'm so glad for you, Mike. I know it has been a terrible struggle." Lily took her friend's hand in hers. "I can't tell you what it has meant to me having you here during all this. I know I could not have made it without you."

"Lily, I can't tell you what it has meant having you here during all of this for me! I know I could not have made it without you!" A warm smile spread across his face as he raised her hand to his lips and kissed it. That day, over a deluxe shrimp basket, Lily and Mike made a vow of friendship and agreed to always stay in touch. They each felt the other was a gift from God to get them through their own personal hell. Lily, however, had no way of knowing her hell was just beginning.

Lily's first day back at the office was more tense than she had expected. After five months of leisure, the hectic pace wore her nerves thin. Having to lie to her friends about her "European tour" filled her with guilt. She plunged into her work, devouring it like a hungry wolf, working long hours equal to those when she first started in the business.

Her emotions were rolling waves in her body. She missed Mike and the happy, carefree days they had spent together. Yet she was glad once again to be with Kathryne. She missed the wonderful house on the beach, but she was so happy to be back home, surrounded by all her things. She missed the ocean, the beautiful sunsets. She missed the peace and solitude, just as she had missed the fast pace of the office and her exciting career when she first, very reluctantly, went to Florida. She missed feeling like her old self. Herself before Alexander.

Each night she fought like a warrior for sleep, but it was hard coming, even with the help of sleeping pills. She thought as she lay in her bed at night that she might have an idea what a soldier just home from Vietnam might feel. How Tommy must have felt. Being able only to think about being home when so far away, counting the days until home was finally where you were, but finding it different. Not like before. An uneasy feeling crept in. Lily wanted something she could never have again. Peace of mind.

Her mind was running a race with her body, and her body was losing. She could not slow down her thoughts. She dropped twenty pounds the first two months she was home. She was thankful that Kathryne had taken that time off to be with Alexander. She could not have withstood one single baby story. Lily avoided talking to Kathryne as much as possible. She returned her phone calls moments before a meeting or so late it was inconvenient to talk. Lily knew her behavior hurt Kathryne. She was hurting as well. But there was no one to talk to about it with. She could not go to Gray Dove. She just wasn't ready to tell the old woman that she had given away Sonny's only grandchild. She refused calls from Andy. Lily hurt inside. Her sense of loneliness was overwhelming. She was losing her best friends, the closeness with her grandmother; in fact, she was losing control of her life. She started smoking, a habit she had always hated with a passion. It made her feel self-destructive, which gave her some type of sick pleasure. Her hair had lost its beautiful luster, and her skin was sallow, with dark, ugly circles under her once sparking eyes.

"Socks," she told her little roommate, "I can't go on like this much longer." She observed her image in the mirror as she talked to her furry companion. "I have got to get control. I have got to talk to someone." She sat on the bed and scratched Socks under the chin. Her thoughts turned to the day she saw Mike hovering over the poor little kitten on the beach. She knew whom she could talk to.

"Mike?"

"Yeah, it's me all right." Lily started to cry uncontrollably when she heard his kind, sweet voice. "Lily, what is it, honey? Go ahead and get it out and then tell me all about it."

She finally calmed down and told him how misplaced she felt. She wanted to come to New York to see him. They made arrangements for him to meet her flight the next day. She left the next morning with no explanation to Kathryne, just a phone call to Theda, their assistant.

Kathryne discussed her concern about Lily's behavior over lunch with Andy the next day. She had been so happy with her new life that she had lost sight of her friend. She could not tell Andy the whole story or what she feared was really bothering Lily. She wondered how she could have been so naïve to think Lily could get over everything so soon. When she returned from New York, she wanted to spend more time with her. She missed their crazy times together.

The six days Lily spent with Mike in New York was the healing she needed. He was devastated by her appearance. He said he almost did not recognize her at the airport.

"Mike, you are staring."

"I'm sorry, Lily, but you have lost so much weight."

"I know. You don't have to apologize. I look like the walking dead. On the other hand, Mike, you've got to admit you are used to seeing me pregnant."

They checked her into the Salisbury Hotel in downtown Manhattan and talked until dawn. She talked, and he listened. She cried, and he held her. This cycle was completed several times before dawn and many more times in the days that followed. Mike was wonderful to her, and Lily knew how blessed she was to have met him when she did. She told him she felt like she had been strapped in a chair and thrown into space. Like she was hurtling aimlessly through time. He understood. She told him she felt use-less and had no reason to go on. He showed her every reason she had to go on.

Then she dropped the bomb. She told him she wanted Alexander back. Her heart was broken, and longing for her son was eating her very being as if it were a cancer in her body. He said, "Get him while you can."

One afternoon while she waited for Mike, Lily called Kathryne. They talked and laughed like old times. Lily felt healed, and Kathryne felt she had regained her old friend. She knew, how-ever, that she was partially to blame for the torment Lily was going through. They had had so little time together since Lily had gotten back home.

Kathryne met Lily's plane. They held each other very close and seemed to know another milestone in their friendship had passed. They went to Lily's and talked the night away. Lily finally asked about Alexander, and Kathryne beamed. Lily knew her son had a wonderful mother and would never want for a single thing in life.

Kathryne asked about Mike, and Lily told her how truly happy he was. He loved the people in his parish and loved help-ing the kids. He was a real person, a real priest. The kind Spencer Tracy would portray. He cared about his people. He got down on their level and brought them back up to his. He played ball in the street with the kids. He talked to their teachers for them. He went to their homes when he knew there was trouble. So many of the kids were on drugs and in gangs. He genuinely grieved when he said the funeral mass for a fifteen-year-old boy who had been stabbed seventeen times in a gang fight. Once by every member of the rival gang.

Mike really cared, and his people knew it. He did not farm his work out to a volunteer committee. He voiced his concern over the incoming seminarians who only seemed interested in themselves and furthering their political status in the church. By constantly voicing his concern, Mike would be kept right where he wanted to be. Where no one else wanted to be. In a small, poor ghetto in the heart of the inner city. Mike was happy. He would not let the Carrozza money pave his way to the Vatican.

Lily began seeing a psychiatrist, and her spirits lightened. She quit smoking, and her skin regained its glow. But she still remained aloof and distant. She hardly saw Andy anymore, and she did not date. Kathryne was hesitant to ask if she was OK. She was still moody and unpredictable.

She told Kathryne one day after a board meeting that she thought Bill was following her. She thought she had seen him twice. Kathryne reasoned that was the cause of Lily's moodiness. She realized it was not the entire reason when she returned to her office after lunch one day and found Lily clutching the latest silver-framed picture of Alexander. Kathryne hurt for her friend, but she did not know what to do.

Over time Lily's emotions seemed to clam down, and she felt like she was getting back to normal. She could talk about her son and look at pictures of him. She seldom saw him, and when she did, she never touched him.

chapter

NINETEEN

Where did the time go?" Kathryne asked herself as she checked the decorations for Alexander's first birthday party.

"Oh no, it's clouding up!" she yelped at Rose. She ran to the window and looked out. "This just has to be a perfect party!"

The patio was decorated from one end to the other with banners, balloons, tablecloths with matching plates, party favors, and presents. Lots and lots of presents. Kathryne had invited seventy-five people. There were friends from the neighborhood, Becky's friends from the clinic, and some of Kathryne and Joe's friends with their families. It was going to be a great day for the kids. Clowns, jugglery, and a magician would be there to entertain them. Kathryne loved to hear children laugh, and she intended to hear them laugh today. The party was no less than a Hollywood production. If it rained—well, it would not; Kathryne just wouldn't permit it.

The past year had been the most wonderful year in her life. Alexander's first tooth, first step, first word. Becky loved him, too. She loved to watch him no matter what he was doing. Sometime she would sit for an hour, just watching him. When Alexander began to recognize Becky and smile and coo at her, it thrilled her into fits of laughter.

Joe had stopped drinking completely. He was enjoying his latest job and was the perfect daddy. He was still the minuteman when it came to sex, but Kathryne didn't care. She had her children, her two best friends, a wonderful career, and Jeff. In the months that followed Alexander's birth, she tried to stop seeing Jeff, but he had become so important to her, such a needed part of her existence, that she could not give him up.

The birthday party was a tremendous success. The children played games and ate hotdogs, cake, and ice cream until they could hold nothing else. Although Alexander was too young to know exactly what it was all about, he loved the attention and excitement of the children. He tried to imitate everything the other children did, from clapping for the magician to laughing at the clowns.

Lily helped serve cake and ice cream and give out party favors to everyone. She was known as Alexander's "Auntie Lily." The weather had indeed cooperated. The jackets came off as the sun came out. It was just what Kathryne had ordered.

"This year has really flown by, huh, KT?" Lily said, smiling. They were doing their share to help Rose clean up some of the mess. "Is everything still going well?" she asked, gathering coffee cups for the dishwasher.

"Unbelievably!" Kathryne replied. The time she had taken off from work when she brought Alexander home had gotten her over the rough spots. She hired a nanny and made sure everything was in capable hands before returning to her busy schedule. She was always home for dinner with the family and to put Becky and Alexander to bed. Then, when necessary, she would return to work and stay until her project was completed. Sometimes the rising sun coming through her office window told her it was time to go home.

Kathryne and Lily continued to work well as a team. They still motivated and inspired each other, but there was an ever-present underlying strain. Kathryne knew Alexander was still a tender subject with Lily and did her best not to talk about him. Even now, as Lily helped her clean up, Kathryne knew she would not have come the party had it not been for her insistence that her absence would look odd.

Kathryne had come to the realization that things would never be exactly the same between them. She could put herself in Lily's position, in a way, and see how it must be for her. Then again, it was Kathryne who begged, assured, and convinced Lily that it would be better if she took the baby. They were both at fault, if you wanted to call it that. She needed to talk to Lily about getting the permanent adoption papers drawn up and everything taken care of legally, but there never seemed to be a proper time to bring it up. And what if Joe found out? Troublesome thoughts seemed to haunt her more and more frequently.

"All in all," Kathryne said, "it has been the best year of my life. Thanks, Lily." Their eyes locked, and Lily knew how deeply she meant it.

Driving back to town after the party, Lily kept thinking of Alexander. She smiled as she thought of him tearing open his presents and squealing with delight at everything. He was a beautiful baby. Black hair and big black eyes, the Gray Dove nose. He was already as sharp as a tack. Kathryne dressed him like a cowboy for the party, in blue denims and a red shirt. He looked like a doll. What was it Mike had said? "Get him while you can."

Lily stepped back quickly from the window, switching off the light on her bedside table. There it was again. The small brown car sitting across the street. The same car she had already seen twice this week. Once in the parking garage at work and once pulling in behind her at the dentist's office. It couldn't be coincidence. Someone was following her. She saw the tiny red glow of a cigarette as the watchdog got comfortable. She would have to remember to rent a car for certain trips from now on.

The only person Lily could think of who would hire a "tail" for her would be Bill. But why? There was only one reason. He couldn't know about Alexander, could he? She sensed danger. She had to get her plan in place and be ahead of Bill if he was onto her.

"Alexander's birthday party last weekend was a riot!" Kathryne told Andy. She and Lily had met him at Pierre's for a late lunch. "Take a look at these pictures!" She gave the pictures to Andy, and she and Lily watched him smile and chuckle at the hordes of children in various stages of playing games and smearing cake on their faces. Kathryne was leaning toward him making oohs and ahs over every picture. He came to a picture of Lily squatting beside Alexander. They were laughing together over a little rocking horse. She was dressed in a white linen pantsuit with her hair in a braid. Andy knew that anyone with half an eye could tell the little cowboy was Lily's child. Thoughts of Alexander's father sent a chill over him.

He had wanted to ask Kathryne about the baby for a long time. Why didn't Lily want her child? He respected their decisions and acted as though he suspected nothing. He could see why Lily would not want to marry a bastard like Bill, but then again, his opinion was somewhat biased.

Rejoining the conversation, Andy assured Kathryne that she had the most beautiful son in all the world. He also went on to say that the women should both be in the modeling business instead of advertising. That was one of the things about Andy they loved so much. He always made them feel so good about themselves, and he never played favorites.

chapter

TWENTY

When Pearl Lewis was in the courtroom, a sense of direction enveloped her. She drew confidence in knowing when the witness was lying, she read the opposing counsel's argument like a premonition, and she never lost a case. She kept her law office efficiently small. She was very selective of the clients she took and never let anyone or anything come before Andy. Andy was, and always had been, the force from which her system received strength. Just the thought of Andy, his pride in her, his need for her, spun Pearl to a level of invincibility.

Although she tried, it proved to be impossible for Pearl to be slim. Plastic surgery had taken care of the ears her mother led her to believe were elephant-like. Her hair was stylishly short, and she dressed like the millionaire she was. She made herself as attractive as possible for Andy, but her weight continued to stay out of control. She always cut the size-fourteen tags from her clothes or had them removed by her seamstress. She knew he loved her as she was, but always, always wished she was prettier, slimmer, more feminine, and fertile.

It was Andy's inability to cope with the prejudices thrust on him as a child that drove Pearl to do everything in her power to establish and promote equal rights for blacks. Putting an end to the plague of illiteracy among down-trodden blacks in America, she felt, was the place to begin.

She knew the answer was within the race itself. Negroes must want it for themselves on an individual, personal level. By installing an eagerness to learn in children, the Negro of tomorrow could have self-respect, goals, and ambition. Pearl was fortunate to have been born with an IQ well above average and a photographic memory, but she knew that her real break was Dr. Drake. Her ambition was the icing on the cake.

One of Pearl's avenues for her fight for equal rights was the Equal Employment Opportunity Commission. The EEOC was a part of the 1964 Civil Rights Act that made it against the law to discriminate against someone in the employment arena because of race, color, religion, sex, or national origin. Most of the complaints about unfair hiring practices and of discrimination on the job involved women and Negroes. EEOC's job was to administer and enforce fair employment practices.

Pearl was the chairman of the EEOC Investigation Committee. She had never experienced the sickening degradation described to her by the black employees she interviewed. White women were also among those feeling the brunt of discrimination on the job. White women who were college graduates bore discrimination because of their sex on a level with black male high-school dropouts. In addition, women were continually faced with verbal and physical sexual encounters. Numerous women recounted details of being raped by bosses who then either fired them or threatened to fire them if they did not provide sexual service upon demand.

Sometimes the stories were so ugly they made Pearl feel guilty to be a successful black woman. But most of the time she felt destined by God as a role model, a savior for those who sought better jobs with equal pay and a lifestyle for her race far removed from "colored town."

Andy had fought prejudice all his life. His light skin made him feel most of the time like a man without a home, without a race. Simply an outcast. He had bucked the system since the day he was born. From what Pearl could piece together about his father in the research she had done, he was an aggressive, never-take-no-for-an-answer kind of guy who still, at age sixty-eight, worked hard, long hours and was never satisfied.

Pearl found Andy's father two years after they were married. She was pregnant and burning with questions about Andy's biological roots that could affect their baby. He was still in Pascagoula and owned most of the town. He had raised three sons and was still married to their mother, a Mississippi socialite. Pearl interviewed Clayton Creel, on the pretense of researching cotton farmers for a college thesis on the South. She sat and talked with him, seeing Andy in Clayton's every expression, every bold statement, and every long-legged stride he took as he showed her his operation. He was damn good-looking, with an electric personality. Pearl liked him very much, and as she drove away, she pondered if she would be able to keep up with the special little person who grew within her.

Since then, so much had happened. She'd lost the baby, and Andy had been elected governor of Texas. She became engrossed in her work and the fight to upgrade her race through education and equal opportunities. These projects and Andy's ambitions were Pearl's life.

"You are sleeping with the next governor of Texas," he had told her four years ago. And, twenty-three months ago, he asked her if making love to a US senator would excite her.

"I don't know. If I ever have sex with a US senator, I'll go over every detail with you." She smiled mischievously.

"I love you, baby," he whispered.

"Andy, my love," she smiled into those gorgeous brown eyes.

She planned the entire campaign around his sincerity, his love of Texas and its people. She structured his speaking engagements to tie in with the president's visit to Texas, union meetings, and other main events. She wrote every speech he made and was by his side every step of the campaign trail. She spoke at women's club luncheons, while he visited hospitals. She attended receptions in his honor if time would not permit his presence. Pearl was every politician's dream wife. Her dream was for Andy to have everything in life he ever wanted.

They traveled from one end of Texas to the other. They talked with wheat farmers in the Panhandle, vegetable and fruit farmers in the Rio Grande and Peco valleys, oil and gas drillers in East Texas, and cattle ranchers in the Great Plains. From the Port of Houston to the capital city of Austin, Andy campaigned his heart out. He kissed old women, held babies, hunkered down with dock workers to discuss minimum wages, state income tax, and unemployment, and walked along the assembly line of major state manufacturing plants, making notes about working conditions, employee benefits, and safety training on the job. He did everything he could, and he called in all of his markers.

Pearl and Andy sat together on the white sectional in the penthouse suite at the Hilton Hotel in Austin as the votes from Texas precincts began to tick into the computerized system. He wanted them to be alone.

As she watched him, her heart ached for the children she could never conceive, for a family to surround them now in the victory she knew was coming. They seemed too alone. Oh, they had many friends, her brothers and, of course, Andy's brother, Todd. But your own children make the difference. Children, the direct bloodline of their parents, gave a sense of completeness, of whole love, that grew from living under the same roof sharing the daily trivia, moods, and sacrifices.

Pearl was painfully aware that Andy did not have progeny. A son. He assured Pearl it did not matter, after she nearly died from a tubal pregnancy that left them hopeless. It mattered to Pearl, though. It mattered a lot. The baby they lost would be in high school now, just right for a political trainee under the wing of his father, the governor of Texas, soon-to-be United States senator.

Her mind was relentless with its memories. Every detail filled her. The joy when she told Andy they were going to have a baby. The planning, caressing her burgeoning tummy, calling the baby by his name, Andrew Monroe Lewis, Jr.

They called him Andrew. The thrill always filled her being when she reflected, as did the ensuing heartsick agony. A violent miscarriage, the formal funeral, and the sight of the name, Andrew M. Lewis, Jr., on the tombstone.

Tears swelled, burning her eyes. The familiar lump in her throat choked her, then the taste of stomach bile. April. He would have been sixteen this April. The same question came to her mind. Why? Why Lord? Lost in the past, Pearl heard the distant television. The volume increased.

"I can't get it loud enough, honey!" The television was deafening. Andy's jubilant cry snapped her back like the fast-forward button of a time machine. What was he saying? She had been so entrenched in her pain.

"Oh, Andy!" She realized what he was saying. "You're in the lead!"

"Andrew Lewis, governor of Texas, is leading the senatorial race by twenty percent. Unless we get some very unexpected surprises, folks, looks like Texas has itself a new senator!" The news reporter went on to say that the campaign and popularity of the first black candidate to enter the senatorial race in Texas had turned the state upside down, much as had happened four years prior, when Andrew Lewis, wealthy Texas oilman, had announced he would run for governor.

"Without a doubt, Andy Lewis is the people's choice!" The commentator gave Andy's background. Elected to the Texas Railroad Commission, elected governor, now on his way to the White House. Andy wanted to remember to give the commentator a bonus in his paycheck this week. He did an excellent job. Owning the television station didn't hurt when it came to plugging yourself. Although it was not known that he owned the station, he could have his manager direct the news as he wanted it.

Pearl was wondering how she could top his present to her when she'd passed her bar exam. He'd bought her a Rolls-Royce and drove her to the spot where they had made love for the first time in the back of his pickup truck. They christened the beautiful new automobile "For The Good Times," and made love just as tenderly and lovingly as they had done so many times before.

He took her hand, and they walked to the elevator, which took them to the lobby and the limousine waiting to deliver the new senator from Texas to campaign headquarters for his acceptance speech.

He delivered a warm, humble acceptance speech, written by Pearl. He added a statement telling everyone that he could not have made it without his wonderful wife, who stood just behind and to the right of him on the podium.

Expressing special thanks to supporters and friends, he added, "Here's to you, son," as he held up the banner that read, Senator Andrew Lewis. Pearl fought dizziness. She thought she would die of love for this man and the heartache of his, their, loss.

chapter

TWENTY-ONE

Kathryne realized that talk of Alexander still bothered Lily even after two years. She surmised that even after two hundred and two years, it would still bother a mother to talk about an adopted child who now belonged to her best friend. It took all of the self-control she had not to share every little detail of Alexander with his biological mother and her best friend. What a combination. Every once in a while, Lily would politely ask about Alexander in a nonchalant manner. Kathryne got the impression she would just as soon talk about anything else.

However, Lily did ask about Joe often and how he was handling the situation. Kathryne assured her that Alexander's entrance into his life had made a new man out of Joe. He was sober, self-confident, and no longer so controlled by Becky, who was also changed. More mature, a big sister. The story they had made up between them to tell Joe had been perfect. Joe himself had lost his parents and had been adopted by a couple from New

England when he was four years old. He had welcomed Alexander into their lives with open arms.

The entire family loved and enjoyed Alexander. They went on picnics, took home movies, and even went horseback riding. Becky was a little afraid of the horses at first, but was OK when she discovered Kathryne would ride on her horse with her. Alexander, approaching two years old, adored them. He cried himself to sleep when they left the stables. They would stay as long as they could and leave as the stables were closing.

"We've got to get a horse for Alexander," Kathryne told Lily on one of the rare occasions they were alone together. And it was still business related. They were on the way to a meeting with Benny's Restaurants for a presentation on their new desserts.

"My God, KT, he's not even two yet," exclaimed Lily.

"Oh, I know. It doesn't have to be tomorrow, but it is coming soon. He is so crazy over horses. He even spots them in magazines and on TV."

"Does he really?" Lily smiled, seeing the little cowboy on a pinto pony in her mind's eye.

"He sure does. We like to take them to the Dixie Stables out on old Dixie Highway. But he cries like his heart is broken when we leave. It really tears us up every time we go out there. Or, when we leave, actually. We've looked at several farms or ranches or whatever they are called in this part of the country. We would like to move out of the city and find a place where the kids can have horses and plenty of room to ride and play. There are some beautiful places available."

"I'm sure there are," Lily said, absent-mindedly staring out of the car window. "We," thought Lily. "Always "we." They really are a family, I guess. I wonder how Jeff fits in, though?" Lily felt bitter.

"She's blocked me out again," thought Kathryne.

Lily was going through her mail as she came in from work when she recognized an envelope with Kathryne's handwriting. "She can be so proper," she said to Socks over the printed invitations to Alexander's second birthday party. Could she endure another day at Kathryne's, the Donna Reed of Atlanta? No, she was sure she could not. Her townhouse seemed to echo, it was so empty. She had almost become a recluse the last couple of years. She never wanted to go anywhere. Home seemed to be a haven for her, and yet, at times like tonight, it could be so silent and lonely.

Lily sat on the window seat in her living room, watching a cold, gray rain sweep over the patio. Holding Socks close, rubbing his furry black tummy, she asked, "Wonder what it would be like to have Alexander live with us, boy. Fun, I bet, huh?" Thoughts of last Saturday's meeting at Kathryne's house to go over some layouts made Lily wince.

As they went over the folder in Kathryne's office, Alexander had come running into the room. When he saw Lily, his face brightened immediately. "Annily!" he squealed happily. He always seemed so excited and happy to see Lily on her infrequent visits. He showed her his new truck, which had a horse trailer attached to it, complete with two plastic horses. He was jabbering away incoherently, trying to tell her about the horse he rode at the stables, when Joe came in.

"Sorry, girls, we didn't mean to interrupt. He got away from me. C'mon pardner." He motioned to Alexander. "Let's hit the kitchen for some grub."

"Wait, Alexander, you dropped one of your horsies," Lily called, handing it to him. As the plump little hand took the horse from Lily's, she drew him close to her and hugged him tightly. It was the first time she had ever hugged her son. Kathryne's heart skipped a beat as she saw the expression in Lily's eyes. It sent a chill over her. The adoption papers had to be finalized. This week, she thought.

After Joe left with Alexander, Kathryne gave Lily a long look and said, "He loves you, 'Auntie' Lily. And so do I."

"No, that will never be enough now!" Lily wanted to scream back at Kathryne. She knew she must follow through with her plan, and as soon as possible. She flashed a half-baked smile to Kathryne and returned to the ad layout in front of them.

"Now, another birthday approaches," Lily said aloud as she dished out Socks' dinner. Socks' dinner bell had sounded in his stomach, and he was meowing at the cabinet door.

"I wonder if it would feel better if he wasn't always so happy to see me," Lily asked Socks. "Anyway, I hope you like Kentucky, pretty kitty." Socks, whose only interest was the foul-smelling glob before him, purred an implied acceptance.

"Thanks, Steve," said Lily as she signed the last of the contracts. "I have waited a long time for this moment. I originally planned it differently, but I guess that's life."

"I'll drive you out to your new farm. Charlie is there with the jeep you wanted to use today." Steve Walker had impressed Lily enough by phone to convince her to fly to Lexington to meet him. She had read an article about him in the *Lexington Herald* she had subscribed to some time back.

Steve was handsome; and mixed with professionalism, knowledge, and down-home wit, became a very successful businessman. His real estate firm specialized in horse farms. He knew where to find even one acre that might possibly be available. He bought, sold, traded, and auctioned. That he loved his work was evident by his success and the high regard the inner sanctum of affluent horse people throughout the state had for him. He had become a good friend to Lily, too.

She enjoyed flying in to look over property he had picked out for her to see. He always went out of his way to accommodate her every wish. His interest in pleasing her seemed to go beyond the boundaries of business. Lily did not seem to mind that idea too much either.

"Well, here it is Lily," he said, pulling his black Jaguar into the tree lined lane that led up to the barn where Charlie waited with the jeep. "It's all yours."

"Isn't this place just gorgeous? You did an excellent job for me, Steve, and I'll always be grateful."

"Well, you have been great to work with, Lily. I've enjoyed every minute of it. I hope you'll be happy here and that your dreams come true.

"I know I'll be happy here," she said as Steve, ever the gentleman, helped her out of the car.

"Promise me, now, that you'll let me come out when you're all settled in," Steve said, shutting the car door behind her.

"It's a promise," Lily said, giving Steve a quick hug. She watched as his car pulled away, not realizing how much he had hoped she would invite him to stay. As if trying to surprise herself, she closed her eyes before she turned back around. She gasped when she opened them again to her magnificent new home. Tears welled in her eyes. She could hardly believe it.

Charlie was waiting for her by the jeep. He worked for Steve's company in a multitude of capacities. He made sure the grounds were kept nice on any vacant property, took clients to and from the airport and, on occasion, would babysit horses or other animals. He did what needed to be done and could do it in a pinch.

"Thanks, Charlie," she said as he dropped the keys to the jeep in her palm. "Well, now, if there's anything else I can do to help you out, ma'am, just give me a holler."

Lily thought for a minute and then told Charlie that she was in need of a good foreman for her horse farm. Someone who could do most anything that came up on a daily basis. Of course the person had to be an expert on horses and had to be reliable and honest—but mostly, trustworthy. Charlie assured her he would think on it. He tipped his hat and mounted his waiting horse.

Lily climbed up into the jeep and began to drive the 550 acres she had just purchased. She wanted to drive every inch of the rolling hills, count every huge oak tree and dunk her feet in the pond. It would make a wonderful horse farm. The house would go just up the hill, the stables off to the right.

She had been buying stock in a Japanese company for the last couple of years. It had proved to be a great investment. With her stock earnings, she had planned to buy some property outside Atlanta, as she had started to do the year Gayle White died. Her plans had changed once again. Oh, how they had changed!

She was scared. More scared than she could ever remember. She drove down the old road through the trees as if she had lived on the property all her life. Her heart began to pound as she thought of what a devastating blow she was planning for her best friend. The truest, dearest friend she had ever known. Her real fear, though, was that something would go wrong, and her plan would fail.

"So, what are you up to?" Lily walked into Kathryne's office, accidentally catching the tail end of a phone conversation between her and Joe.

"Oh, Joe is taking Becky on one of those Little Princess camp-outs for YMCA this weekend. I don't understand for the life of me why he enjoys those damn things so much."

"So?"

"Of all weekends for a camp-out."

"Why? What's the problem?"

"Way before this camp-out was set up, I planned the presentation for the new pantyhose company in New York. You know the one we had the plastic eggs made for? The one we busted our non-existent balls for? Anyway, I had it planned for this Friday afternoon. Peter—their advertising manager with whom I have been working—and I wanted to have an early dinner with the president and then meet with their layout technician on Saturday morning. I can't get home until Saturday evening, and I just don't like leaving Alexander with Rose on the weekends. I just feel Joe or I should be there. Alexander and Rose see so much of each other during the week.

"I'm free Friday and Saturday. I would be glad to stay with Alexander. Maybe the change of routine would do me good." Had she sounded too anxious? Was her voice unsteady? Could Kathryne hear her heart pounding?

Lily knew this was the chance she had been waiting for. With the help of Charlie and Steve, the old frame house was ready to move into. Charlie had gotten painters, carpenters, plumbers, and everyone else he needed. He rode herd on them like a plantation boss at harvest time. "ASAP!" Charlie loved that acronym. She had been back to Lexington one time since she had signed the final papers and driven over her beautiful farm. The remodeled farmhouse would do nicely until she could build the kind of house she wanted.

She had all the legal work regarding her part of the agency completed. Her town house had been sold, and the new owners had given her sixty days to move. She was down to her last two weeks. Everything was perfect.

The brown car was still following her, but she had been able to outsmart him so far. She would park at a downtown office complex, leave by the rear entrance and get a taxi. She would have to lead the watchdog on a merry chase the day the movers came.

Kathryne was hesitant at first. She had a bad feeling about the whole thing, but she finally put the bad thoughts out of her mind and agreed with Lily. They decided it would be best for everyone if she kept Alexander for the weekend. She would stay at Kathryne's.

"Give Momma a big ol' kiss and hug before she goes to work," Kathryne said, bending down to Alexander. The scene tore Lily's heart apart. She had to look away.

"Lily," Kathryne said softly, "I left those papers you need to sign for Alexander in an envelope on the desk. I think it's time we got that matter behind us, don't you?"

"Yes...yes, of course," Lily stammered. The dream she had been creating for so long was becoming a reality. Kathryne had no idea that Lily's dream would become her worst nightmare.

chapter

TWENTY-TWO

As she walked into Alexander's room, a myriad of toys began to suck the air from her lungs. The force of what Lily had done was sinking in, and Kathryne began to realize that it had been cleverly arranged.

Lily had discreetly planned this for many months. When had it started? When did she begin her plot and why? Couldn't they have talked it over? Surely another solution could have been found.

Now, the little boy who claimed her heart the day he was born was gone from her life. "Ms. Gray cannot be reached," the attorney told Kathryne when she called him from the airport.

Kathryne opened the handwritten letter her driver gave to her when he picked her up at the airport.

Dear KT:

My dear, dear friend, I am so very sorry for what I am about to do to you. I won't go into how much you mean to me and how special you have become over the years. It won't be important to you after you read this.

I have taken my son to be with me, as it should have been from the beginning. I know you cannot understand, but let me appeal to you as a mother to try. It hurt so much to see Alexander growing up and being unable to share in it. Try to picture being around Becky, seeing her raised by another person. It was a terrible mistake on both our parts from the start.

We are going faraway to start our lives over. I know you will be able to find us, but please don't, for all our sakes. Please find it in your heart someday to forgive me.

All the papers for the agency are with my attorney, Herb Grossman.

I am sorry, KT, truly sorry. I knew no other way.

Lily

Racing home from the airport, Kathryne told herself, "This has to be some kind of cruel joke. Please God, a mistake."

"Kathryne, where are you?" Joe called from the kitchen. "Your warrior and little princess are home."

There was no answer. Just sounds of sobbing. Joe followed the sounds from the kitchen through the house to Alexander's room. By the time he reached Kathryne, she was an uncontrollable wild woman, screaming, "Damn you to hell, Lily Gray!"

"Kathryne, what in God's name is wrong with you?" Joe shouted rushing into the room. She was wild, crazy. Shaking her by the shoulders, he noticed the crumbled letter clutched in her hand. He had to struggle to get it away from her to read.

"What the hell does she mean, *her son?*" he said, his teeth clenched.

Kathryne, sprawled across Alexander's bed, only continued to sob.

"Dammit! Answer me, Kathryne! I said answer me. Now." Joe grabbed his wife's arm, pulling her up from the blue teddy-bear comforter. "You just better calm your ass down and start explaining. What"—he spoke to her through his teeth, his jaws tight, "does Lily mean, her son?"

"Lily is Alexander's mother. She—"

"What do you mean? We adopted him. His parents are dead."

"No."

"She kidnapped him! The bitch just stole our son and took off with him. I'm calling the police."

"Joe, listen to me. Put the phone down." Kathryne had regained her control. The tone in her voice got Joe's attention, and he slowly lowered the phone. "Lily got pregnant, had the baby, and I took him. No parents were killed. There was no adoption. No papers of any kind were ever signed." Kathryne watched Joe pace the room. He was a time bomb whose time was up.

"You stupid bitch!" He slapped Kathryne hard across the face. They weren't aware Becky was watching until she started screaming. She had slipped into the room unnoticed. Seeing Daddy slap Mommy was the scariest thing she had ever witnessed.

Rose appeared in the doorway, looking for Becky. "Get her outta here, Rose."

Kathryne started to go with them. "Like hell, you lying bitch!" Joe slammed her against the wall. "You've got a lot of explaining to do, Miss Big Businesswoman, some big damn explaining!" He slapped her harder this time. Grabbing her hair, he pulled her head back until she thought her neck was going to snap. "Tell me all about it, bitch! How you lied to me, how you and your deceitful little partner set me up. I'd like to slit your damn throat. Fix you so you couldn't tell me another lie, by God!" He ran a finger across her throat like a knife.

He spit in her face and threw her back on the bed. He slapped her again and again. Wrapping his fingers around her throat, he screamed, "I can't believe you did this to me." He bounced her head off the bed with every word. "You stinking, lying scum! He's just a baby. Where is he...? What has she done with him?" His voice cracked, and he started to cry, releasing the suffocating grip on her neck. Kathryne lay motionless, racked by pain inside and out. He was crying as he looked around the room. Joe started to leave, but instead went back in the bedroom and slammed the door behind him.

Rose, huddled in the kitchen with Becky, didn't know what to do. Each time she had Becky calmed down, something would crash against the wall, sending the child into a crying fit all over again. Joe's voice rose and fell like waves on an ocean. Vulgar names filled the air.

Just as Rose picked up the phone to call for help, Joe stomped violently down the stairs and out of the house, knocking over everything in his path. He slammed the front door so hard that the family portrait, as if making a statement, fell from the foyer wall, sending broken glass everywhere.

Kathryne slowly regained mobility, groaning with every move. It took some time for everything to register—what had happened, and why every inch of her body hurt so badly. The pain in her throat was so excruciating she could hardly move her head. She found the letter Joe had tried to stuff down her throat. Pulling herself up on a pillow, she read and reread the letter.

"How could you do this to me, Lily?" She looked around the ransacked room. A room that only last night had been the center of love and joy. The taste of blood on her cut lip, her torn clothes, her aching body did not matter as much as finding Alexander.

The house was dead quiet. Not knowing where Joe might be, she slipped out of the house and drove to Lily's town house where she was greeted with a sold sign in the front yard. Unable to give up, she drove to the stables where Lily boarded her horse.

"No, ma'am, Miss Gray come in, paid her bill, and sold the mare to Mr. Phillips. He still boards her here, though."

"Could I get in touch with this Mr. Phillips?" Kathryne was grasping for straws.

"He ain't in town. He's gone on business for several months."

"Can you tell me anything else? A forwarding address. Did she leave a forwarding—" Kathryne knew the answer.

"I'm sorry, ma'am. She didn't leave no for'arding address or nothin'."

"Thanks," whispered Kathryne. Tears spilled from her eyes. Driving in desperation to the last place she knew to look, she entered Lily's office to find absolutely nothing to show that Lily Gray ever existed. It looked like a showroom in an office furniture store. No personal items. Everything gone. Exhaustion and defeat overcame Kathryne, and she lay on the powder-blue couch in the empty office and cried until dawn. She prayed as she drove home in the early morning light that Lily would come to her senses and bring Alexander back to her.

"Lily, please!" She begged the sky, as if to send her a message by telepathy.

Wiping tears from her cheeks, she winced at the pain from the bruises where Joe had hit her. She quietly entered the house and silently ascended the stairs to her bedroom. Kathryne opened the door to the work of a madman. Joe had torn all her clothes to shreds. It must have taken him hours. Everything from her beautiful sequined gowns to her pantyhose was destroyed. Her makeup smeared the white walls in words of "liar," "whore," "slut," and "bitch." The plush floral comforter that covered the bed soaked up the many bottles of dumped nail polish. The dresser mirror was smashed, the phone disassembled, every glass object in the room was broken. Even the wallpaper was pulled away in huge strips.

"Oh my God." Kathryne mouthed as she slumped against the doorway.

"Mrs. Langford," Rose whispered putting her arm around Kathryne's shoulder. "He's gone now. Let's go to the kitchen, and I'll fix some coffee. You poor thing. Let me help you." Kathryne leaned against her, and they walked down the stairs to the kitchen. Over coffee, Kathryne heard how Joe returned to the house and began destroying the bedroom. Rose gave Becky a sedative. She was spared the violence.

"Mrs. Langford, he was a wild man. He cried and screamed for that baby and beat his fists on the walls. It was a pitiful thing. Thank goodness Becky was fast asleep back in my apartment. I stayed there with her with all my doors locked. He finally tore out of here, driving real crazy. When I heard your car in the driveway, I was afraid it was him coming back." Rose was trying to make a pot of coffee as she talked. She was still shaking all over.

"Oh, Rose. What have I done?"

"Don't think about it now, honey. Drink this coffee. You'll feel better. You'll figure it out."

"Thanks, Rose. Has anyone called?" She suddenly felt a little hopeful Lily had tried to reach her.

"No, ma'am," Rose replied sympathetically. "Is it true? Can she take the baby away from us? Is he really her child?"

"I am afraid so, Rose. I made the stupidest mistake of my life." Sobs overtook her voice. Rose cradled Kathryne's head against her bosom, smoothing the unruly mass of red hair.

It had been a long, tiring, and stressful day for Lily. The drive from Atlanta made her feel like a fugitive. The ride was long for

Alexander, but Lily kept him occupied. When he began to get restless and fussy, she would play singing games with him and make him laugh. By the time they reached the lane at Gray Meadow Farms, their new home just outside of Lexington, Kentucky, Lily and Alexander were both exhausted. It was a little after eight that evening. She was relieved to see that Charlie had been there and turned the outside lights on for her.

Alexander started crying just after they arrived. Lily carried the suitcase in, while Alexander stood in the doorway, crying. Nothing she could say or do would quiet him. He wouldn't eat the McDonald's burger they had stopped to get. He followed her around crying as she got his room settled with all his things. She didn't know what to do, so she picked him up and carried him everywhere she went in the house.

She gave him a warm bath, and he cried for the ducky he didn't have. She rocked him in the big oak chair on the front porch, and he cried for Becky. She took him in the yard to see the fireflies against the beautiful night sky, and he cried for Dada. But it was when she put him to bed and sang soft lullabies to him, and he cried for Mommy, that Lily cried with him.

She willed herself not to picture what his mama was going through at this moment. Even though she was close to the breaking point, Lily knew it was so much worse for Kathryne.

"Mommy!" He raged until his face became red and hot. She walked him and rocked him, and finally, he fell asleep with "Mommy" on his lips. It was three in the morning. Lily stood in total relief at the wonderful sound of silence. She bent to kiss him gently on the cheek but at the last second decided against it, not wanting to take a chance on waking him.

Downstairs in the kitchen, Lily smiled when she saw the Folgers on the counter next to a new coffee pot. "Welcome home, Lil." The note from Steve was printed on the back of a small brown bag. Never in her life had she had a cup of coffee that tasted so good. She leaned back in the kitchen chair, wondering if she had done the right thing. She assured herself that Alexander would be better tomorrow. She checked the locks on all the doors, looked in on her son, and went to bed in the room next to his.

She was awakened at five in the morning when Alexander began screaming like a wild animal. She ran into his room, sure she would find his head caught in the bed rail or something worse. He was standing in his bed, crying "Mommy" at the top of his lungs. There was no doubt he sensed something was dead wrong.

Lily picked him up and began to soothe him. "I'm here," she assured him. "I'll take care of you."

"No!" He shook his head. "Mommy."

"I'm here now," she repeated. He cried all morning. Lily was at her wit's end. She had the house to get in order, and the movers were due this afternoon. The movers had agreed to let Socks ride up in the cab with them. She hoped his arrival would get Alexander's attention and cheer him up.

"How can he cry so loud and so long?" Lily wondered in desperation. She couldn't help but wonder what was going through his little mind.

She finally got him quiet, and he fell asleep on a blanket on the floor. She was afraid to move. He was surely exhausted, and she didn't want to cut his nap time short. If he got some sleep he would be fine, she tried to convince herself.

She pounced at the front door in answer to a heavy knock. "If this wakes him up…" Lily's caller was Tom McNally. He had come in answer to the ad Charlie placed in the *Horse Trader.* Trying to stay quiet, she stepped onto the porch to talk to Tom. It took only a few minutes for Lily to know he was the man she wanted. She hired him as foreman of Gray Meadows Farms. Then Alexander's screams cut the conversation short.

She began to plan her time around his naps. She would meet with Tom and try to do everything she could in small amounts of time each day. Lily would begin each day with new hope that Alexander would be better. She found a pediatrician and took him in for a checkup just to make sure he wasn't sick. He wasn't. Lily knew in her heart her son was grieving for the only mother and family he had ever known. She began to doubt herself. Did she really have the right to do this?

Tom got the first of the horses in and Lily took Alexander to the barn to see them. She was sure this would be the answer. He only cried harder for his mommy. It seemed to remind him of Kathryne and the times she had taken him riding.

Each time Lily would patiently assure him, "I'm here. I'll take care of you." She began to call herself Mommy to him.

Night after night Lily tossed and turned, tormented by guilt. She could see the look on Kathryne's face when she took Alexander home from the hospital. She saw the joy in Joe's eyes as he watched Alexander play. She could even hear Becky's laughter filling the house as they played together. And, most of all, she kept seeing Alexander's happy little face when he was with them.

Lily hurt inside. It was a different hurt than she had ever felt. She didn't like herself very much anymore. How could she do this to her best friend? How could she do this to an innocent baby? How could she rationalize the whole thing? First not wanting him, then wanting him.

And through it all, she could not forget the debt she owed Kathryne. If it wasn't for her, the woman she loved more than anyone in the world, her baby would have been given away to strangers, his whereabouts unknown, lost forever.

She got up at the usual five o'clock reveille when Alexander began his day, crying for his mommy. He was losing weight and his little eyes, once so big and bright, had dark circles under them and were streaked with red from crying so much.

"God help me today, please. Don't forget me here. I need you so badly. I know I have been wrong and made such a mess of things. It seemed like a good idea at the time. I need to know what to do." She was at the end of her rope.

Alexander cried all morning. Lily tried ignoring him as a last ditch effort. She saw Tom coming up the lane. He had the horse trailer hooked to the back of his truck and stopped by the back porch. He opened the back and brought out a beautiful brown pony he had found at the morning auction. Lily's hopes soared! She gathered her son in her arms and rushed to the pony to show him.

"This is your very own pony, Alexander." She told him excitedly.

He looked the pony over from head to tail. He checked out Tom's truck and the trailer he brought the pony in. He looked Tom over as if he'd never seen him before, and he turned and looked deep into Lily's eyes. Tom and Lily held their breath. Then he started crying.

Without saying a word, Lily carried Alexander into the house and up to his room. She sat him on the floor and gave him his teddy bear. She took a long look at his precious face, streaked with tears.

Then she went to his closet, reached far in the back, and brought out his suitcase. "This is ridiculous," she said. Her trembling hands filled it with his little shirts and jeans. "I'll just take him back. It was wrong. I know it. I just can't go on like this." She opened the drawer to his blue pajamas with brown and black ponies on them. She wanted to die.

Suddenly, she felt a tiny hand slip into hers. Tugging toward the door, Alexander said, "Mommy, come ride horsey."

chapter

TWENTY-THREE

Kathryne lay motionless in her dark bedroom while Joe pounded away on top of her. It started two weeks after Lily took Alexander away. He snuck into her room in the early hours of the morning. At first she'd thought he wanted to talk. Then she realized he was naked. Having her was his only interest.

"Don't, Joe. No, I'm not—" She realized he was going to have it with or without her cooperation. To keep him from hurting her, she cooperated. As soon as he was finished, without saying a word, he returned to his room next to Becky's. He asked Rose to move all of his things to that room when he returned to the house the morning after the horrible scene.

He was so rough she always had bruises on her legs. Sometimes she was so sore when he finally stopped that she would have to soak in a tub of warm water and Epsom salts. She knew it was all her fault. She should have never deceived him the way she did. She deserved every miserable moment he gave her. She never cried or felt sorry for herself. She was numb. Alexander had been gone six months. Joe came to her room every night.

One afternoon when she came home from the office, he was waiting for her in the garage. "Why haven't you gotten pregnant?" He demanded as soon as her car door opened.

"Wha—?"

"Are you using anything for birth control?" His face was distorted, his voice mean and angry.

She had never told Joe that she had her tubes tied after they found out about Becky's problems. She sure wasn't about to tell him now, either.

"No, I'm not. Why?" she asked.

"You should have been pregnant by now, that's why." He grabbed up a bag of chemicals for the pool and stomped out.

So, that's it, she thought. He's trying to get me pregnant. He wants to replace Alexander. She felt so sorry for him. Maybe he wanted to try to start over with their own child. She found him at the pool checking the water chemistry.

"Are you trying to get me pregnant, Joe?" she asked softly.

He gave her a long, hard look and then smiled. But his smile turned to a horrible sneer as he spoke, "Yeah, you stupid, selfish bitch. I want you to have another baby so I can have you declared an unfit mother and take it and Becky away from you. I want you to hurt so much that you die of grief. I want you to cry until you are sick. Do you hear me? I want you to cry and cry and cry until you puke and lay in your sour puke until…"

Kathryne could no longer hear him. She was in her car, the radio on high volume. He had followed her back into the garage, and she got a glimpse of his distorted face in the rearview mirror as she raced to an unknown destination.

It was all her fault. Poor Joe. He was so heartbroken over Alexander that it was making him crazy. She had made such a mess of their lives. How could she expect them to forgive her when she couldn't forgive herself? Joe's words rang in her ears. "Cry until you puke!" he had screamed. Is that what he did the night they found out that Alexander was gone?

As she drove, she relived reading the note from Lily telling her that she had taken Alexander and gone away. The weeks that followed were unclear in her mind. She was on and off pills like a junkie. She would try to do without them, and then something would remind her of her precious baby. She cried for Alexander and reached for the pills. She couldn't exist without them. She just wanted the days to come and go until the proverbial time of healing had passed, as so many people said it would.

She thought about Gayle White and how drugs had become her everything. Yes, Gayle, she understood better now. They eased so much pain. She began to think about them while she was at work. Her thoughts would fill with dreams of a warm bath, her snuggly pajamas, and those two capsules of escape. They were her best friends now, those beautiful allies. There were mornings she couldn't even remember if Joe had been in her room.

Although Jeff begged her to talk to him, to see him, let him help, she felt so guilty about their relationship that she tied it to the reason her baby was gone and tried to cut it off. But she needed him so badly. He became her rock. She would get spaced out on her little capsules and call him. He would pretend with her that it was before Alexander and talk to her about a trip they were planning or something fun they had done. She would pass out with happy thoughts.

The agency was so well established that it seemed to run itself. It was a good thing, too, because although it had always been her refuge, Kathryne had more than she could handle.

It was Jeff who took her to detox the morning she found Gayle's picture. Someone must have put it on her desk. When she sat down in her chair, Gayle was looking right at her. Kathryne felt a chill hit her. She heard Gayle's words, "Don't do this, Kathryne."

She had suddenly felt transported to the bedroom where Gayle died. Kathryne again stood with Lily beside Gayle's bed, looking into Gayle's glazed dead eyes. She screamed and looked around herself, happy to see she was back at her desk. She was perspiring. She trembled. She was scared, very scared.

When Jeff answered his phone, her mouth was so dry she could hardly speak. "Hi, um, Jeff. It's Kathryne. I, um…Jeff?"

"Kathryne, what is it? Tell me. It's OK, tell me what it is.

"Jeff"—she straightened herself in her chair—"I need to go to a hospital, and I am not sure I can drive, much less get myself out of the office. I don't want anyone here to see me like this." She began to sob.

"Listen, Kathryne, we can work this out. We can do this. You just sit right where you are. You are at the office, right? OK, stay right there, and I'll come over and fix everything. Promise you'll sit right there."

"I promise. Jeff, please hurry," she whispered.

Somehow they got out of the office and to Jeff's apartment, where the doctor he called on the way to Kathryne's office waited for them. Kathryne was able to call Rose on the way to tell her about an account that was in serious jeopardy in Arizona. She would be back in three or four days. It was four days before Kathryne could call Rose again. When she did, she asked Rose to cover for her so she could get straightened out. Rose knew what was going on and took care of everything.

The last three months she had been faithful to therapy and stayed off the pills. Now this with Joe. She knew she deserved it, but how much more could she take? Since it was apparent she wasn't going to get pregnant, maybe she should make up yet another lie about the reason. She had to find a way to make him leave her alone.

⚬✗⚬

"With Tom running things so smoothly now, I have a chance to take Alexander to visit his great-grandmother," Lily told Steve Walker on one of his now frequent visits to Gray Meadows.

Steve's son, Kyle, was a year older than Alexander, and they played well together. Lily liked the idea of her son being around other children his own age. She worried that he would grow up too fast being around adults too much of the time.

Lily saw the pain in Steve's eyes when he told her about the death of his wife. She was paying her parking meter when a drunk driver lost control of his car and passed out. She was eight months pregnant with Kyle. The impact of the car slammed her against another car, severing her right arm. The shock sent her into labor. Kyle was born healthy, but the trauma threw Teresa into cardiac arrest within moments of his birth. Lily told Steve that Alexander's father had been killed in Vietnam, making reference to the picture of Tommy she always kept on her mantel.

"How long will you be away?" Steve inquired, motioning Kyle toward the door.

"Just a week or two. I'll call you when we get back," Lily answered, giving Kyle a quick kiss on the cheek. She had mixed feelings about going to Gray Dove's. She felt like a bad child going home to own up to a crime, but on the other hand, she couldn't wait for her grandmother to see her great-grandson.

Lily and Alexander left early the next morning on their way to see Gramma Dove. She relaxed and enjoyed the trip until they were about thirty miles from their destination. Lily's hands became sweaty, and her heart began to pound.

"Let's stretch our legs," she said to her agreeable companion as she pulled into a roadside rest area. She got them a root beer out of the machine. Alexander would take a sip and take off running. "Watch how fast, Mommy!"

She would clap and yell, "Yeah!" and his little legs would bring him back for another sip. It wasn't long until he was tired and ready to get back in the car and finish their journey. With regained courage, she continued on.

Lily didn't tell her grandmother they were coming to visit. Her intention was to bring her back with them to Gray Meadows Farms to stay. She was afraid Gray Dove would read between the lines of a letter or detect something in her voice if she phoned. When they pulled into the driveway, Gray Dove was sweeping her front porch. She slowly leaned the broom against the railing as she watched Lily come up the walk with a child in her arms. Lily walked straight to her grandmother and gave her Alexander.

"Momma, this is Sonny's grandson, Alexander Michael Gray."

The old woman's hands were strong as she took the child in her arms. She studied him carefully, as he did her. She ran her fingers over his temple, and Alexander squealed with delight at the colorful beads he found around Momma's neck.

"Alexander Gray?"

"Yes, Momma."

"Sonny's grandson?"

Alexander smiled at Gray Dove as if he had known her all his young life and put his arms around her. He hugged her with all his might.

After Lily put Alexander to bed and Gray Dove finished the supper dishes, the two sat down with a cup of herb tea and talked. Lily told her grandmother the whole story and how she had anguished over her every decision.

"It was so hard, Momma, not being able to tell you. I couldn't bear for you to suffer as I was. Finally, I'm able to tell you."

"I felt things were not right with you. I could tell by the infrequent letters and the way you could not hold a thought when we talked by phone the few times."

"Momma, what else could I have done?"

"You did what you thought was best for you and the child. That's the main thing. Nothing else matters. I know it was a very trying time for you and a difficult task. Now it is done. Put it away and concentrate on your new life."

"Oh, Momma, what would I ever do without you?" She kissed her grandmother gently on the cheek and hugged her.

They talked long into the night. Lily described Gray Meadows down to the last fence post. With very little persuasion, Gray Dove agreed to return home with Lily and Alexander to stay.

"By the time you finished describing the place," Gray Dove laughingly admitted, "I was planning my move."

By the end of the week, everything was boxed and ready for transport. Lily's station wagon was filled to capacity when they pulled onto the narrow road that led to the highway. Lily was as close to complete happiness as she had ever been. Grief over the loss of Kathryne, however, hung in the bottom of her soul like a bullet embedded in a nerve, inoperable.

chapter

TWENTY-FOUR

Kathryne had dreaded Christmas terribly. She could disappear with Jeff for several days after Christmas but wanted to be with Becky until then. Becky was extremely excited to be in a Christmas play at her school. She was one of three angels who brought the wise men to baby Jesus. After the play, Kathryne planned to take Becky to her mother's in Waleska for the weekend. Joe could stay home and drink. She would concentrate on her plans to divorce him as a diversion.

It was as if Becky had totally forgotten Alexander. Her therapist said she was blocking it out in order to deal with it. Becky's play turned into a disaster for Kathryne. The manger scenes reminded Kathryne of Alexander, and in her head she replayed the scene of his birth in the ambulance. The memory of his little face peeping out of the sheet wrapped around him, and those black eyes! She cried throughout the whole program.

Packing for her mother's, Kathryne ran across a photograph in the back of her closet. It was a picture of Lily. The gypsy hairdo she

wore spun Kathryne back in time. She touched the diamond bracelet she wore and reminisced about the morning she took the picture.

Kathryne rolled over in her king-size bed and pulled the pale-
blue comforter over her head, wanting to sleep a little longer.

"Ooh," she moaned as she stretched and yawned. She and Lily
had been out late the night before, celebrating Lily's first account.
After going to P J's for an extravagant meal, both calorically and
monetarily, they wound up at Pinky's, and it seemed everyone was
in the mood to dance. Pinky's had opened up on Third Street
with the new rage called disco. Larry and Scott, stockbrokers from
the seventh floor of their office building, showed up to dance the
disco with them.

When Pinky's closed, Kathryne and Lily decided to come to
Kathryne's house, a comfortable two-story ranch in the suburbs
with a screened pool and recreation room. Joe was out of town and
Becky and Rose were asleep upstairs, so she and Lily had the run
of the house.

On the way home, they picked up a couple of bottles of
Boone's Farm wine. When Lily lived in Kentucky, she and her girlfriends always drank Boone's Farm at the horse races. Lily was not
much of a drinker since, true to the stereotype of her Indian heritage, she seemed to get drunk and throw up very easily. But they
thought it brought them luck, since they always won a little money
at every race.

"Oh my God, Lily!" Kathryne screeched, scaring Dusty, her
beautiful honey-colored tabby. She was sitting straight up now,
stricken with horror as her head began to clear, and she remembered what she had done to Lily the night before. Kathryne sprang
from her bed.

"What got into me!" she said, racing down the stairs. "Lily!
Lily!" She could hear nothing. There were no sounds of life in
the house. The silence made Kathryne feel as if she were lost in
another dimension.

Rushing to the patio, she saw the scissors still lying on the
floor. The floor, a beautiful, coral Spanish tile, was covered in
hair. Lily's hair! Lily's long, gorgeous, black hair! She fell to

her knees and groaned. They had gotten the bright idea, after killing the bottle of Boone's Farm, to give Lily a new hairdo. That month's *Harper's Bazaar* magazine showed Jane Fonda in a curly, layered, shoulder-length hairstyle called "the gypsy." All the models wore it. Why did Kathryne ever think she could cut hair? Or do anything to hair, remembering the Toni Home Perm they had raced to the overnight supermarket to get at four in the morning.

Lily's hair was like a black-velvet curtain that had hung almost to her waist. Kathryne, who had always wanted straight hair, envied her. When she was a teenager, she would iron her hair or roll it on soda cans. She even had it straightened professionally once, but it never held. The curl was just too stubborn.

Now she had ruined Lily. How did she get so bold? What would she try next—an appendectomy? She heard the roar of Lily's Corvette coming up the driveway.

"Kathryne?" Lily called from the garage.

"She went to get someone to come in here and beat me to a pulp," Kathryne murmured aloud. "She is so particular about her hair!" She remembered the story Lily told her about the time her mother cut her hair, when she was a little girl. Lily hated it so much she wore a scarf for six weeks and would not take it off for anything or anybody.

There Kathryne stood. She was barefoot, in her white silk gown on her sunlit patio in the midst of the scissors, the hair, and the little pieces of paper from the Toni Home Perm kit. She saw the door opening slowly and heard Lily screaming her name. Kathryne could not believe her eyes! A more perfect and beautiful gypsy hairstyle she had never seen in her life.

"Kathryne, isn't it beautiful! You are so talented. Are you sure you never went to beauty school or anything?" Lily twirled, flipping and fluffing her hair with her hand like a prissy little girl.

Kathryne stood frozen. Her mouth was hanging so far open, she looked like someone doing a comedy routine. "Lily, I..." she stammered. "Did you go to the beauty shop this morning?"

"Heavens no, Kathryne. I went to get donuts," beamed Lily. She held out the Krispy Kreme box. "You did this last night. You do remember, don't you? You got all the perm rods out and put the neutralizer on just before you conked out."

Kathryne started giggling, then Lily started. Soon, they were laughing together as they realized what they had done.

Kathryne sat on the floor in her bedroom resting her back against the bed, smiling at her memories. She loved Lily. Nothing would ever change that. Yes, she probably would have done the same thing. Lily had tried to tell her, warn her it wouldn't work. And hadn't she known all along it was an impossible situation? She found peace, realizing at last that Lily was doing everything in her power to make her baby, their baby, happy. She knew also that love for her was buried deep within Alexander's little heart and would always be there, no matter what. She began to forgive Lily. It was the only way she could survive the loss of two people she loved so very, very deeply.

The snow began to fall, turning Gray Meadows Farms into a winter wonderland. Lily's heart ached as the memories of the many Christmases shared with Kathryne flooded her mind. Had she not been so coldhearted toward her baby, they could all be together now sharing with each other the love and peace the Christmas season was supposed to bring.

"Oh, KT," she asked the falling snow. "Where are you?" This first Christmas alone had been so empty. Alexander, just about to turn three, was so much fun. He told Santa when he saw him at the mall in Lexington that all he wanted for Christmas was cowboy boots. Gray Dove beaded him a pair of moccasins with the head of a falcon on them. Alexander loved the moccasins but wanted boots when he rode his horse. He rode every day, either with Lily or her foreman, Tom.

Tom had taken Alexander under his wing. He worked with Alexander and his pony every day. The pony was the bridge she needed. Her son was finally a happy child, growing and learning new things constantly. She set up sessions with a child psychologist after he calmed down to make sure he was not suppressing feelings or missing Kathryne in a way that would be emotionally detrimental to him later. Lily told the psychologist that, due to a serious health problem, her girlfriend kept Alexander his first two years, and she wanted to make sure he was dealing with the change OK. There seemed to be no problem whatsoever.

Lily worked wonders with the farm. The new house was under construction, the barn was finished, and beautiful horses were the pride of Gray Meadows.

"That must be Steve," she told Alexander when the headlights of an approaching car lit the windows. He was playing by the fireplace with a bionic horse Santa left under the tree for him. It was a wonderful Christmas Day, followed by a meal with all the hands in the dining room of the new house. The house was framed up enough to run space heaters and play country music. They danced in the big family room on the rough wood floor and laughed about the fact that Lily wouldn't let them stomp around in there like that once the house was finished. She saw Steve often. He took her to a concert in Lexington the first of December, and she fixed dinner for him last week. She did not invite him to Christmas dinner yesterday and expected him to drop in today.

She caught her breath. The car approaching, she could now see, was a white limousine. She watched it approach. There could only be one person who would come to see her in a car like that.

He got out of the car and strolled up the steps to the front door. She could not move. It had been so long since she had seen him. Her emotions were crazy and mixed up. She was excited, yet she dreaded old feelings and vulnerabilities.

"Mommy, Mommy, someone's here!"

She hesitated...couldn't move. He slowly opened the door and the same wonderful smile that charmed her from the beginning poked its way through a huge basket of white poinsettias.

"Anybody home?" Andy kidded her as their eyes met.

Alexander's arms circled her legs. "Hi," she said limply.

"I'm really sorry to barge in. You know, I was in the neighborhood." he teased

"Heh." She tried to appreciate his joke. He looked so good! She hadn't seen him in almost a year. Since she left Atlanta. She could not let down her guard.

"Come on, Lily," he said softly. "I am your friend. Let me in. It's OK. Everything is OK. Can we sit down?"

He navigated them to the sofa, and Alexander crawled into Lily's lap. He seemed to be under the same spell as Lily was. He kept very quiet and leaned back against Lily like she was a chaise lounge and relaxed as if to say, "OK, Bub, let's hear it."

They talked about the weather, the season, the poinsettias he brought. He said he loved the house, the horses looked grand, and so did she. Alexander fell asleep, and she stretched him out on the sofa and covered him with her sweater.

They moved to the kitchen. She poured them each a brandy and, as they sipped it, she told him that Gray Dove lived with her now, that she had a foreman named Tom, and Socks had a wife and family.

He told her he had seen Kathryne. She was trying to move on, working hard. She hung on his every word about the dear friend she loved and missed so much.

The tension eased the more they talked, and before she knew it, the daylight had slipped away. Alexander had awakened and was playing with his toy horses. From time to time he would just stroll through the kitchen with his play horsey running across the counter and through the air around Lily and Andy.

Lily didn't like the way Andy looked at Alexander, but she knew he would never say anything to Bill about him. They hated each other. She didn't know anyone who even *liked* Bill, much less wanted to talk to him.

He said he had to go, and she walked him to the door. "I'll always be your friend, Lily Gray." He kissed her on the cheek and walked to his car. She closed the door behind him, leaned against it, and slid to the floor. He was such a part of her and Kathryne. Kathryne. How she longed for, ached for Kathryne. The tears swelled. From deep in her soul they came. Deep wails came as her body heaved with emotion. Lily was unaware of how much time passed when she felt her presence. Gray Dove squatted beside her and stroked her hair.

"It is time to rebuild. The time for closing yourself off has ended. Let us go now and have some tea." Gray Dove pulled her from the floor with the strength of a young warrior.

"Alexander?" Lily whispered.

"He is in his bed."

The herbal tea she drank, along with Gray Dove's calmness, affected her like a sedative.

"Tomorrow you will start anew." Gray Dove whispered as she tucked Lily into bed.

chapter

TWENTY-FIVE

Lily pulled the old blue cardigan tight around her shoulders and locked the back screen door. Dusk covered the trees and hillsides. The full moon peaked out from behind billowy dark clouds as a restless wind gave movement to every branch and fallen leaf. There was a certain uneasiness in the cool night air. The horses were snorting and whinnying in their stalls. Even George, usually content to sleep, was pacing the basement floor where Alexander, now five, was doing his homework.

Tom had been away for a few days in Maryland, checking out two mares he wanted to buy, and was due back anytime now. Lily usually did not mind being alone when Tom and his assistant were gone, but tonight was different. All the help was gone. She felt anxious, apprehensive. About two months ago she started getting phone calls. When she answered, there would be a long silence or heavy breathing. She received one such phone call tonight. Lily wished Tom would come on back.

She shut the back door to the kitchen and started downstairs when Alexander called up for another order of hot cocoa.

Smiling, Lily did an about face and walked up the stairs. Out the kitchen window—did she see a shadow by the big oak tree? Probably just a branch or reflection. George had taken his place in front of the stove to oversee the cocoa making. Actually, his favorite part was the marshmallows. Against the vet's advice, she always slipped him one.

Reaching for cups from the cabinet above the microwave, Lily saw a light flicker at Tom's. Breathing a heavy sigh of relief, she dialed his house from the wall phone beside the door. No answer. Thinking he must be on the way to the house, she poured the steamy cocoa and started to the basement. There, again, a shadow, a stealthy movement. On the edge of fright, she dialed Tom's number again. Still no answer. She tried the big barn. No answer.

George had begun a low growl that came from way down in his gut. He stood and slowly moved toward the back door, ears perked, body alert.

"What is it, boy?" Lily whispered, turning off the kitchen light. With the room darkened, she could see out of the window into the night. Yes, she saw a light, only this time it was from Arizona's barn. She saw a vehicle, but couldn't make out exactly the type.

"It must be Tom, and he's unloading the new mares," she murmured, straining to see outside. George had begun to bark madly to get out and bolted into the night as soon as the door was opened.

Judging from George's behavior, Lily wasn't sure now who was in the barn. She picked up the phone again, this time to dial the equipment barn, only to find the line from the house was dead.

"Oh God, someone is trying to steal Arizona!" It would be a good theft, too. Arizona was pregnant and expected to deliver a derby winner. Lily slipped out the back door quickly, running into the chilly wind with cat-like deftness. As she rounded the corner of the barn, she slowed to a silent creep. She saw no one outside. Only an unfamiliar, old green truck. She crouched silently, leaning against the outer barn wall. The door was half open, and she listened to hear if she recognized any voices. There were none. Only rustling noises in the hay, and George's barking from somewhere in the back of the barn. She heard Arizona begin to kick her stall.

"Easy girl, easy." That voice. Bill. What was he doing here? Lily could feel the cool dampness of the earth penetrating the knee of her pants as she tried to gather her wits. Suddenly, she felt Alexander's warm body slide in close to her. All the things he had seen and learned about cowboys and horse thieves were actually happening. Lily always taught her son to do exactly as she or Tom said in the face of an emergency, no questions asked. He was very mature for a 5 year old. His mother discussed things about the farm with him, often asking his opinion.

He was silent. She signaled to him to get the hay rake leaning behind them about ten feet away. Seconds later he placed the sturdy wooden handle in her hand. Whispering directly into his ear, Lily told her excited young son to run to the equipment barn after she went inside and got Bill's attention. Only after she had gone inside, she stressed. Try the phone there and call the sheriff. Stay there, out of sight, until help arrives. She kissed his ear after her last word and slowly slid her back up the wall.

Taking a deep breath, she walked to the door. As she made herself visible, she saw that Bill's plan was not to steal Arizona, but to shoot her. She surveyed the area quickly. Bill must have lured George to a stall and locked him in instead of drawing attention to the barn with a premature bullet.

"What the hell do you think you are doing?!" Lily demanded, walking out of the shadows into the barn, hay rake in hand.

"Oh, Lily, my ladylove, just in time for the show. I'm going to shoot your precious horse and along with it, your chances for the derby. You won't have a thing left to love on this farm when I'm finished, including that bastard of yours!" There was no doubt Bill was certifiably insane. She had seen it coming. Why hadn't she realized how deeply losing the election and her in the same year had affected him? She kept thinking that he would get over it.

"No." Her steel-firm voice covered her panic as she slowly moved toward Bill. "I don't think so. Tom has a rifle pointed right at the back of your head. He can drop you like a rock."

Knowing Tom was nowhere in sight, Lily had to make her move count, and it had to be fast. Bill, taken off guard by the threat, turned slightly to where Lily's eyes were focused behind him. At that second, Lily ran at him with the rake, knocking him and the gun to the ground. The impact caused the gun to fire. As

Bill tried to stumble to his feet, Lily turned Arizona out of her stall and sent her running from the barn with a hard slap on the rump.

Alexander had reached the equipment barn moving swiftly along in the dark shadows. Breathlessly he stretched for the phone only to find the cord had been neatly clipped. Panic raced through his mind, and he wondered what his hero, John Wayne, would do in this situation. When the shot rang out from Arizona's barn, his only thought was getting to his mommy.

He ran cautiously toward the barn, stopping just outside. He peeked in through the crack in the hinge of the half-open door. The scene inside the barn was unbelievable to his young eyes. His mother lay on her stomach on the dirt floor. Her feet were tied. Her mouth gagged. He saw blood on her beautiful face. The man was walking around her with a rifle, taunting her with the barrel. Poking at her face, then sticking it in her back.

"Oh, Mommy!" His heart pounded. He must keep his cool. He had always been taught the importance of a level head in a crisis. His eyes quickly scanned the area for a weapon of some sort. There was nothing within reach. His only hope was to enter the small service door at the other end of the barn, crawl behind the assailant, knock him down, and grab the gun. But could he do it? Sure! He began his mission, sliding along quietly until reaching the door. He pulled it open quickly to quiet the inevitable squeak. The jeering banter of the attacker gave him the sound cover he needed. He eased to the floor and crawled combat style through straw and dust, trying to hold his breath to ward off a sneeze. As he drew closer, he met his mother's eyes, telling her not to move.

Alexander saw his mother close her eyes tightly as he rolled his strong little body into the back of the intruder's legs sending him face down into the dirt. Bill grabbed Alexander by the ankle and caught a small boot in his face. They rolled in the dirt, Alexander fought back with everything he had. He kicked, bit, and clawed like a tiger.

Lily managed to sit up and was butt-hopping toward the two in hopes of diverting Bill until Alexander could get away. All at once, Bill grabbed Alexander by the arm and threw him across the barn like an old sack. She heard him scream as the weight of his body hit the wall and then the breath went out of him. As he fell, his head hit a sharp corner pole. Blood turned the hay crimson as he lay motionless on the floor.

Her heart was racing. Bill grabbed Lily around the waist and was dragging her to the old truck outside the barn. She was doing everything she could to break his grasp when suddenly Bill's arm went limp and he fell, pulling her on top of him. She looked up to see Tom, still holding the tire iron with one hand, reaching for her with the other. He took the scarf from across her mouth.

"Tom, Alexander! He's hurt! The barn! Quick, untie me!" Alexander was groaning as Lily reached him. Tom called for help on the CB radio in his truck. Within minutes, it seemed, help was there.

Somehow, in all the turmoil, Bill had managed to slither away as a serpent into the night. As Lily looked out at the witching moon, she felt as if the devil had set out on the land to do more evil. She knew his sickness would again touch her life.

chapter

TWENTY-SIX

When Pearl Lewis hired Gene Madison to follow Andy two months ago, she never really expected to receive the call she got this morning. Pearl had not wanted to use anyone in Texas, so she located a detective out of New Jersey. She overheard a conversation in which Gene Madison's name was mentioned as the most discreet private investigator available.

This morning Gene called to ask Pearl to meet him in Atlanta. He had the information she wanted. The information she wanted? What Pearl really wanted was no information at all. Why had she hired him, anyway? Damn, she had ruined everything now.

Andy was life to Pearl. She could not believe it when he had asked her to marry him eighteen years ago. She adored him then, and she still felt she was the luckiest woman on earth. The fact that she could never conceive a child had made her insecure over the years. Lately, that insecurity had begun to fester like a sore. She seemed to look for ways to feed it. She became obsessed with feeding it.

Now she had found the payload. Buy why? Why had she sought evidence? Even now, trying to find an excuse to put off talking to Gene, she was anxious as a drug addict for an injection.

She met her detective early in the morning at an out-of-the-way café in a section of Atlanta she had never seen. Pearl found out that Andy not only had a girlfriend, he had two of them. Somehow, he had managed a continuing relationship with two women for quite some time. One was in Atlanta and the other in Kentucky. And worse of all for Pearl, they were white.

Slowly making her way through the airport to board her flight back to Texas, she stopped at the phone to call her husband.

"Hi, baby," Andy crooned into the phone.

Pearl's voice was quivering. "Andy, I am in Atlanta. I will be in Dallas in a hour. Meet my plane—Delta flight 141."

"Why in the world did you go to Atlanta? I didn't know you were going. Listen, baby, I'd love to pick you up, but I have a meeting with—"

"Cancel it!" She had not meant to scream.

"What's wrong, baby?" Andy was so startled he sat upright in his chair. Was it a meeting with the NAACP? Or was that next week? Wasn't she going to speak…yes, he was going with her.

"Well, Andy," she said in a voice as sharp as a razor. "There are two things wrong. Lily Gray and Kathryne Langford." With that statement, Pearl hung up the phone and walked to her gate.

Not much of a drinker, Pearl had a glass of wine on takeoff, one of the advantages of traveling first class. It went right to her head. Tears burned her eyes as she tried to focus her mind on the devastation she would bring to his career. She fought thoughts of him being a warm loving husband. She wished she had never called Gene Madison.

He would be destroyed politically. She had helped him in every campaign. She visualized the sweet victory she would have detailing his affairs to the papers, the disappointing despair. Her pain-ridden eyes looked out over the clouds. Her heart told her she would rather be dead.

Bill Dressler had lost all direction. He was obsessed by thoughts of Lily. Stretched out on the bed in his cheap, dirty motel room, he went over and over his new plan to hurt her. His hair was long and greasy. Food wrappers covered the dilapidated bed. He still could not believe he had seen her with Andy Lewis last weekend. That black bastard! He would fix him.

At the end of the workers' lunch break, he entered Field Number 20 dressed as an oilman. He rechecked the package tucked inside his shirt. One little spark was all it took in an oil field. The owner of the badge he wore lay in a ditch with his head caved in. He would have paid him to use the badge if he had not been so righteous about it.

Red Sanderson felt uneasy. Something was wrong. Andy always told him he was part cat. He seemed to be able to smell trouble, and something didn't smell right today. He was looking for Andy to discuss his feelings when he saw the bomb.

"Son of a bitch!" He was running now, screaming. "She's gonna blow! Run like hell!" He spotted Andy standing in front of the shed. Waving and shouting to him, Red tried to reach him in time. "Andy! A bomb! Get out, get out!"

Flight 141 had left Atlanta on schedule at 11:30 a.m., about the time Andy Lewis told his secretary to cancel all his appointments for the afternoon as well as for the following day. He went looking for Red to tell him he was leaving, knowing it would take him a little under an hour to get to the airport. He drove to Field Number 20. Old Twenty, as they called it, had been good to them. It just seemed to keep on coming on. He parked his jeep in front of the foreman's shed and hopped out.

"What's the matter with Red?" he asked one of the men. He had called Red on his CB and asked him to meet him at the shed. Red was running toward them through a forest of derricks, dust flying from his heels, waving his arms.

"What tha hell?" The words, "She's gonna blow!" reached his ears. His arms positioned to run, he turned toward the man next to him.

"Get outta here!" he yelled. Words that were never heard.

chapter

TWENTY-SEVEN

She understood the high altitude was probably hurting his ears, but if that baby two seats back did not stop crying soon, Kathryne would have to start crying herself. The staff parties seemed to last longer than they used to. The headaches, too. But as soon as this 747 got her to Jeff and one of his wonderful massages, she would feel like a different woman. Kathryne needed this long weekend with Jeff. She had worked so hard to land the South Central Air account, and now she could forget the office, and Joe, for four whole days. Jeff. Mm, the thought of him made her feel better already.

"This man has all I will ever really want," Kathryne thought as she pushed the button on her armrest and leaned her seat back. While the wonderful invention by the Wright Brothers soared toward her paradise destination, she closed her eyes and began her favorite pastime. Daydreaming about her new life without Joe.

She was relaxed and smiling when the pilot announced the approach to Charlotte Airport. This morning's meeting with the design concept coordinator had really screwed up her flight. The delay made it impossible to catch the nonstop flight to Nassau. The only flight she could get had a change of planes and a layover in Charlotte. At least it would give her a chance to give Theda a call and check on things at the office. Kathryne always traveled first class, so she was the first one off the plane.

"Theda, how's the world treating you today?" Kathryne said fondly. Theda was a great assistant and had saved her life more than once.

Theda sounded upset. "Kathryne, I am so glad you called. Red has been trying to reach you. He says it is extremely urgent."

"Thanks, Theda, I'll call you back." Kathryne was really curious about this. Red never called her. "Oh my God. It's Andy. Something has happened to him!" She was fumbling through the buttons on the phone, and it seemed to take hours for the system to process the numbers.

"Lord, please, he has got to be all right!" She could not lose another best friend. She thought of all the things that could be wrong, but none of them prepared her for what Red was going to tell her.

"Hello." Red's voice came through the receiver.

The sound of Red's voice sent fear through Kathryne. She knew something was wrong, and as her mind raced across a thousand possibilities, she said, "Red, this is Kathryne. Theda said it was urgent I call you. Is everything OK? Andy OK? Red?"

Red drew in a deep breath and said, "Kathryne, where are you?"

"Red, I'm at the Charlotte Airport on my way to Nassau. Dammit, what's wrong?!" Kathryne had not realized she was shouting until several people in the Delta Crown Room turned to see who was causing the commotion.

As the words Red was saying began to pierce her, Kathryne knew she was dying. The room began to spin, and she was losing control. She couldn't hold the phone, she couldn't stand up. Everything went black.

Red awoke early in the morning of what was to be a long and tiring day and sat down with his first cup of coffee and a cigarette.

The sun was just beginning to appear on the horizon. The usual gentle breeze had retired with the darkness of the night before. Outside the breakfast-nook window, the tall moss-covered trees stood as if still asleep. Not a leaf moved. It was like the world stood still waiting for the first tinge of fall. Only the faint coo of a dove somewhere in the distance could be heard as it broke the silence of the new day.

Red lingered, thinking of Andy. The day Andy came to juvenile hall, looked him straight in the eye, and said, "Want a job?" Before Red could answer, Andy continued, "Good. Let's go."

Andy could have left Red in jail that day twenty years ago, when he was caught stealing generators from his oil docks. Instead, Andy saw a little of himself at that age in Red and gave him the opportunity to work off the cost of the generators. The court released him in Andy's custody, and that is where Red had been ever since.

For more than twenty years, Red Sanderson had been Andy Lewis's troubleshooter. Broken down into the daily order of things, that could mean anything from riding herd on an oil crew to being his personal friend and confidant. Red always admired Andy and perhaps tried to copy as much of his charisma and finesse as he could. Red knew he owed everything he had and everything he was to Andy Lewis.

He chuckled at the fun they had enjoyed. He grimaced to think about him really being gone. Glancing at the kitchen clock, he knew it was time.

"Oh, shit," muttered Red. If he couldn't get to the funeral home to intercept Lily and Kathryne, there might be a bad scene. It would be the first time they had seen each other after their big split three years before. Andy had stayed in touch with them both. When Andy made the tape for them, Red did not know.

Andy's untimely death early yesterday morning had thrown the entire operation of Lewis Enterprises into Red's lap. But Lewis Enterprises, with all its holdings and operations, was a piece of cake compared to the situation he was racing toward.

266

"Where in God's name does the traffic come from?" he grumbled. The new beltway was supposed to take traffic off Texas Boulevard, but it seemed worse than ever to Red. As he inched along the boulevard, he could feel his anxiety heighten.

Red's black Bronco slid to a stop in front of Vance Funeral Home. Located in a magnificent old building, it reminded him of a miniature version of Elvis's Graceland in Memphis. Stepping up to the door, Red checked his tie.

"Damn things are uncomfortable as hell," he murmured. Something else to worry with. The whole situation would be easier if he were in his jeans. He wiped off the toes of his boots on the back of his pants legs and took a deep breath. A glance around the parking lot had given him the dreaded answer. They were there. Looking toward the heavens as if asking for help, he took a long breath and went inside.

As Red walked into the funeral home, the marquis hit him in the face: Andrew M. Lewis—Chapel A. His eyes burned, and he softly mumbled, "It's real. It's really real." At Pearl's request, Red had made all the arrangements. But this was the end, the final product. He wasn't prepared for it, but then again, he never would be. He leaned against the cool mahogany door and took another deep breath. He felt like time was frozen, the world at a standstill. He realized he was trying to force it all away. The explosion. Andy...

Voices from Chapel A hit him like an alarm clock. He had to wake up, but pushing away the nightmare was difficult to do. He knew that once he did, he would never be able to get it back again. But as he stood, hanging onto a wonderful mental picture of Andy laughing and talking to him, the voices and the floral aroma forced his illusions further and further away.

When Red entered Chapel A, the two beautiful women Andy had loved for so many years stood by his casket. The casket was surrounded by flowers of every description. The casket itself, at Red's request, was covered in a blanket of bright-red roses.

After an awkward greeting, Red told Lily and Kathryne that Andy had left a cassette tape for them to hear in the event of his death. Shocked to hear this news, they looked at each other, and Red was shocked to see Lily take Kathryne's hand for a moment.

"I knew you would be anxious to hear it and brought it with me, as well as the tape player," he explained, his voice more than normally husky. They were indeed anxious to hear it.

The trio found a private room. Red closed the door and invited them to sit together to listen to Andy's taped message. Red had no intention of handing the player and tape over to Lily and Kathryne and not hearing what was on it. He hit the button to turn it on.

Both women caught their breath as the sound of Andy's voice sprang from the recorder, making them feel as if he had just stepped into the room. The tape began with Andy's recount of meeting each of them and then continued.

"My dearest, dearest darlings. I have always loved you both. With all my heart I have loved you both. By now you know that I have continued my relationship with each of you during this horrible time of your estrangement. But step into my shoes for a moment. The hurt you are feeling now reflects only part of the hurt I would feel losing one of you.

"Choose between you? How could I? Can you choose one eye over another? One body part over another? My precious ones, both of you are too special to me.

"You know how lovable you are, because you love each other. I have witnessed your love and friendship for each other. It is a friendship I have never seen anyone else share.

"I have also seen you grieve for each other these last few years. My love seemed to be the only key to your relief."

He recounted the times Lily cried in despair wanting so badly to see Kathryne, and the times he held Kathryne as she cried violently, not for Alexander, but for Lily.

They listened intently, hanging onto every incredible word, glancing at one another, tears spilling from their sad eyes.

"I know all about Alexander and how you tried to do the very best you could with the situation. Let's not dwell in the past and talk about 'I should have or why didn't I.' Alexander needs you both, as I always have. The love you have for him and each other will be a special blessing for him throughout his life. I know. I have experienced it.

I love you both so very, very much."

When the tape ended, no one could speak. They sat in silence for a long time, weeping softly. Kathryne and Lily were not aware when Red had slipped away.

"Have you been well?"

"Yes."

"I've missed you terribly."

"Lily, I don't understand all I know at this point, but I do know one thing. I can't get through this without you." Sobbing, shaking, and muttering incoherent words, they stared at each other, immobile.

Finally, Kathryne slowly got up. She turned to leave and steadied herself. She looked over at Lily and said in a soggy voice, "We need a drink."

And so they left their beloved Andy, found a little tavern, and spent the entire night talking and drinking. Once Lily had to excuse herself to the ladies' room to throw up. Kathryne helped her, and they laughed about how it reminded them of old times. They continued their wake until their throats were sore.

They found a little park after the bar closed and continued the vigil until dawn. They were a pretty rumpled-looking pair when the sun came up.

"KT?"

"What?" Kathryne answered, thinking how the nickname Lily had given her years ago sounded like music to her ears.

"After the funeral today, will you come home with me?"

"Are you kidding?" Kathryne answered excitedly. "Does a dog have fleas? I thought you'd never ask!"

"Oh, KT," Lily sobbed as they embraced for hundredth time. The unconditional forgiveness of a true friend has no comparison. Lily felt the warmth of that forgiveness flow through her heart.

The funeral that afternoon was a simple ceremony, but hundreds of people showed up. Oil people, politicians, civil rights activists, lots of young black people Andy and Pearl had mentored and put through college.

There were also cops. An explosion in the oil fields demanded a full investigation. They were dressed as mourners, but they were there. An all-out search was in progress for the afternoon stranger to Field Number 20. Lily thought she saw Bill Dressler. Thinner, stooped. She wasn't sure. He wore a hat.

Lily and Kathryne sat together a few rows back, reflecting with the minister as he bragged of Andy's accomplishments. They stayed seated until everyone left the church and then approached the closed casket for a final farewell.

There was a framed picture of Andy placed in the center of the red roses on the casket. He was dressed in a black tuxedo, a white pleated shirt, and a red cummerbund, with a red rose bud in his lapel. Andy was, without a doubt, handsome beyond description. It was always the way he walked, the things he said, and those wonderful brown eyes that brought his good looks to life. There just did not seem to be enough strength left in the women to cry anymore. They felt peace entwine their heartache as they turned and walked out, hand in hand. They were going home.

The car topped the brow of the hill. Lily exclaimed, "There it is, KT!" Kathryne looked through the windshield and saw the softly rolling hills, the whitewashed barns, and a mother horse and colt grazing alongside of the white fence. It was Lily's place, for sure.

"Alexander is dying to see you!"

Lily had explained to Kathryne that night in Dallas that she had always kept her picture on the dresser and they called her Aunt KT, which Alexander pronounced Katie. Pulling up to the beautiful white house with the horn on high, Lily jumped out, yelling, "Alexander! We're home!"

As Kathryne crawled from the car, she heard the front door open and turned to feast her eyes on the precious baby she had never stopped loving as her very own. Her heart pounded furiously. She stepped toward him and caught her breath. There on the steps, with a broad, charming smile and wonderful, warm dark eyes stood, unmistakably the son of Andy Lewis.

The End